NNEWTS

BOOK TWO
THE RISE OF HERK

DOUG TENNAPEL
WITH COLOR BY KATHERINE GARNER

An Imprint of

The publisher does not have any control over and does not assume any responsibility
for author or third-party websites or their content.

Library of Congress Control Number: 2015940673

ISBN 978-0-545-67652-6 (Hardcover)
ISBN 978-0-545-67654-0 (Paperback)
12 11 10 9 8 7 6 5 4 3 2 1   16 17 18 19 20
Printed in China   62

First edition, February 2016
Edited by Adam Rau
Book design by Phil Falco
Creative director: David Saylor

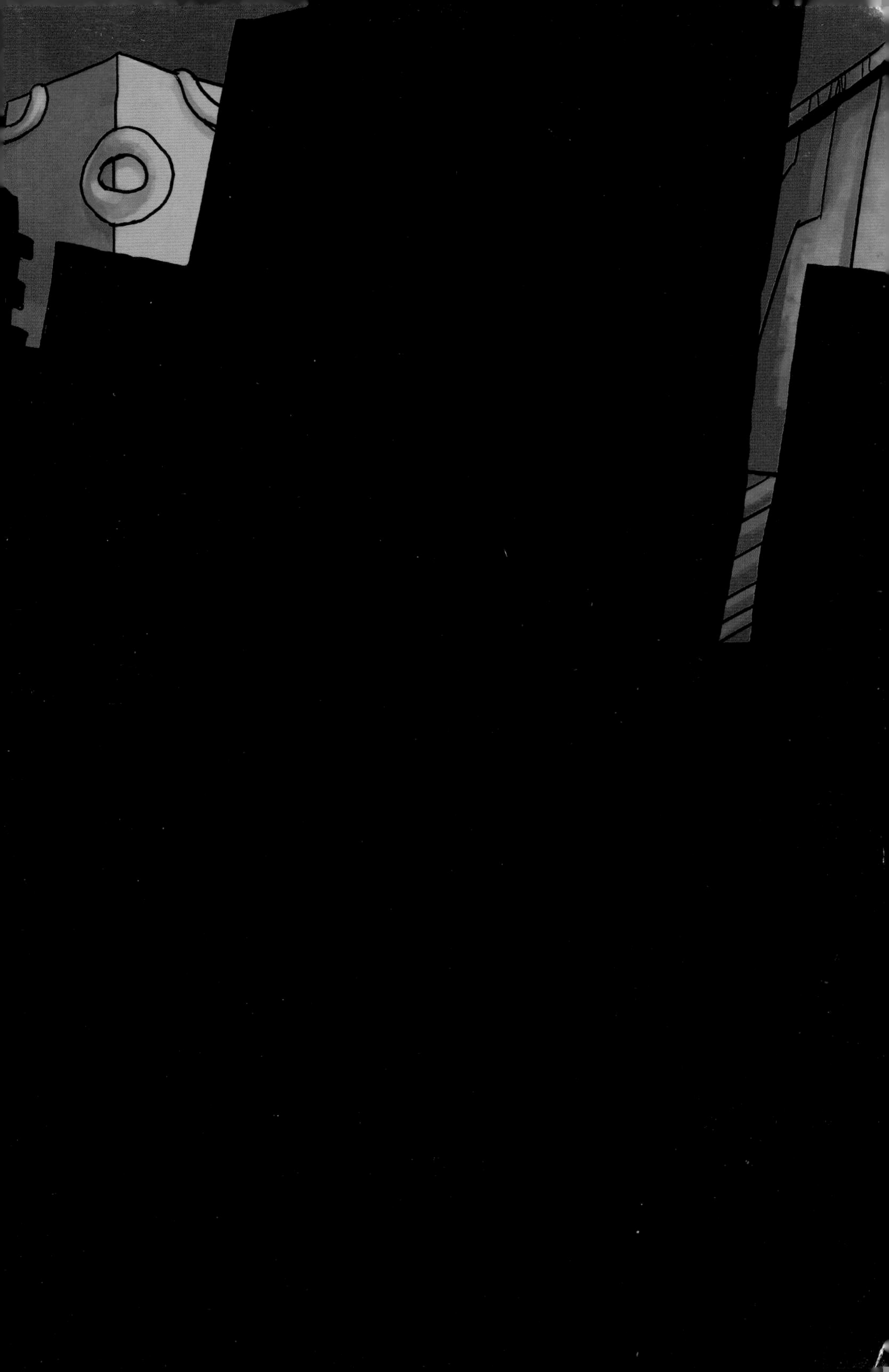

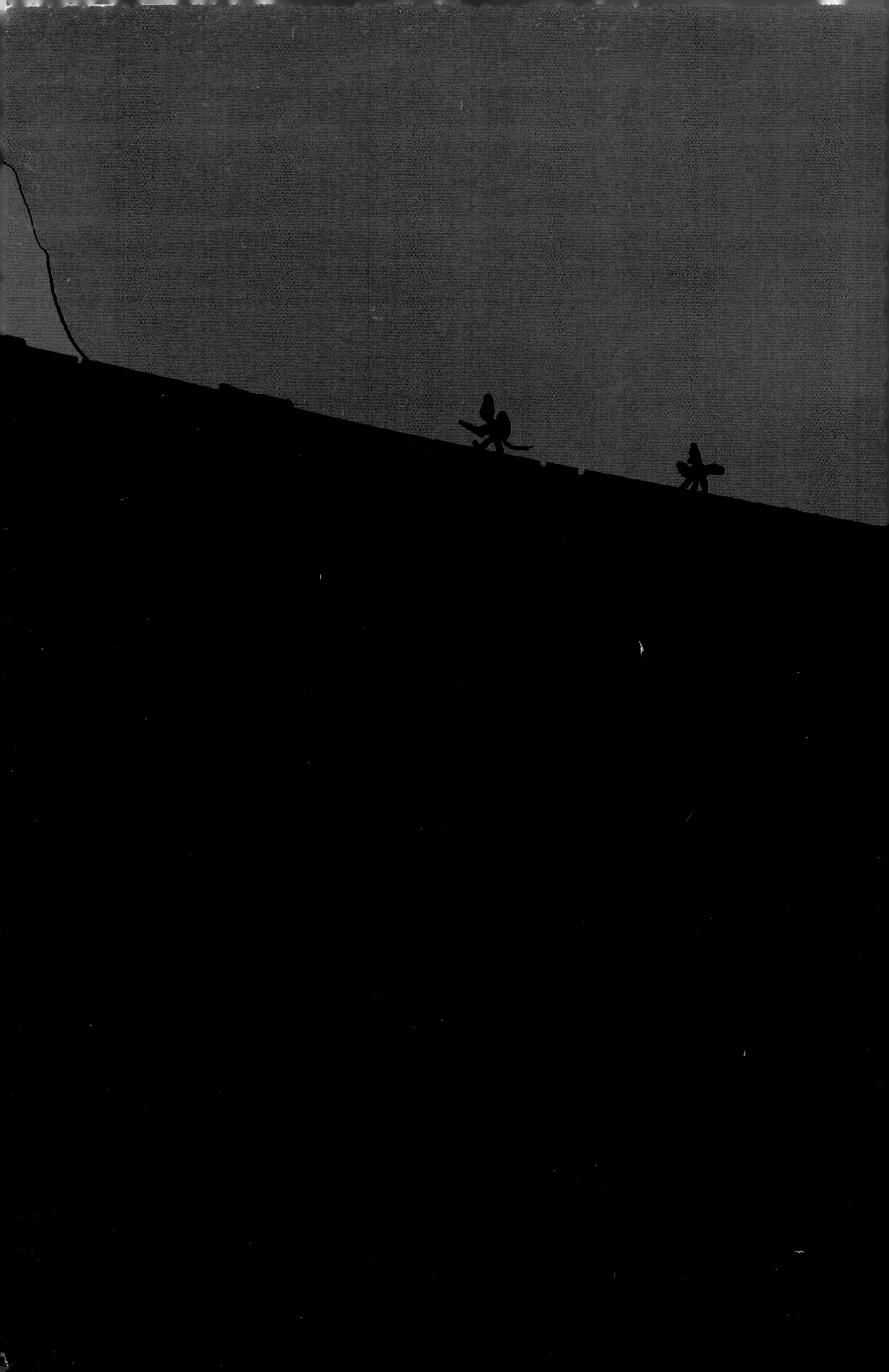

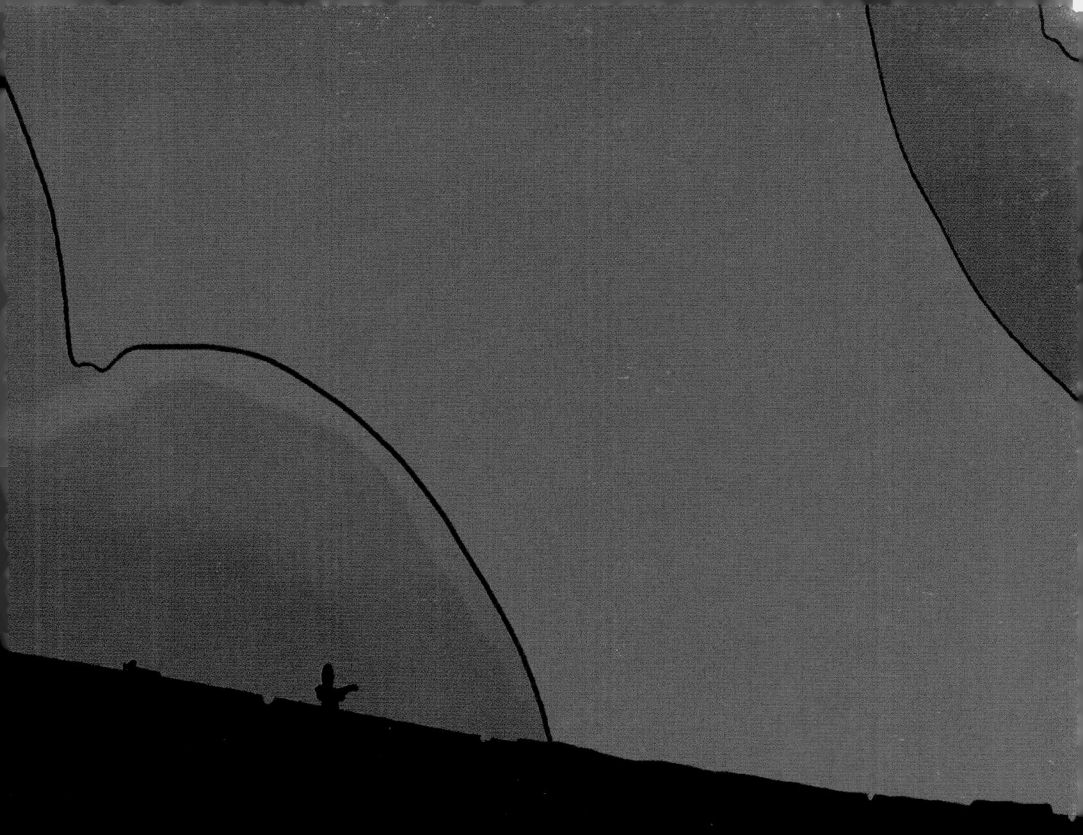

For Rick

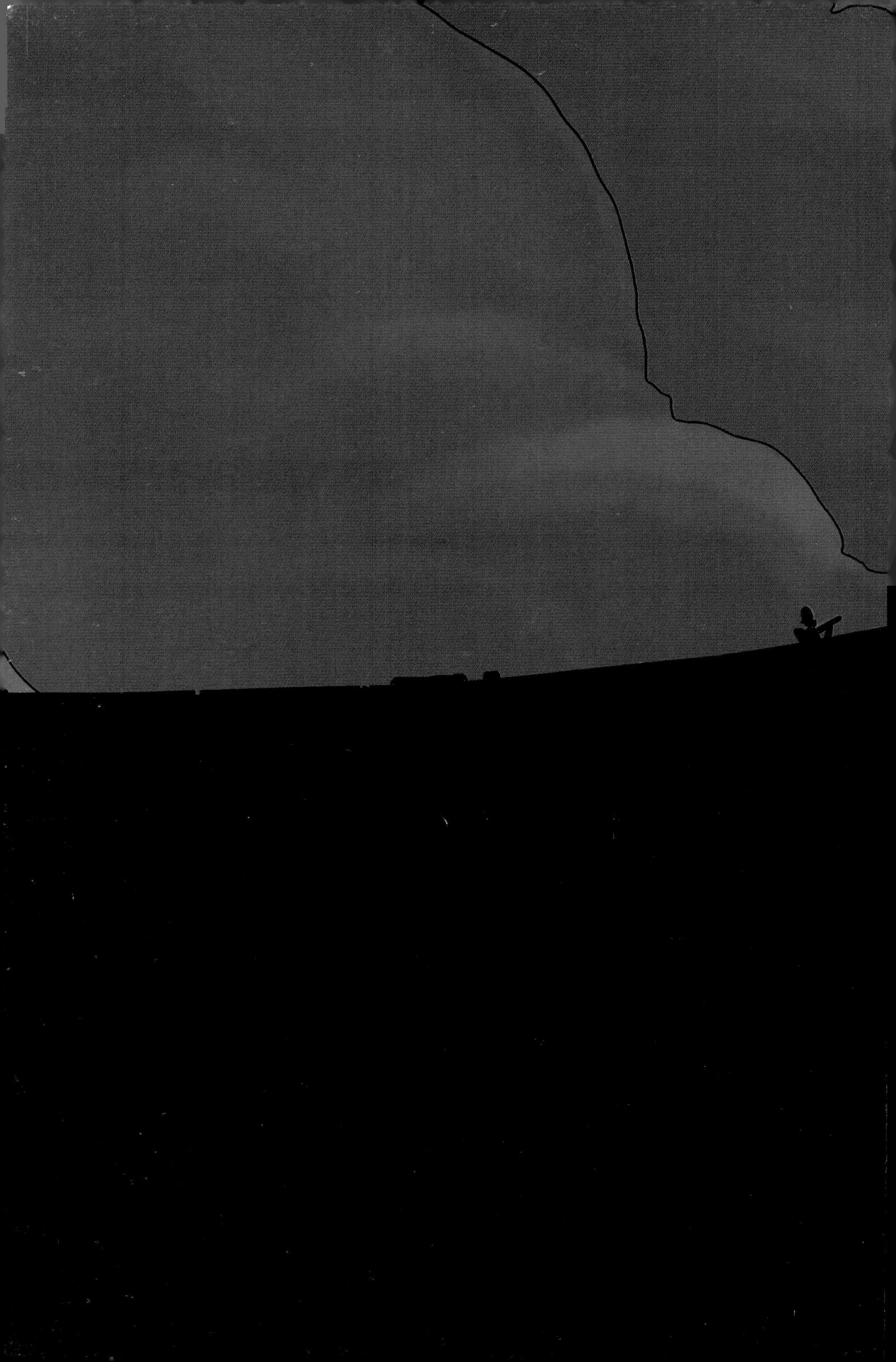

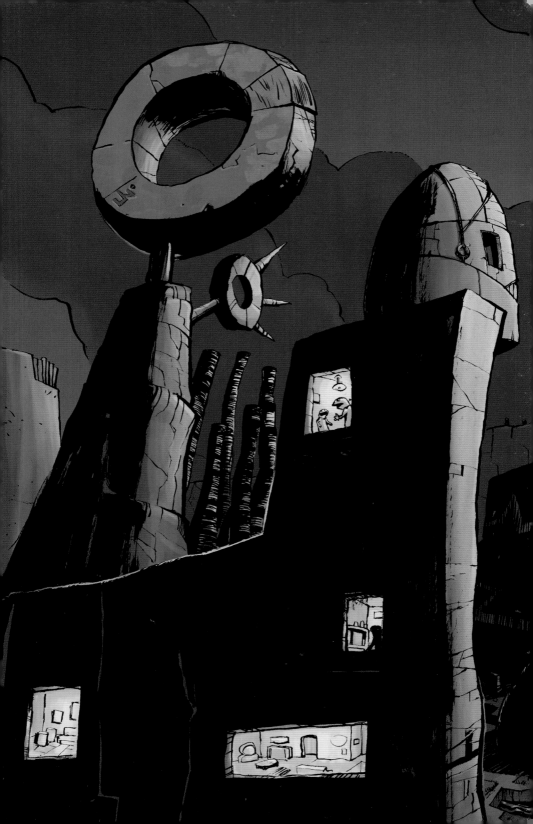

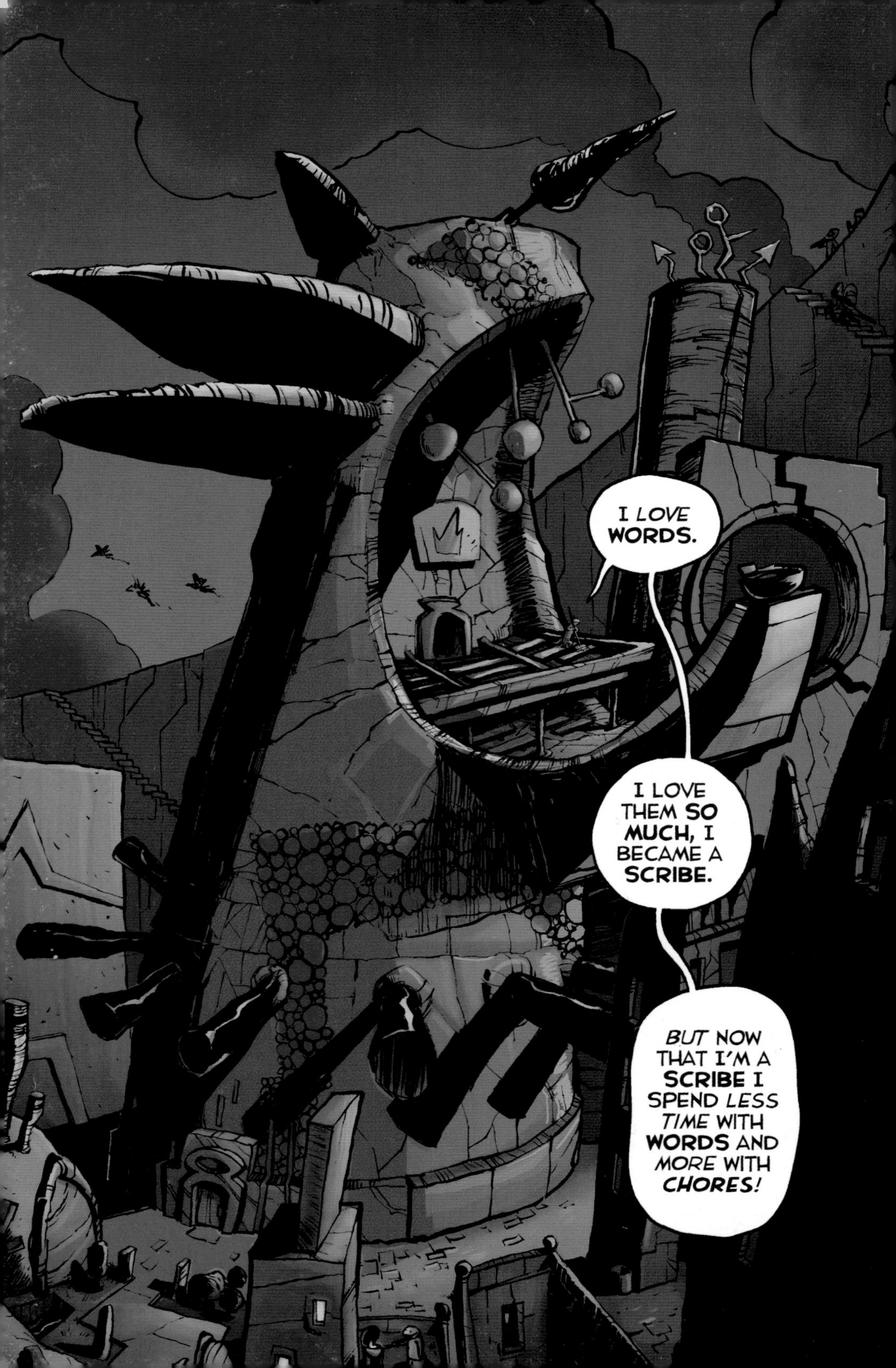
I *LOVE* **WORDS.**
I LOVE THEM **SO MUCH,** I BECAME A **SCRIBE.**
BUT NOW THAT I'M A **SCRIBE** I SPEND *LESS TIME* WITH **WORDS** AND *MORE* WITH ***CHORES!***

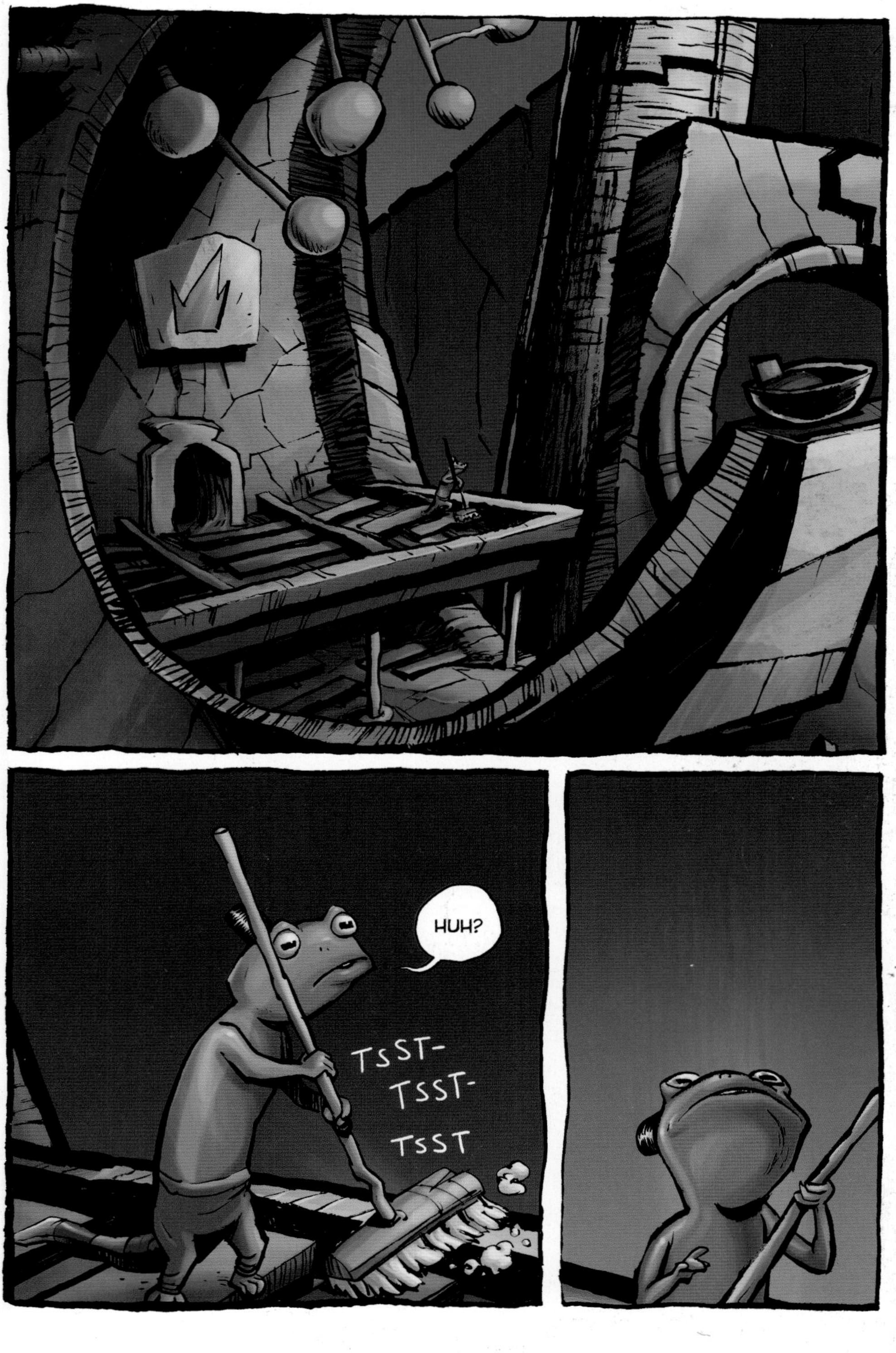
HUH?
TSST-
TSST-
TSST

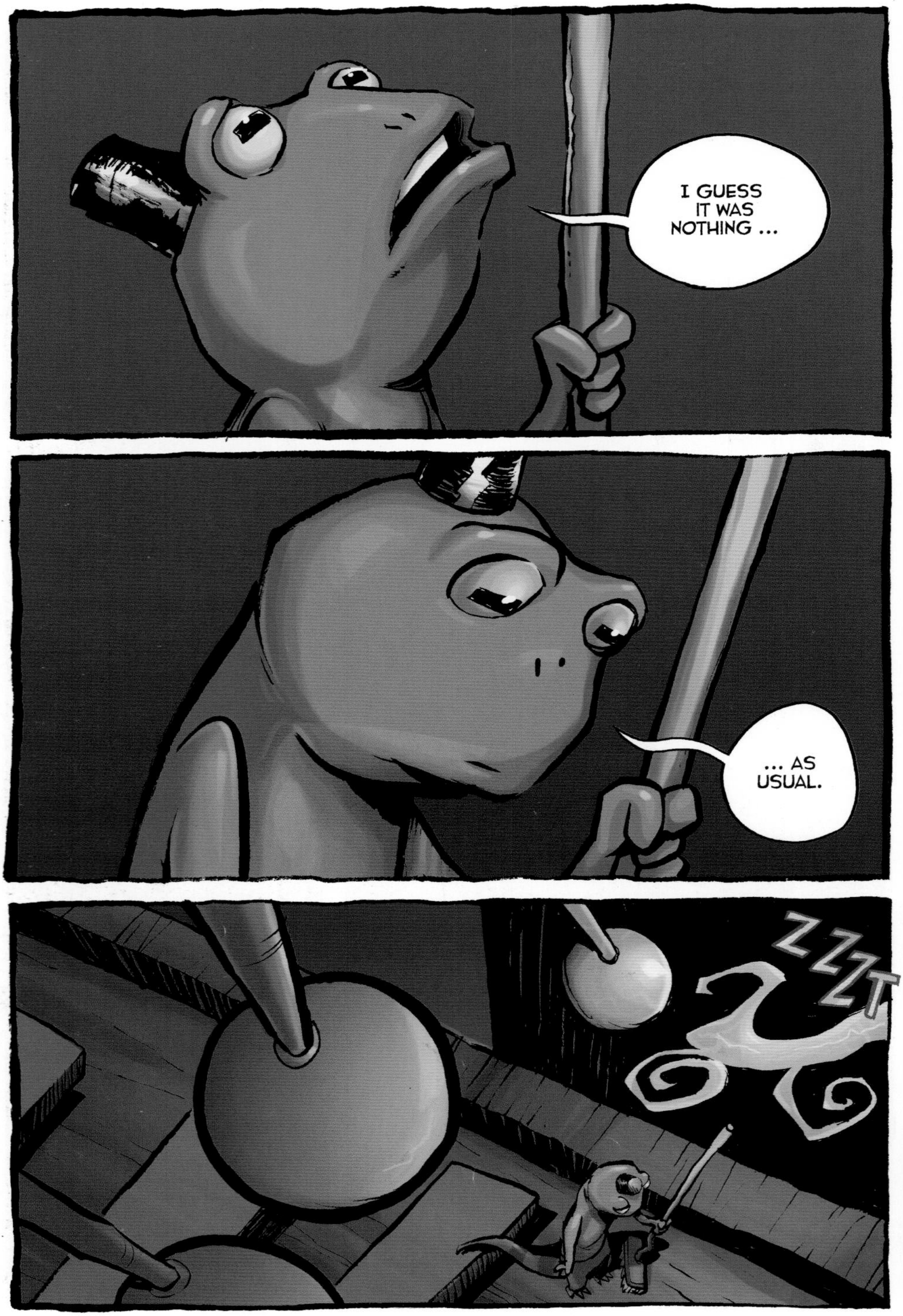
I GUESS IT WAS NOTHING ...
... AS USUAL.
ZZZT

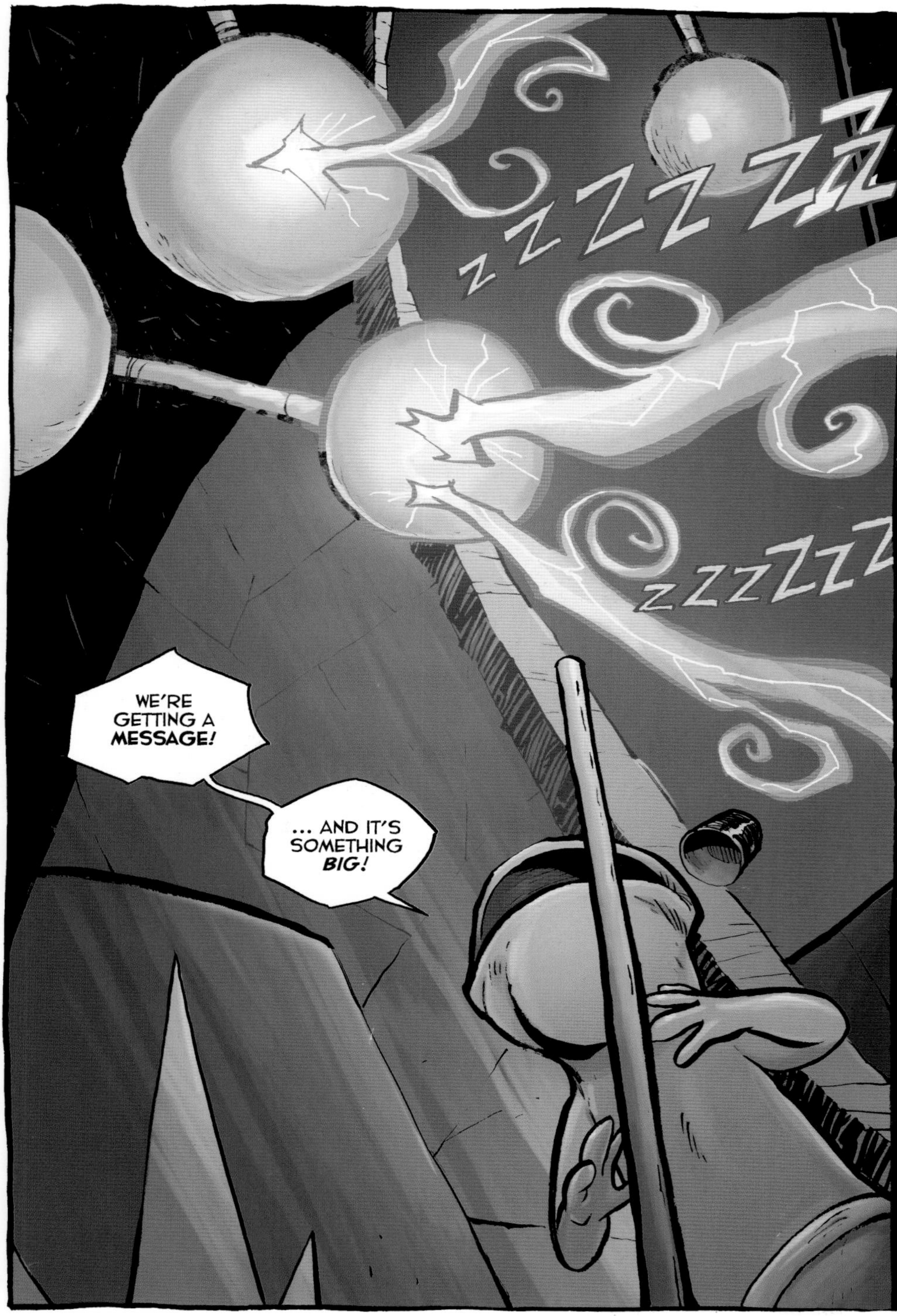
ZZZZZZZ
ZZZZZZZZ
WE'RE GETTING A MESSAGE!
... AND IT'S SOMETHING BIG!

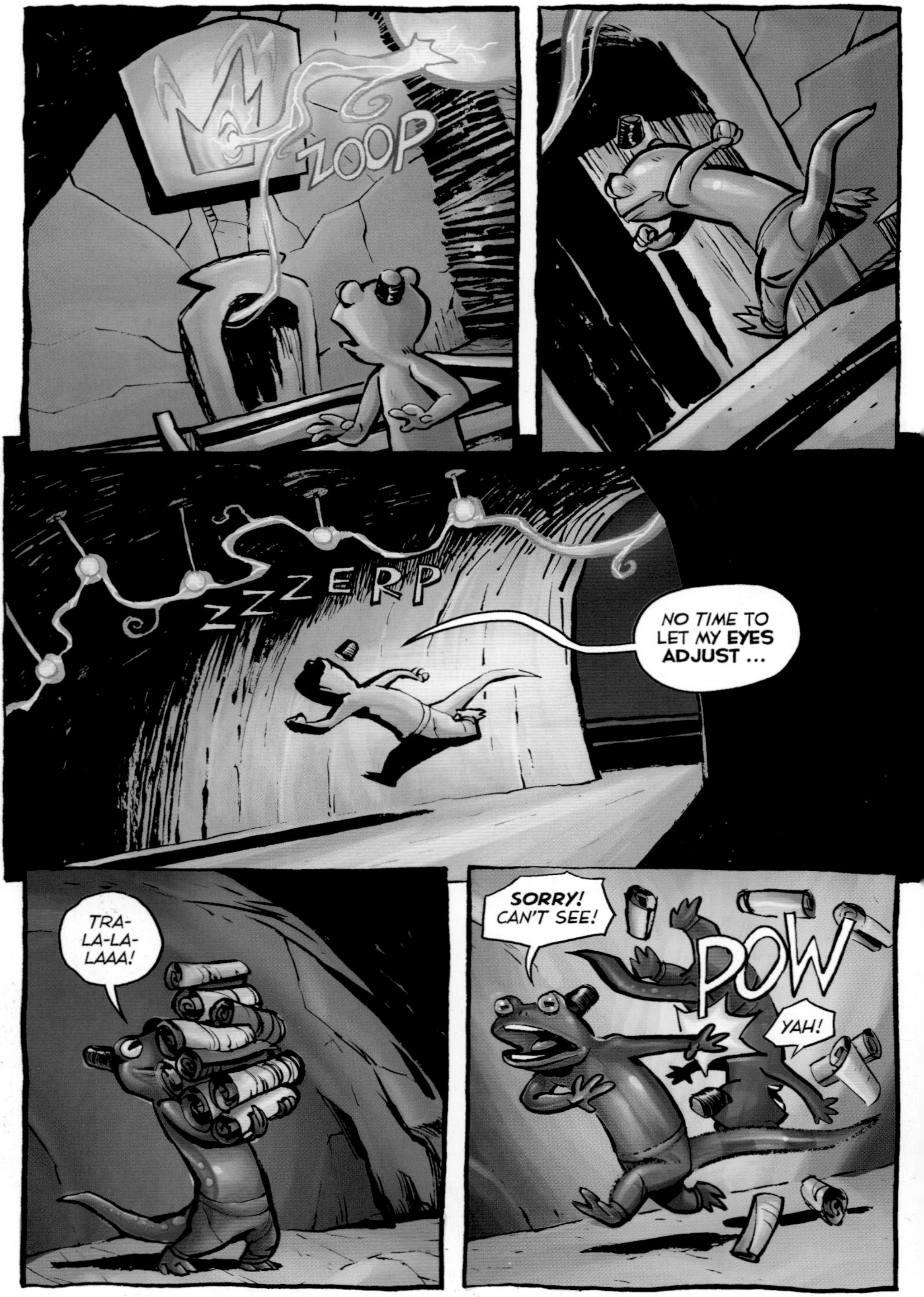
ZOOP
ZZZZERP
NO TIME TO LET MY EYES ADJUST ...
TRA-LA-LA-LAAA!
SORRY! CAN'T SEE!
POW
YAH!

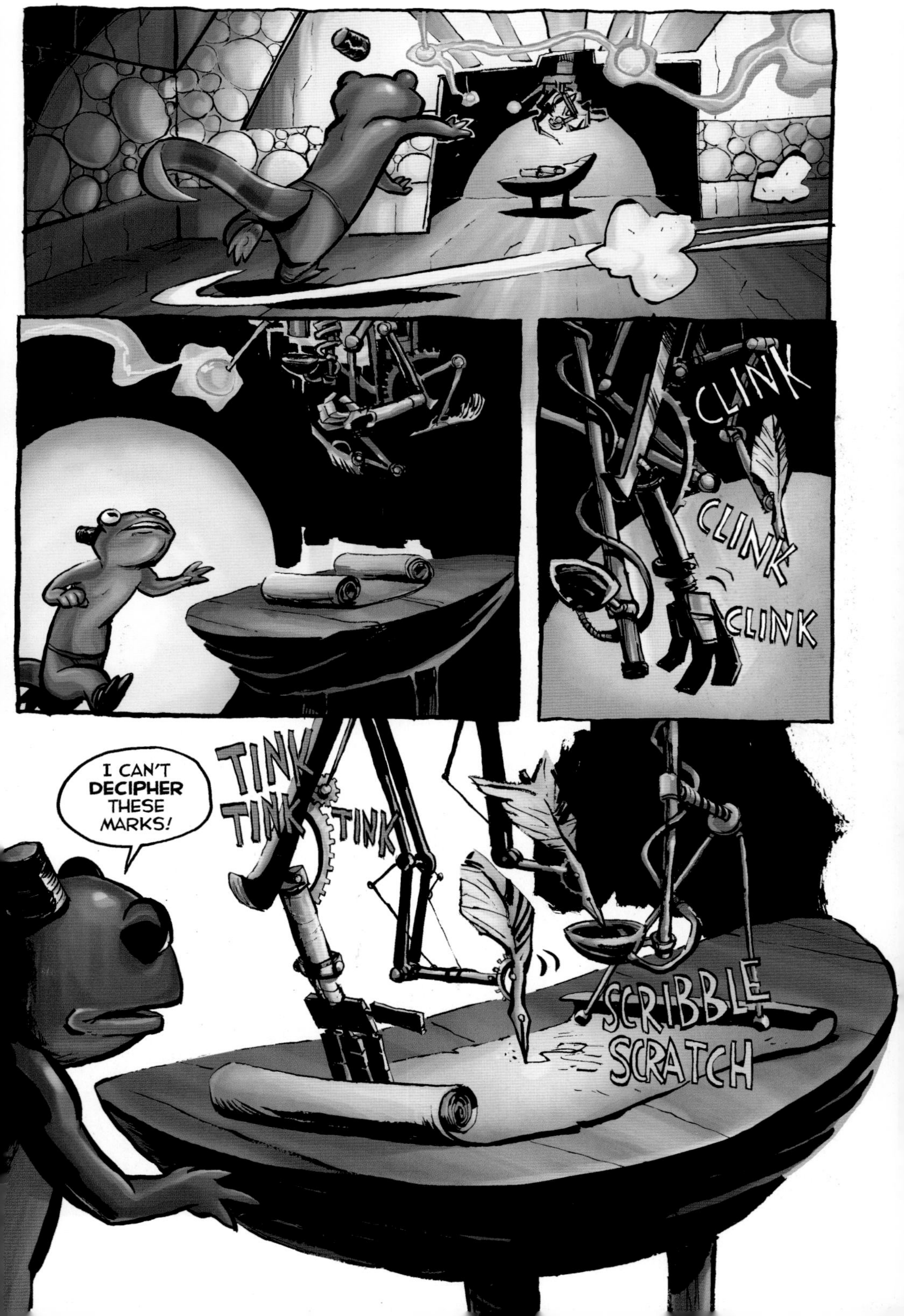

CLINK
CLINK
CLINK
I CAN'T DECIPHER THESE MARKS!
TINK
TINK
TINK
SCRIBBLE
SCRATCH

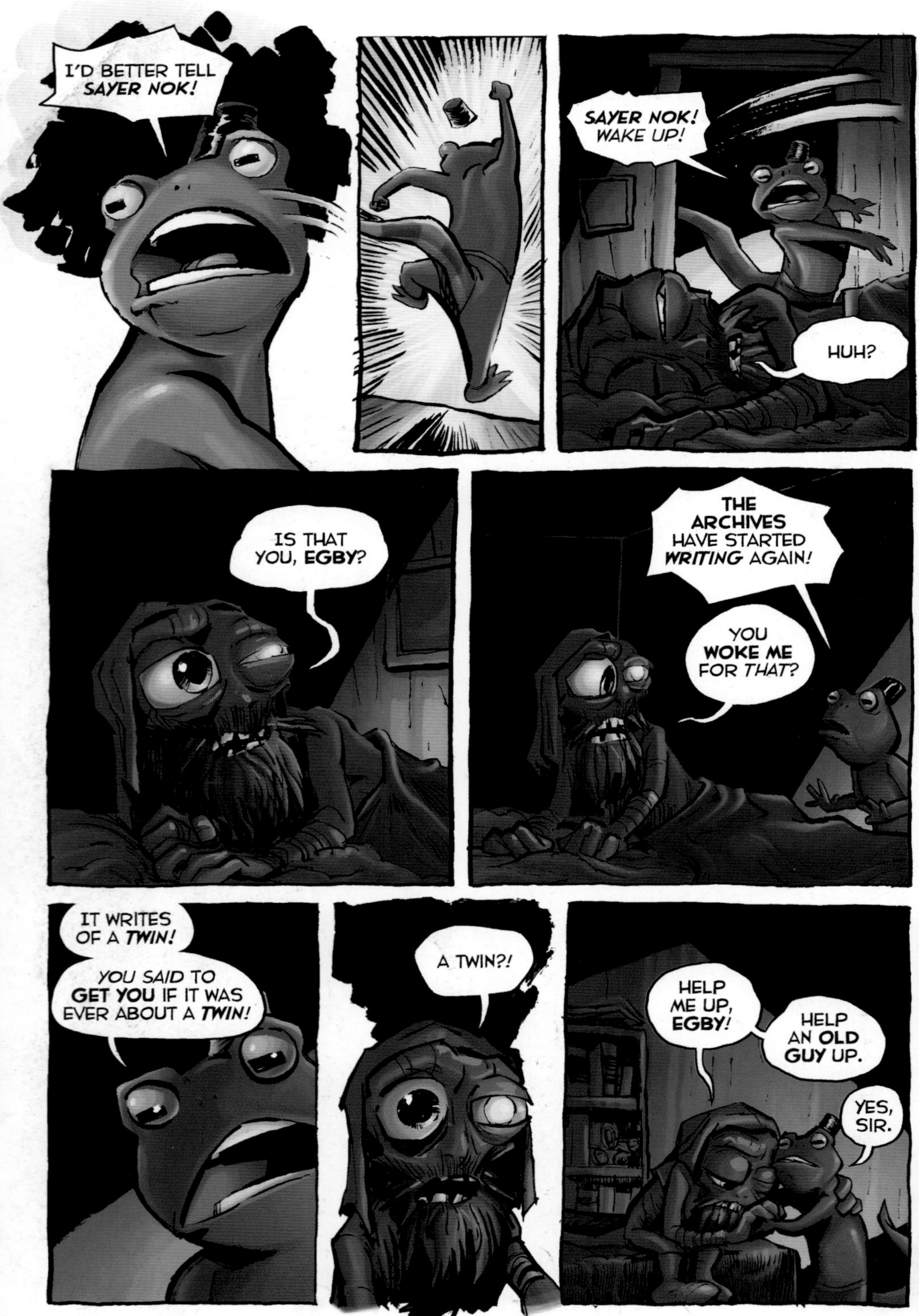

I'D BETTER TELL SAYER NOK!
SAYER NOK! WAKE UP!
HUH?
IS THAT YOU, EGBY?
THE ARCHIVES HAVE STARTED WRITING AGAIN!
YOU WOKE ME FOR THAT?
IT WRITES OF A TWIN!
YOU SAID TO GET YOU IF IT WAS EVER ABOUT A TWIN!
A TWIN?!
HELP ME UP, EGBY!
HELP AN OLD GUY UP.
YES, SIR.

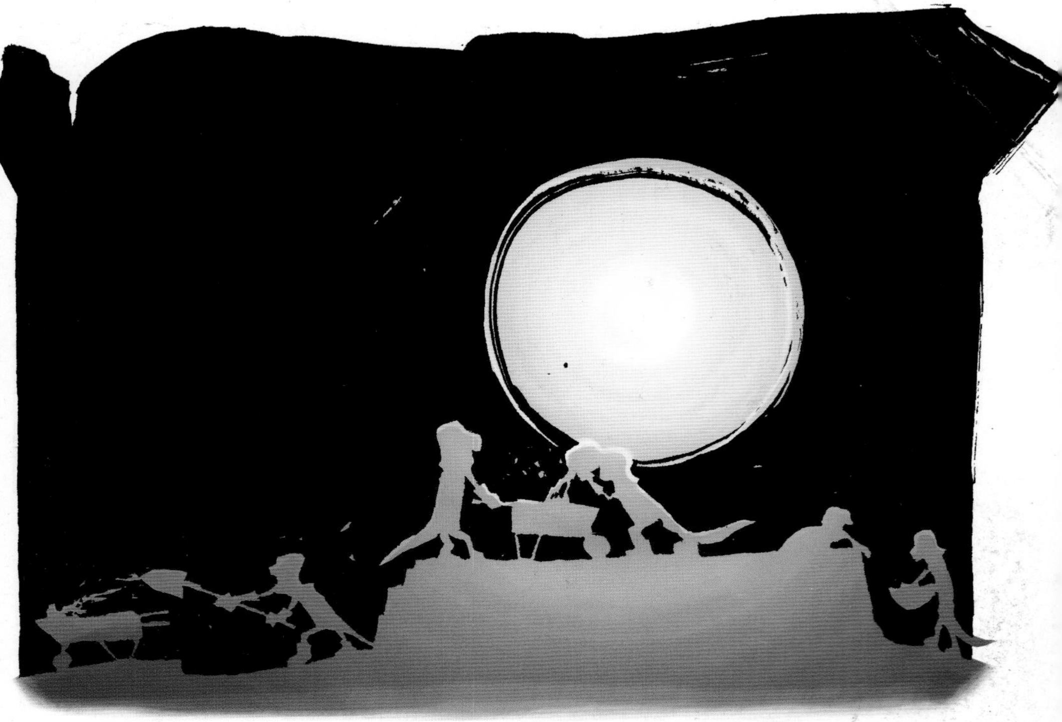

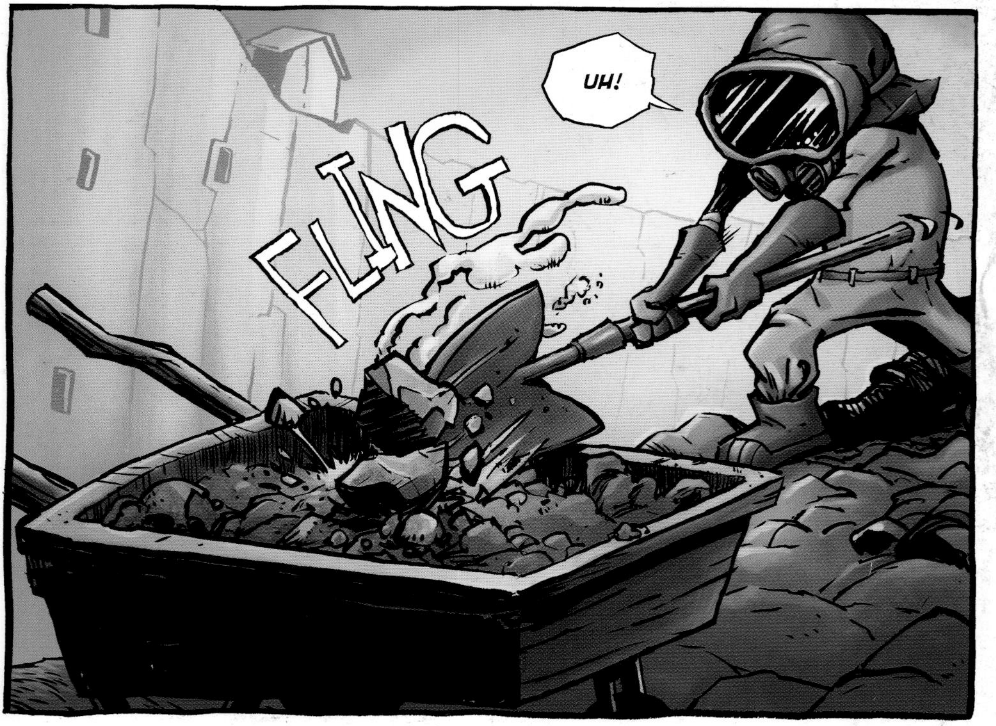
UH!
FLING

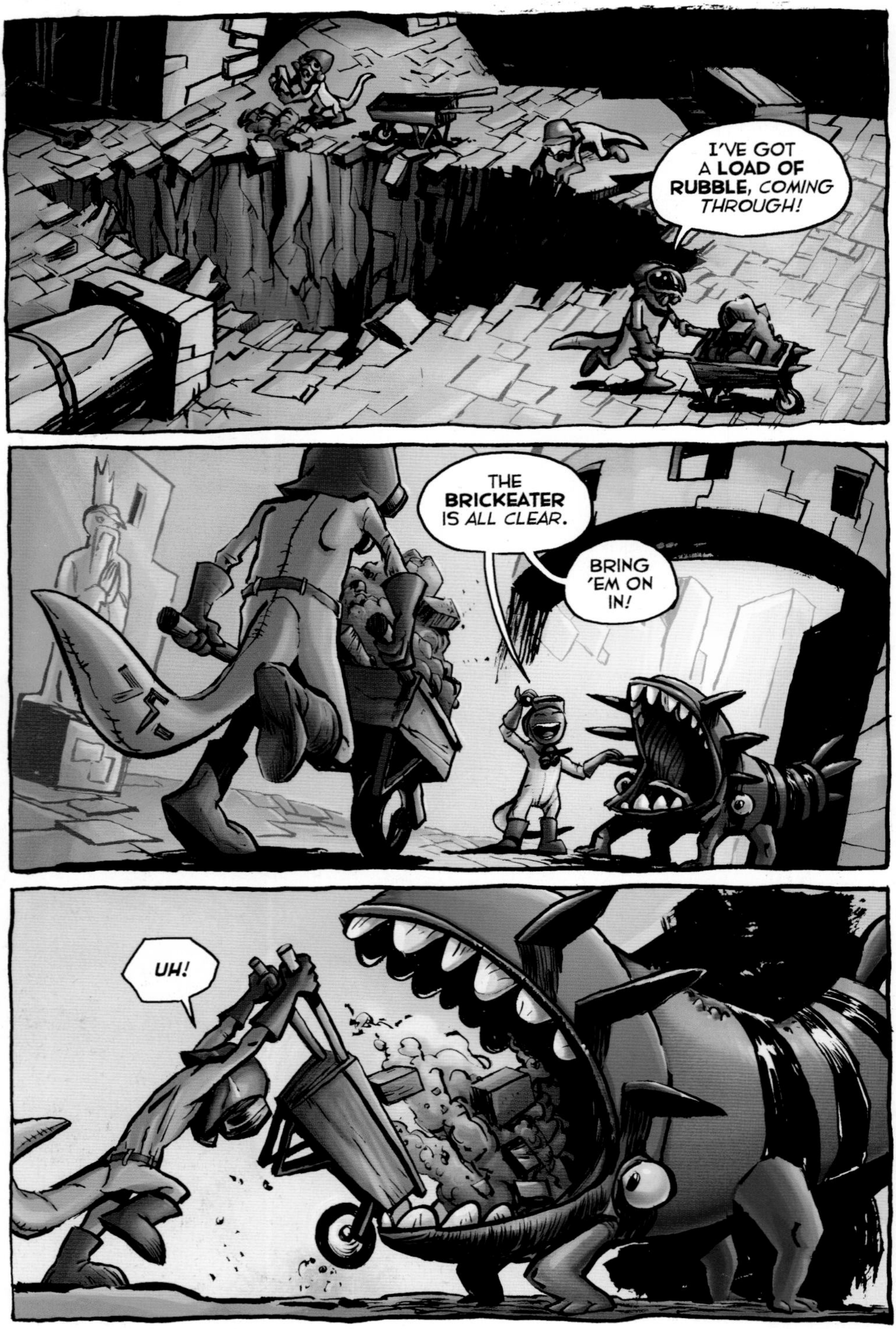
I'VE GOT A **LOAD OF RUBBLE**, *COMING THROUGH!*
THE **BRICKEATER** IS *ALL CLEAR*.
BRING 'EM ON IN!
UH!

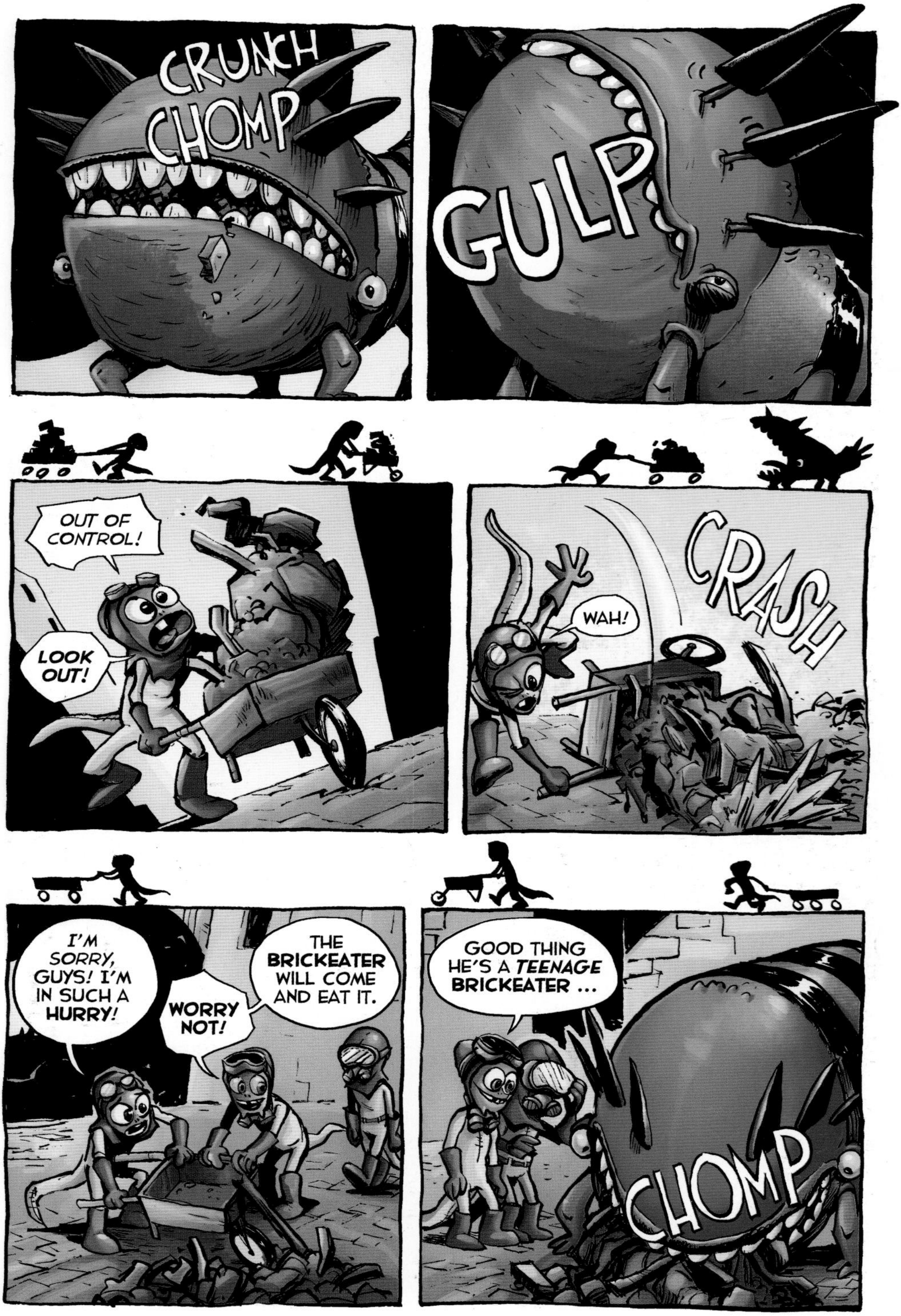
CRUNCH
CHOMP
GULP
OUT OF CONTROL!
LOOK OUT!
WAH!
CRASH
I'M SORRY, GUYS! I'M IN SUCH A **HURRY!**
WORRY NOT!
THE **BRICKEATER** WILL COME AND EAT IT.
GOOD THING HE'S A *TEENAGE* **BRICKEATER ...**
CHOMP

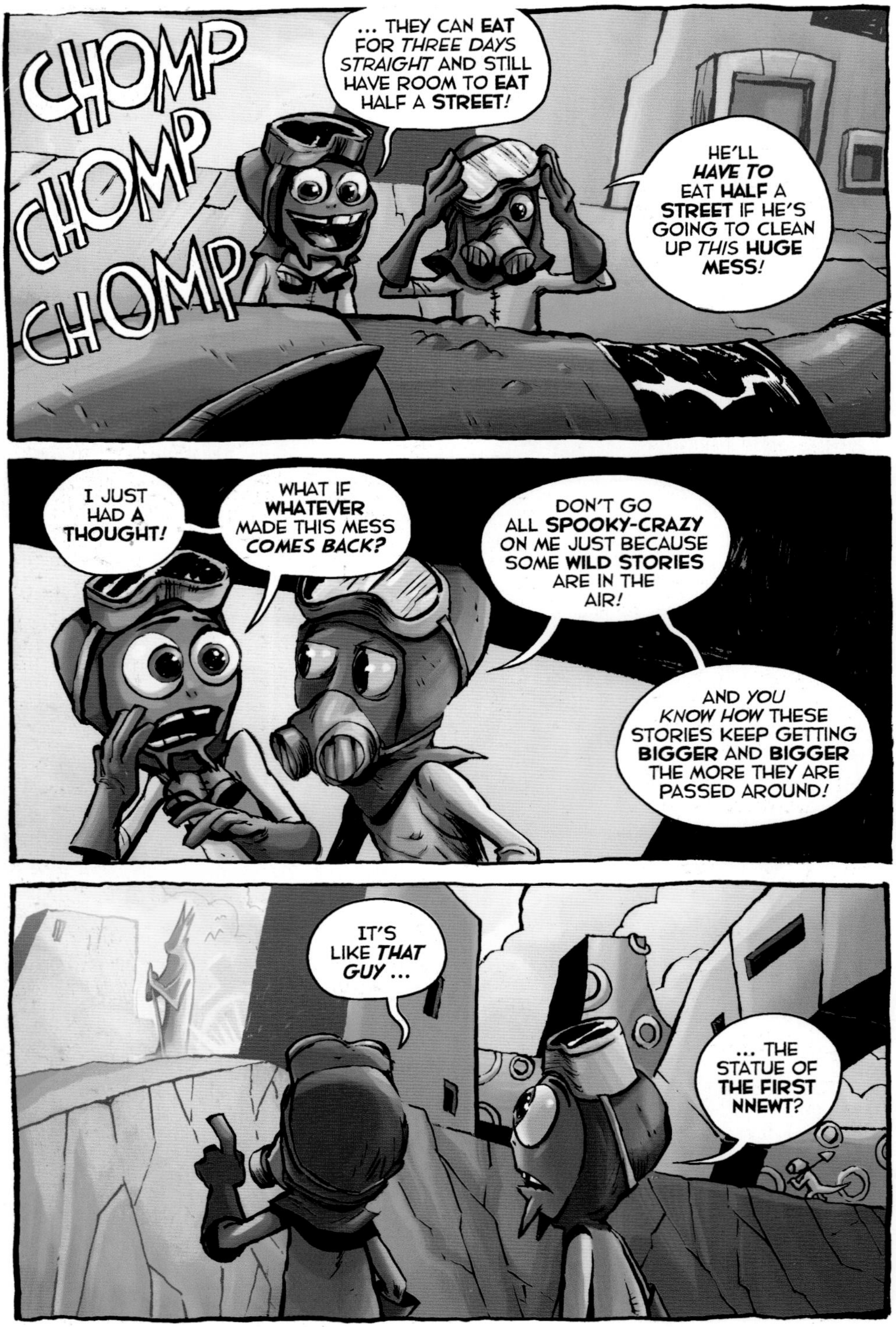
CHOMP CHOMP CHOMP
... THEY CAN EAT FOR THREE DAYS STRAIGHT AND STILL HAVE ROOM TO EAT HALF A STREET!
HE'LL HAVE TO EAT HALF A STREET IF HE'S GOING TO CLEAN UP THIS HUGE MESS!
I JUST HAD A THOUGHT!
WHAT IF WHATEVER MADE THIS MESS COMES BACK?
DON'T GO ALL SPOOKY-CRAZY ON ME JUST BECAUSE SOME WILD STORIES ARE IN THE AIR!
AND YOU KNOW HOW THESE STORIES KEEP GETTING BIGGER AND BIGGER THE MORE THEY ARE PASSED AROUND!
IT'S LIKE THAT GUY ...
... THE STATUE OF THE FIRST NNEWT?

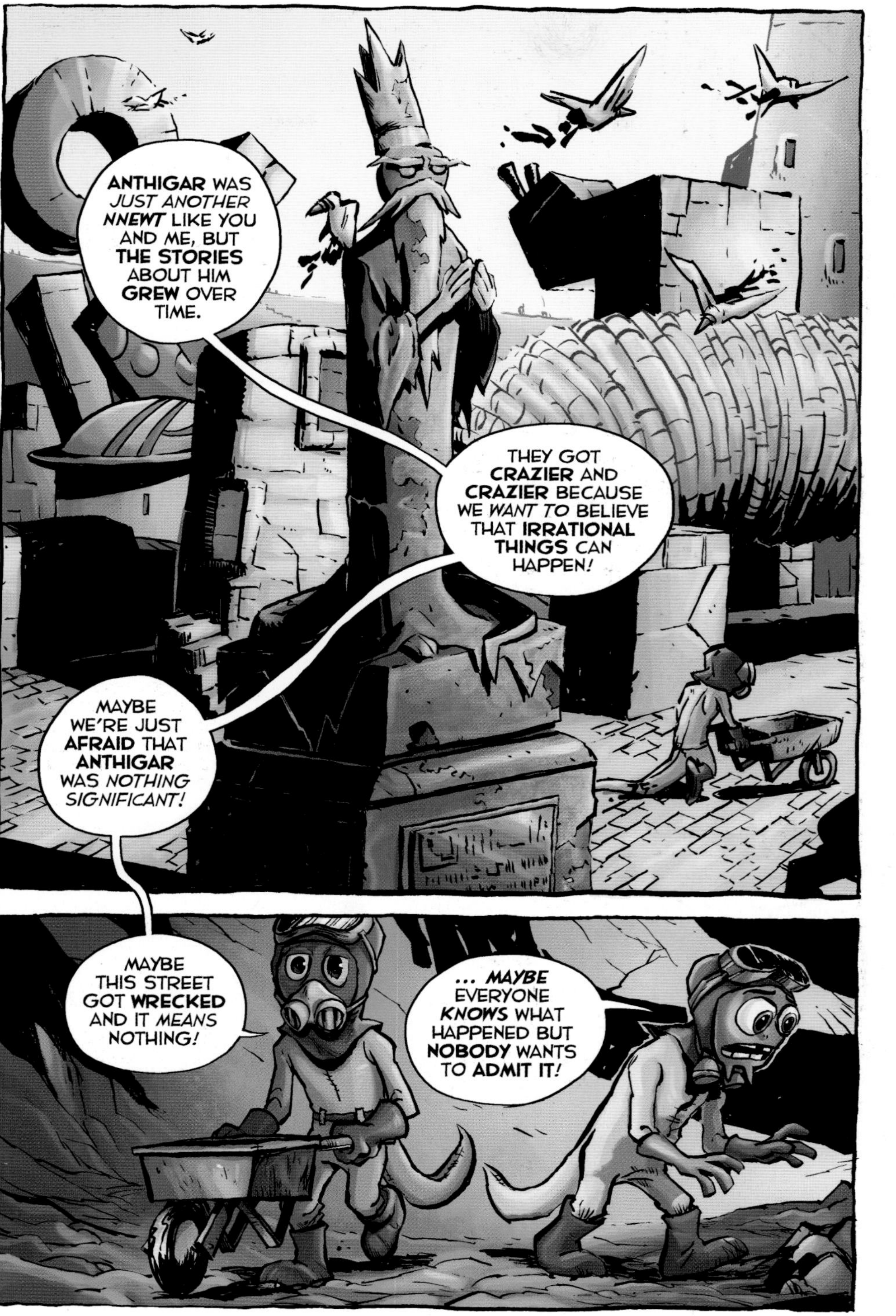
ANTHIGAR WAS JUST ANOTHER NNEWT LIKE YOU AND ME, BUT THE STORIES ABOUT HIM GREW OVER TIME.
THEY GOT CRAZIER AND CRAZIER BECAUSE WE WANT TO BELIEVE THAT IRRATIONAL THINGS CAN HAPPEN!
MAYBE WE'RE JUST AFRAID THAT ANTHIGAR WAS NOTHING SIGNIFICANT!
MAYBE THIS STREET GOT WRECKED AND IT MEANS NOTHING!
... MAYBE EVERYONE KNOWS WHAT HAPPENED BUT NOBODY WANTS TO ADMIT IT!

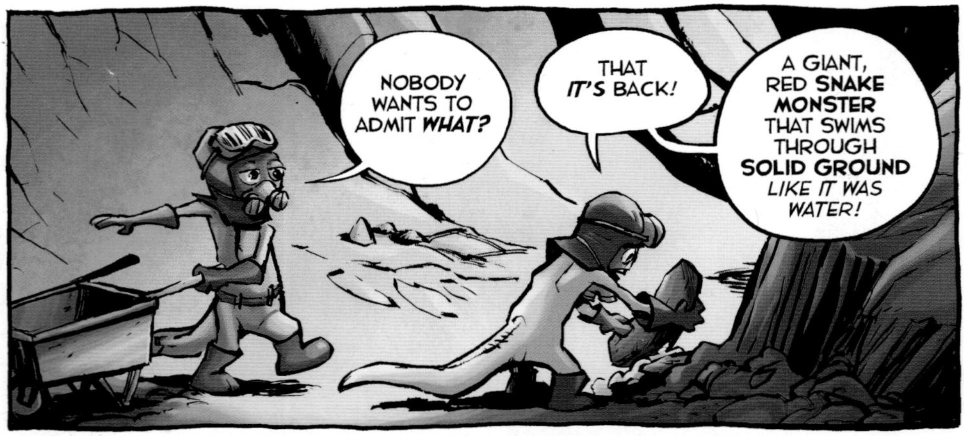
NOBODY WANTS TO ADMIT *WHAT?*
THAT *IT'S* BACK!
A GIANT, RED **SNAKE MONSTER** THAT SWIMS THROUGH **SOLID GROUND** *LIKE IT WAS WATER!*

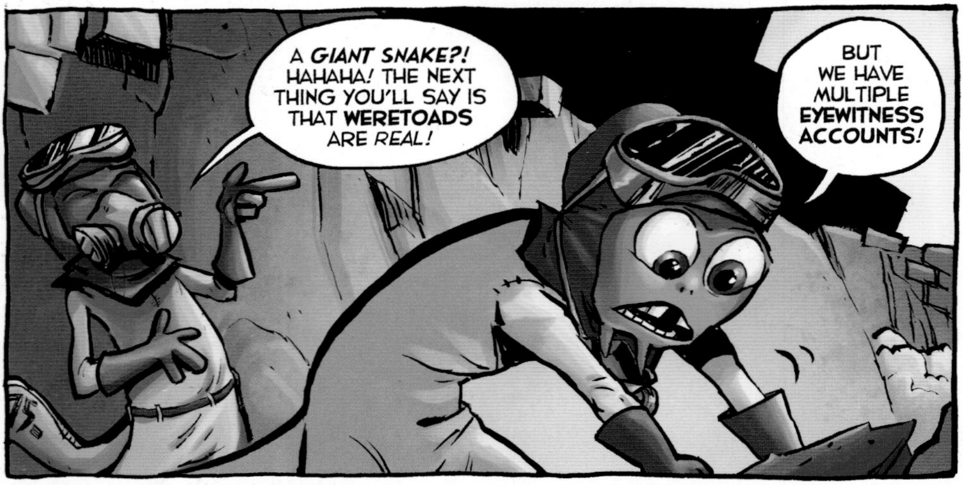
A *GIANT SNAKE?!* HAHAHA! THE NEXT THING *YOU'LL* SAY IS THAT **WERETOADS** ARE *REAL!*
BUT WE HAVE MULTIPLE **EYEWITNESS ACCOUNTS!**

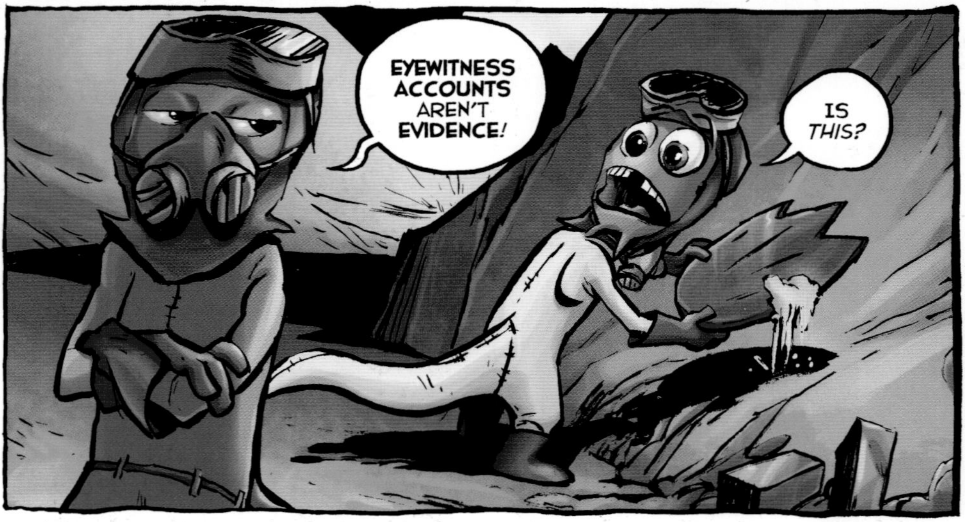
EYEWITNESS ACCOUNTS AREN'T **EVIDENCE!**
IS *THIS?*

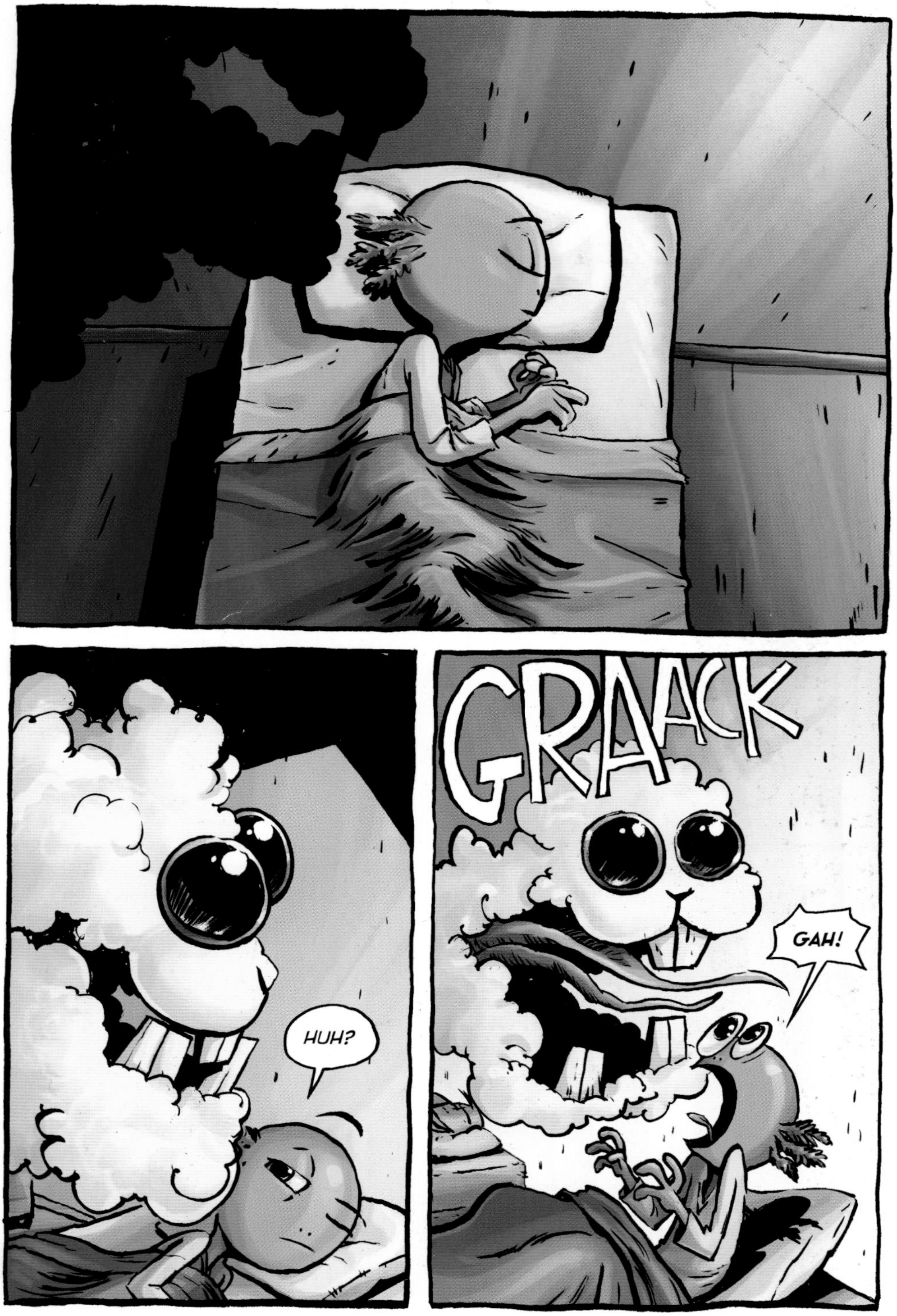
HUH?
GRAACK
GAH!

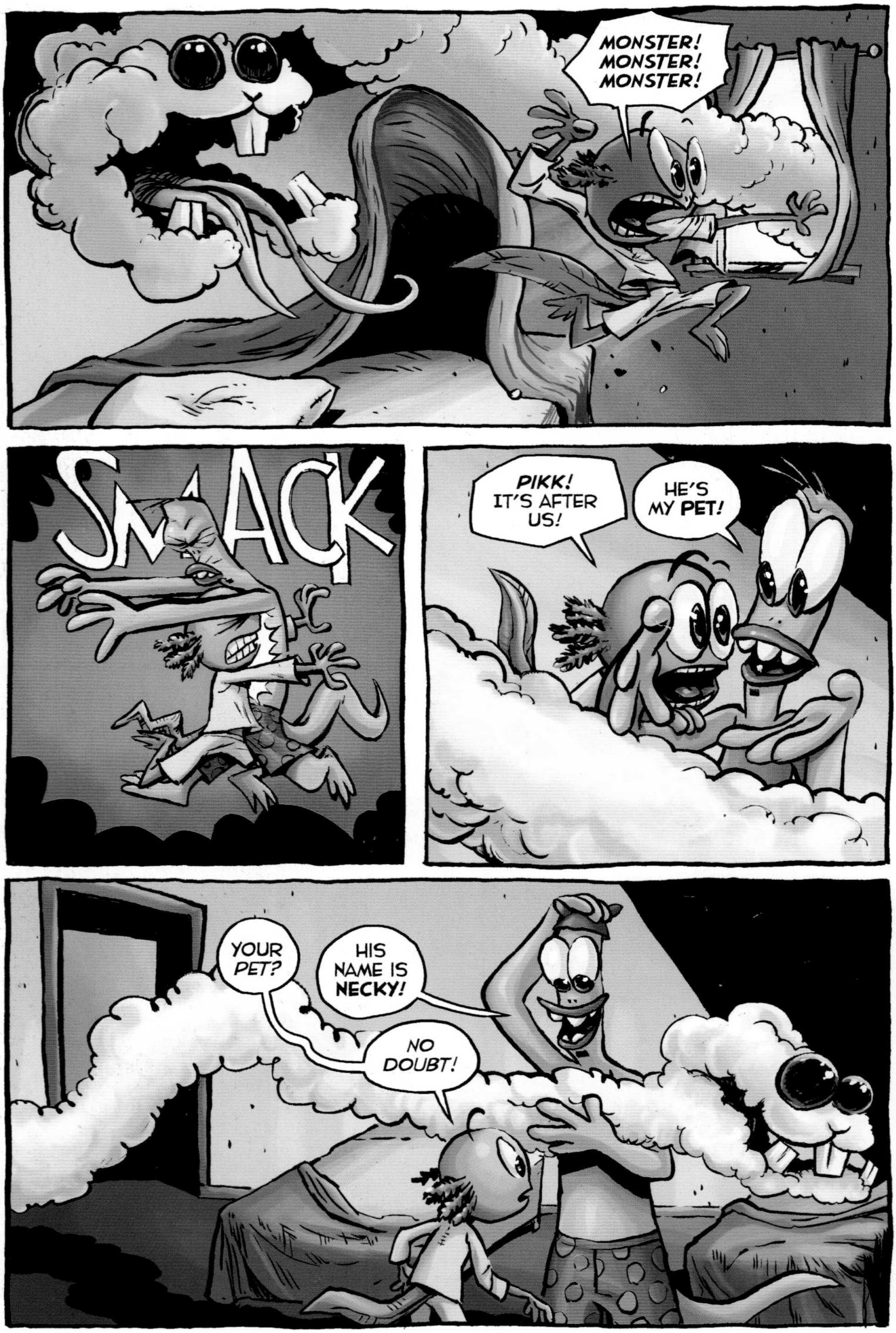
MONSTER! MONSTER! MONSTER!
SMACK
PIKK! IT'S AFTER US!
HE'S MY PET!
YOUR PET?
HIS NAME IS NECKY!
NO DOUBT!

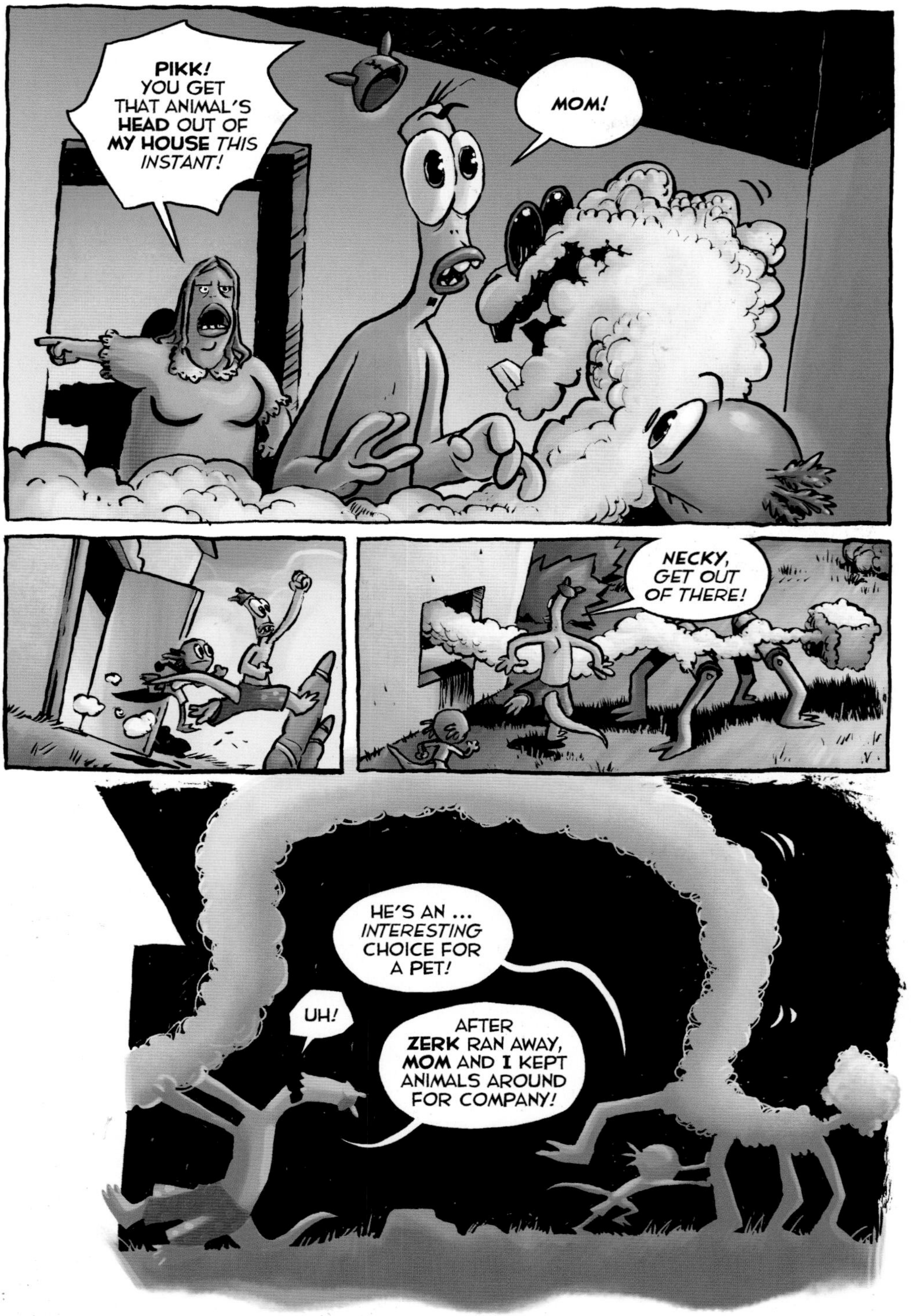
PIKK! YOU GET THAT ANIMAL'S HEAD OUT OF MY HOUSE THIS INSTANT!
MOM!
NECKY, GET OUT OF THERE!
HE'S AN ... INTERESTING CHOICE FOR A PET!
UH!
AFTER ZERK RAN AWAY, MOM AND I KEPT ANIMALS AROUND FOR COMPANY!

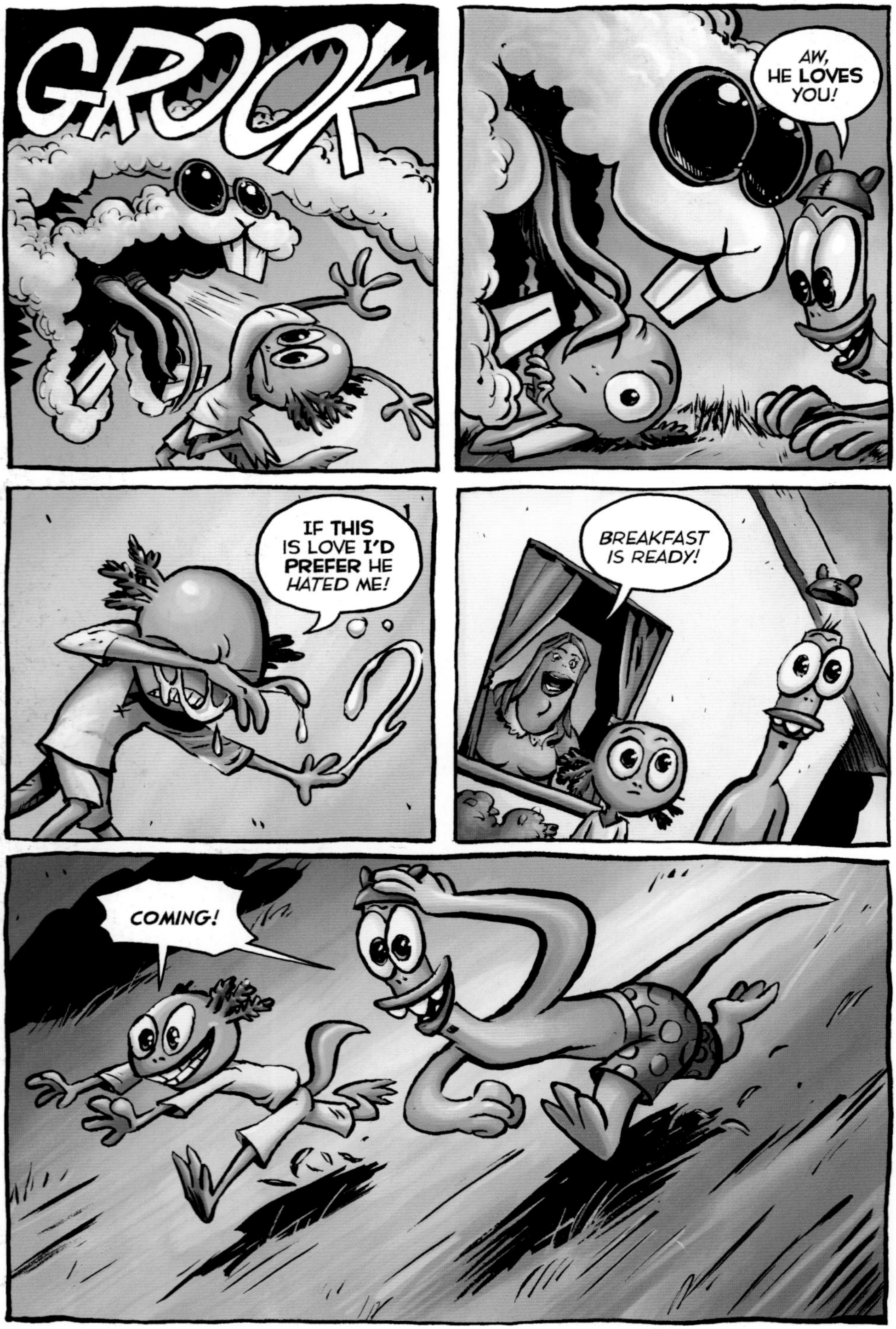
GROOK!
AW, HE LOVES YOU!
IF THIS IS LOVE I'D PREFER HE HATED ME!
BREAKFAST IS READY!
COMING!

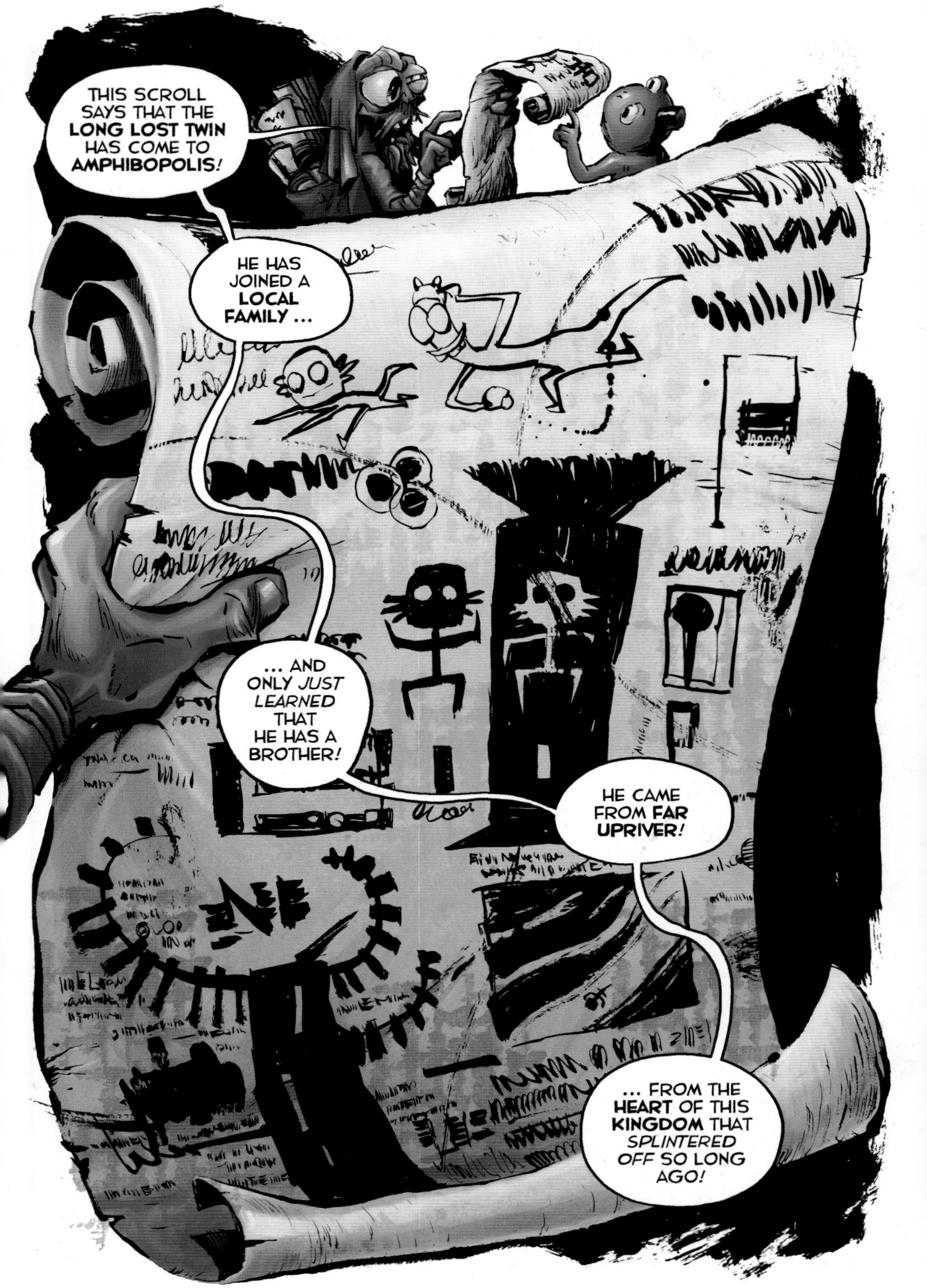
THIS SCROLL SAYS THAT THE **LONG LOST TWIN** HAS COME TO **AMPHIBOPOLIS**!
HE HAS JOINED A **LOCAL FAMILY** ...
... AND ONLY *JUST LEARNED* THAT HE HAS A **BROTHER**!
HE CAME FROM **FAR UPRIVER**!
... FROM THE **HEART** OF THIS **KINGDOM** THAT *SPLINTERED OFF* SO LONG AGO!

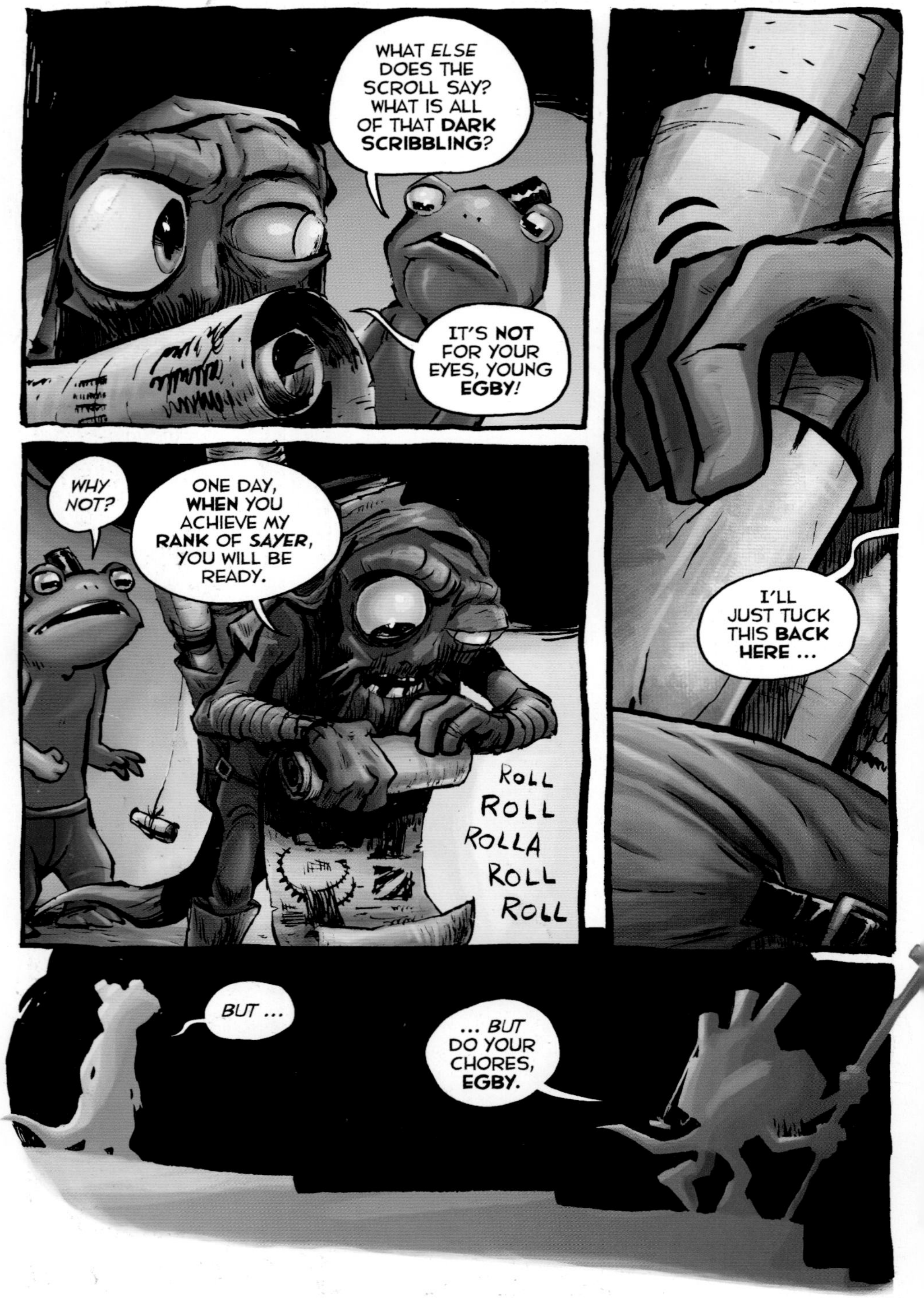
WHAT *ELSE* DOES THE SCROLL SAY? WHAT IS ALL OF THAT **DARK SCRIBBLING**?
IT'S **NOT** FOR YOUR EYES, YOUNG **EGBY**!
WHY NOT?
ONE DAY, **WHEN** YOU ACHIEVE MY **RANK** OF ***SAYER***, YOU WILL BE READY.
ROLL ROLL ROLLA ROLL ROLL
I'LL JUST TUCK THIS **BACK HERE ...**
BUT ...
... *BUT* DO YOUR CHORES, **EGBY**.

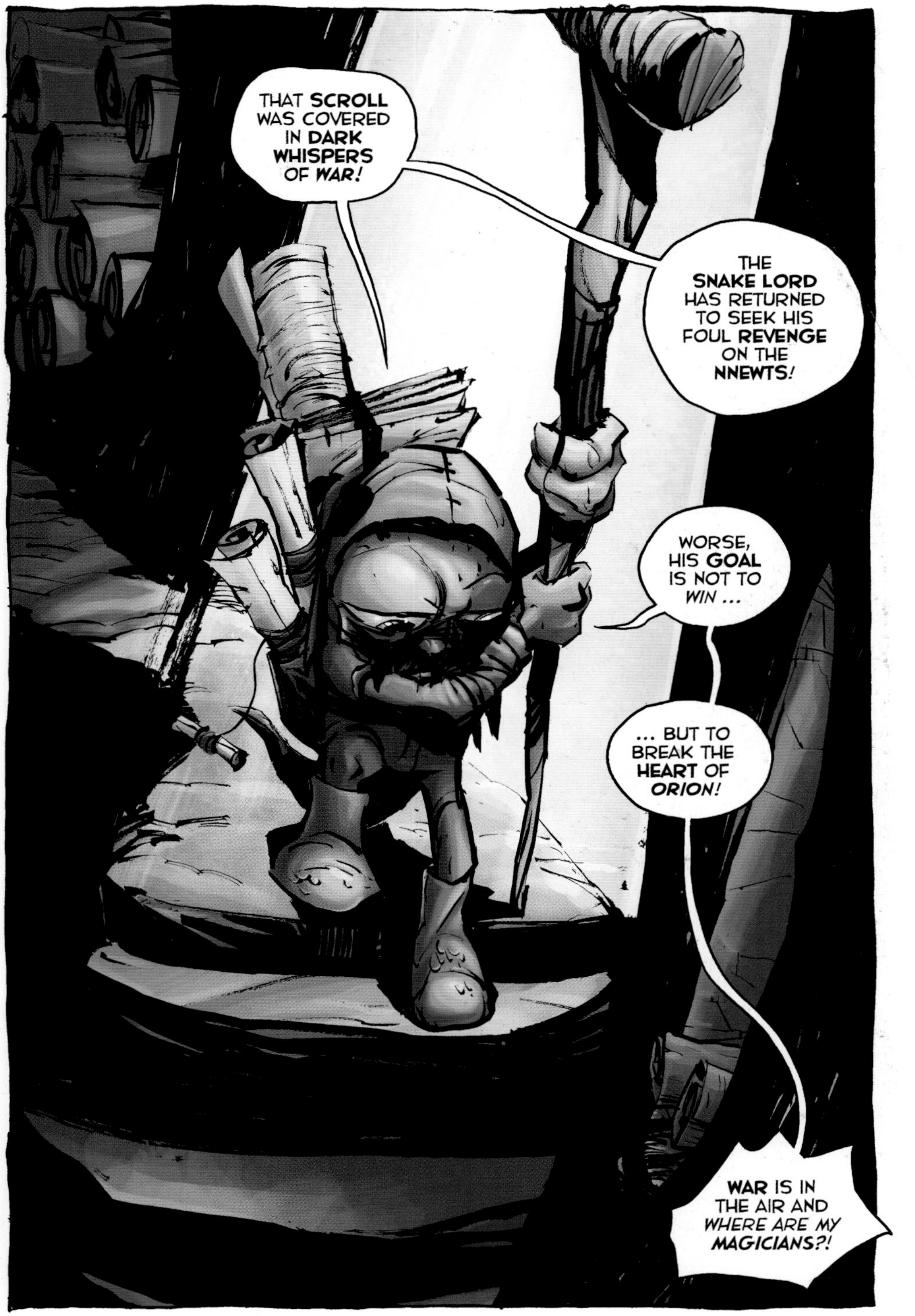
THAT **SCROLL** WAS COVERED IN **DARK WHISPERS** OF ***WAR!***
THE **SNAKE LORD** HAS RETURNED TO SEEK HIS FOUL **REVENGE** ON THE **NNEWTS!**
WORSE, HIS **GOAL** IS NOT TO *WIN ...*
... BUT TO BREAK THE **HEART** OF ***ORION!***
WAR IS IN THE AIR AND *WHERE ARE MY* ***MAGICIANS?!***

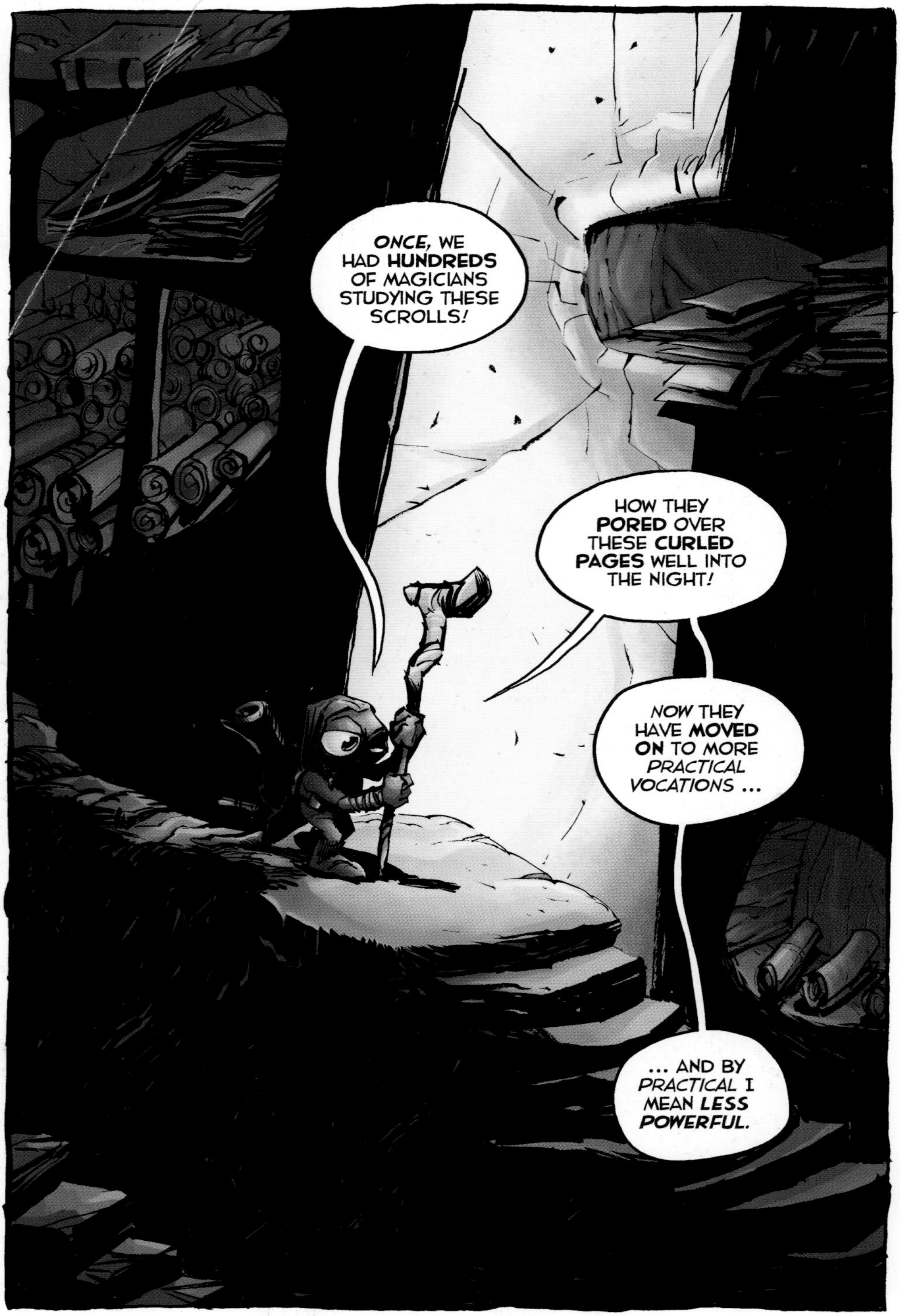
ONCE, WE HAD **HUNDREDS** OF MAGICIANS STUDYING THESE SCROLLS!
HOW THEY **PORED** OVER THESE **CURLED PAGES** WELL INTO THE NIGHT!
NOW THEY HAVE **MOVED ON** TO MORE *PRACTICAL VOCATIONS* ...
... AND BY *PRACTICAL* I MEAN **LESS POWERFUL.**

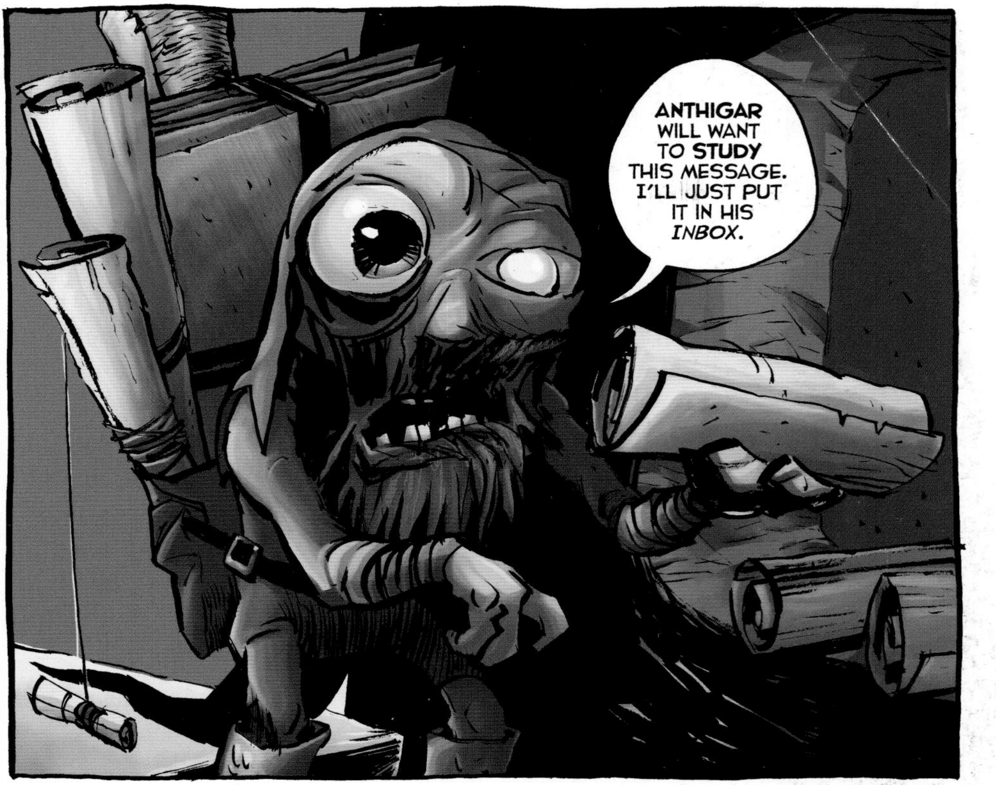
ANTHIGAR WILL WANT TO **STUDY** THIS MESSAGE. I'LL JUST PUT IT IN HIS *INBOX*.

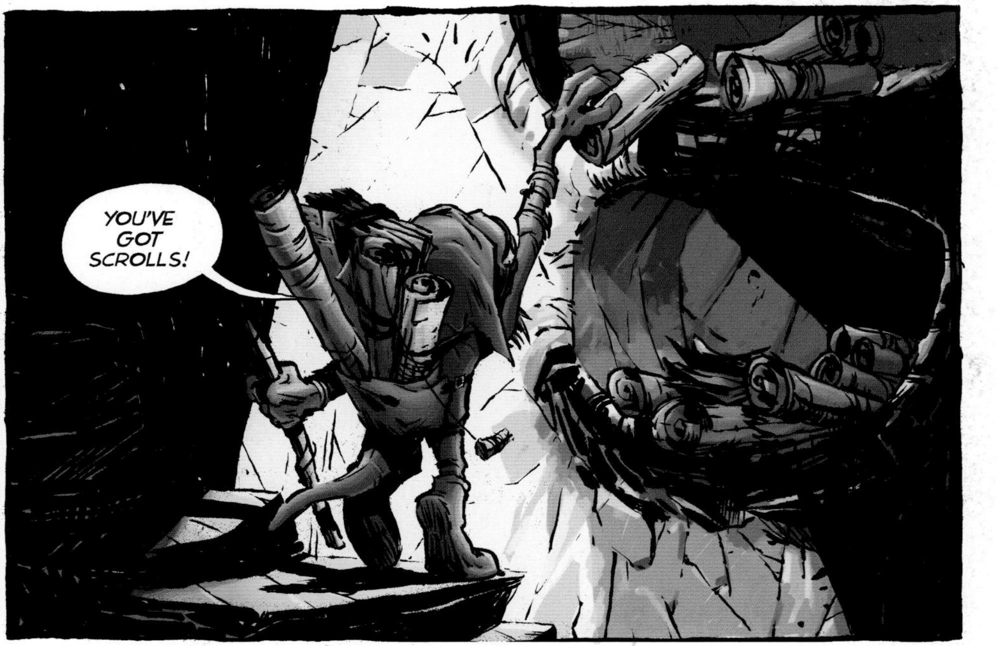
YOU'VE GOT SCROLLS!

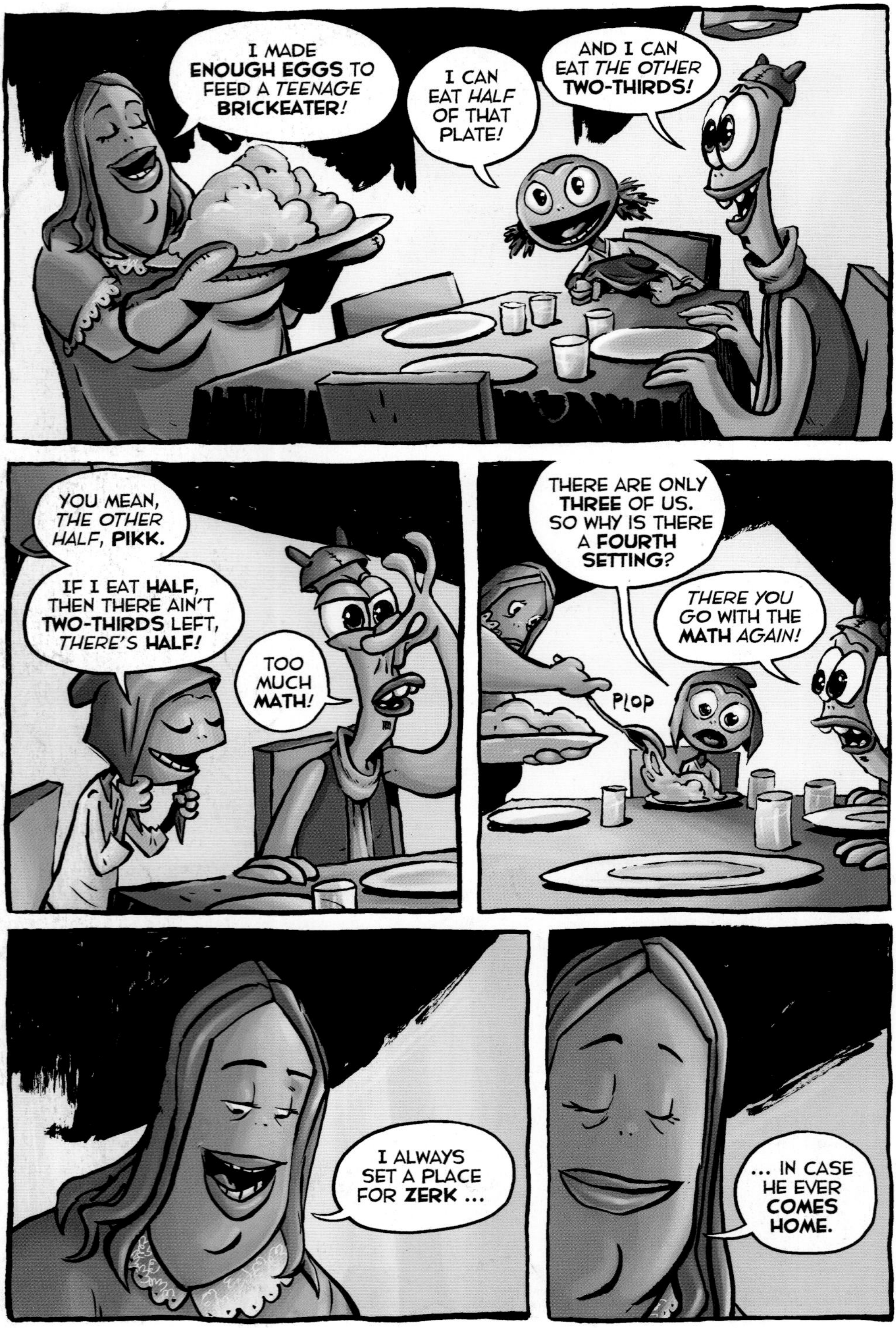
I MADE ENOUGH EGGS TO FEED A TEENAGE BRICKEATER!
I CAN EAT HALF OF THAT PLATE!
AND I CAN EAT THE OTHER TWO-THIRDS!
YOU MEAN, THE OTHER HALF, PIKK.
IF I EAT HALF, THEN THERE AIN'T TWO-THIRDS LEFT, THERE'S HALF!
TOO MUCH MATH!
THERE ARE ONLY THREE OF US. SO WHY IS THERE A FOURTH SETTING?
PLOP
THERE YOU GO WITH THE MATH AGAIN!
I ALWAYS SET A PLACE FOR ZERK ...
... IN CASE HE EVER COMES HOME.

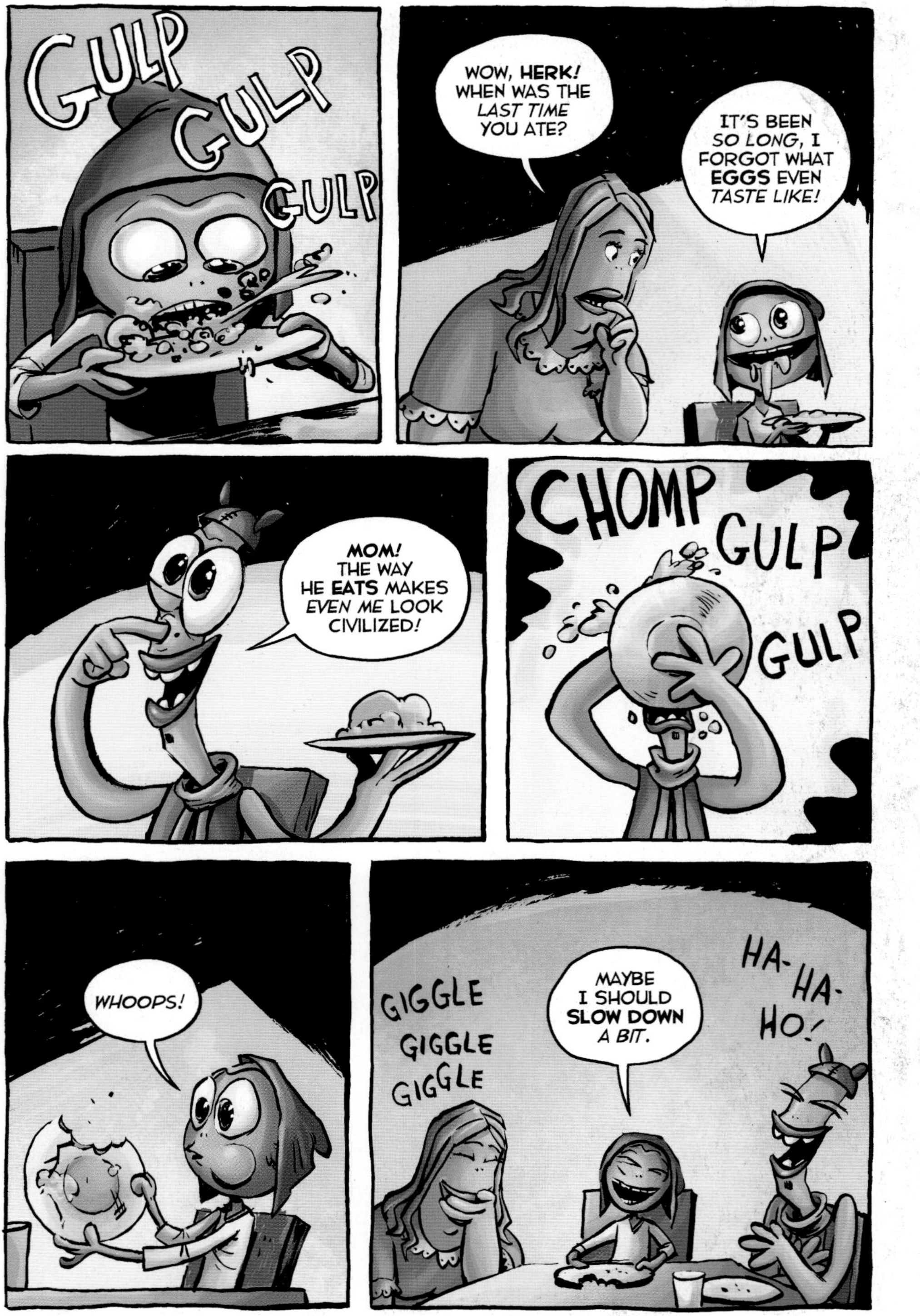
GULP GULP GULP
WOW, HERK! WHEN WAS THE LAST TIME YOU ATE?
IT'S BEEN SO LONG, I FORGOT WHAT EGGS EVEN TASTE LIKE!
MOM! THE WAY HE EATS MAKES EVEN ME LOOK CIVILIZED!
CHOMP GULP GULP
WHOOPS!
GIGGLE GIGGLE GIGGLE
MAYBE I SHOULD SLOW DOWN A BIT.
HA-HA-HO!

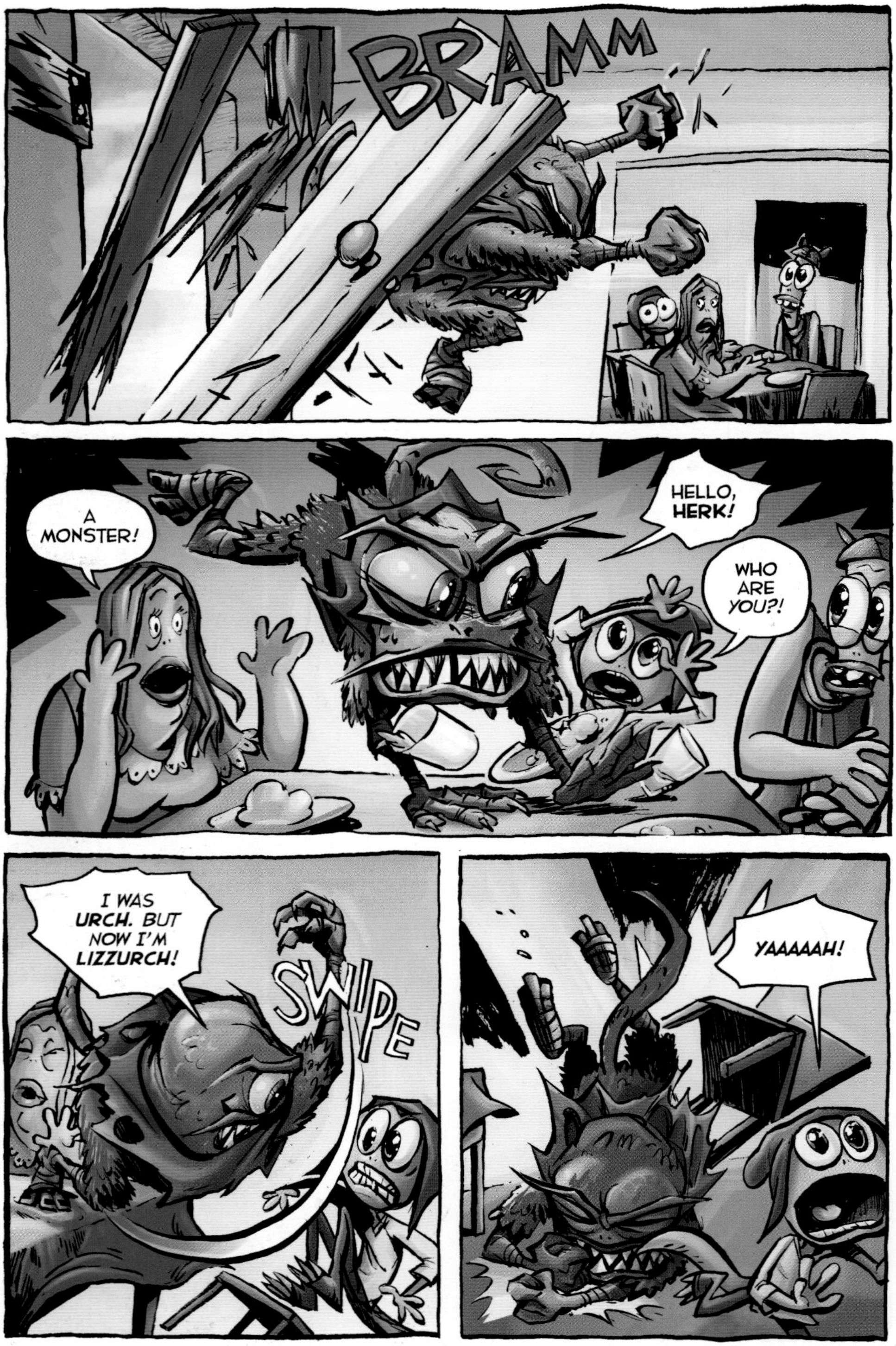
BRAMM
A MONSTER!
HELLO, HERK!
WHO ARE YOU?!
I WAS URCH. BUT NOW I'M LIZZURCH!
SWIPE
YAAAAAH!

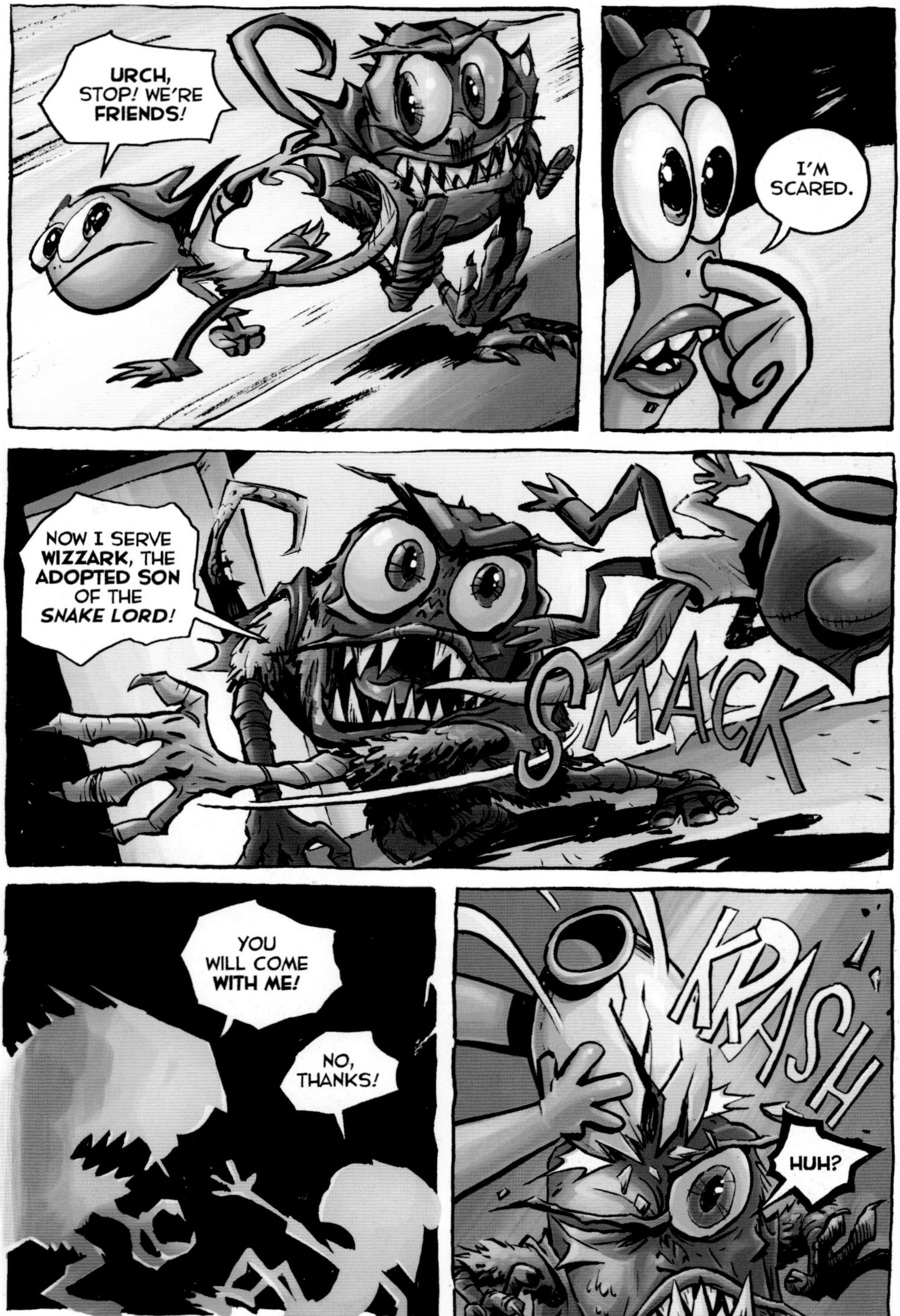
URCH, STOP! WE'RE FRIENDS!
I'M SCARED.
NOW I SERVE WIZZARK, THE ADOPTED SON OF THE SNAKE LORD!
SMACK
YOU WILL COME WITH ME!
NO, THANKS!
KRASH
HUH?

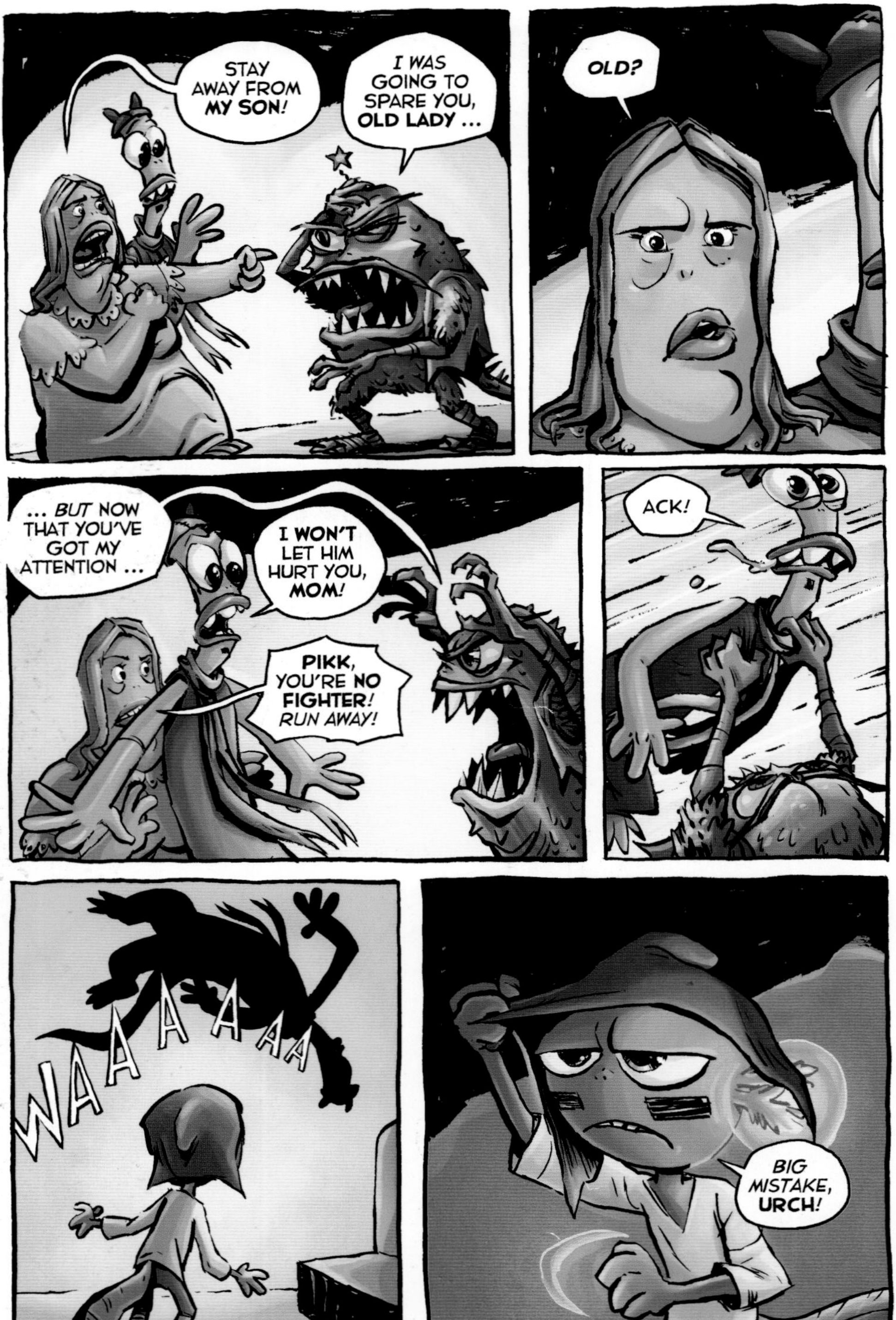
STAY AWAY FROM **MY SON**!
I WAS GOING TO SPARE YOU, **OLD LADY ...**
OLD?
... *BUT* NOW THAT YOU'VE GOT MY ATTENTION ...
I WON'T LET HIM HURT YOU, **MOM**!
PIKK, YOU'RE **NO FIGHTER**! *RUN AWAY!*
ACK!
WAAAAAAA
BIG MISTAKE, **URCH!**

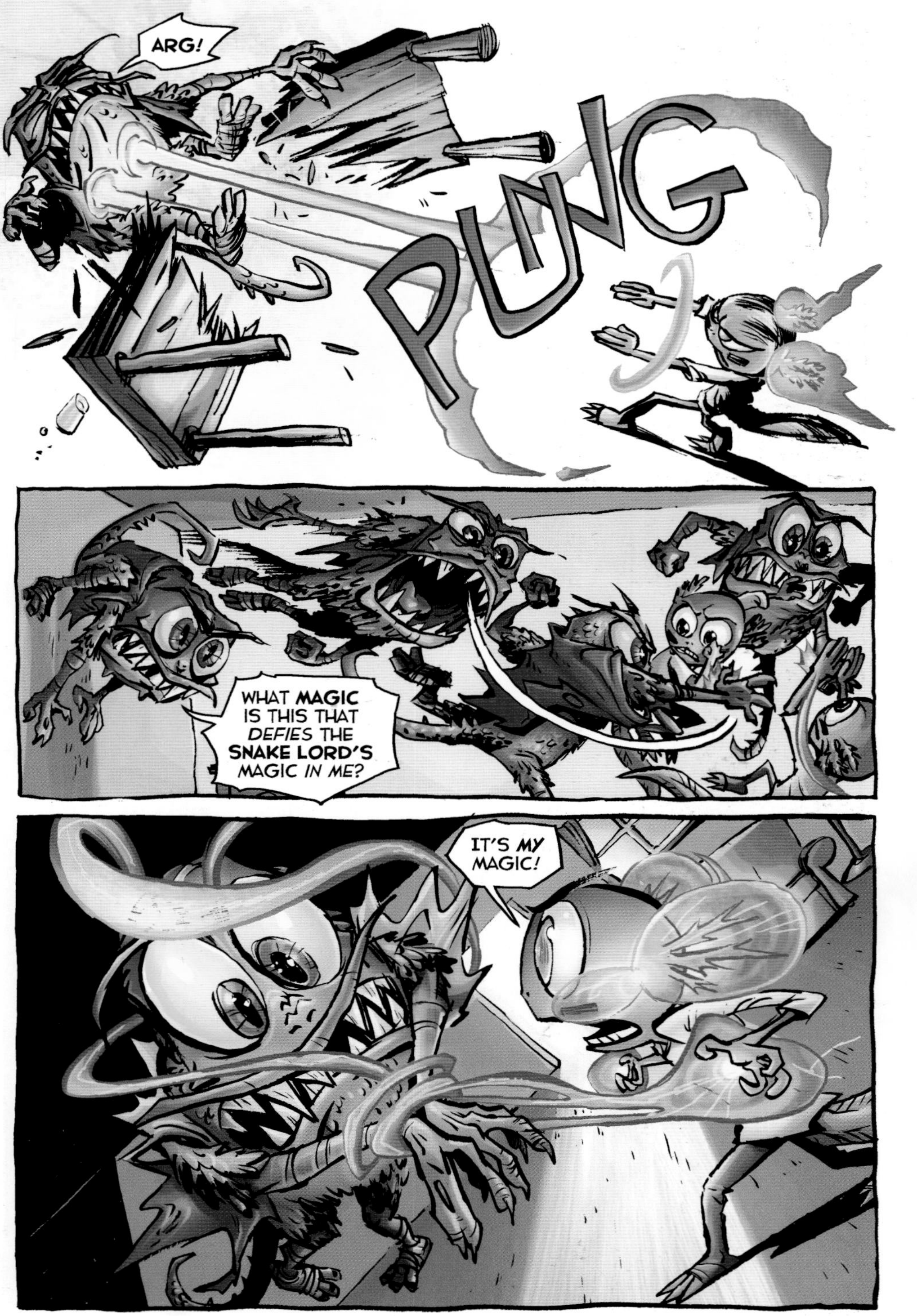
ARG!
PLUNG
WHAT **MAGIC** IS THIS THAT *DEFIES* THE **SNAKE LORD'S** MAGIC *IN ME*?
IT'S *MY* MAGIC!

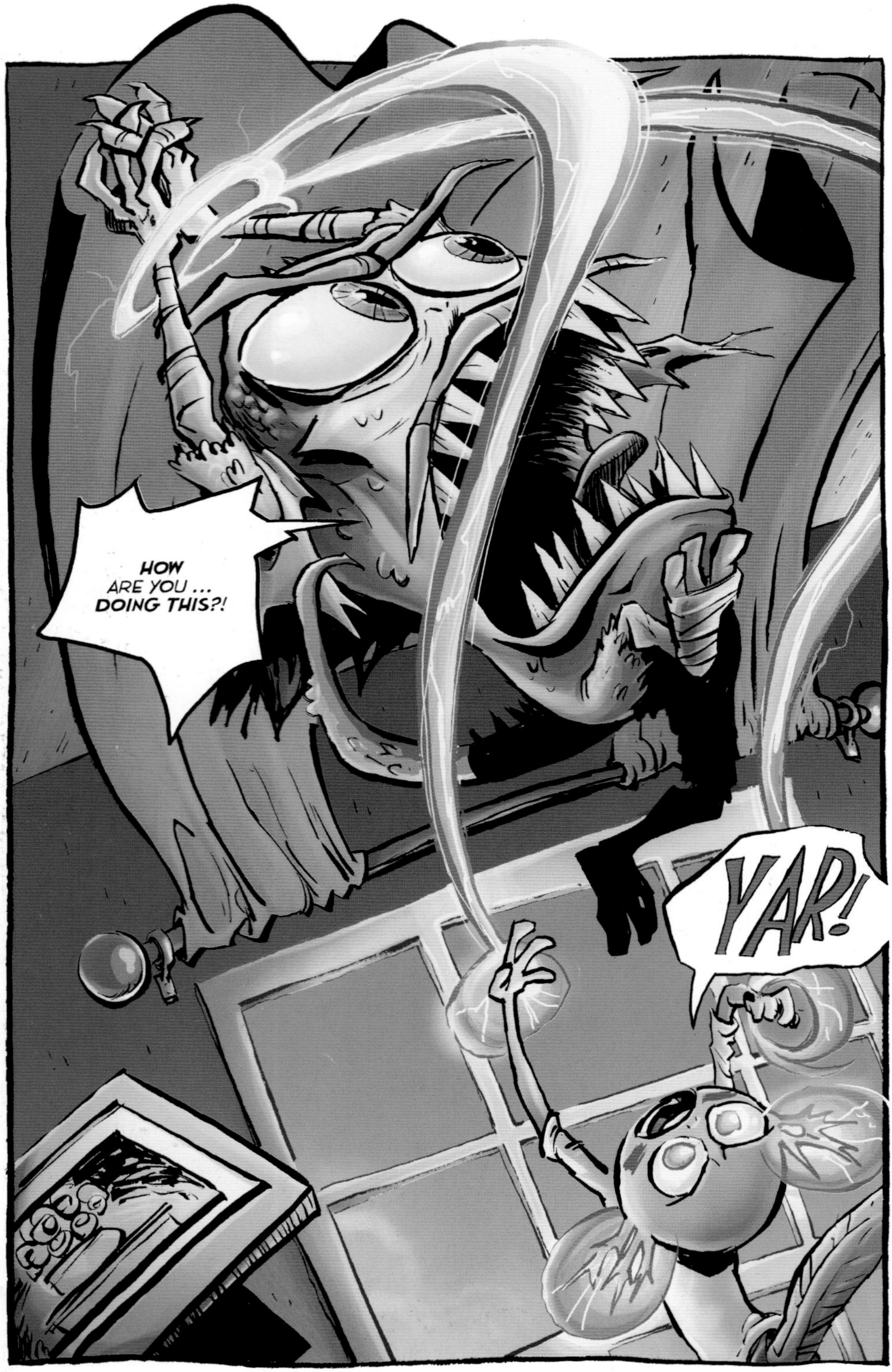
HOW ARE YOU ... DOING THIS?!
YAR!

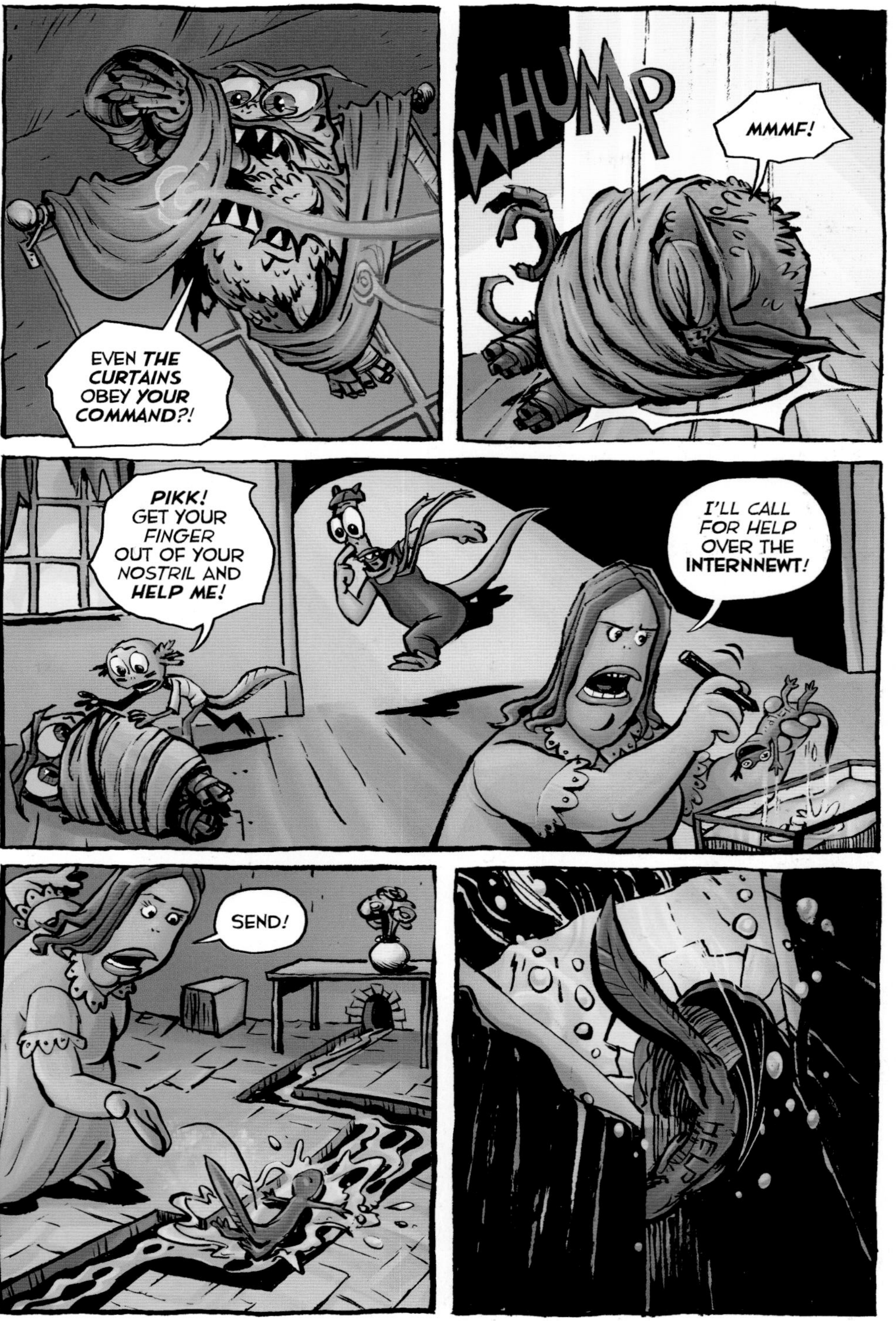
EVEN THE CURTAINS OBEY YOUR COMMAND?!
WHUMP
MMMF!
PIKK! GET YOUR FINGER OUT OF YOUR NOSTRIL AND HELP ME!
I'LL CALL FOR HELP OVER THE INTERNNEWT!
SEND!
HELP

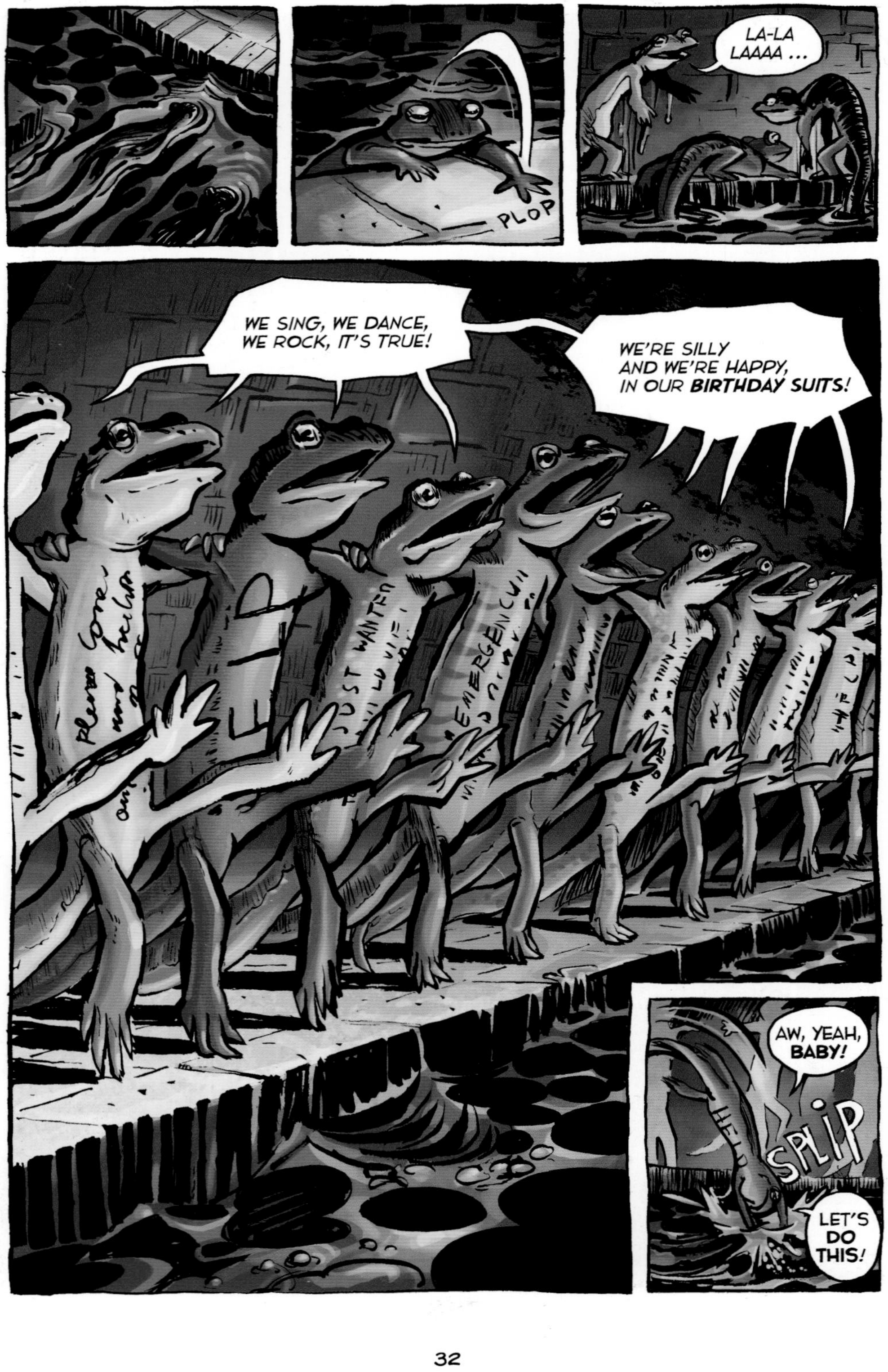
PLOP
LA-LA LAAAA ...
WE SING, WE DANCE, WE ROCK, IT'S TRUE!
WE'RE SILLY AND WE'RE HAPPY, IN OUR **BIRTHDAY SUITS!**
AW, YEAH, **BABY!**
SPLIP
LET'S **DO THIS!**

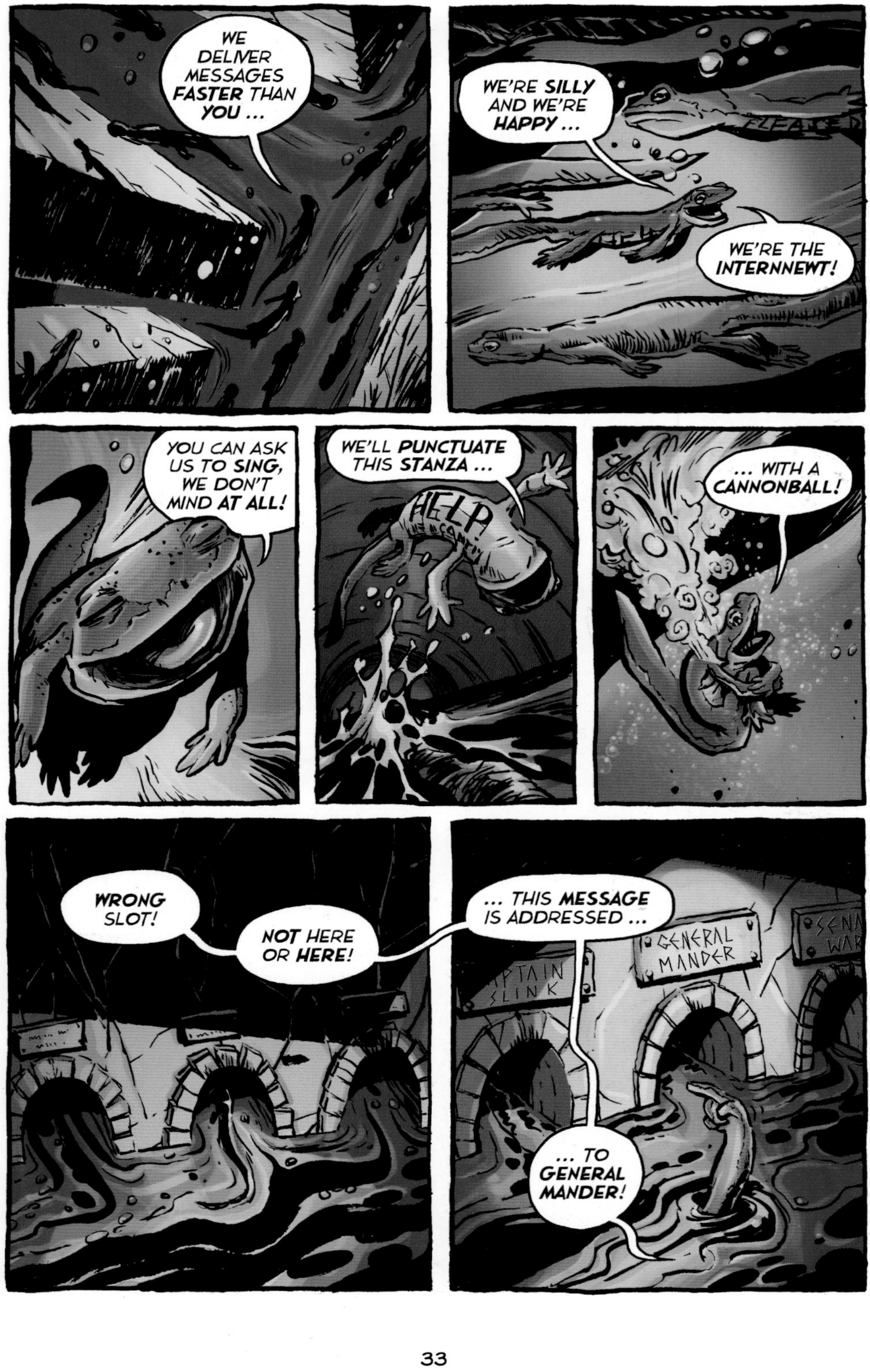
WE DELIVER MESSAGES FASTER THAN YOU ...
WE'RE SILLY AND WE'RE HAPPY ...
WE'RE THE INTERNNEWT!
YOU CAN ASK US TO SING, WE DON'T MIND AT ALL!
WE'LL PUNCTUATE THIS STANZA ...
HELP
... WITH A CANNONBALL!
WRONG SLOT!
NOT HERE OR HERE!
... THIS MESSAGE IS ADDRESSED ...
GENERAL MANDER
... TO GENERAL MANDER!

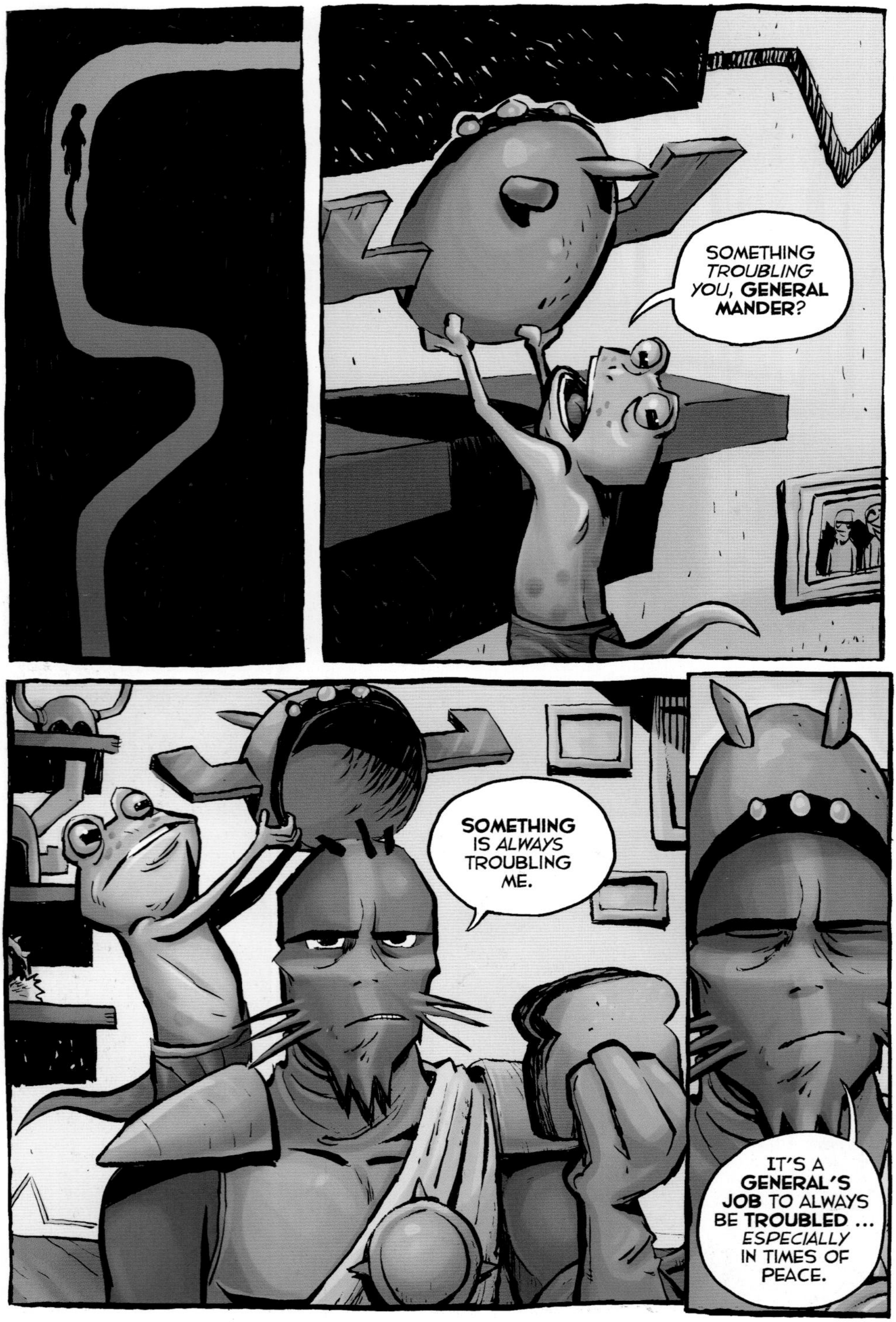
SOMETHING *TROUBLING* *YOU*, **GENERAL MANDER**?
SOMETHING IS *ALWAYS* TROUBLING ME.
IT'S A **GENERAL'S JOB** TO ALWAYS BE **TROUBLED** ... *ESPECIALLY* IN TIMES OF PEACE.

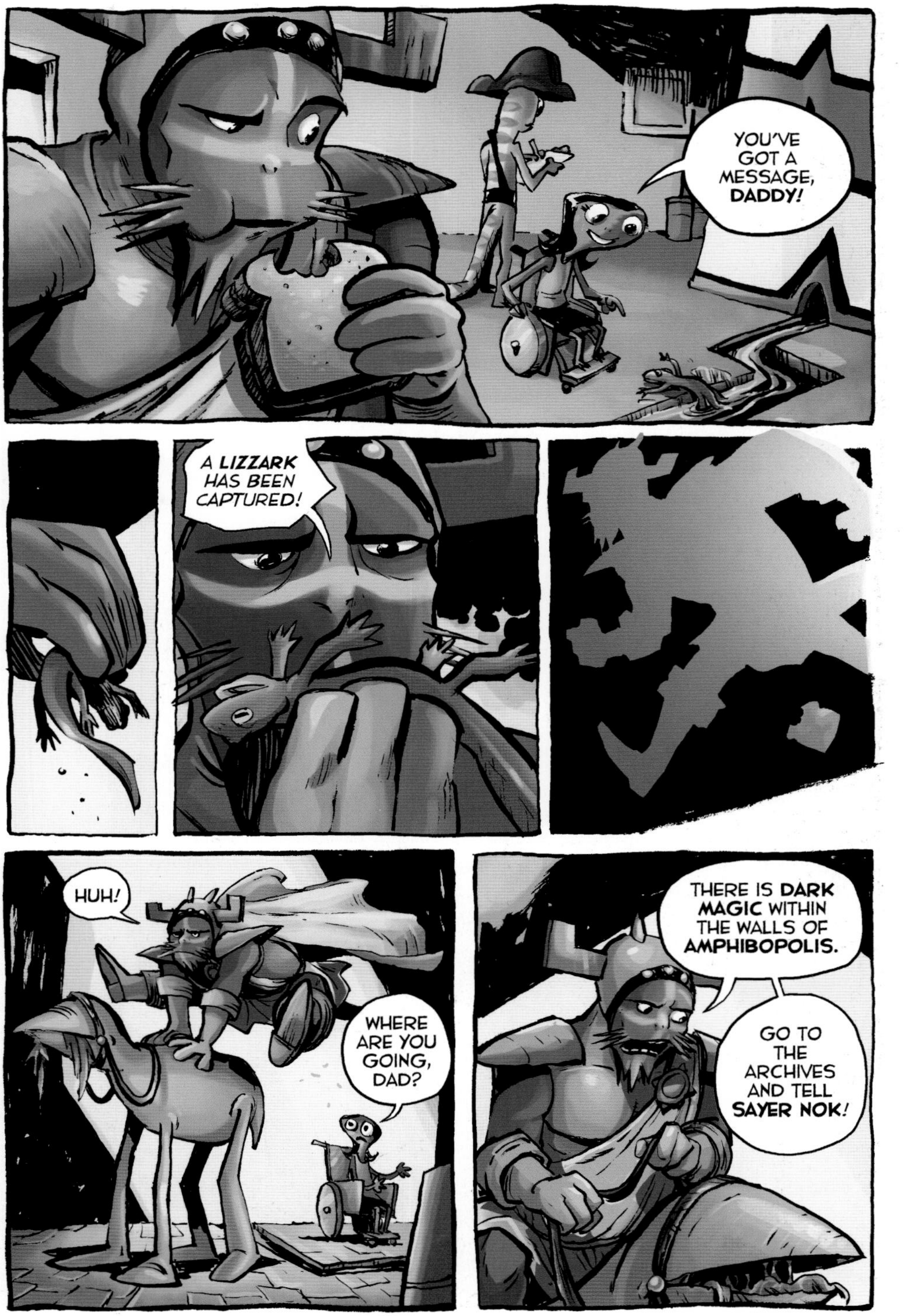
YOU'VE GOT A MESSAGE, **DADDY!**
A **LIZZARK** HAS BEEN CAPTURED!
HUH!
WHERE ARE YOU GOING, DAD?
THERE IS **DARK MAGIC** WITHIN THE WALLS OF **AMPHIBOPOLIS.**
GO TO THE ARCHIVES AND TELL **SAYER NOK!**

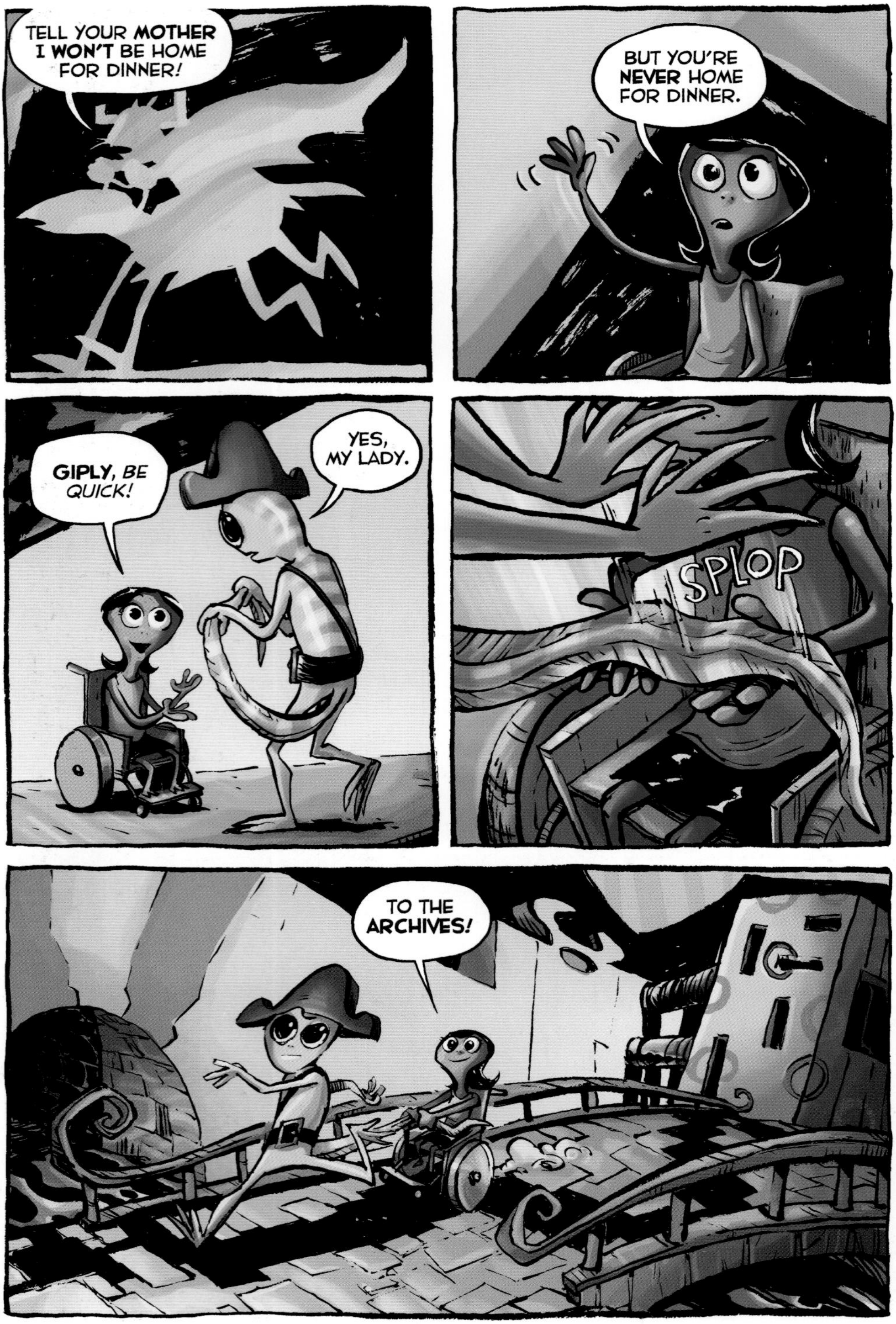

TELL YOUR **MOTHER** **I WON'T** BE HOME FOR DINNER!
BUT YOU'RE **NEVER** HOME FOR DINNER.
GIPLY, *BE QUICK!*
YES, MY LADY.
SPLOP
TO THE **ARCHIVES!**

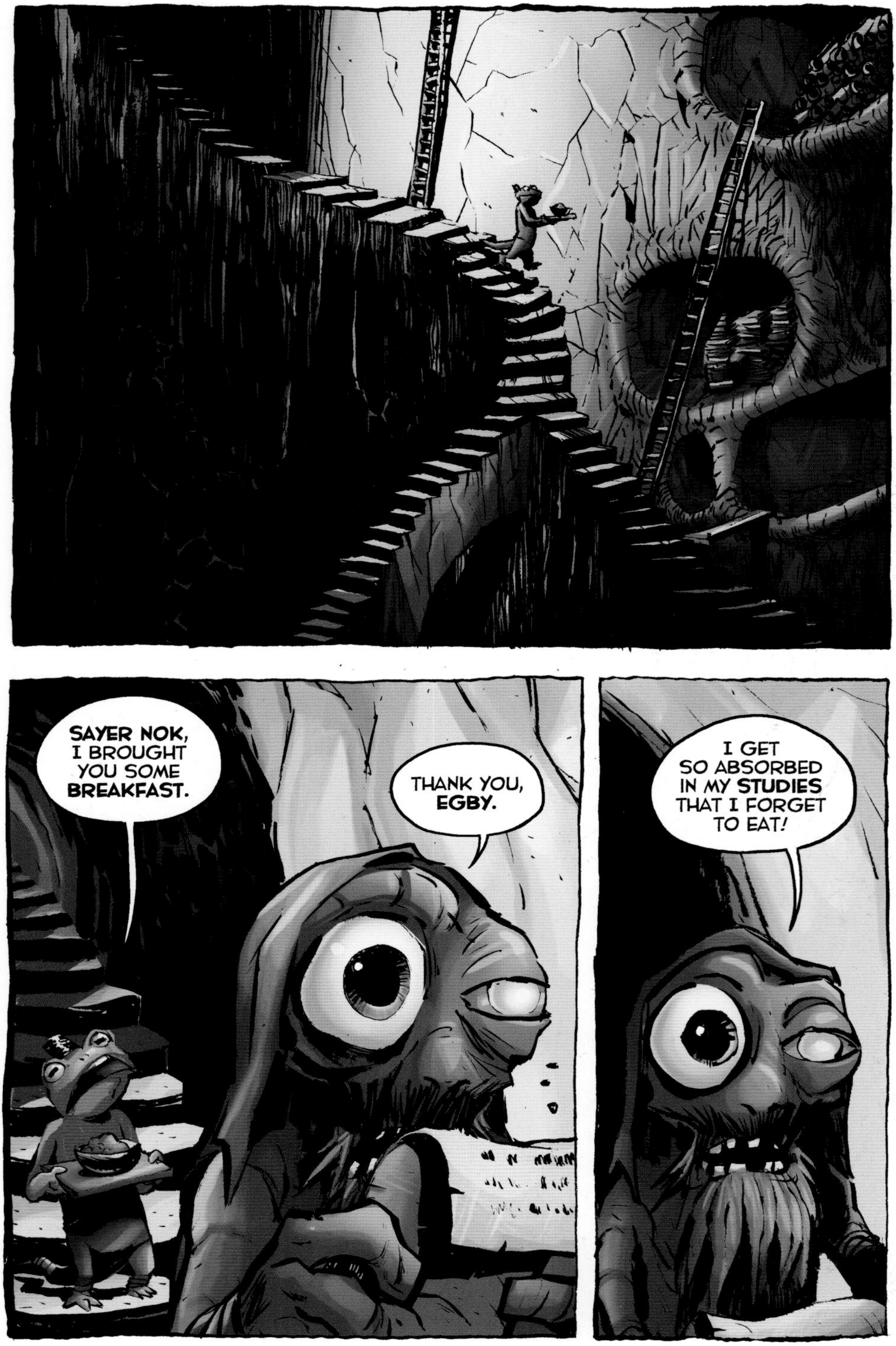
SAYER NOK, I BROUGHT YOU SOME BREAKFAST.
THANK YOU, EGBY.
I GET SO ABSORBED IN MY STUDIES THAT I FORGET TO EAT!

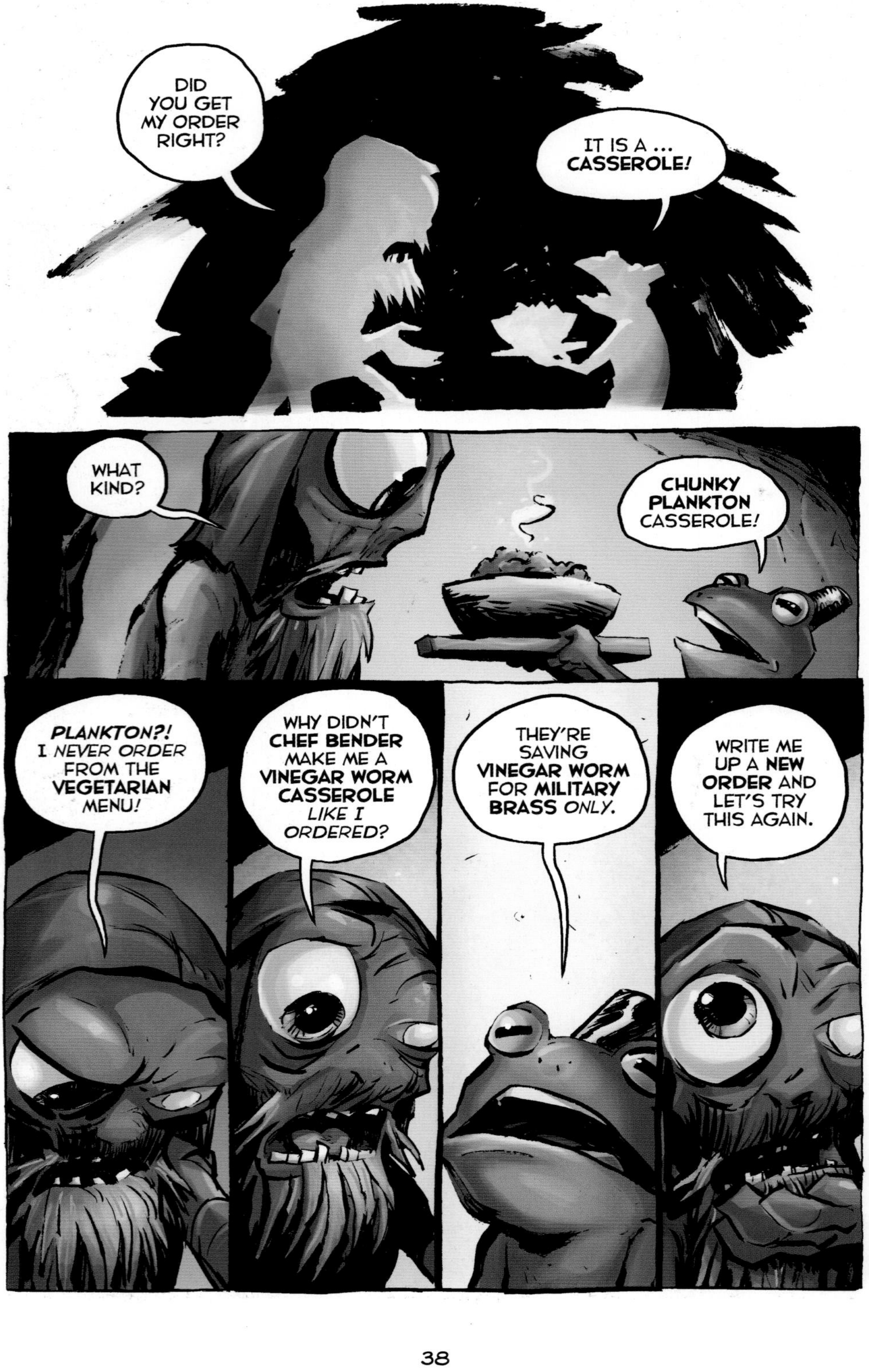
DID YOU GET MY ORDER RIGHT?
IT IS A ... **CASSEROLE!**
WHAT KIND?
CHUNKY PLANKTON CASSEROLE!
PLANKTON?! I *NEVER ORDER* FROM THE **VEGETARIAN** MENU!
WHY DIDN'T **CHEF BENDER** MAKE ME A **VINEGAR WORM CASSEROLE** *LIKE I ORDERED?*
THEY'RE SAVING **VINEGAR WORM** FOR **MILITARY BRASS** *ONLY.*
WRITE ME UP A **NEW ORDER** AND LET'S TRY THIS AGAIN.

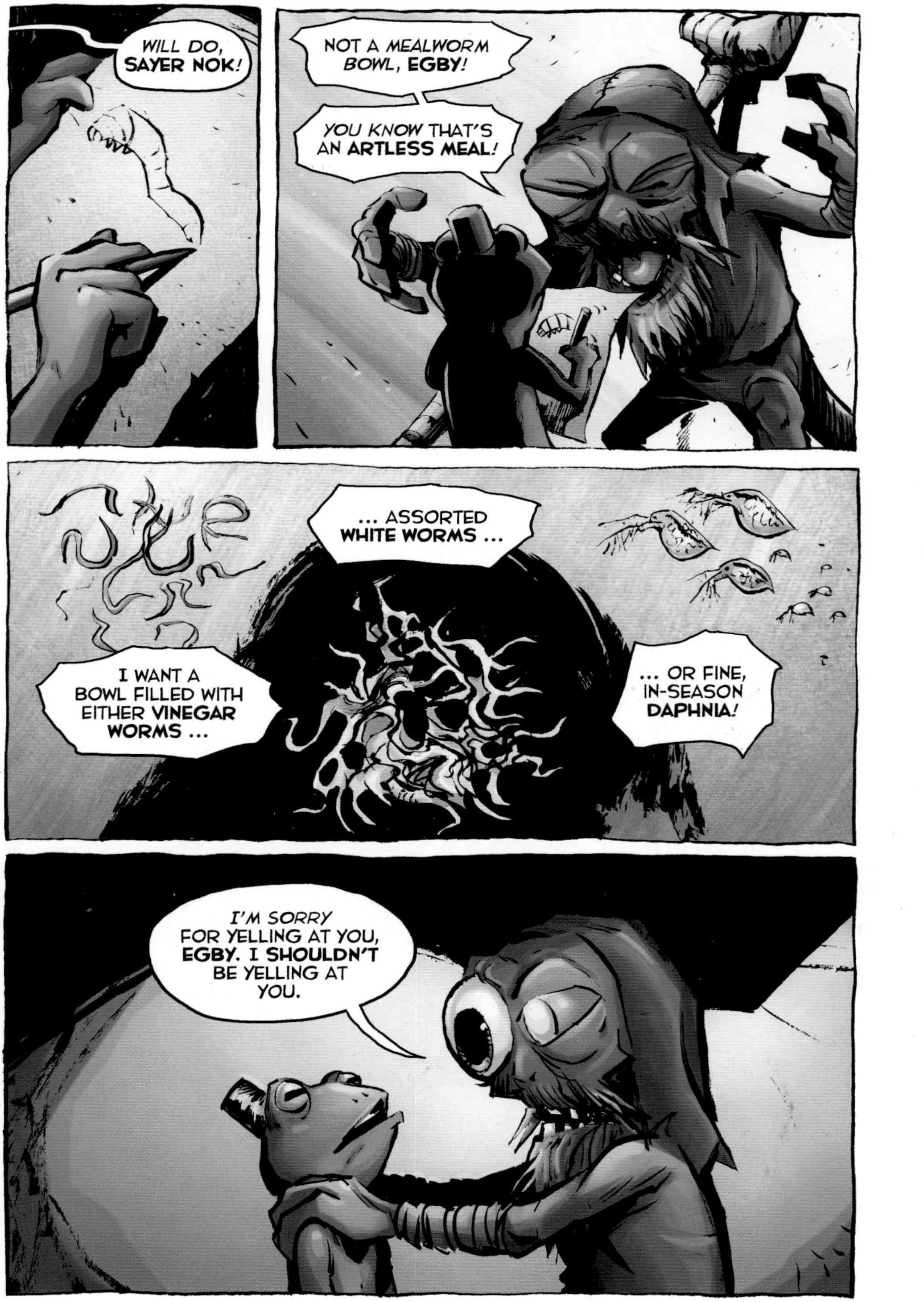
WILL DO, SAYER NOK!
NOT A MEALWORM BOWL, EGBY!
YOU KNOW THAT'S AN ARTLESS MEAL!
I WANT A BOWL FILLED WITH EITHER VINEGAR WORMS ...
... ASSORTED WHITE WORMS ...
... OR FINE, IN-SEASON DAPHNIA!
I'M SORRY FOR YELLING AT YOU, EGBY. I SHOULDN'T BE YELLING AT YOU.

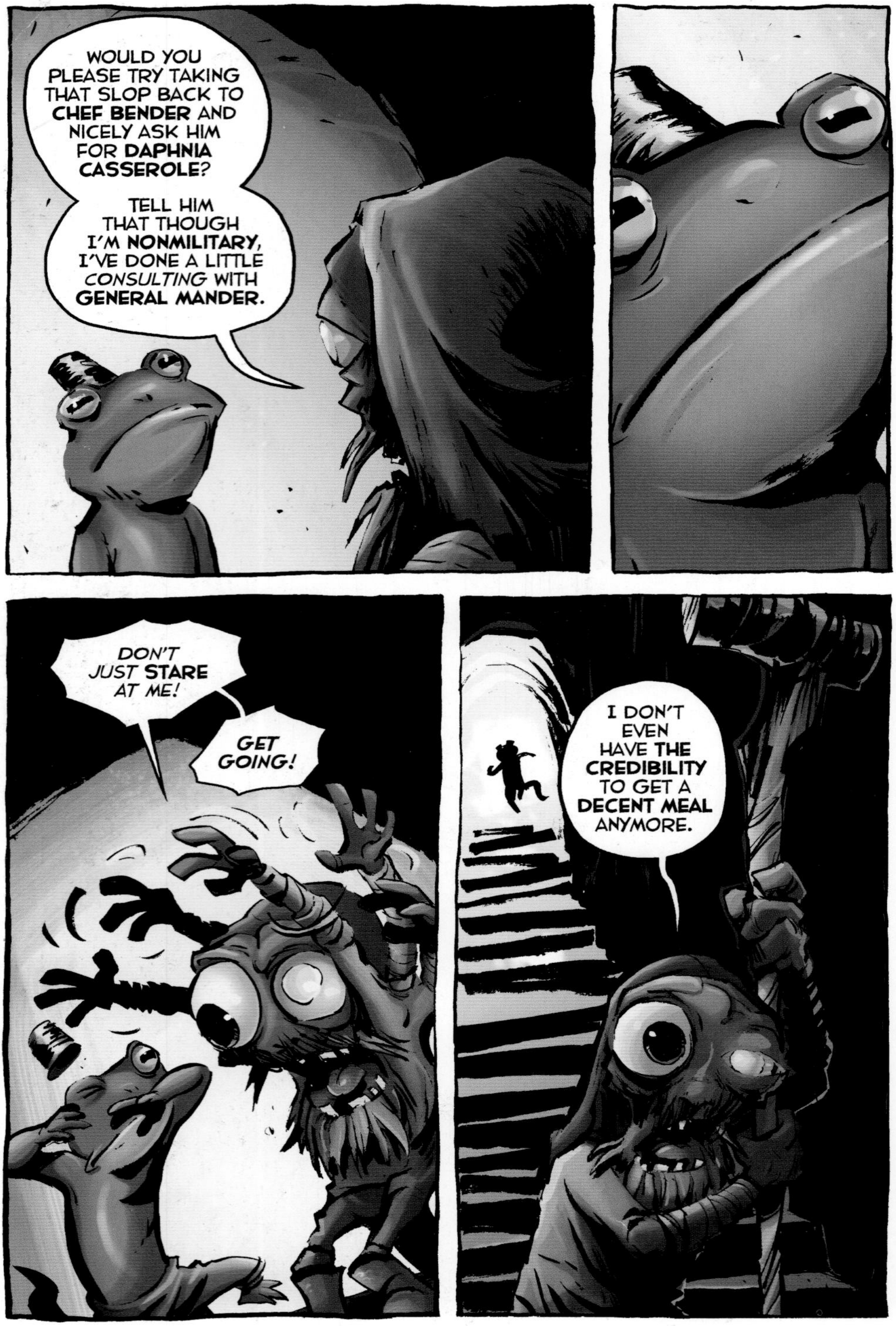

WOULD YOU PLEASE TRY TAKING THAT SLOP BACK TO CHEF BENDER AND NICELY ASK HIM FOR DAPHNIA CASSEROLE?
TELL HIM THAT THOUGH I'M NONMILITARY, I'VE DONE A LITTLE CONSULTING WITH GENERAL MANDER.
DON'T JUST STARE AT ME!
GET GOING!
I DON'T EVEN HAVE THE CREDIBILITY TO GET A DECENT MEAL ANYMORE.

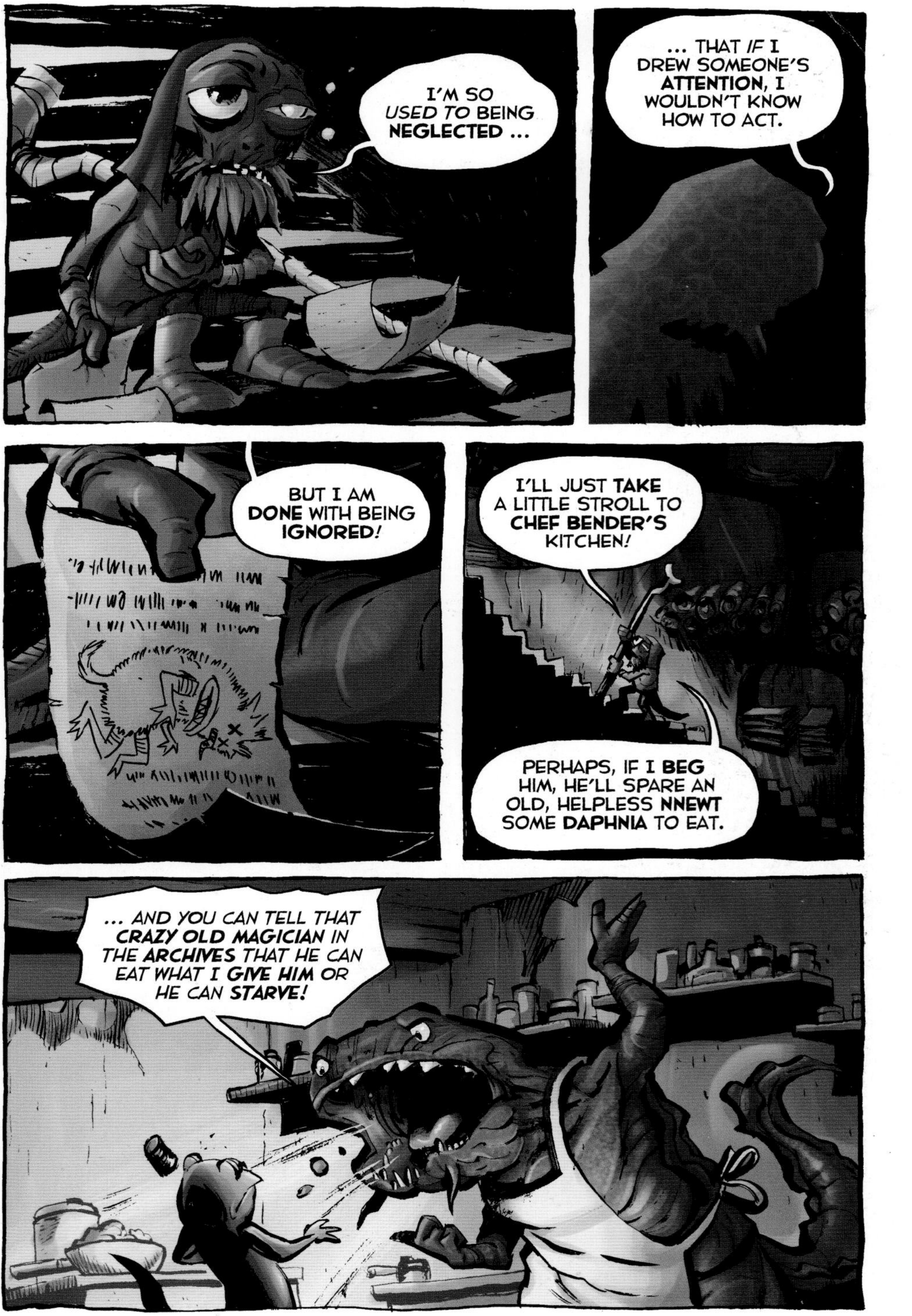
I'M SO *USED TO* BEING **NEGLECTED** ...
... THAT *IF* I DREW SOMEONE'S **ATTENTION**, I WOULDN'T KNOW HOW TO ACT.
BUT I AM **DONE** WITH BEING **IGNORED**!
I'LL JUST **TAKE** A LITTLE STROLL TO **CHEF BENDER'S** KITCHEN!
PERHAPS, IF I **BEG** HIM, HE'LL SPARE AN OLD, HELPLESS **NNEWT** SOME **DAPHNIA** TO EAT.
*... AND YOU CAN TELL THAT **CRAZY OLD MAGICIAN** IN THE **ARCHIVES** THAT HE CAN EAT WHAT I **GIVE HIM** OR HE CAN **STARVE!***

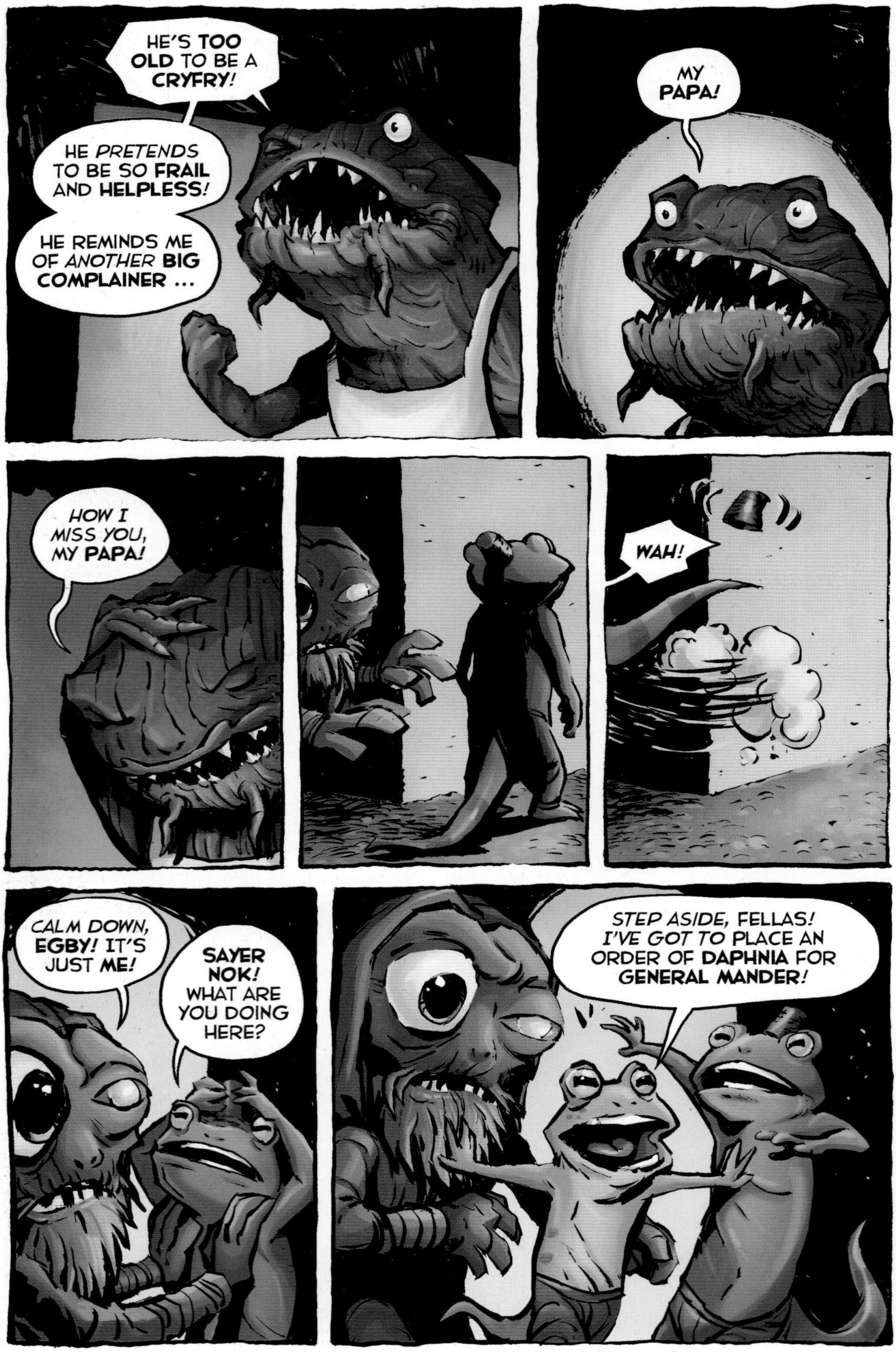
HE'S TOO OLD TO BE A CRYFRY!
HE PRETENDS TO BE SO FRAIL AND HELPLESS!
HE REMINDS ME OF ANOTHER BIG COMPLAINER ...
MY PAPA!
HOW I MISS YOU, MY PAPA!
WAH!
CALM DOWN, EGBY! IT'S JUST ME!
SAYER NOK! WHAT ARE YOU DOING HERE?
STEP ASIDE, FELLAS! I'VE GOT TO PLACE AN ORDER OF DAPHNIA FOR GENERAL MANDER!

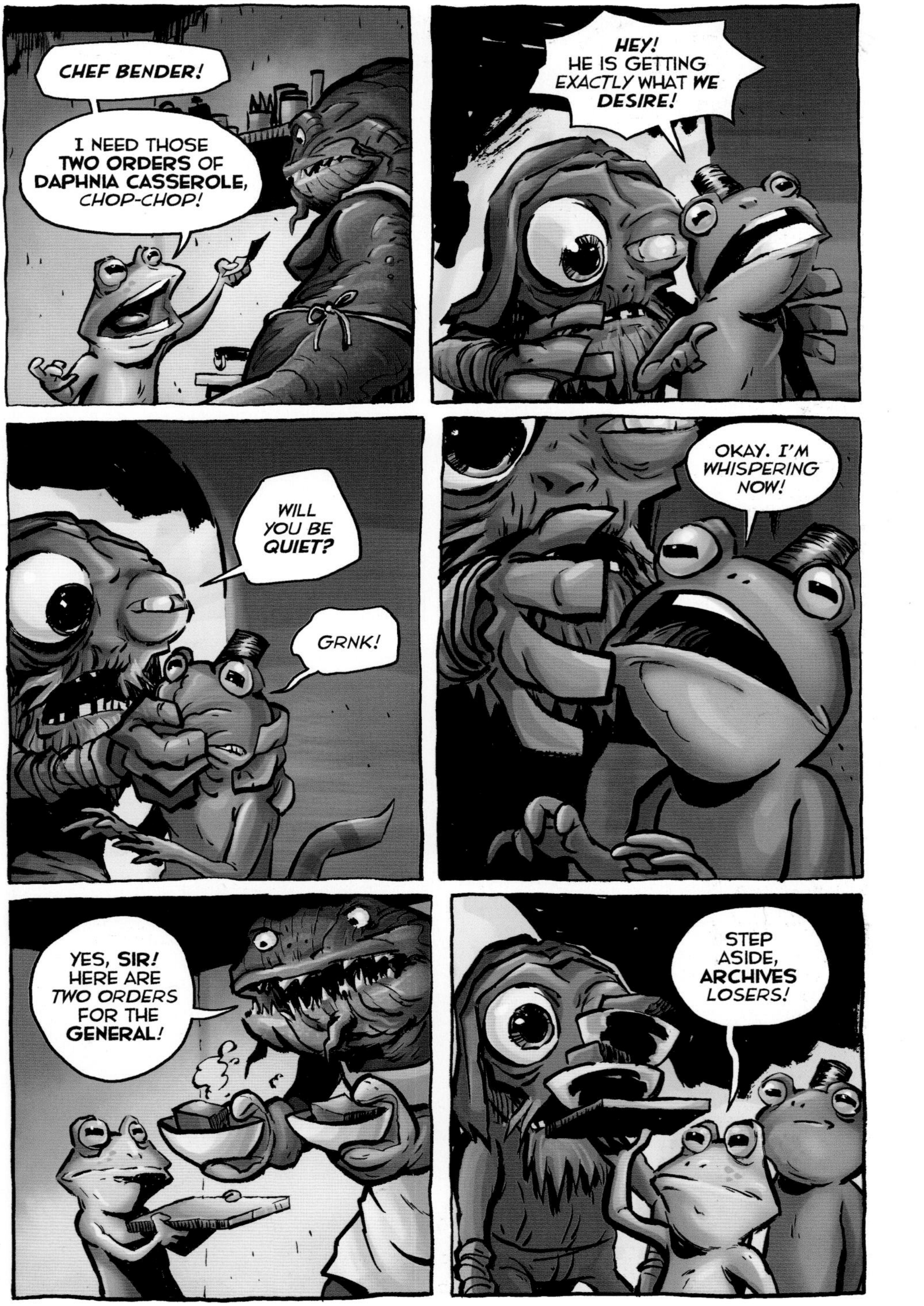
CHEF BENDER!
I NEED THOSE TWO ORDERS OF DAPHNIA CASSEROLE, CHOP-CHOP!
HEY! HE IS GETTING EXACTLY WHAT WE DESIRE!
WILL YOU BE QUIET?
GRNK!
OKAY. I'M WHISPERING NOW!
YES, SIR! HERE ARE TWO ORDERS FOR THE GENERAL!
STEP ASIDE, ARCHIVES LOSERS!

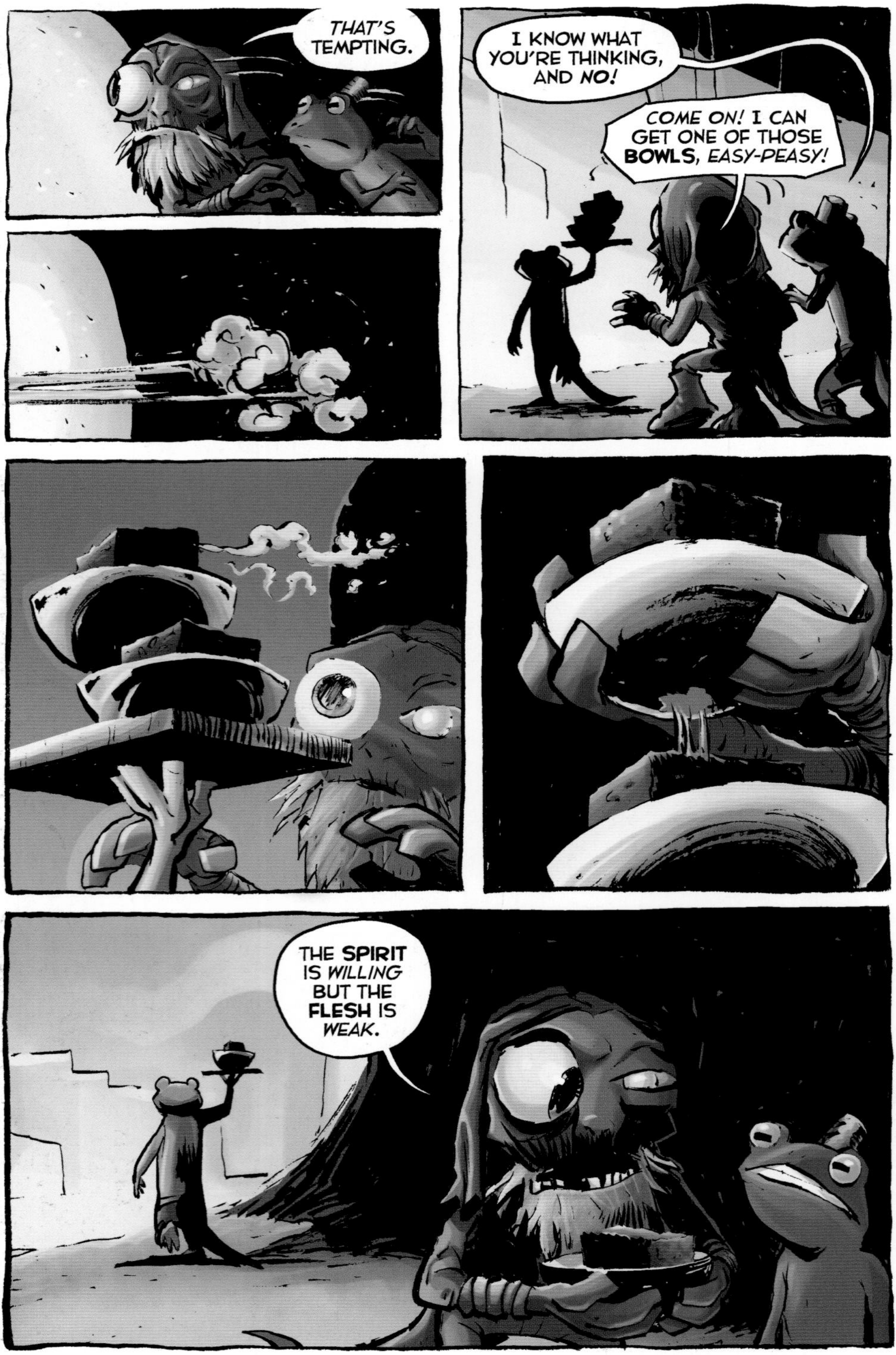
THAT'S TEMPTING.
I KNOW WHAT YOU'RE THINKING, AND NO!
COME ON! I CAN GET ONE OF THOSE BOWLS, EASY-PEASY!
THE SPIRIT IS WILLING BUT THE FLESH IS WEAK.

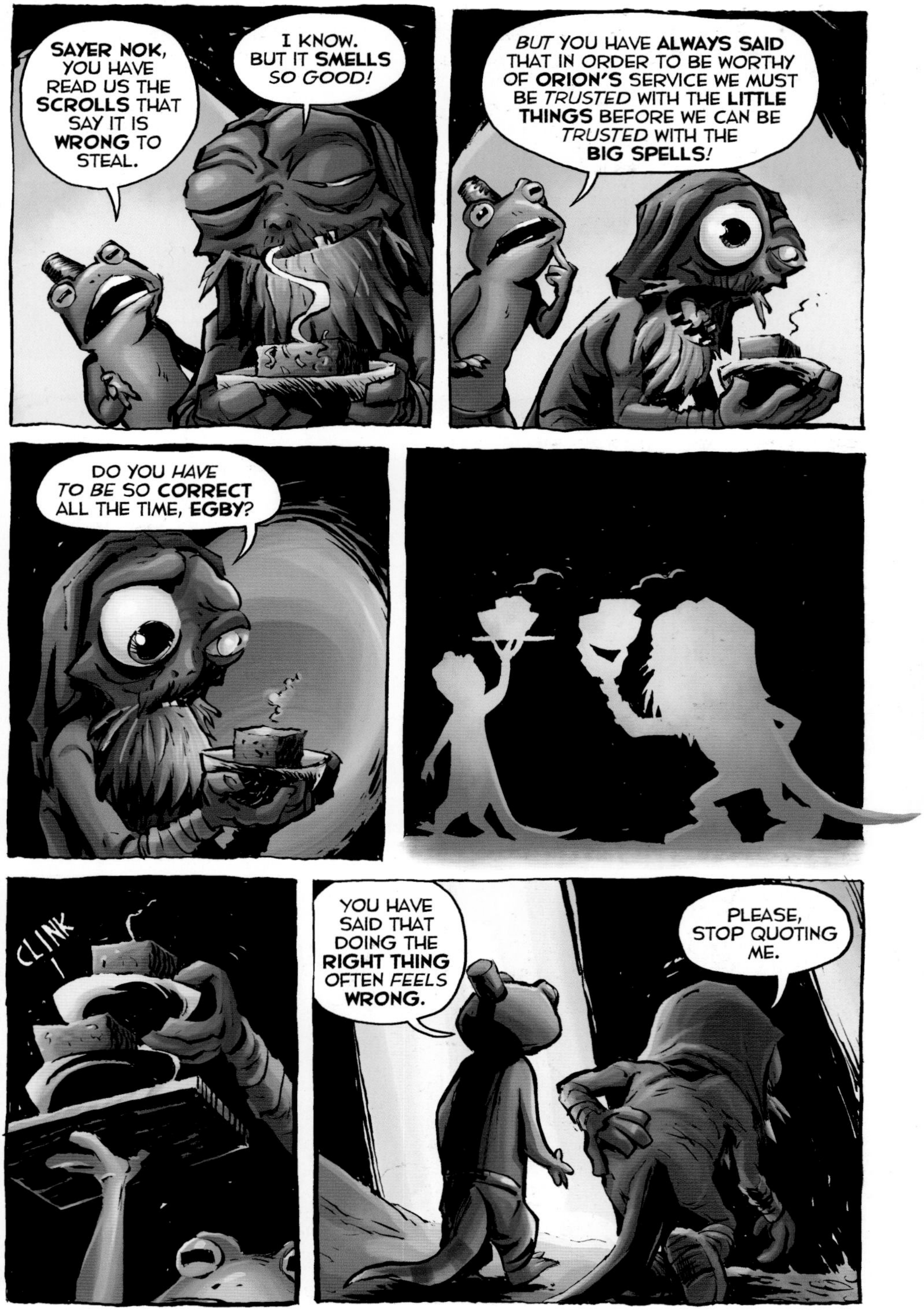
SAYER NOK, YOU HAVE READ US THE SCROLLS THAT SAY IT IS WRONG TO STEAL.
I KNOW. BUT IT SMELLS SO GOOD!
BUT YOU HAVE ALWAYS SAID THAT IN ORDER TO BE WORTHY OF ORION'S SERVICE WE MUST BE TRUSTED WITH THE LITTLE THINGS BEFORE WE CAN BE TRUSTED WITH THE BIG SPELLS!
DO YOU HAVE TO BE SO CORRECT ALL THE TIME, EGBY?
CLINK
YOU HAVE SAID THAT DOING THE RIGHT THING OFTEN FEELS WRONG.
PLEASE, STOP QUOTING ME.

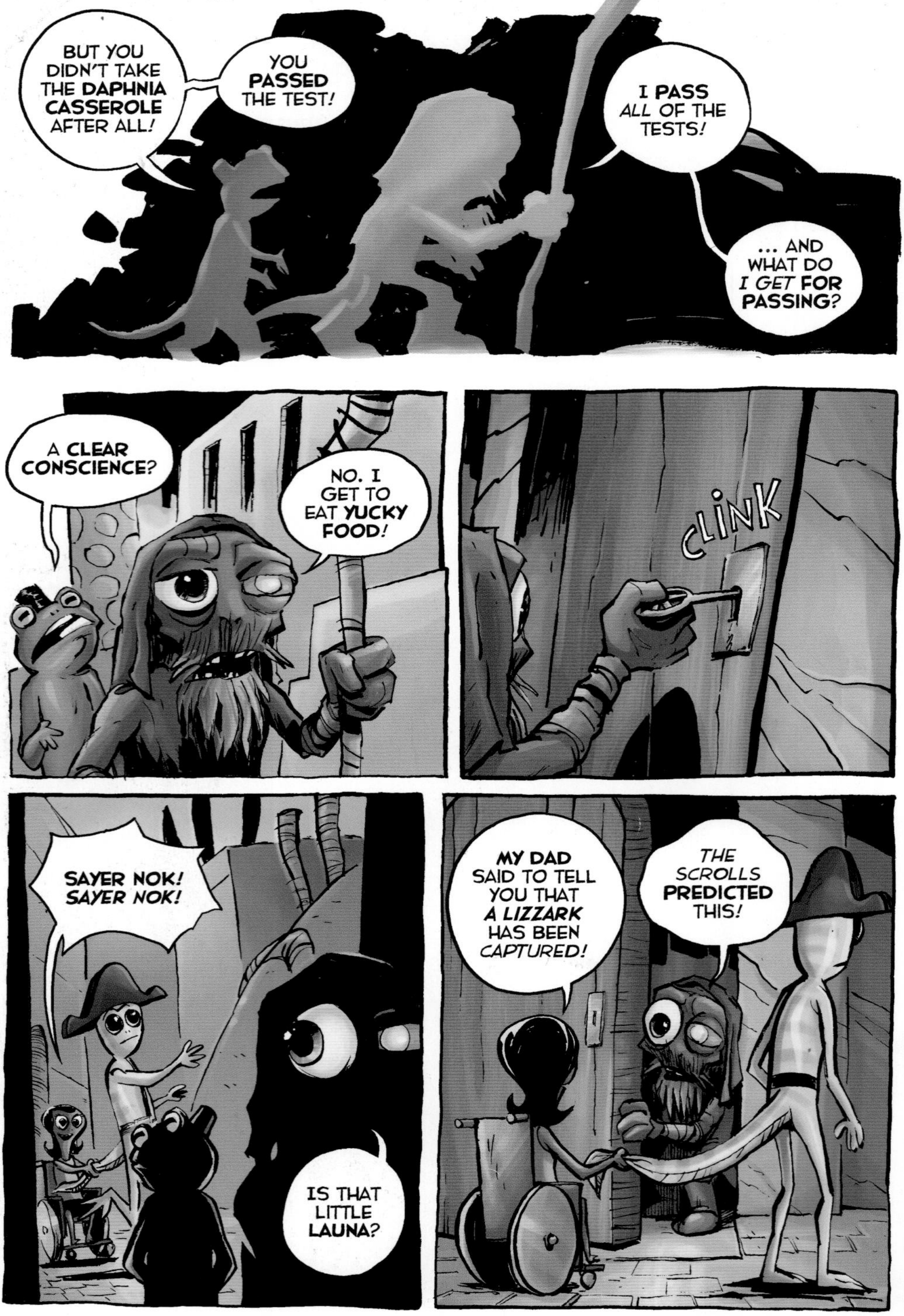
BUT YOU DIDN'T TAKE THE DAPHNIA CASSEROLE AFTER ALL!
YOU PASSED THE TEST!
I PASS ALL OF THE TESTS!
... AND WHAT DO I GET FOR PASSING?
A CLEAR CONSCIENCE?
NO. I GET TO EAT YUCKY FOOD!
CLINK
SAYER NOK! SAYER NOK!
IS THAT LITTLE LAUNA?
MY DAD SAID TO TELL YOU THAT A LIZZARK HAS BEEN CAPTURED!
THE SCROLLS PREDICTED THIS!

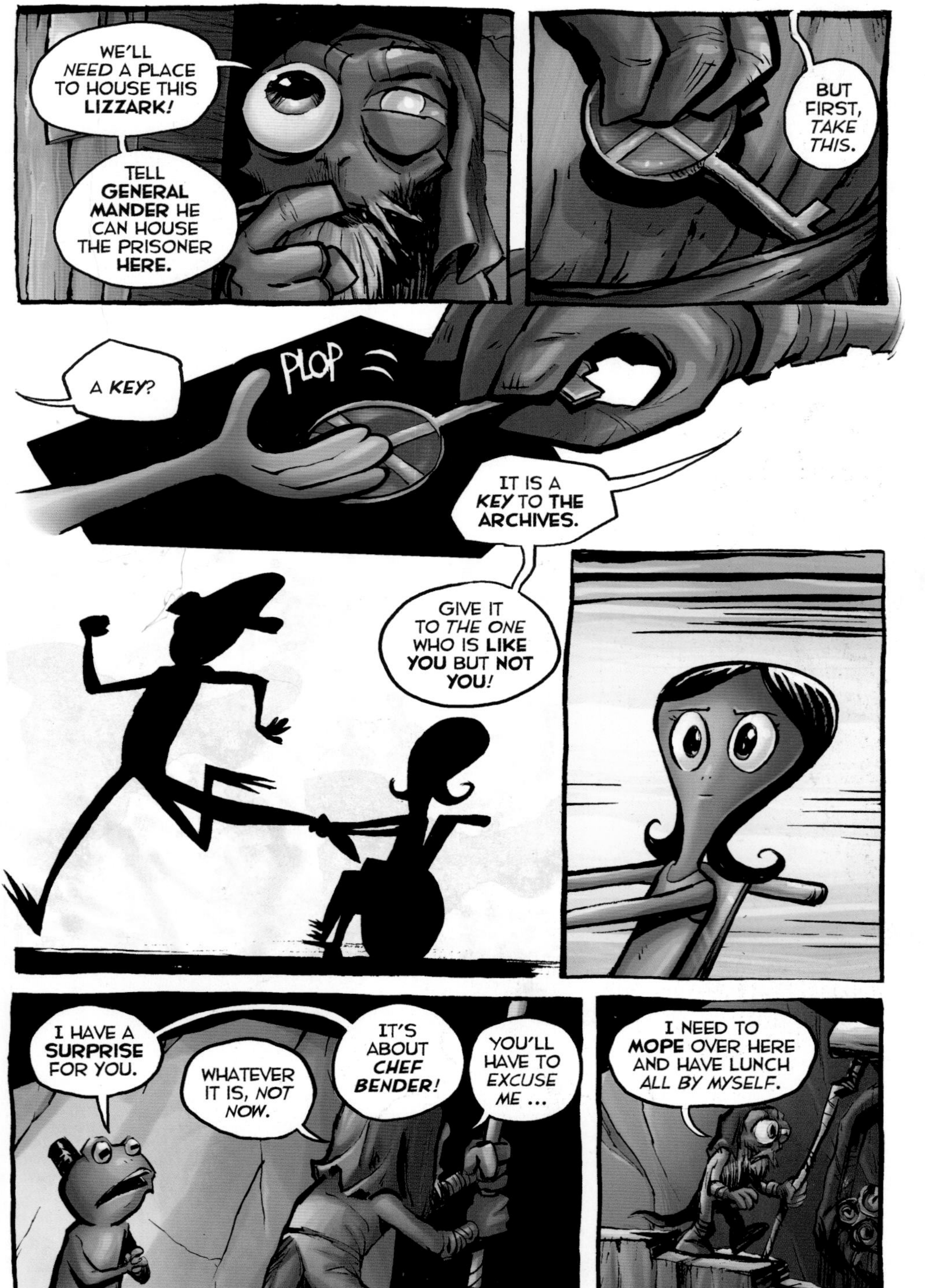
WE'LL *NEED* A PLACE TO HOUSE THIS **LIZZARK!**
TELL **GENERAL MANDER** HE CAN HOUSE THE PRISONER **HERE.**
BUT FIRST, *TAKE THIS.*
PLOP
A *KEY?*
IT IS A *KEY* TO **THE ARCHIVES.**
GIVE IT TO *THE ONE* WHO IS **LIKE YOU** BUT **NOT YOU!**
I HAVE A **SURPRISE** FOR YOU.
WHATEVER IT IS, *NOT NOW.*
IT'S ABOUT ***CHEF BENDER!***
YOU'LL HAVE TO *EXCUSE ME ...*
I NEED TO **MOPE** OVER HERE AND HAVE LUNCH *ALL BY MYSELF.*

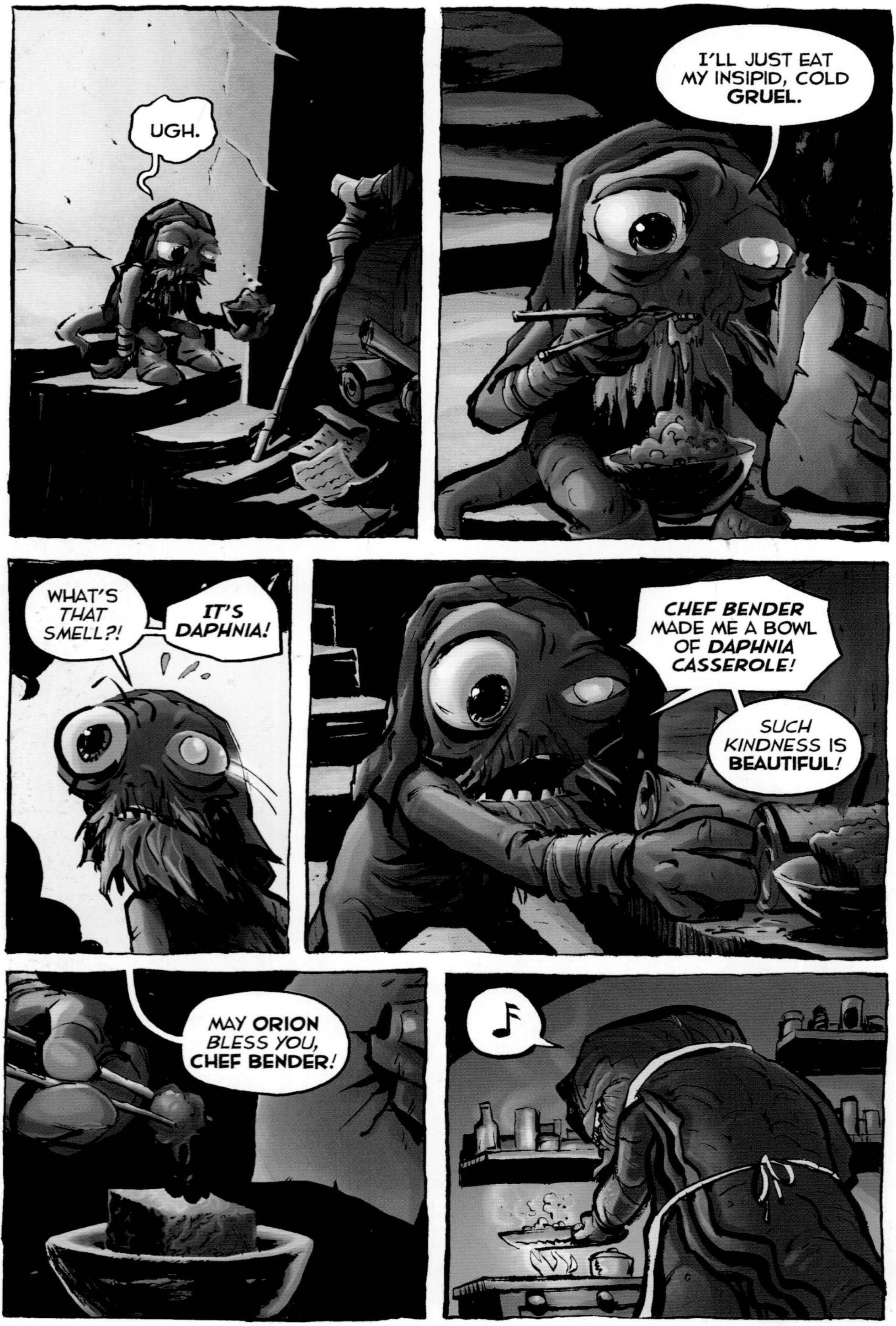
UGH.
I'LL JUST EAT MY INSIPID, COLD **GRUEL.**
WHAT'S *THAT* SMELL?!
IT'S DAPHNIA!
CHEF BENDER MADE ME A BOWL OF ***DAPHNIA CASSEROLE!***
SUCH KINDNESS IS ***BEAUTIFUL!***
MAY **ORION** *BLESS YOU,* ***CHEF BENDER!***
♪

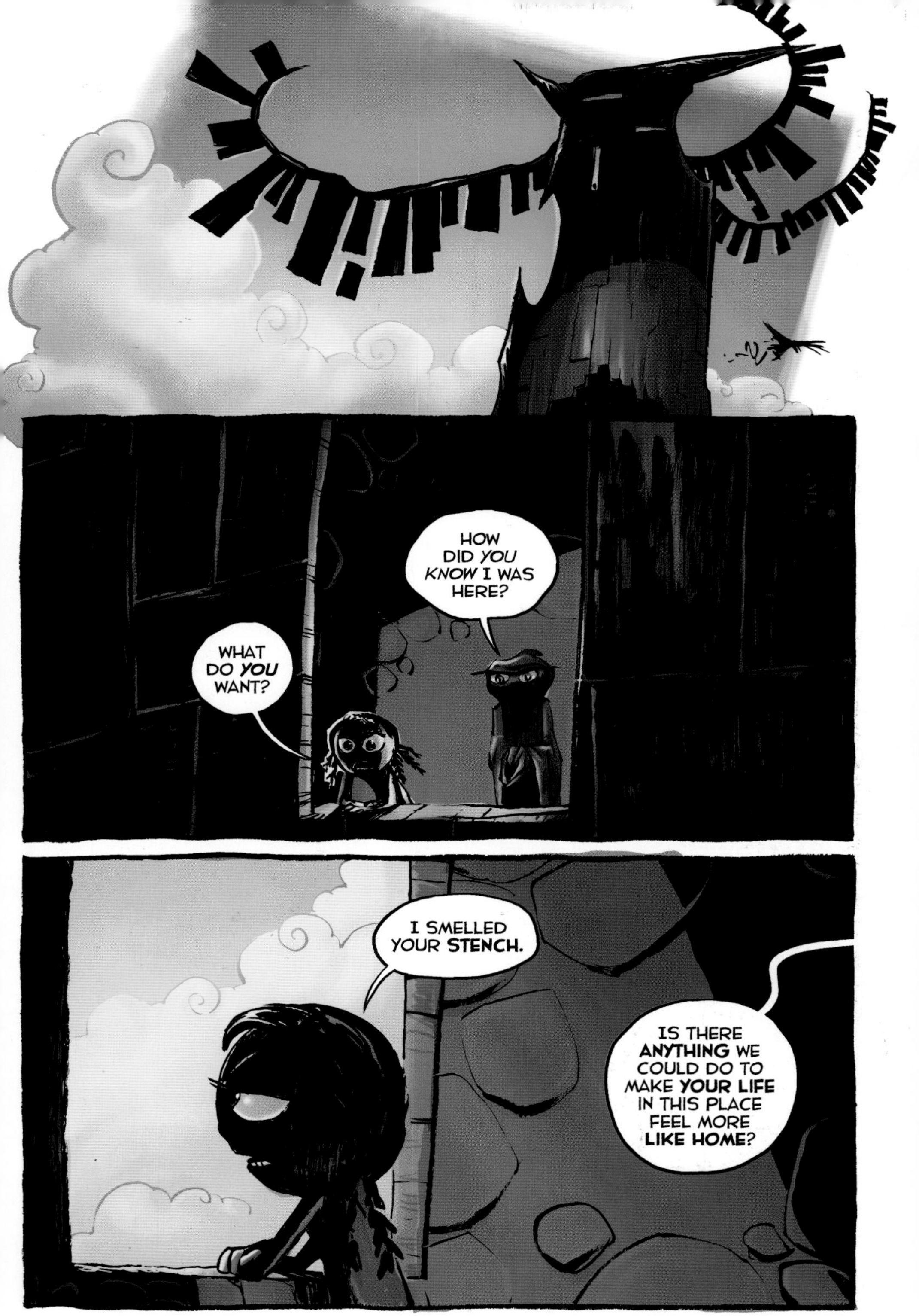

WHAT DO *YOU* WANT?
HOW DID *YOU* *KNOW* I WAS HERE?
I SMELLED YOUR **STENCH.**
IS THERE **ANYTHING** WE COULD DO TO MAKE **YOUR LIFE** IN THIS PLACE FEEL MORE **LIKE HOME?**

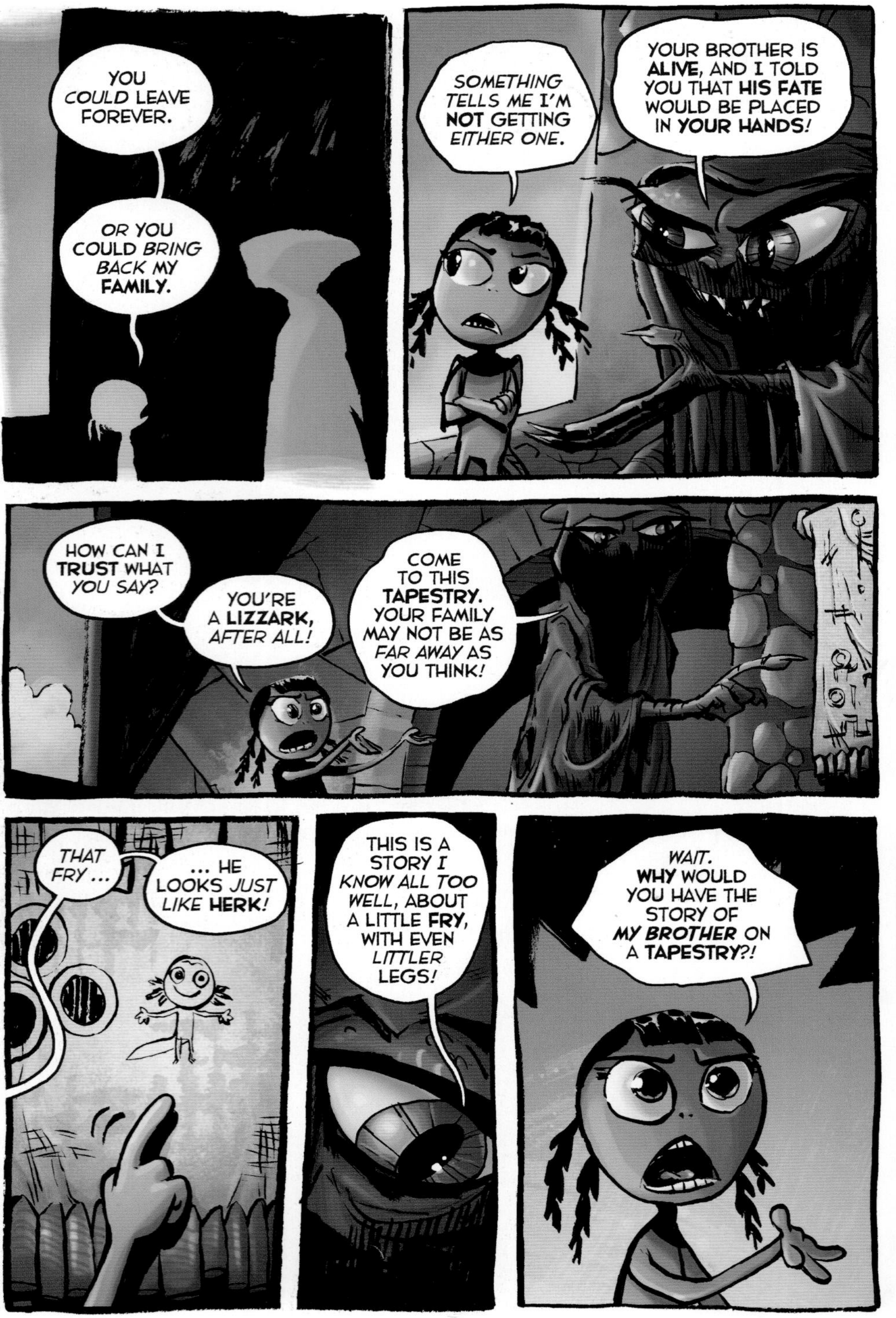
YOU *COULD* LEAVE FOREVER.
OR YOU COULD *BRING BACK* MY **FAMILY.**
SOMETHING TELLS ME I'M **NOT** GETTING *EITHER ONE.*
YOUR BROTHER IS **ALIVE**, AND I TOLD YOU THAT **HIS FATE** WOULD BE PLACED IN **YOUR HANDS**!
HOW CAN I **TRUST** WHAT *YOU SAY?*
YOU'RE A **LIZZARK,** *AFTER ALL!*
COME TO THIS **TAPESTRY.** YOUR FAMILY MAY NOT BE AS *FAR AWAY* AS YOU THINK!
THAT FRY ...
... HE LOOKS *JUST* LIKE **HERK**!
THIS IS A STORY *I KNOW ALL TOO* WELL, ABOUT A LITTLE **FRY,** WITH EVEN *LITTLER* LEGS!
WAIT. **WHY** WOULD YOU HAVE THE STORY OF ***MY BROTHER*** ON A **TAPESTRY**?!

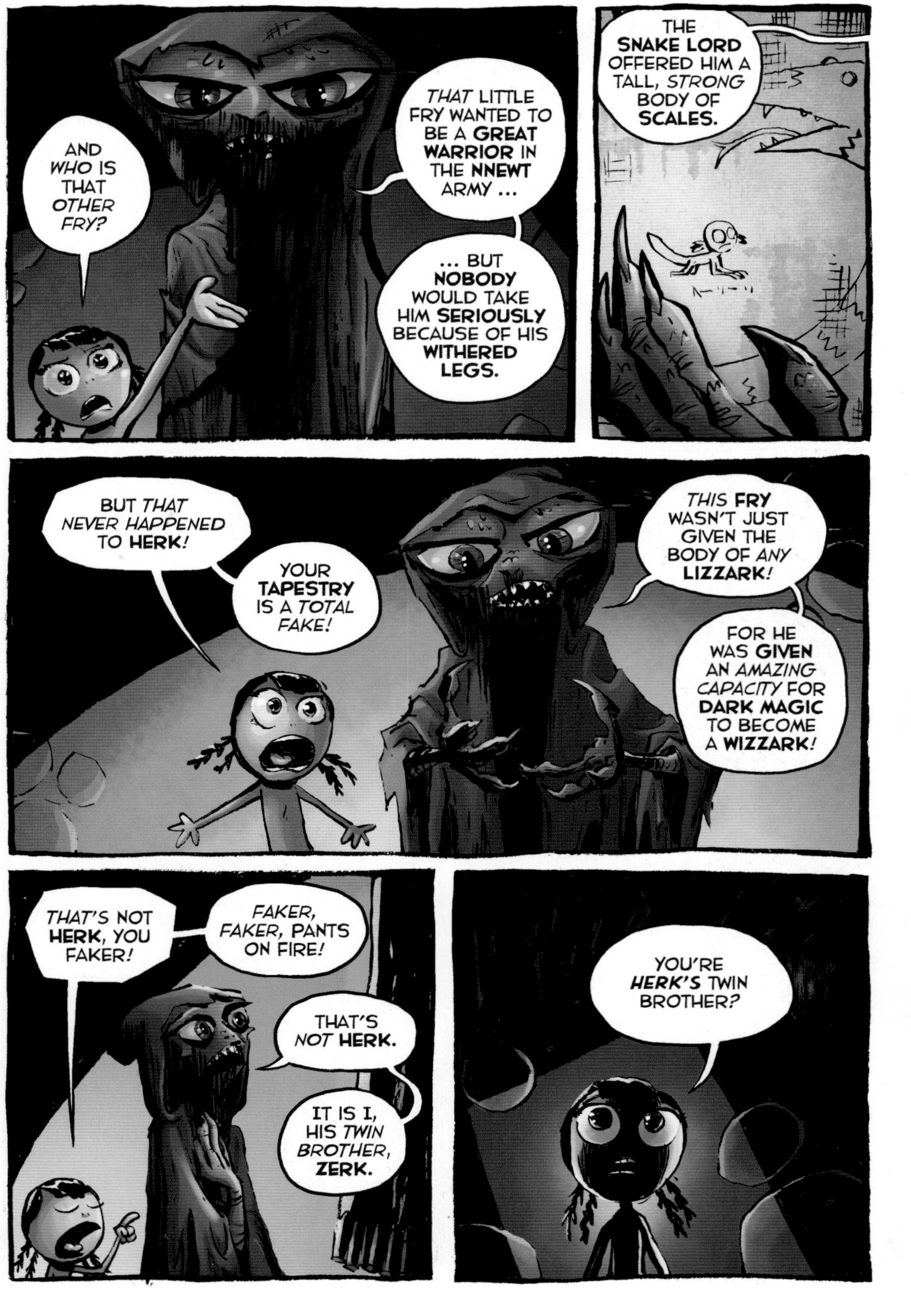
AND WHO IS THAT OTHER FRY?
THAT LITTLE FRY WANTED TO BE A GREAT WARRIOR IN THE NNEWT ARMY ...
... BUT NOBODY WOULD TAKE HIM SERIOUSLY BECAUSE OF HIS WITHERED LEGS.
THE SNAKE LORD OFFERED HIM A TALL, STRONG BODY OF SCALES.
BUT THAT NEVER HAPPENED TO HERK!
YOUR TAPESTRY IS A TOTAL FAKE!
THIS FRY WASN'T JUST GIVEN THE BODY OF ANY LIZZARK!
FOR HE WAS GIVEN AN AMAZING CAPACITY FOR DARK MAGIC TO BECOME A WIZZARK!
THAT'S NOT HERK, YOU FAKER!
FAKER, FAKER, PANTS ON FIRE!
THAT'S NOT HERK.
IT IS I, HIS TWIN BROTHER, ZERK.
YOU'RE HERK'S TWIN BROTHER?

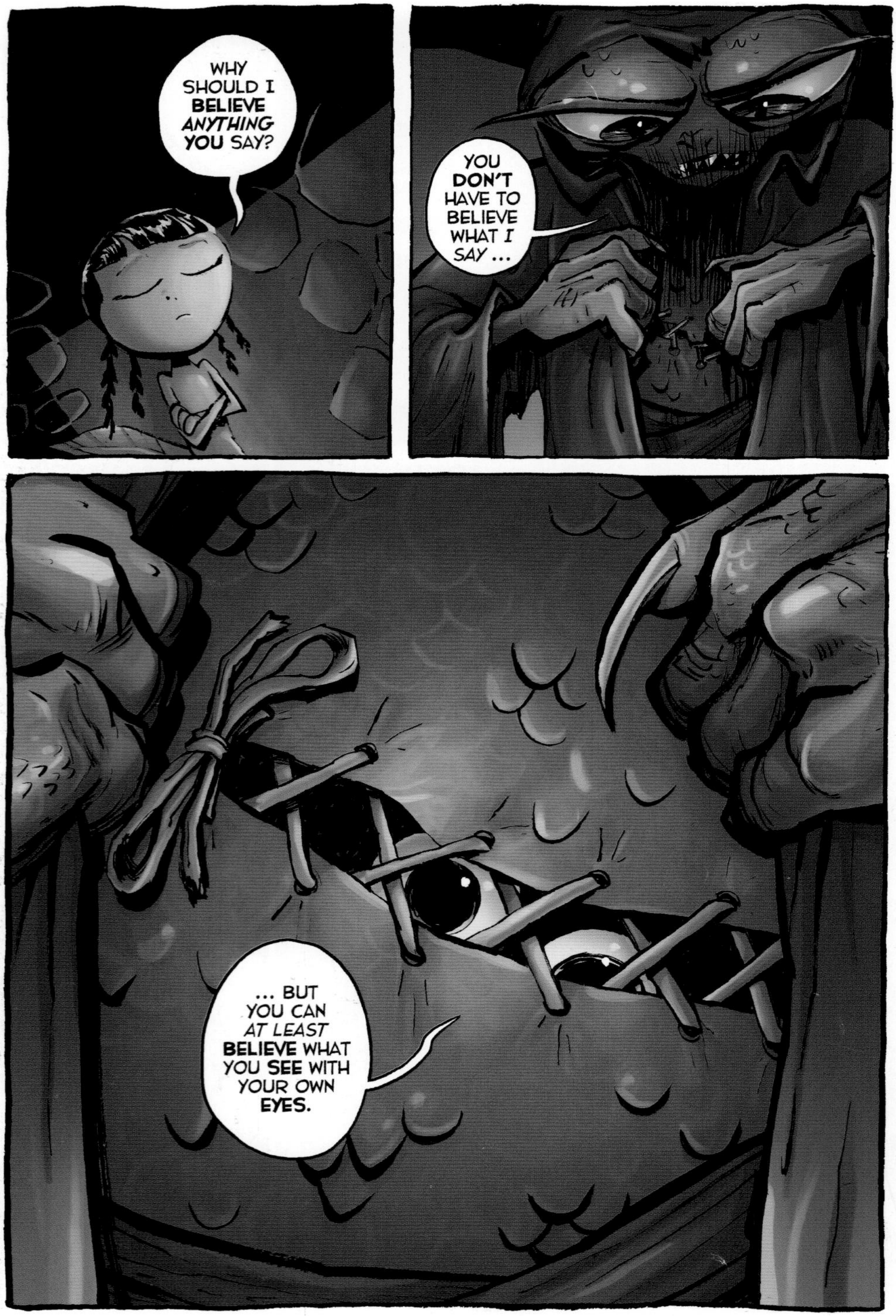
WHY SHOULD I BELIEVE ANYTHING YOU SAY?
YOU DON'T HAVE TO BELIEVE WHAT I SAY ...
... BUT YOU CAN AT LEAST BELIEVE WHAT YOU SEE WITH YOUR OWN EYES.

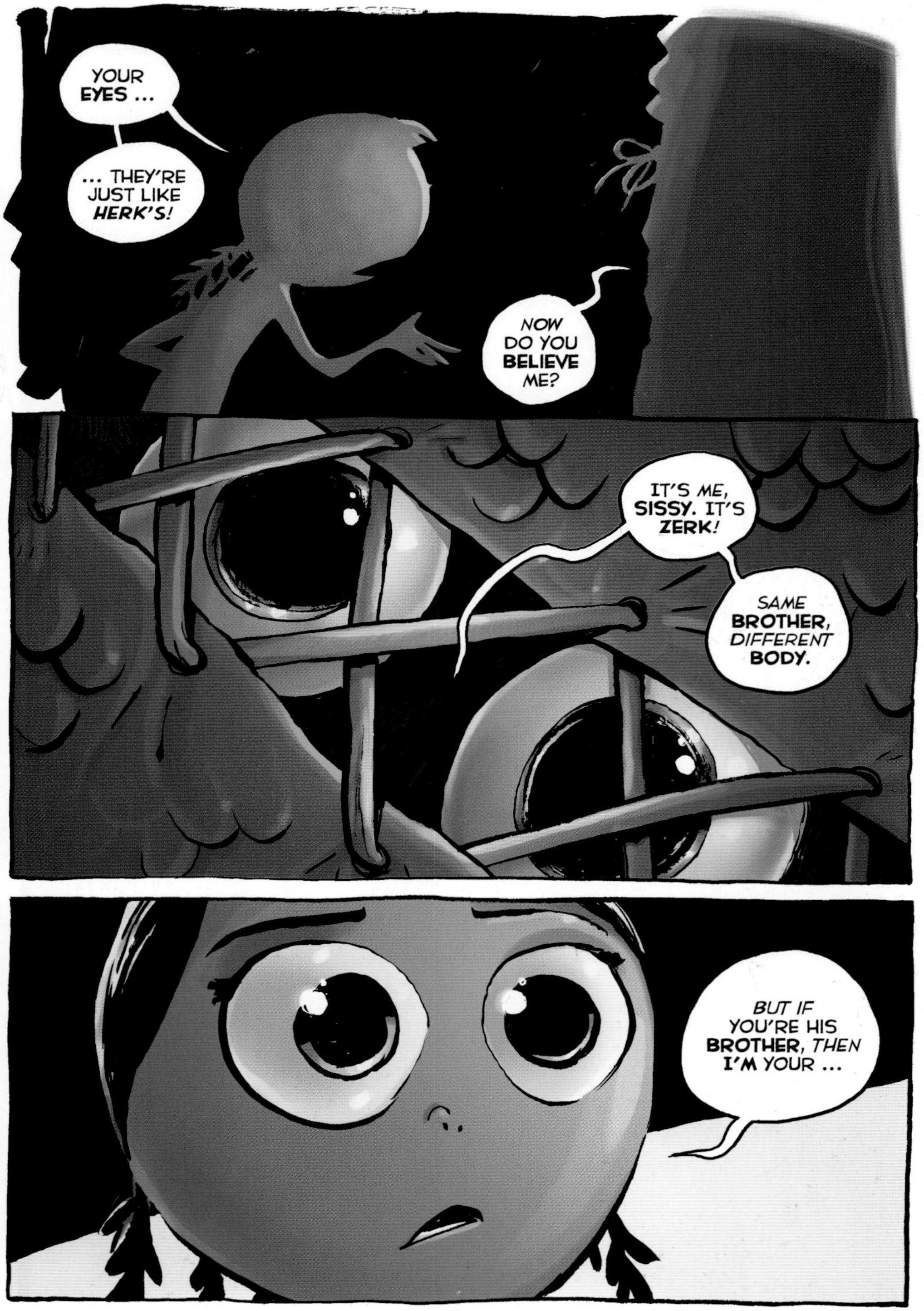
YOUR **EYES** ...
... THEY'RE JUST LIKE ***HERK'S!***
NOW DO YOU **BELIEVE** ME?
IT'S *ME*, **SISSY.** IT'S **ZERK!**
SAME **BROTHER,** *DIFFERENT* **BODY.**
BUT IF YOU'RE HIS **BROTHER,** *THEN* **I'M** *YOUR* ...

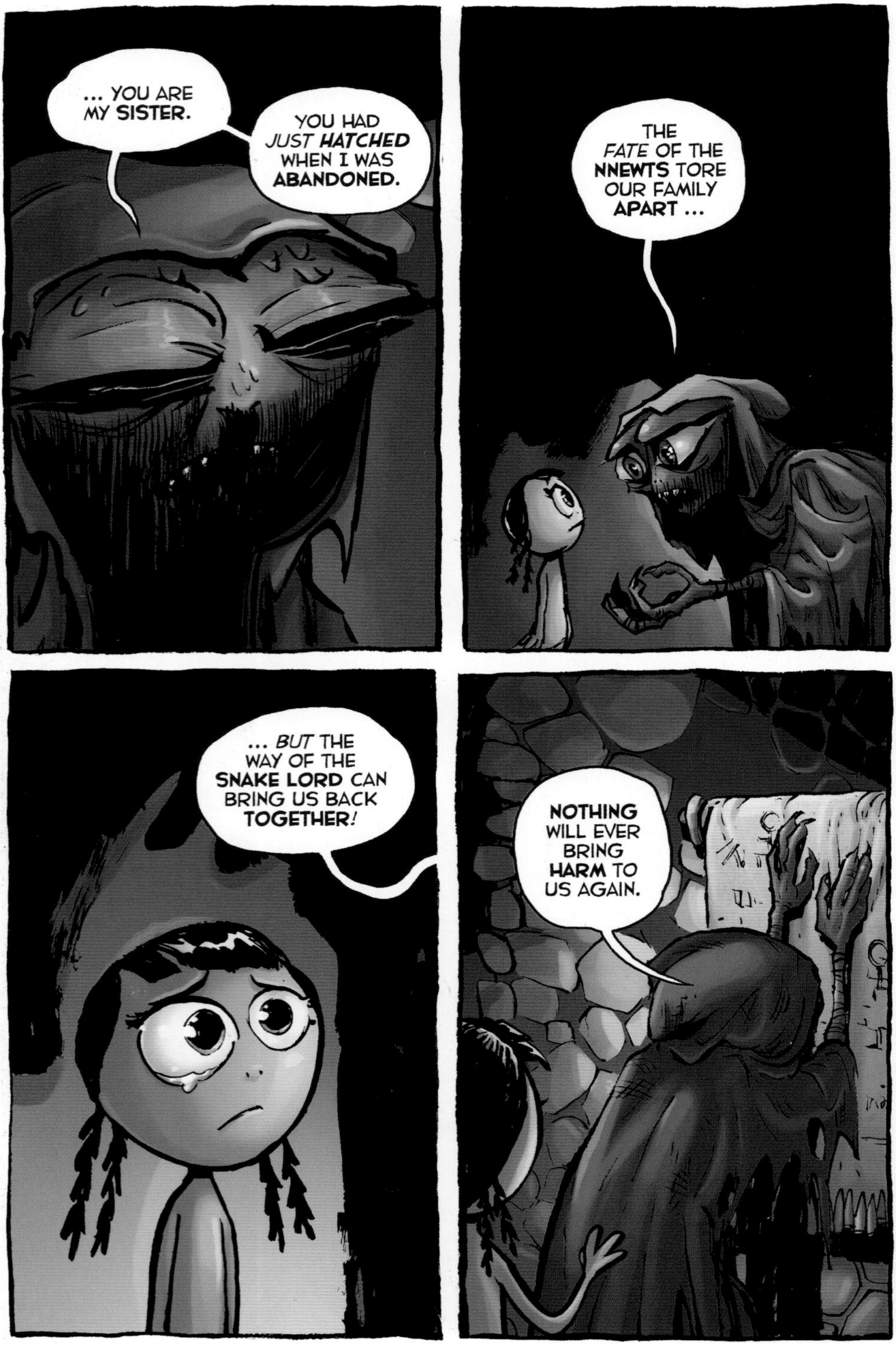

... YOU ARE MY SISTER.
YOU HAD JUST HATCHED WHEN I WAS ABANDONED.
THE FATE OF THE NNEWTS TORE OUR FAMILY APART ...
... BUT THE WAY OF THE SNAKE LORD CAN BRING US BACK TOGETHER!
NOTHING WILL EVER BRING HARM TO US AGAIN.

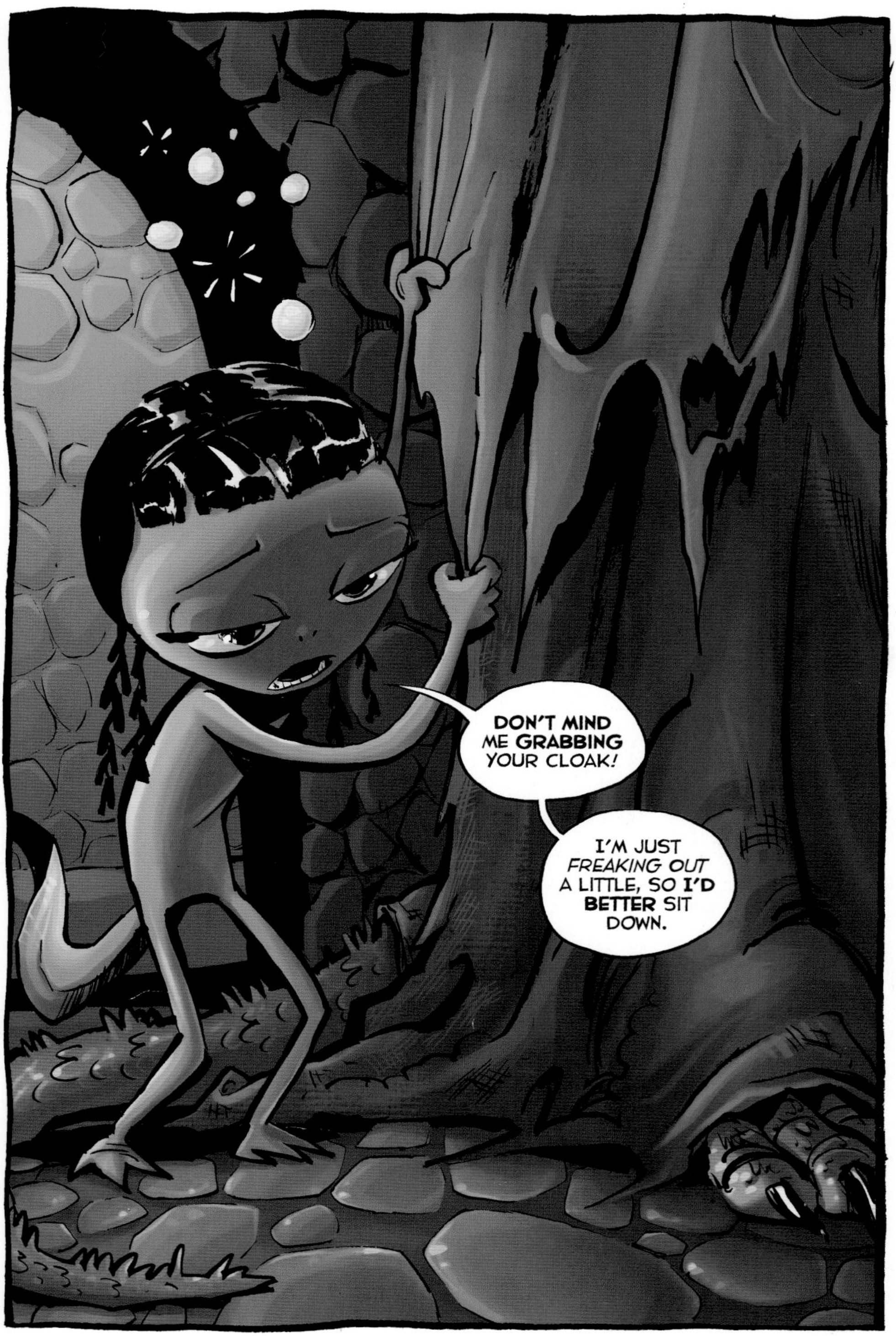
DON'T MIND ME GRABBING YOUR CLOAK!
I'M JUST FREAKING OUT A LITTLE, SO I'D BETTER SIT DOWN.

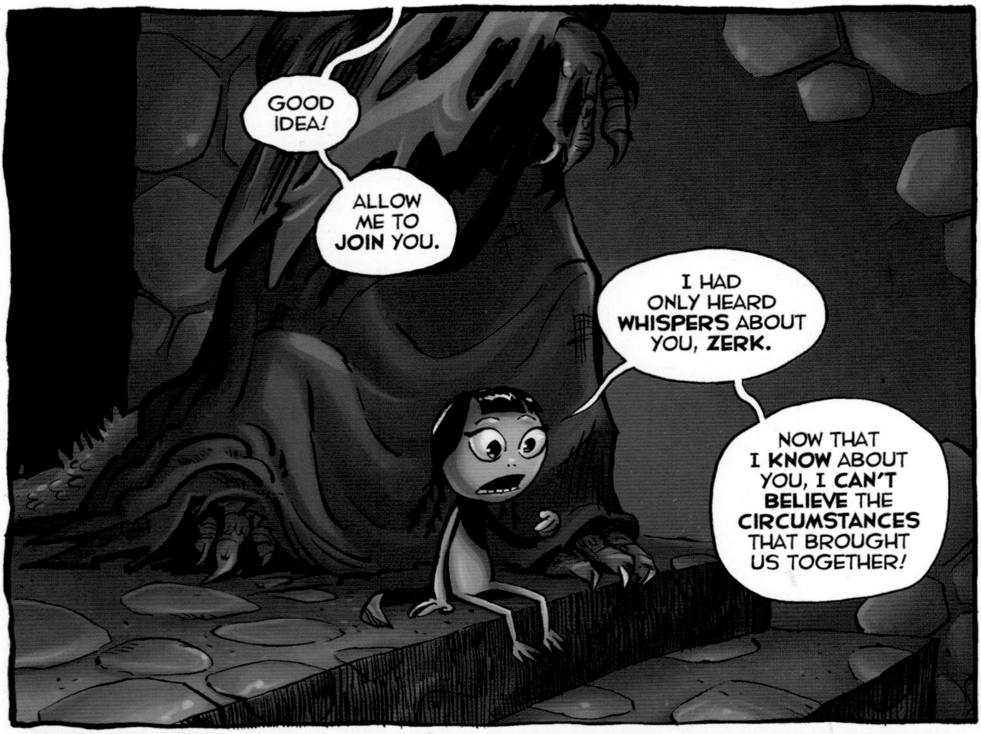
GOOD IDEA!
ALLOW ME TO JOIN YOU.
I HAD ONLY HEARD WHISPERS ABOUT YOU, ZERK.
NOW THAT I KNOW ABOUT YOU, I CAN'T BELIEVE THE CIRCUMSTANCES THAT BROUGHT US TOGETHER!

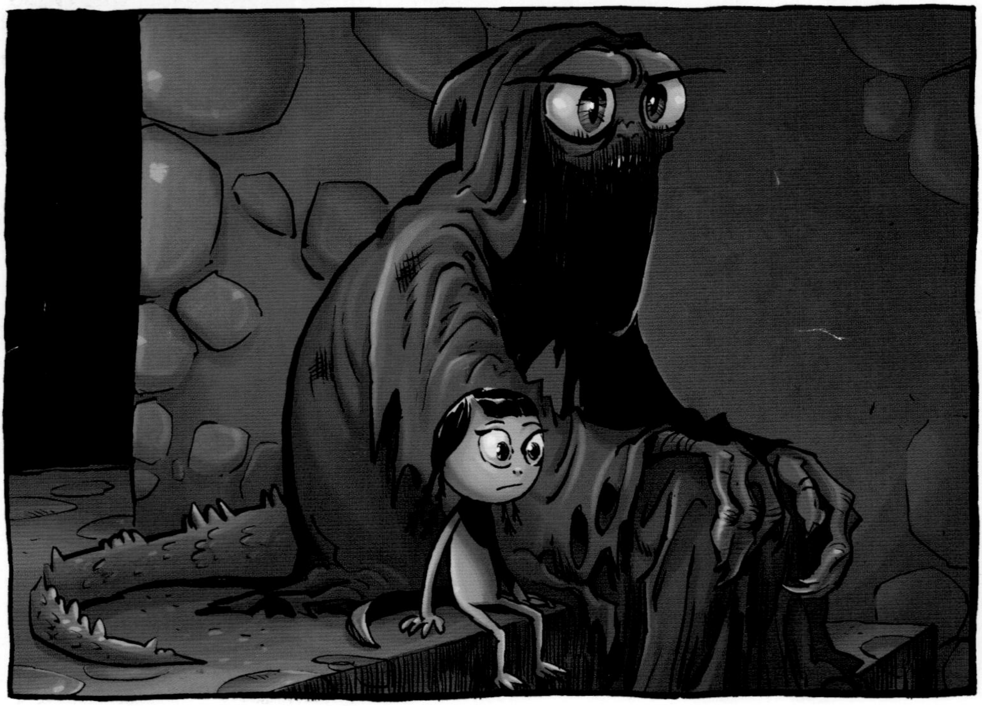

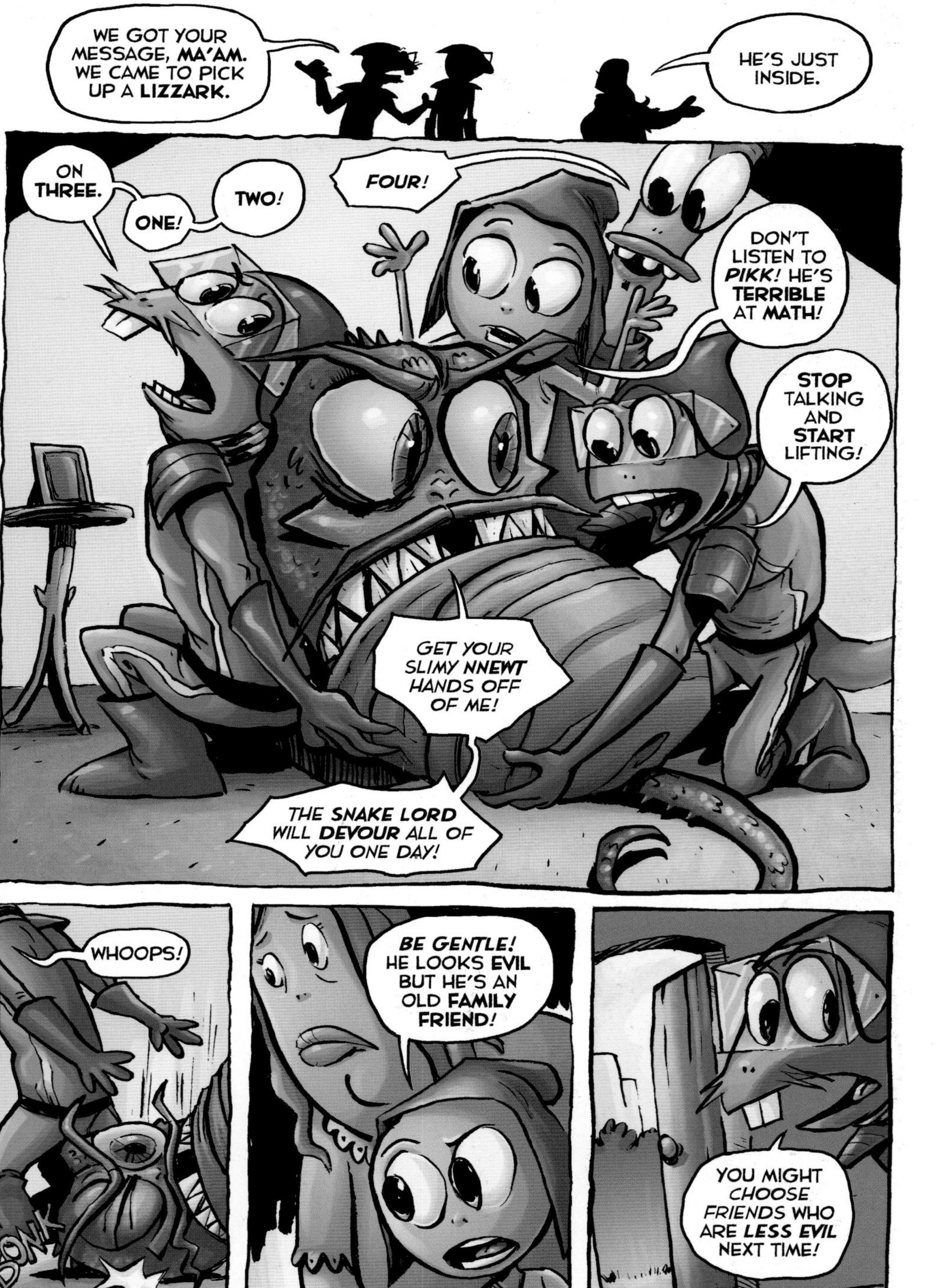
WE GOT YOUR MESSAGE, MA'AM. WE CAME TO PICK UP A LIZZARK.
HE'S JUST INSIDE.
ON THREE.
ONE!
TWO!
FOUR!
DON'T LISTEN TO PIKK! HE'S TERRIBLE AT MATH!
STOP TALKING AND START LIFTING!
GET YOUR SLIMY NNEWT HANDS OFF OF ME!
THE SNAKE LORD WILL DEVOUR ALL OF YOU ONE DAY!
WHOOPS!
BONK
BE GENTLE! HE LOOKS EVIL BUT HE'S AN OLD FAMILY FRIEND!
YOU MIGHT CHOOSE FRIENDS WHO ARE LESS EVIL NEXT TIME!

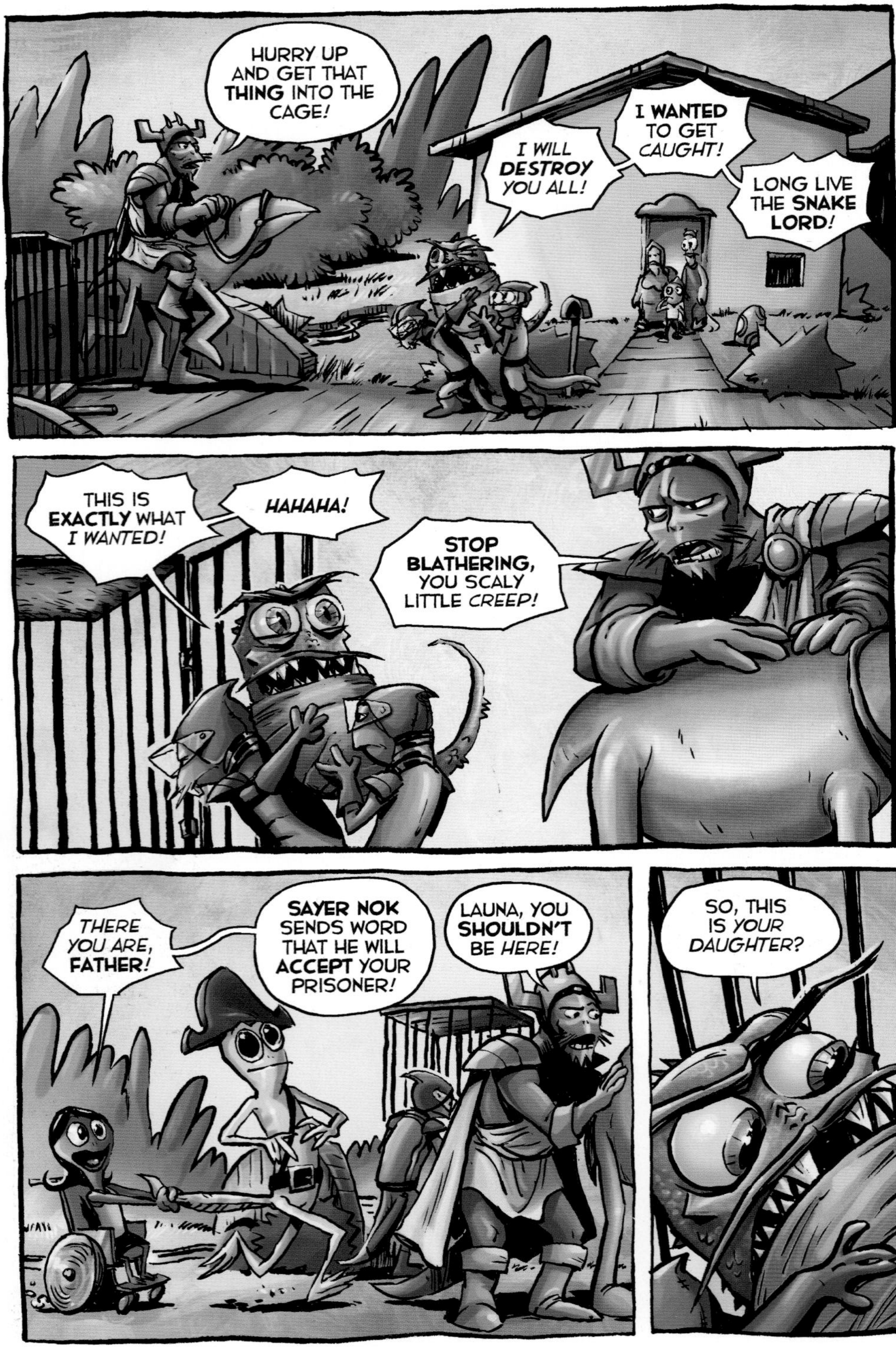
HURRY UP AND GET THAT **THING** INTO THE CAGE!
I WILL **DESTROY** *YOU ALL!*
I WANTED TO GET *CAUGHT!*
LONG LIVE THE **SNAKE LORD**!
THIS IS **EXACTLY** WHAT *I WANTED!*
HAHAHA!
STOP BLATHERING, YOU SCALY LITTLE *CREEP!*
THERE YOU ARE, **FATHER**!
SAYER NOK SENDS WORD THAT HE WILL **ACCEPT** YOUR PRISONER!
LAUNA, YOU **SHOULDN'T** BE *HERE!*
SO, THIS IS *YOUR* DAUGHTER?

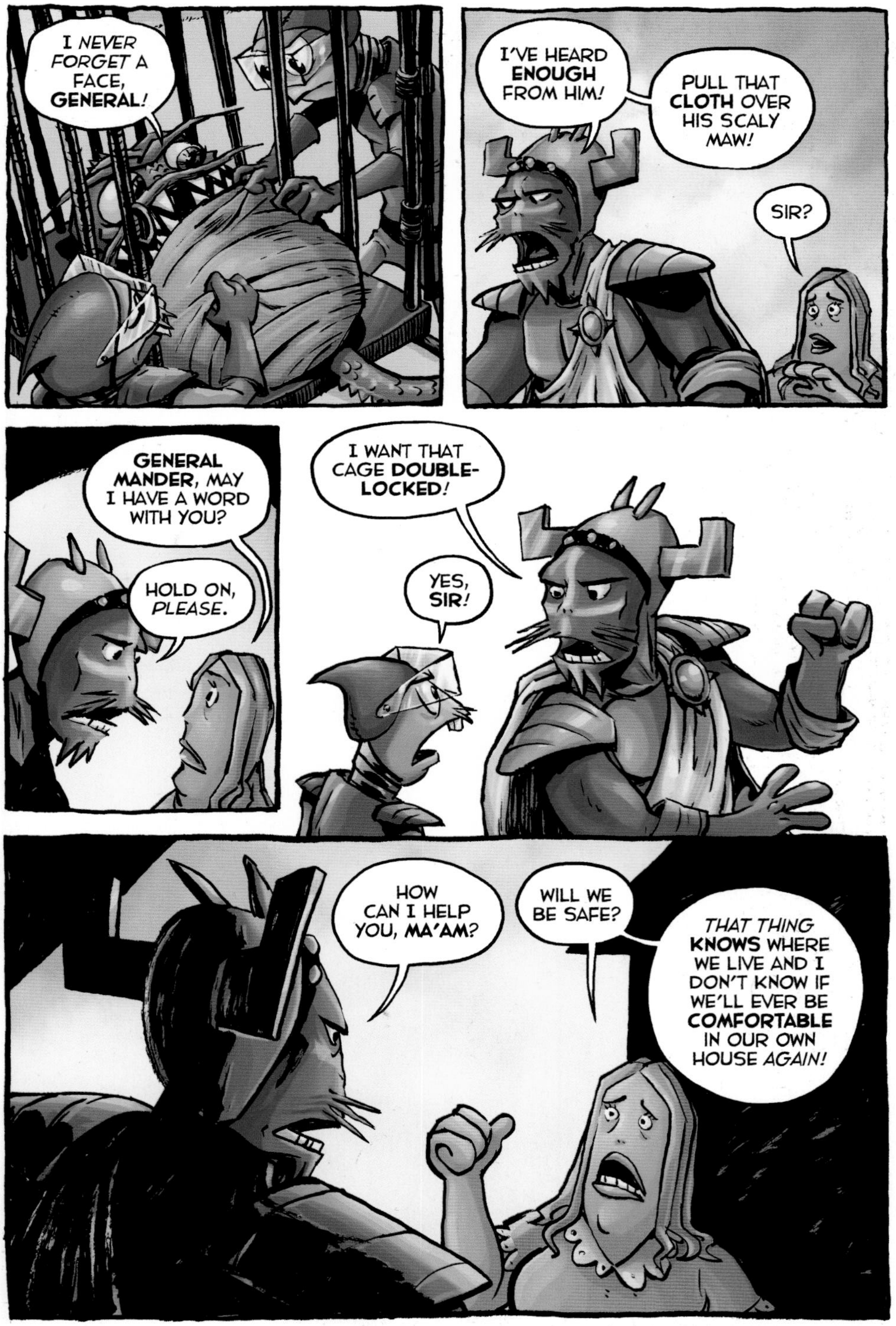
I *NEVER* *FORGET* A FACE, **GENERAL**!
I'VE HEARD **ENOUGH** FROM HIM!
PULL THAT **CLOTH** OVER HIS SCALY MAW!
SIR?
GENERAL MANDER, MAY I HAVE A WORD WITH *YOU*?
HOLD ON, *PLEASE*.
I WANT THAT CAGE **DOUBLE-LOCKED**!
YES, **SIR**!
HOW CAN I HELP YOU, **MA'AM**?
WILL WE BE SAFE?
THAT THING **KNOWS** WHERE WE LIVE AND I DON'T KNOW IF WE'LL EVER BE **COMFORTABLE** IN OUR OWN HOUSE *AGAIN*!

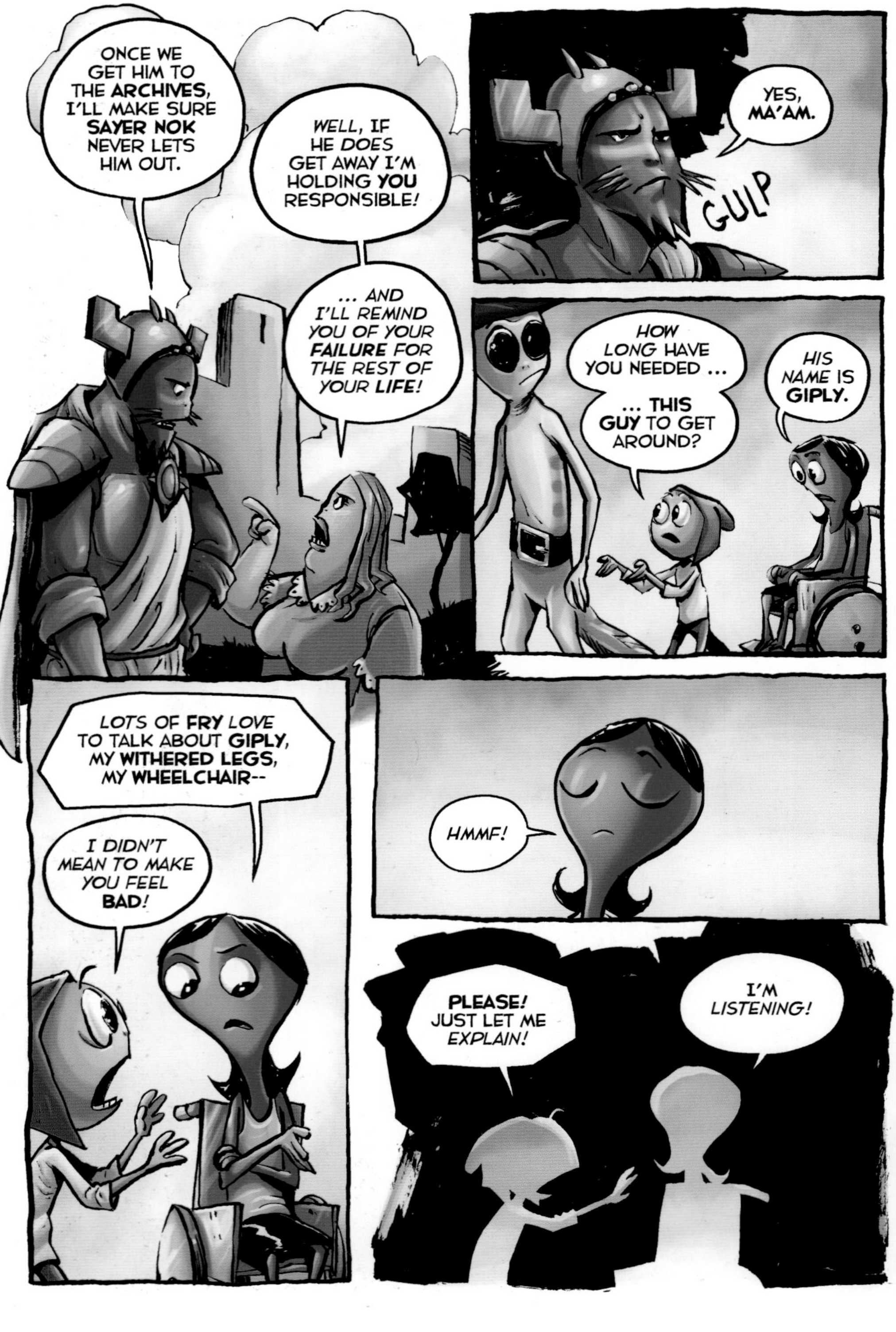
ONCE WE GET HIM TO THE ARCHIVES, I'LL MAKE SURE SAYER NOK NEVER LETS HIM OUT.
WELL, IF HE DOES GET AWAY I'M HOLDING YOU RESPONSIBLE!
... AND I'LL REMIND YOU OF YOUR FAILURE FOR THE REST OF YOUR LIFE!
YES, MA'AM.
GULP
HOW LONG HAVE YOU NEEDED ...
... THIS GUY TO GET AROUND?
HIS NAME IS GIPLY.
LOTS OF FRY LOVE TO TALK ABOUT GIPLY, MY WITHERED LEGS, MY WHEELCHAIR--
I DIDN'T MEAN TO MAKE YOU FEEL BAD!
HMMF!
PLEASE! JUST LET ME EXPLAIN!
I'M LISTENING!

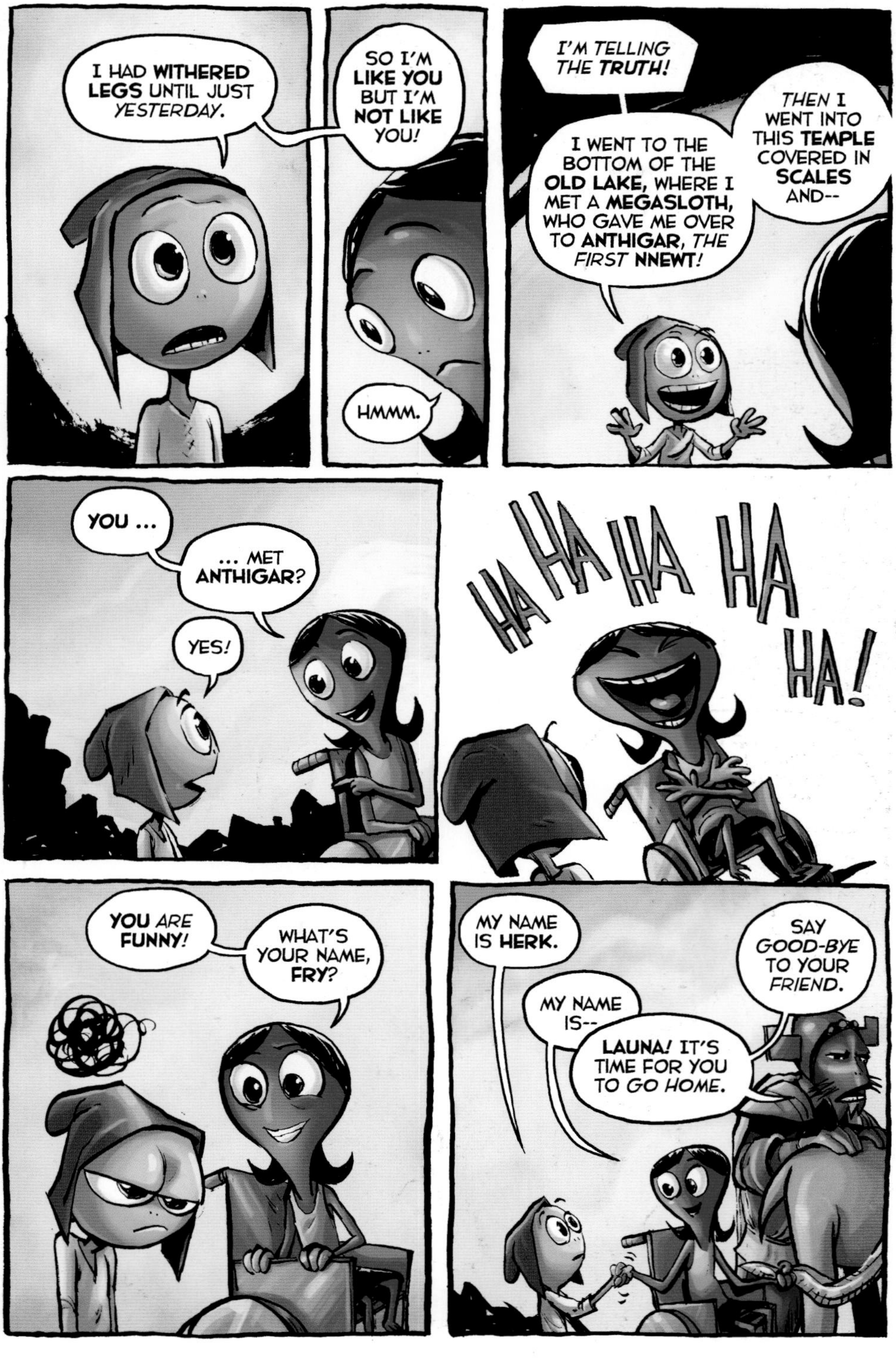
I HAD WITHERED LEGS UNTIL JUST YESTERDAY.
SO I'M LIKE YOU BUT I'M NOT LIKE YOU!
HMMM.
I'M TELLING THE TRUTH!
I WENT TO THE BOTTOM OF THE OLD LAKE, WHERE I MET A MEGASLOTH, WHO GAVE ME OVER TO ANTHIGAR, THE FIRST NNEWT!
THEN I WENT INTO THIS TEMPLE COVERED IN SCALES AND--
YOU ...
... MET ANTHIGAR?
YES!
HA HA HA HA HA HA!
YOU ARE FUNNY!
WHAT'S YOUR NAME, FRY?
MY NAME IS HERK.
MY NAME IS--
SAY GOOD-BYE TO YOUR FRIEND.
LAUNA! IT'S TIME FOR YOU TO GO HOME.

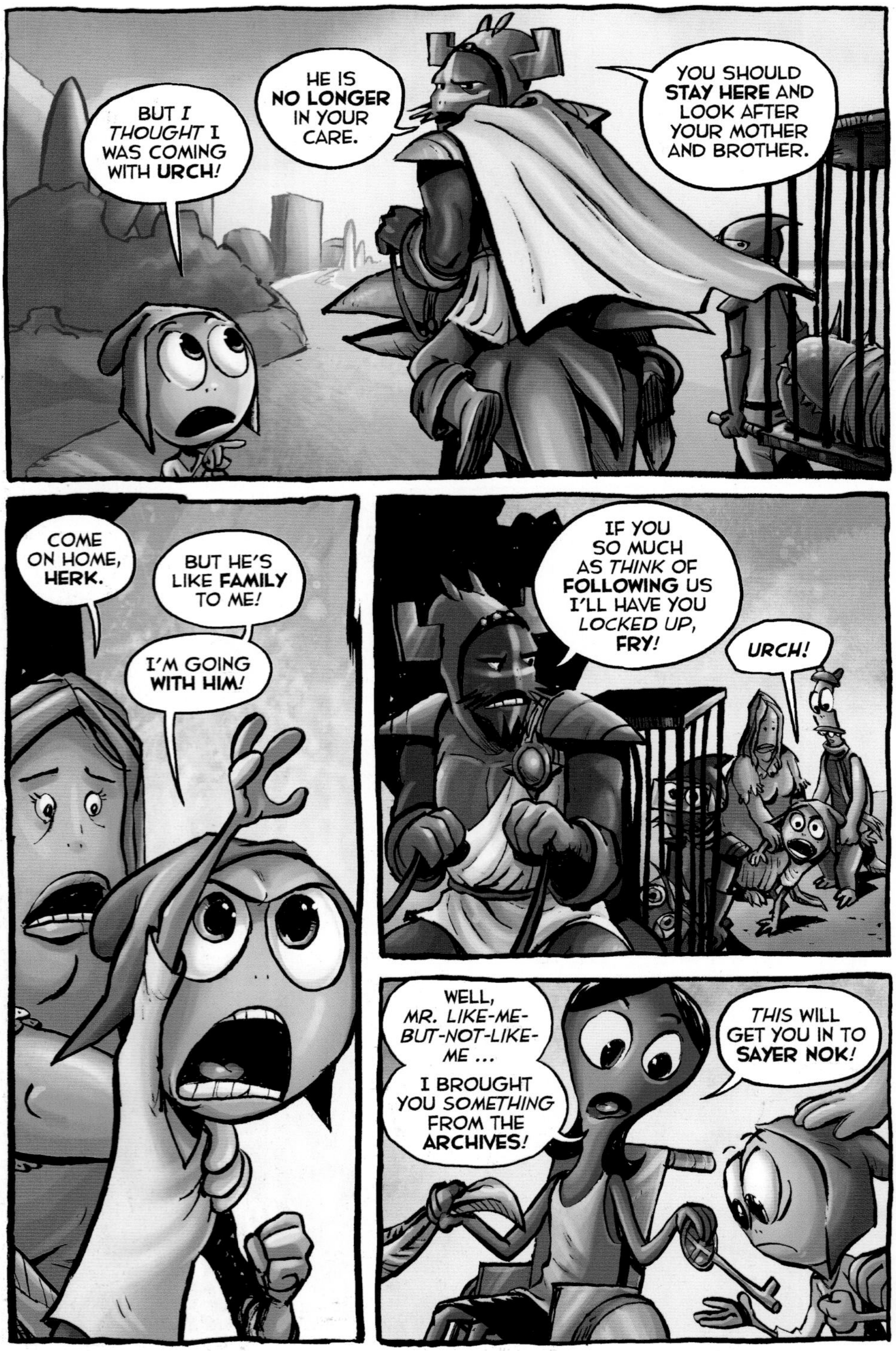
BUT *I* *THOUGHT* I WAS COMING WITH **URCH**!
HE IS **NO LONGER** IN YOUR CARE.
YOU SHOULD **STAY HERE** AND LOOK AFTER YOUR MOTHER AND BROTHER.
COME ON HOME, **HERK.**
BUT HE'S LIKE **FAMILY** TO ME!
I'M GOING **WITH HIM**!
IF YOU SO MUCH AS *THINK* OF **FOLLOWING** US I'LL HAVE YOU *LOCKED UP*, **FRY**!
URCH!
WELL, *MR. LIKE-ME-BUT-NOT-LIKE-ME* ...
I BROUGHT YOU *SOMETHING* FROM THE **ARCHIVES**!
THIS WILL GET YOU IN TO **SAYER NOK**!

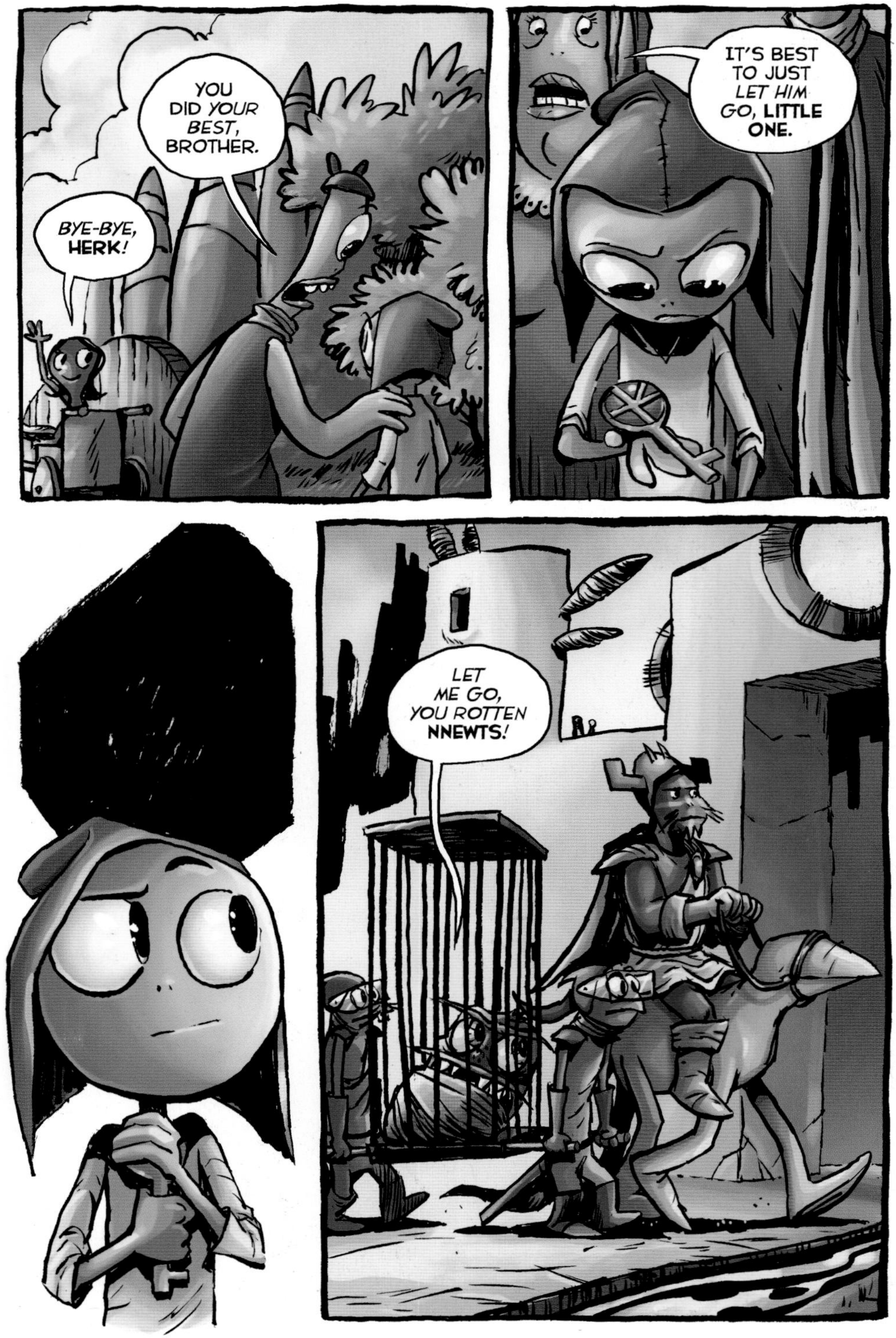
YOU DID YOUR BEST, BROTHER.
BYE-BYE, HERK!
IT'S BEST TO JUST LET HIM GO, LITTLE ONE.
LET ME GO, YOU ROTTEN NNEWTS!

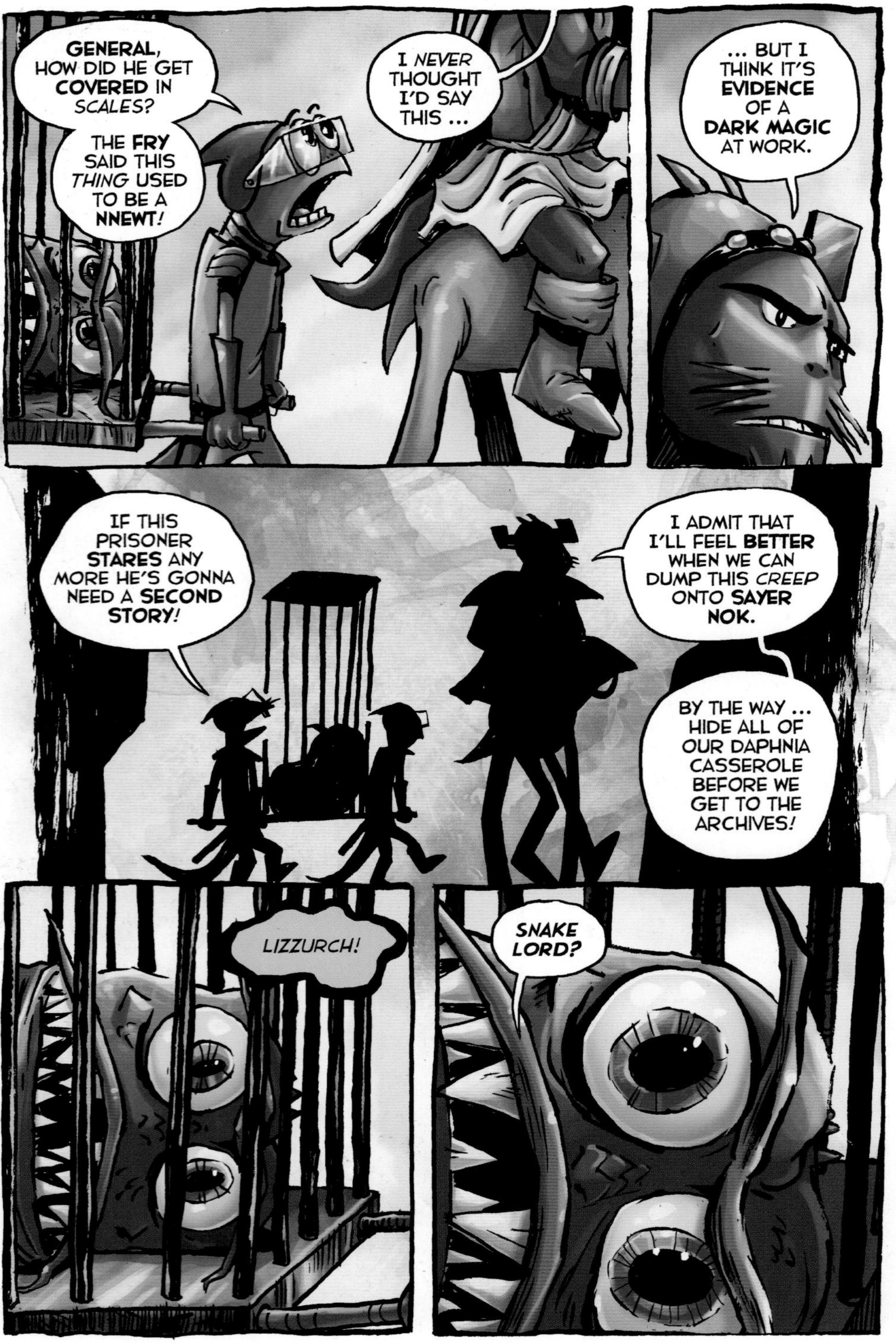
GENERAL, HOW DID HE GET COVERED IN SCALES?
THE FRY SAID THIS THING USED TO BE A NNEWT!
I NEVER THOUGHT I'D SAY THIS ...
... BUT I THINK IT'S EVIDENCE OF A DARK MAGIC AT WORK.
IF THIS PRISONER STARES ANY MORE HE'S GONNA NEED A SECOND STORY!
I ADMIT THAT I'LL FEEL BETTER WHEN WE CAN DUMP THIS CREEP ONTO SAYER NOK.
BY THE WAY ... HIDE ALL OF OUR DAPHNIA CASSEROLE BEFORE WE GET TO THE ARCHIVES!
LIZZURCH!
SNAKE LORD?

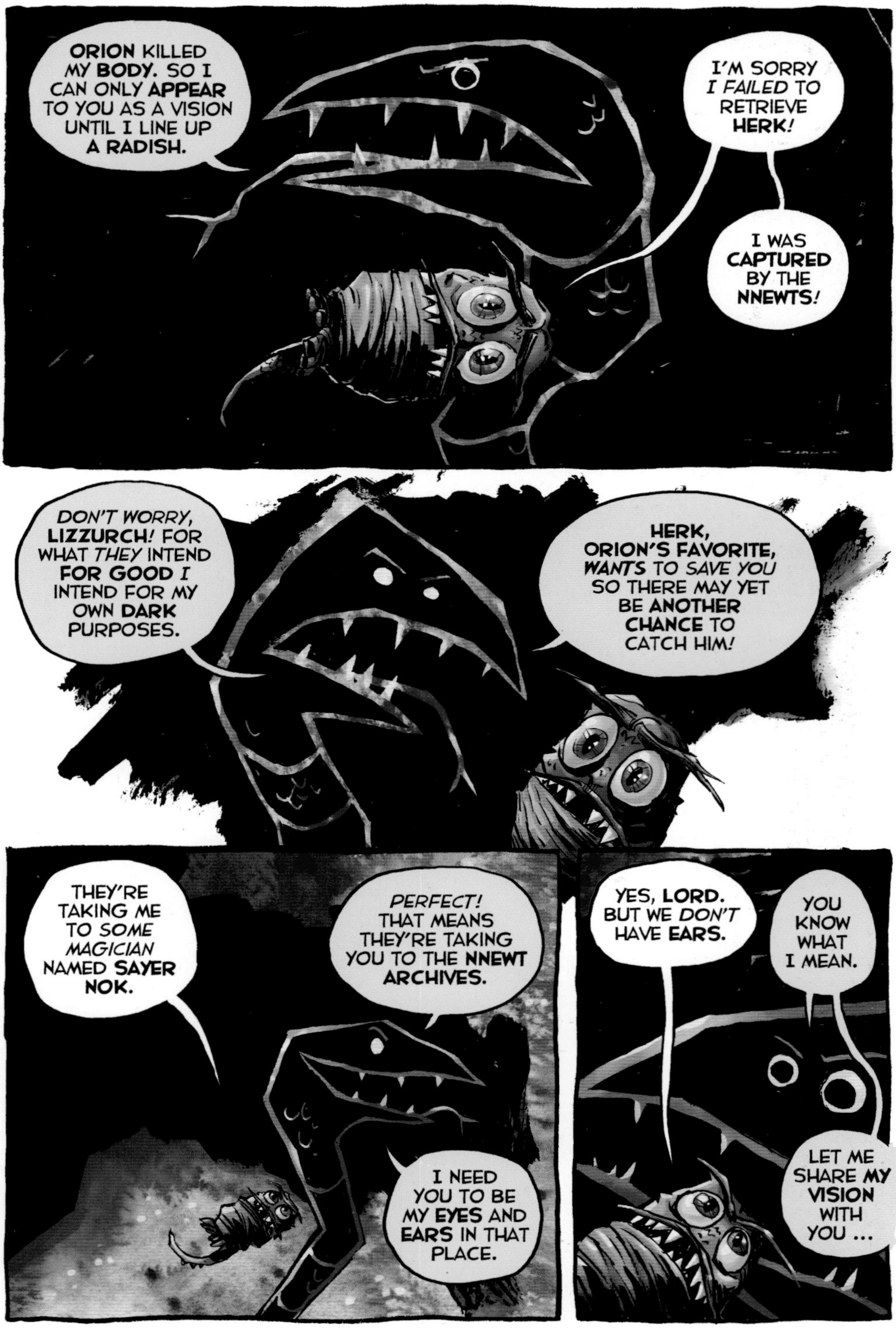
ORION KILLED MY BODY. SO I CAN ONLY APPEAR TO YOU AS A VISION UNTIL I LINE UP A RADISH.
I'M SORRY I FAILED TO RETRIEVE HERK!
I WAS CAPTURED BY THE NNEWTS!
DON'T WORRY, LIZZURCH! FOR WHAT THEY INTEND FOR GOOD I INTEND FOR MY OWN DARK PURPOSES.
HERK, ORION'S FAVORITE, WANTS TO SAVE YOU SO THERE MAY YET BE ANOTHER CHANCE TO CATCH HIM!
THEY'RE TAKING ME TO SOME MAGICIAN NAMED SAYER NOK.
PERFECT! THAT MEANS THEY'RE TAKING YOU TO THE NNEWT ARCHIVES.
I NEED YOU TO BE MY EYES AND EARS IN THAT PLACE.
YES, LORD. BUT WE DON'T HAVE EARS.
YOU KNOW WHAT I MEAN.
LET ME SHARE MY VISION WITH YOU ...

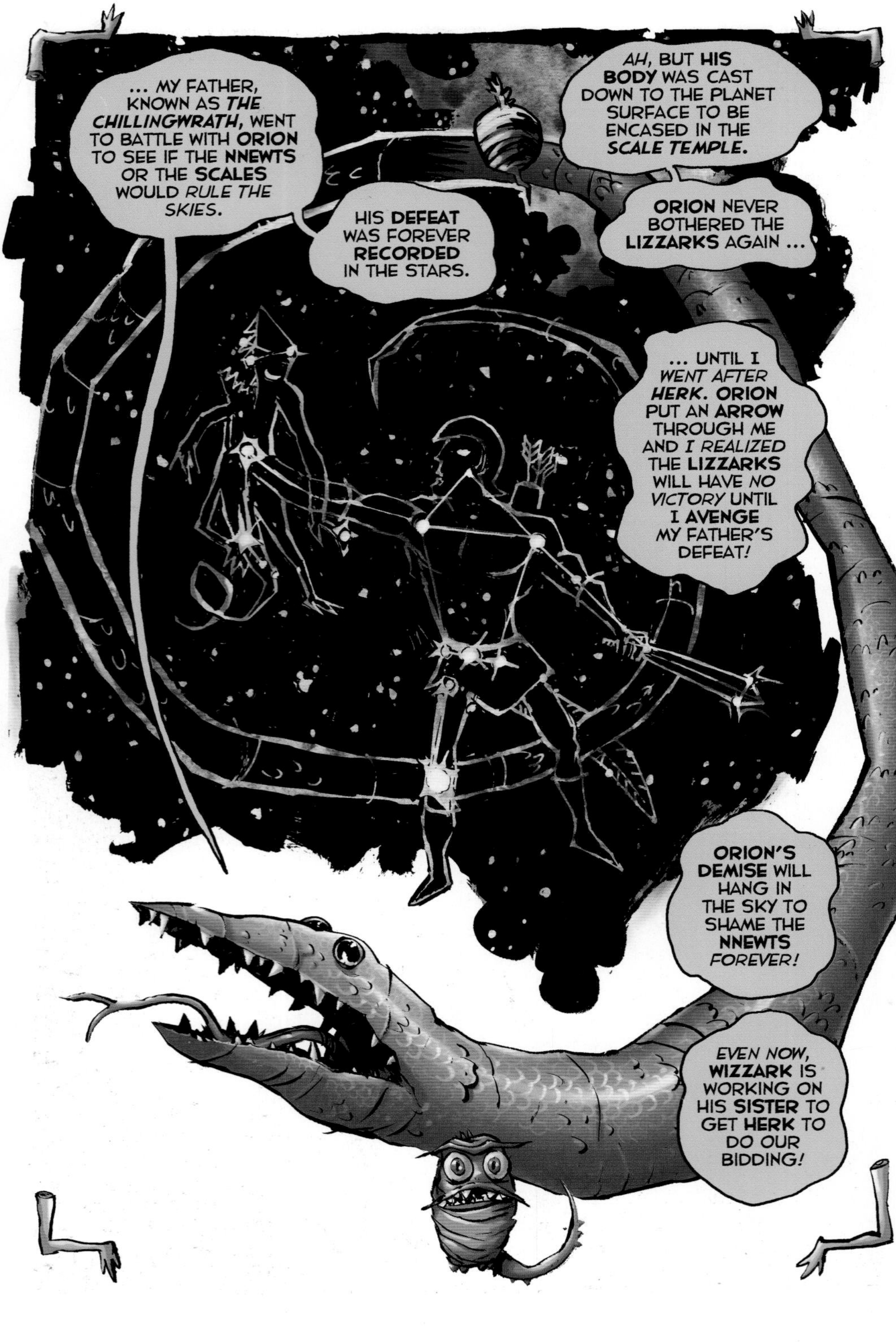
... MY FATHER, KNOWN AS *THE CHILLINGWRATH*, WENT TO BATTLE WITH **ORION** TO SEE IF THE **NNEWTS** OR THE **SCALES** WOULD *RULE THE SKIES*.
HIS **DEFEAT** WAS FOREVER **RECORDED** IN THE STARS.
AH, BUT **HIS BODY** WAS CAST DOWN TO THE PLANET SURFACE TO BE ENCASED IN THE ***SCALE TEMPLE***.
ORION NEVER BOTHERED THE **LIZZARKS** AGAIN ...
... UNTIL I *WENT AFTER* ***HERK***. **ORION** PUT AN **ARROW** THROUGH ME AND *I REALIZED* THE **LIZZARKS** WILL HAVE *NO VICTORY* UNTIL **I AVENGE** MY FATHER'S DEFEAT!
ORION'S DEMISE WILL HANG IN THE SKY TO SHAME THE **NNEWTS** *FOREVER!*
EVEN NOW, **WIZZARK** IS WORKING ON HIS **SISTER** TO GET **HERK** TO DO OUR BIDDING!

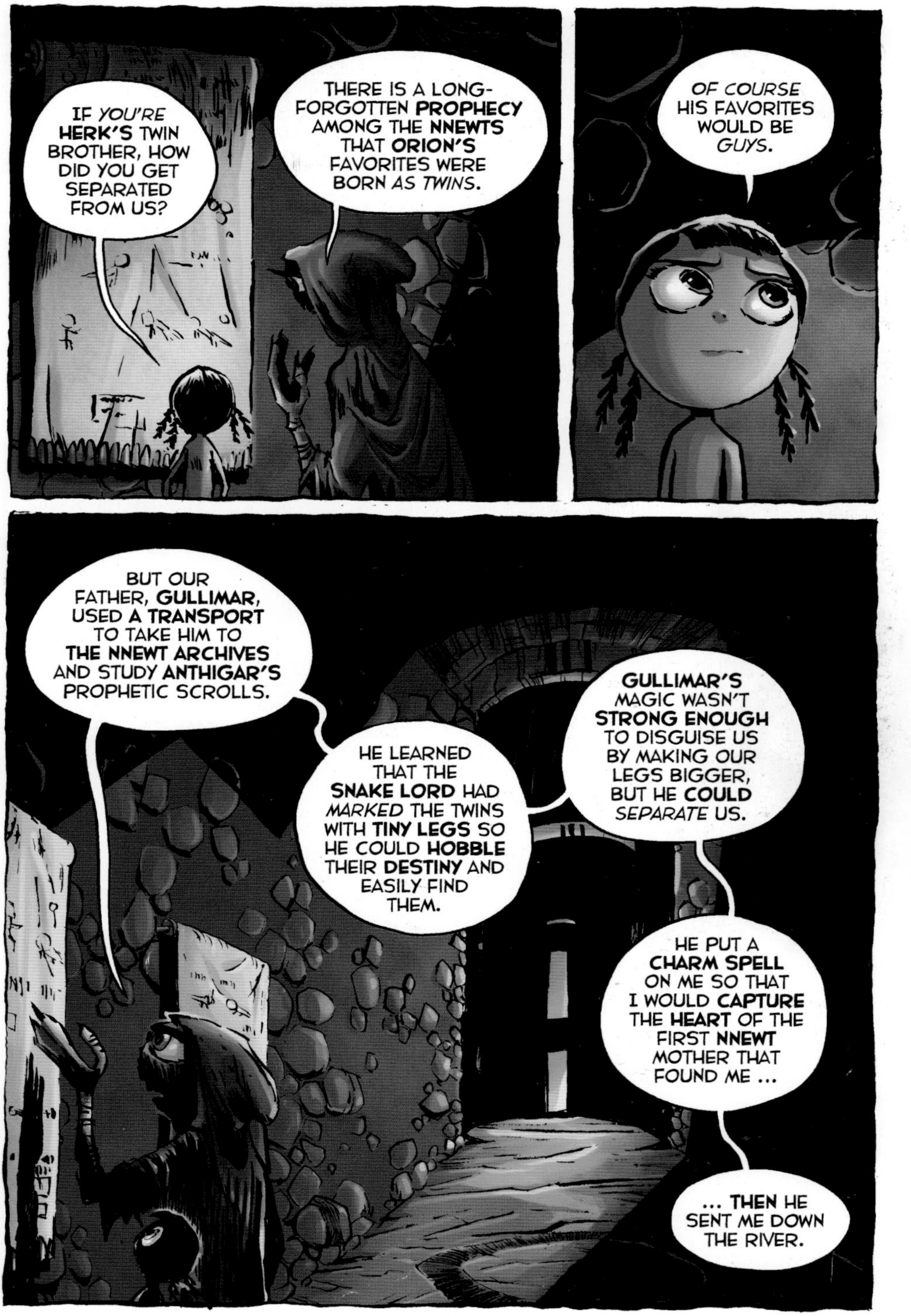
IF YOU'RE HERK'S TWIN BROTHER, HOW DID YOU GET SEPARATED FROM US?
THERE IS A LONG-FORGOTTEN PROPHECY AMONG THE NNEWTS THAT ORION'S FAVORITES WERE BORN AS TWINS.
OF COURSE HIS FAVORITES WOULD BE GUYS.
BUT OUR FATHER, GULLIMAR, USED A TRANSPORT TO TAKE HIM TO THE NNEWT ARCHIVES AND STUDY ANTHIGAR'S PROPHETIC SCROLLS.
HE LEARNED THAT THE SNAKE LORD HAD MARKED THE TWINS WITH TINY LEGS SO HE COULD HOBBLE THEIR DESTINY AND EASILY FIND THEM.
GULLIMAR'S MAGIC WASN'T STRONG ENOUGH TO DISGUISE US BY MAKING OUR LEGS BIGGER, BUT HE COULD SEPARATE US.
HE PUT A CHARM SPELL ON ME SO THAT I WOULD CAPTURE THE HEART OF THE FIRST NNEWT MOTHER THAT FOUND ME ...
... THEN HE SENT ME DOWN THE RIVER.

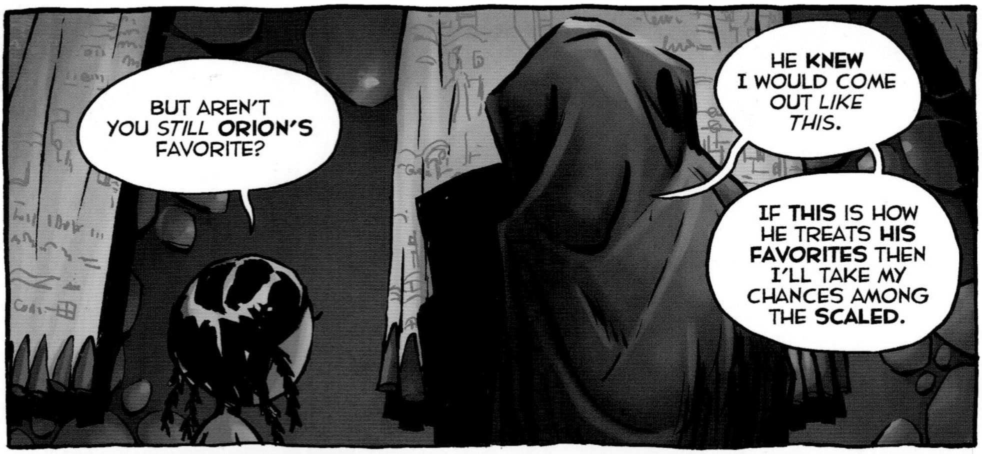
BUT AREN'T YOU STILL ORION'S FAVORITE?
HE KNEW I WOULD COME OUT LIKE THIS.
IF THIS IS HOW HE TREATS HIS FAVORITES THEN I'LL TAKE MY CHANCES AMONG THE SCALED.

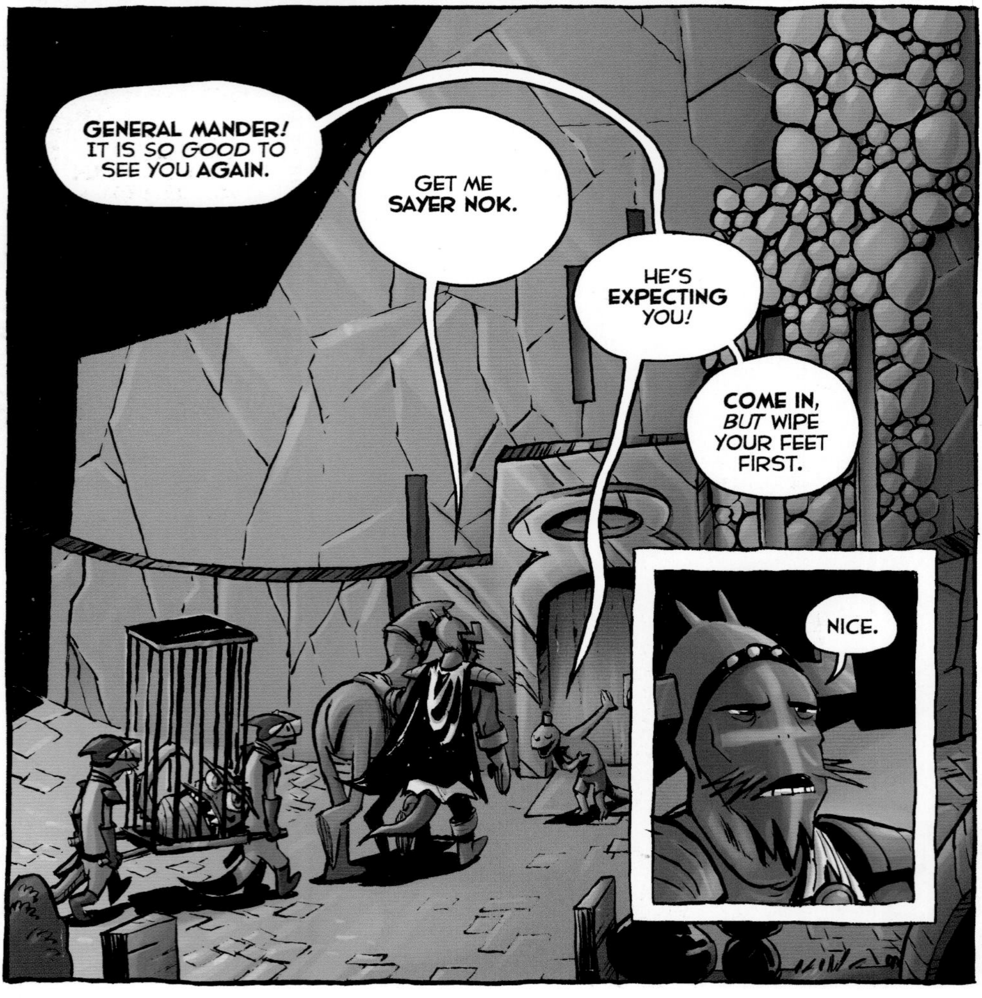
GENERAL MANDER! IT IS SO GOOD TO SEE YOU AGAIN.
GET ME SAYER NOK.
HE'S EXPECTING YOU!
COME IN, BUT WIPE YOUR FEET FIRST.
NICE.

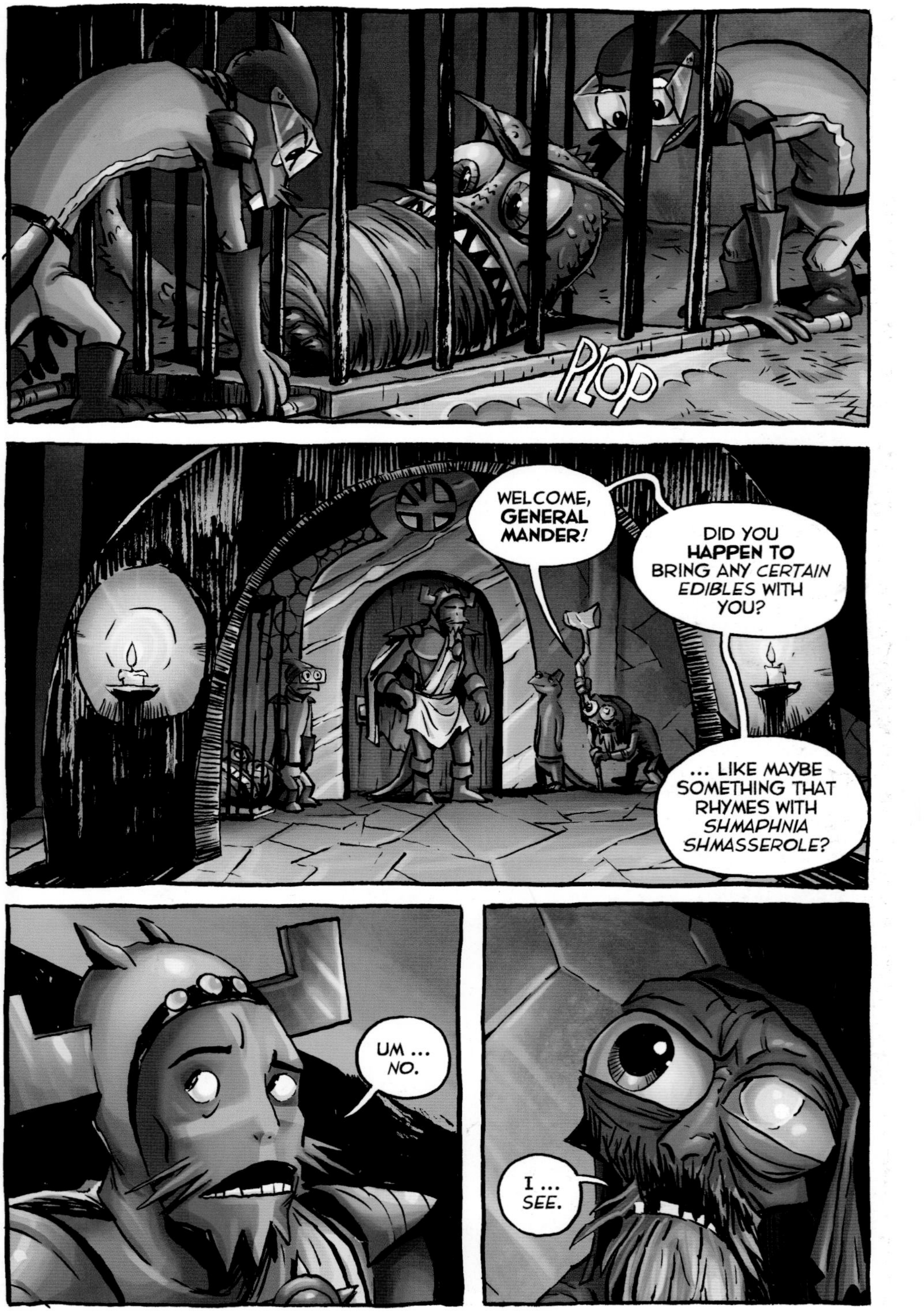
PLOP
WELCOME, GENERAL MANDER!
DID YOU HAPPEN TO BRING ANY CERTAIN EDIBLES WITH YOU?
... LIKE MAYBE SOMETHING THAT RHYMES WITH SHMAPHNIA SHMASSEROLE?
UM ... NO.
I ... SEE.

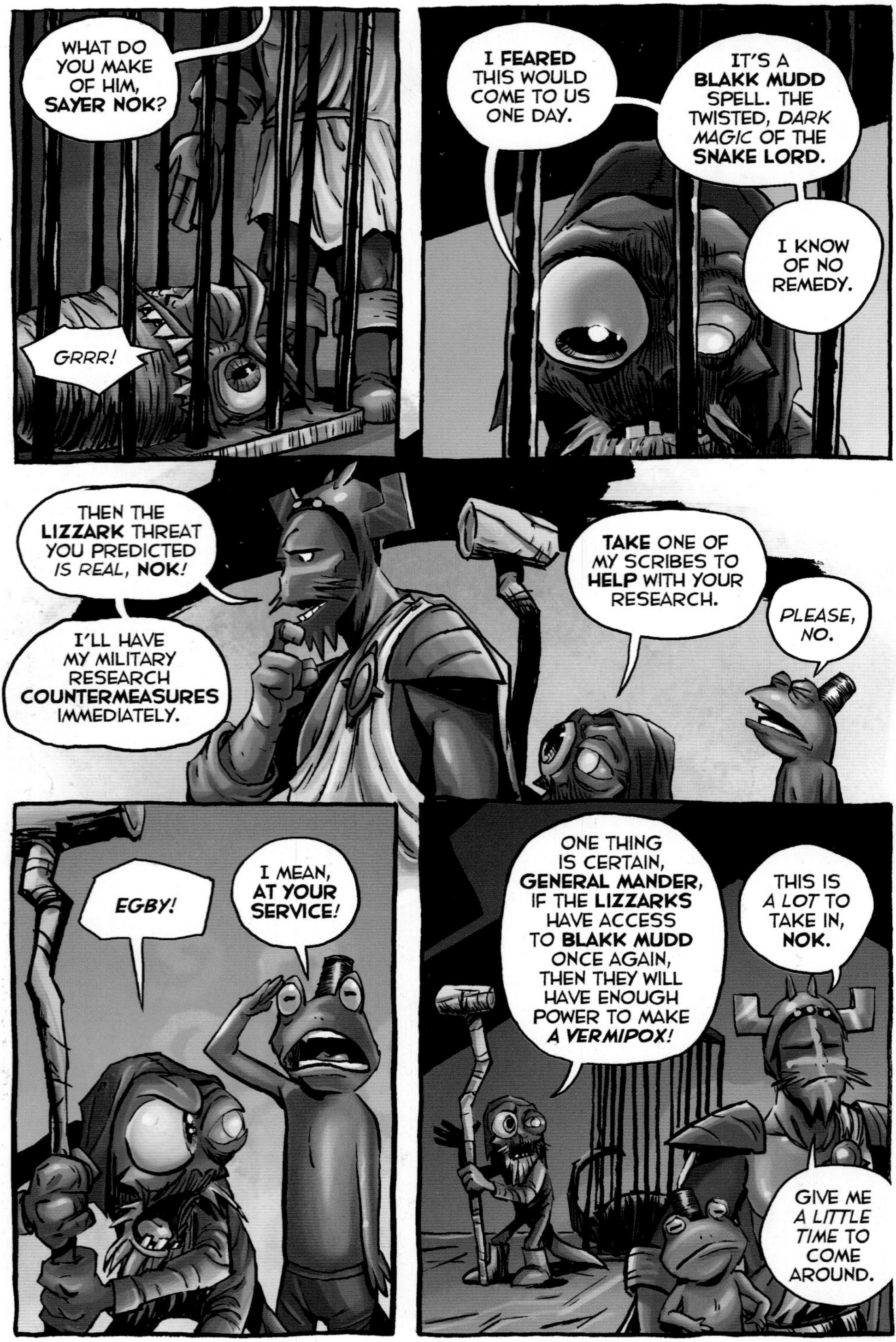
WHAT DO YOU MAKE OF HIM, SAYER NOK?
GRRR!
I FEARED THIS WOULD COME TO US ONE DAY.
IT'S A BLAKK MUDD SPELL. THE TWISTED, DARK MAGIC OF THE SNAKE LORD.
I KNOW OF NO REMEDY.
THEN THE LIZZARK THREAT YOU PREDICTED IS REAL, NOK!
I'LL HAVE MY MILITARY RESEARCH COUNTERMEASURES IMMEDIATELY.
TAKE ONE OF MY SCRIBES TO HELP WITH YOUR RESEARCH.
PLEASE, NO.
EGBY!
I MEAN, AT YOUR SERVICE!
ONE THING IS CERTAIN, GENERAL MANDER, IF THE LIZZARKS HAVE ACCESS TO BLAKK MUDD ONCE AGAIN, THEN THEY WILL HAVE ENOUGH POWER TO MAKE A VERMIPOX!
THIS IS A LOT TO TAKE IN, NOK.
GIVE ME A LITTLE TIME TO COME AROUND.

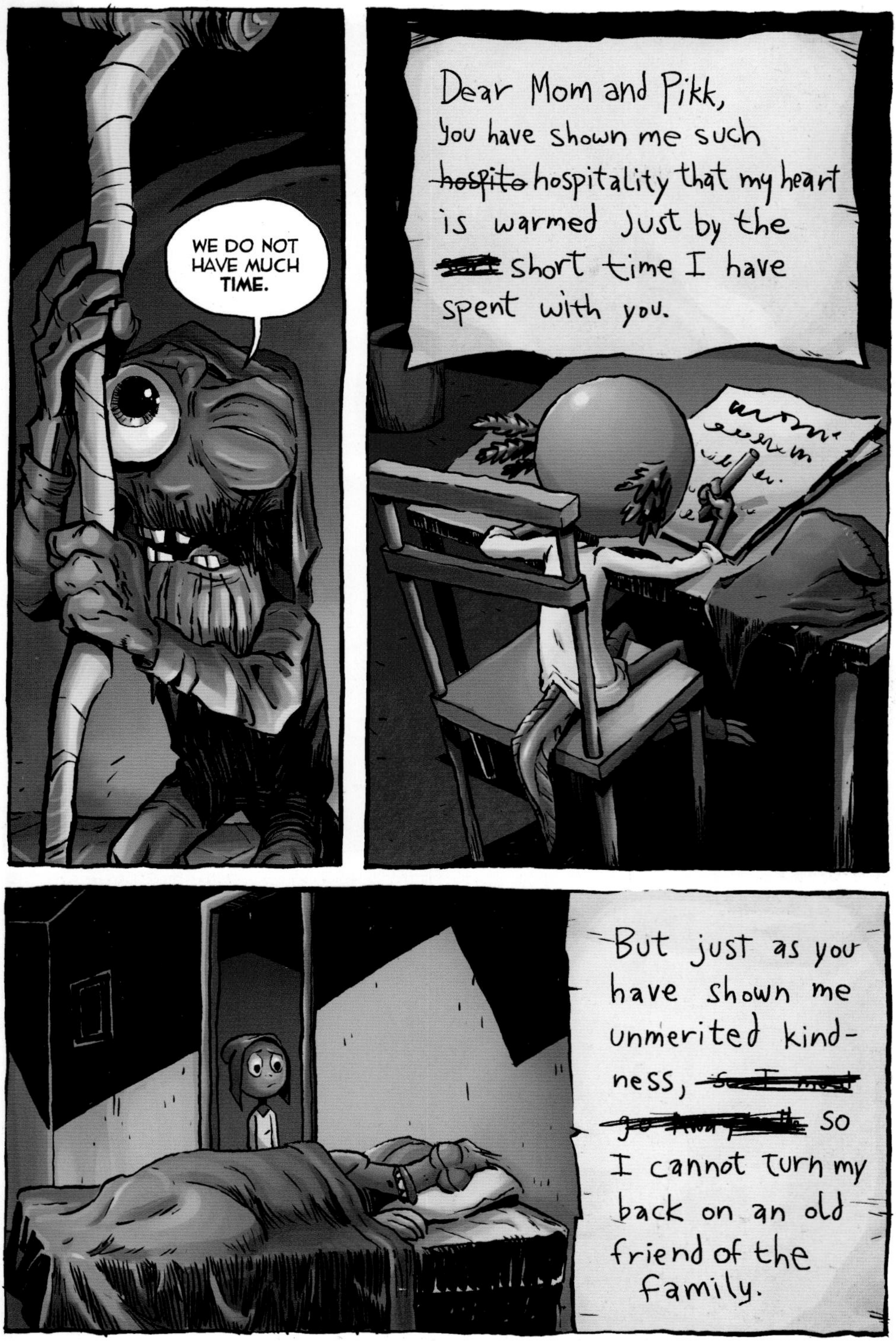
WE DO NOT HAVE MUCH TIME.
Dear Mom and Pikk,
You have shown me such ~~hospito~~ hospitality that my heart is warmed just by the short time I have spent with you.
But just as you have shown me unmerited kindness, so I cannot turn my back on an old friend of the family.

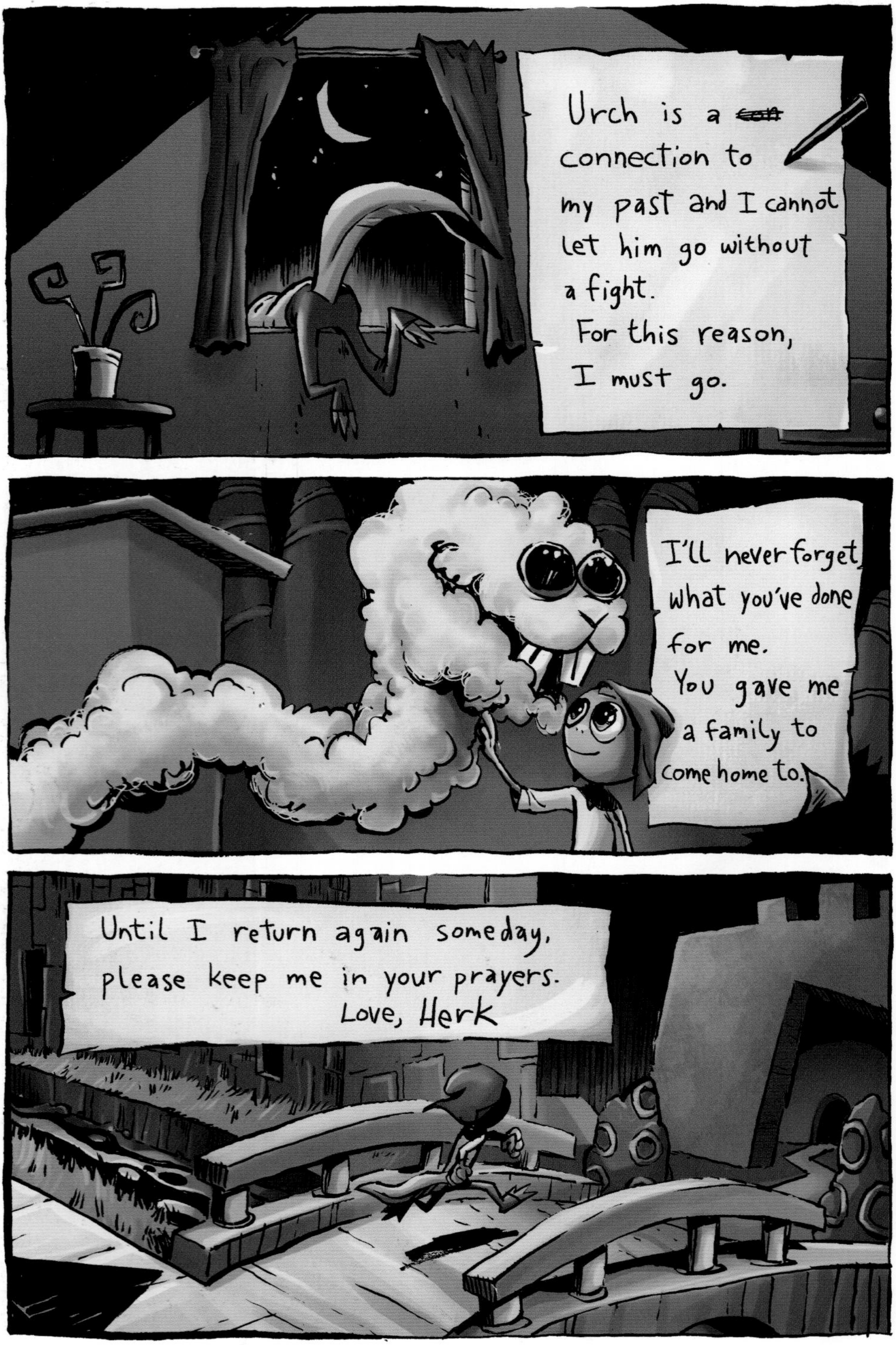
Urch is a ~~con~~ connection to my past and I cannot let him go without a fight. For this reason, I must go.
I'll never forget what you've done for me. You gave me a family to come home to.
Until I return again someday, please keep me in your prayers. Love, Herk

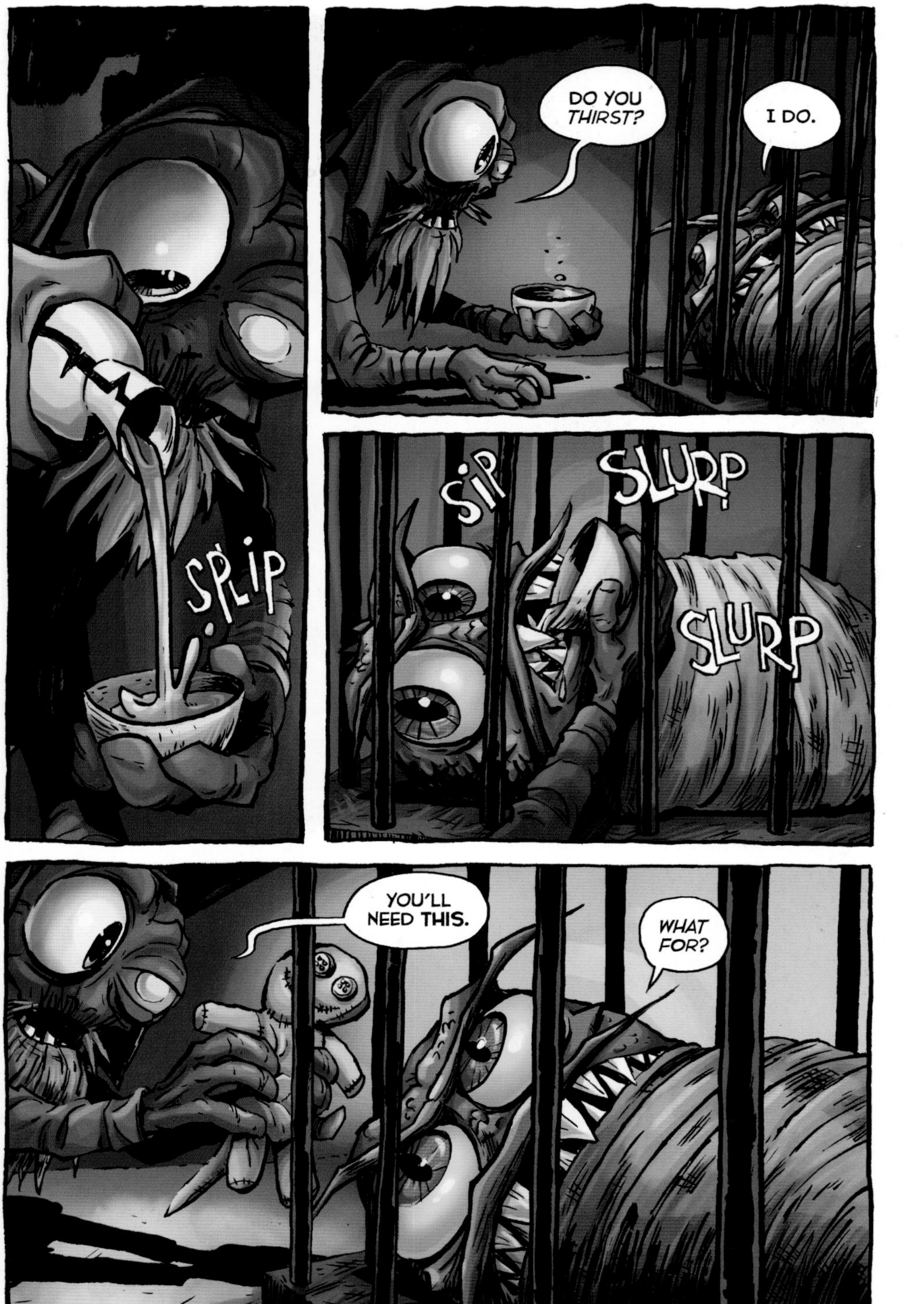
SPLIP
DO YOU THIRST?
I DO.
SIP
SLURP
SLURP
YOU'LL NEED THIS.
WHAT FOR?

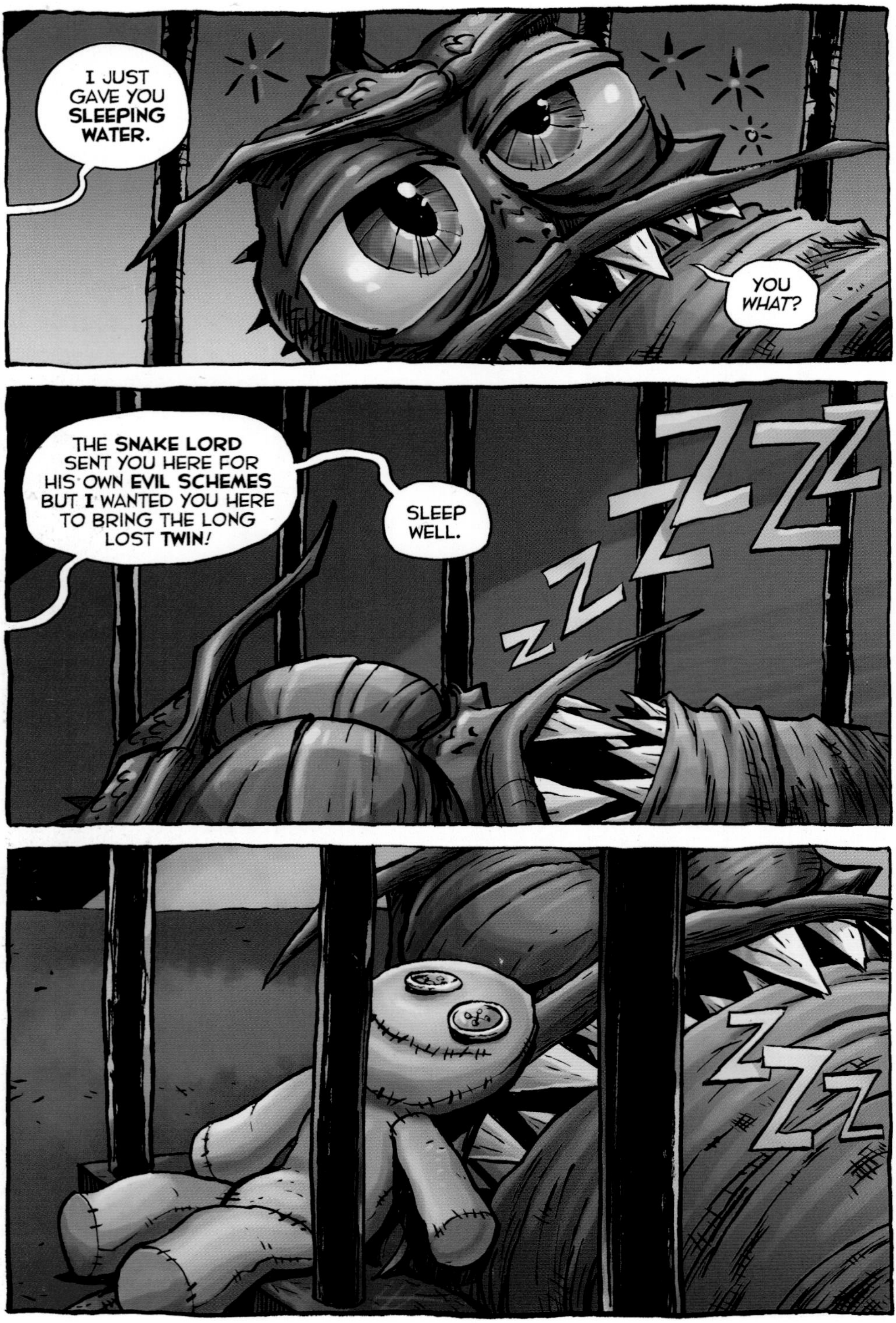
I JUST GAVE YOU SLEEPING WATER.
YOU WHAT?
THE SNAKE LORD SENT YOU HERE FOR HIS OWN EVIL SCHEMES BUT I WANTED YOU HERE TO BRING THE LONG LOST TWIN!
SLEEP WELL.
zZZZZ
ZZZ

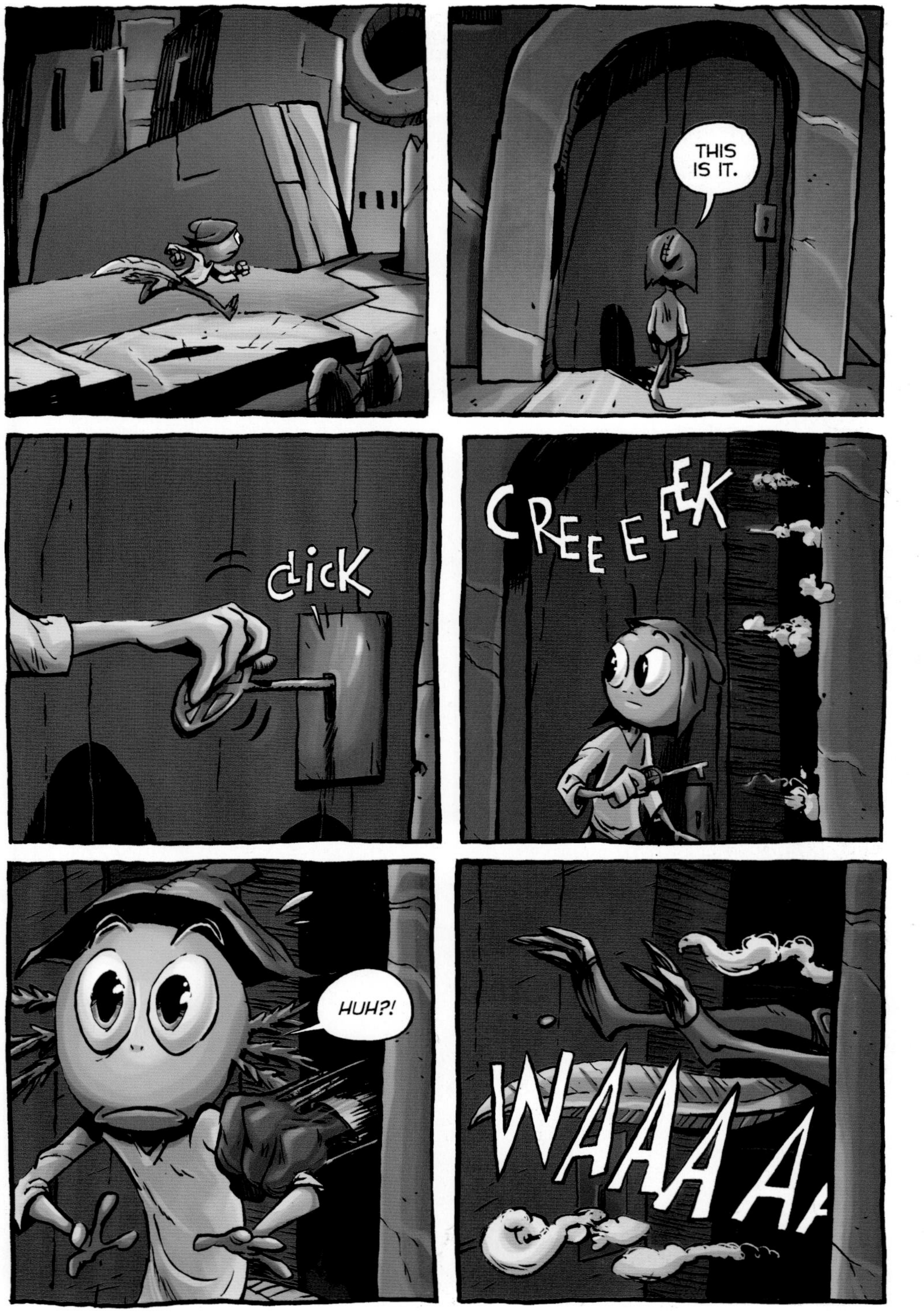
THIS IS IT.
CLICK
CREEEEEK
HUH?!
WAAAAA

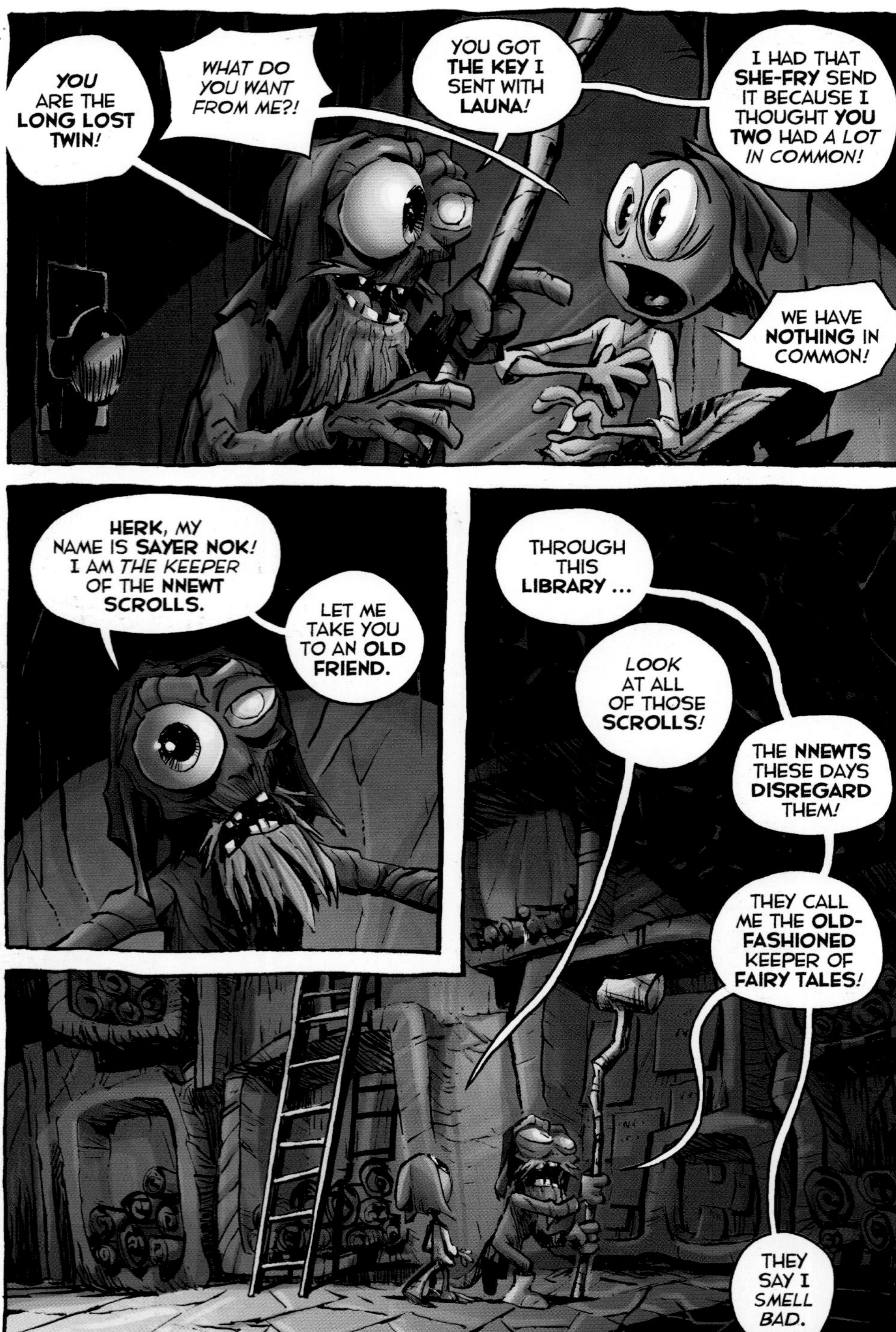

YOU ARE THE **LONG LOST TWIN**!
WHAT DO YOU WANT FROM ME?!
YOU GOT **THE KEY** I SENT WITH **LAUNA**!
I HAD THAT **SHE-FRY** SEND IT BECAUSE I THOUGHT **YOU TWO** HAD *A LOT IN COMMON!*
WE HAVE **NOTHING** IN COMMON!
HERK, MY NAME IS **SAYER NOK**! I AM *THE KEEPER* OF THE **NNEWT SCROLLS.**
LET ME TAKE YOU TO AN **OLD FRIEND.**
THROUGH THIS **LIBRARY ...**
LOOK AT ALL OF THOSE **SCROLLS**!
THE **NNEWTS** THESE DAYS **DISREGARD** THEM!
THEY CALL ME THE **OLD-FASHIONED** KEEPER OF **FAIRY TALES**!
THEY SAY I *SMELL BAD.*

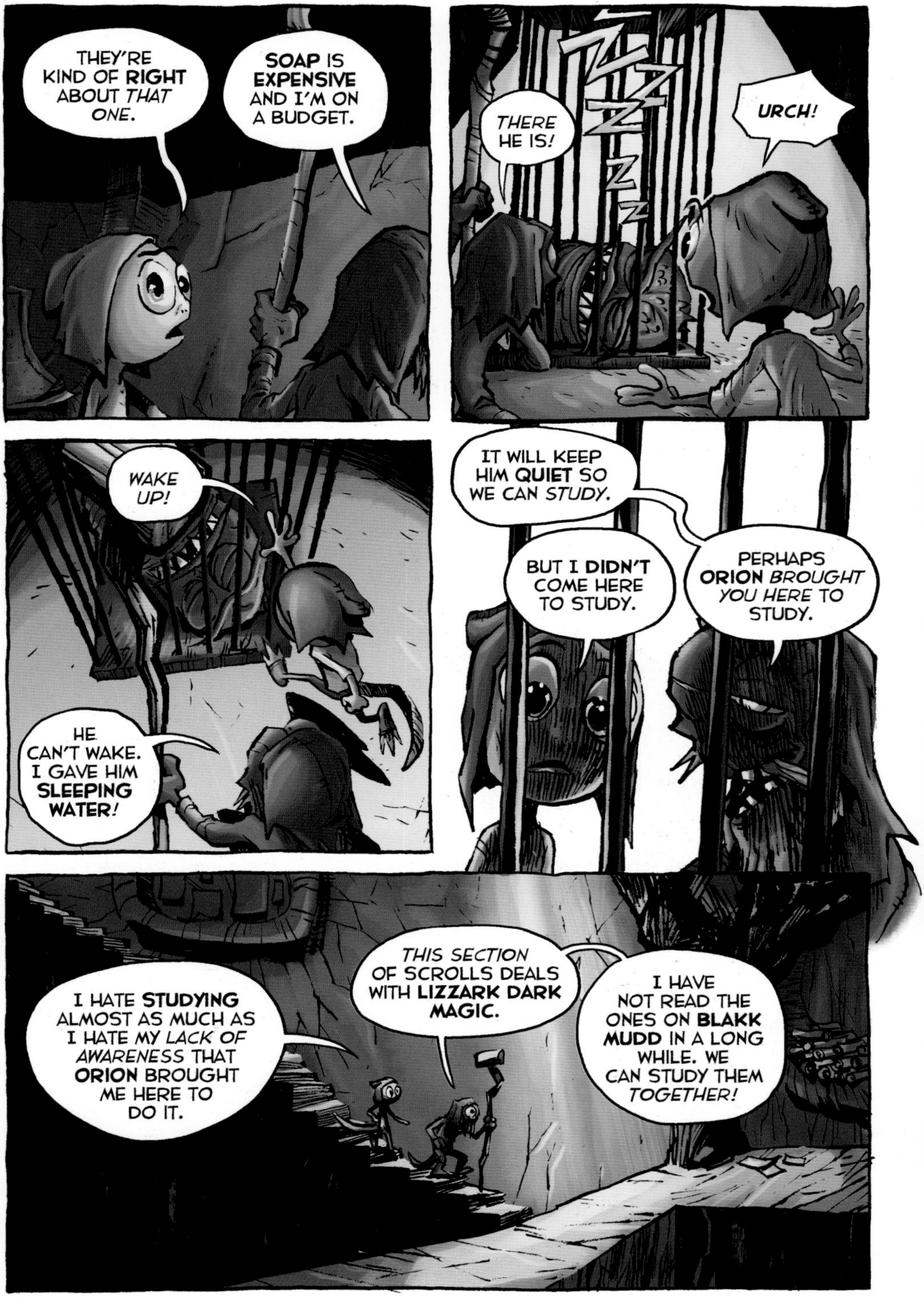
THEY'RE KIND OF **RIGHT** ABOUT *THAT* ONE.
SOAP IS **EXPENSIVE** AND I'M ON A BUDGET.
THERE HE IS!
ZZZZZ
URCH!
WAKE UP!
HE CAN'T WAKE. I GAVE HIM **SLEEPING WATER!**
IT WILL KEEP HIM **QUIET** SO WE CAN *STUDY*.
BUT I **DIDN'T** COME HERE TO STUDY.
PERHAPS **ORION** *BROUGHT YOU HERE* TO STUDY.
I HATE **STUDYING** ALMOST AS MUCH AS I HATE MY *LACK OF AWARENESS* THAT **ORION** BROUGHT ME HERE TO DO IT.
THIS SECTION OF SCROLLS DEALS WITH **LIZZARK DARK MAGIC.**
I HAVE NOT READ THE ONES ON **BLAKK MUDD** IN A LONG WHILE. WE CAN STUDY THEM *TOGETHER!*

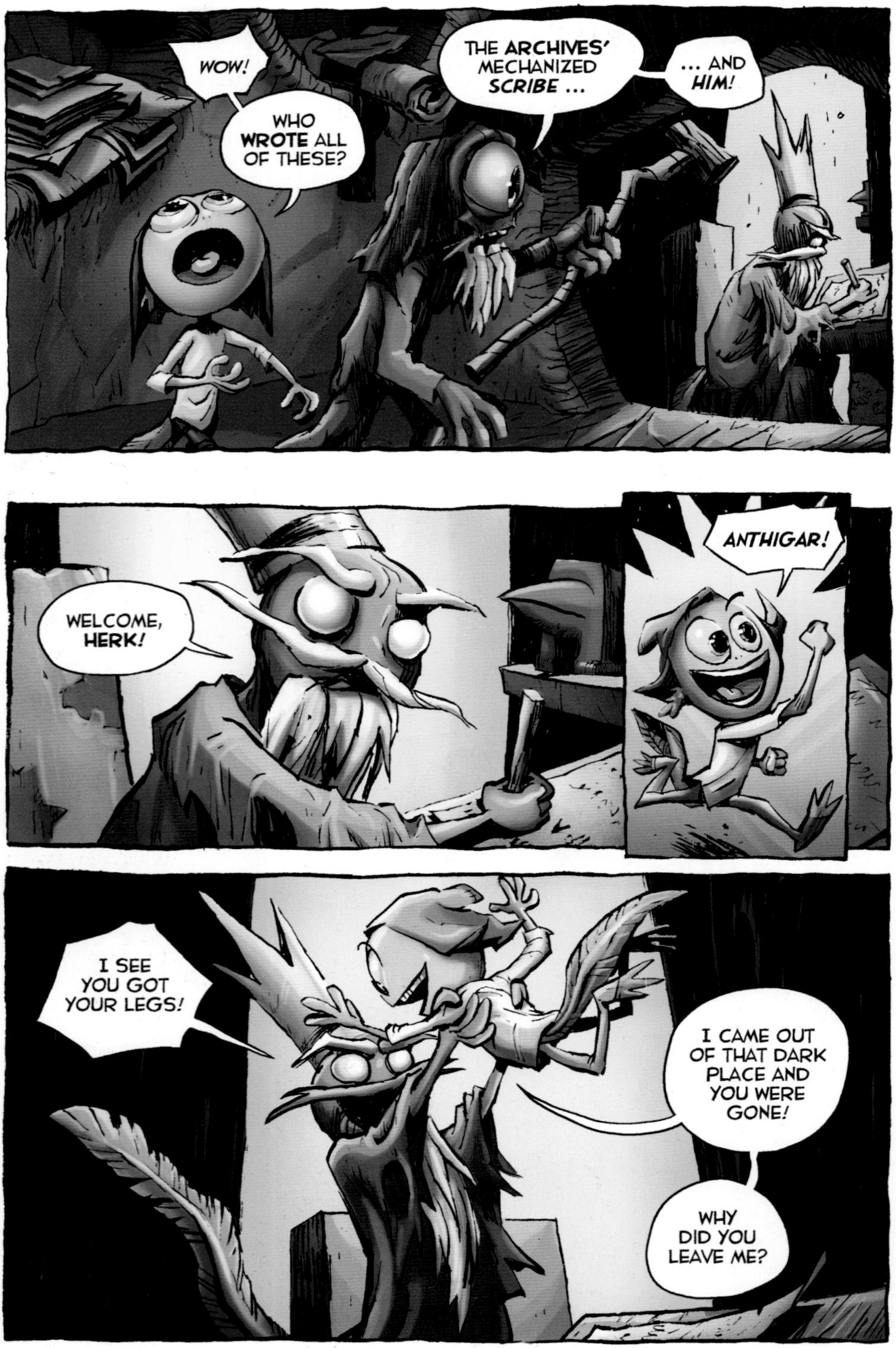
WOW!
WHO WROTE ALL OF THESE?
THE ARCHIVES' MECHANIZED SCRIBE ...
... AND HIM!
WELCOME, HERK!
ANTHIGAR!
I SEE YOU GOT YOUR LEGS!
I CAME OUT OF THAT DARK PLACE AND YOU WERE GONE!
WHY DID YOU LEAVE ME?

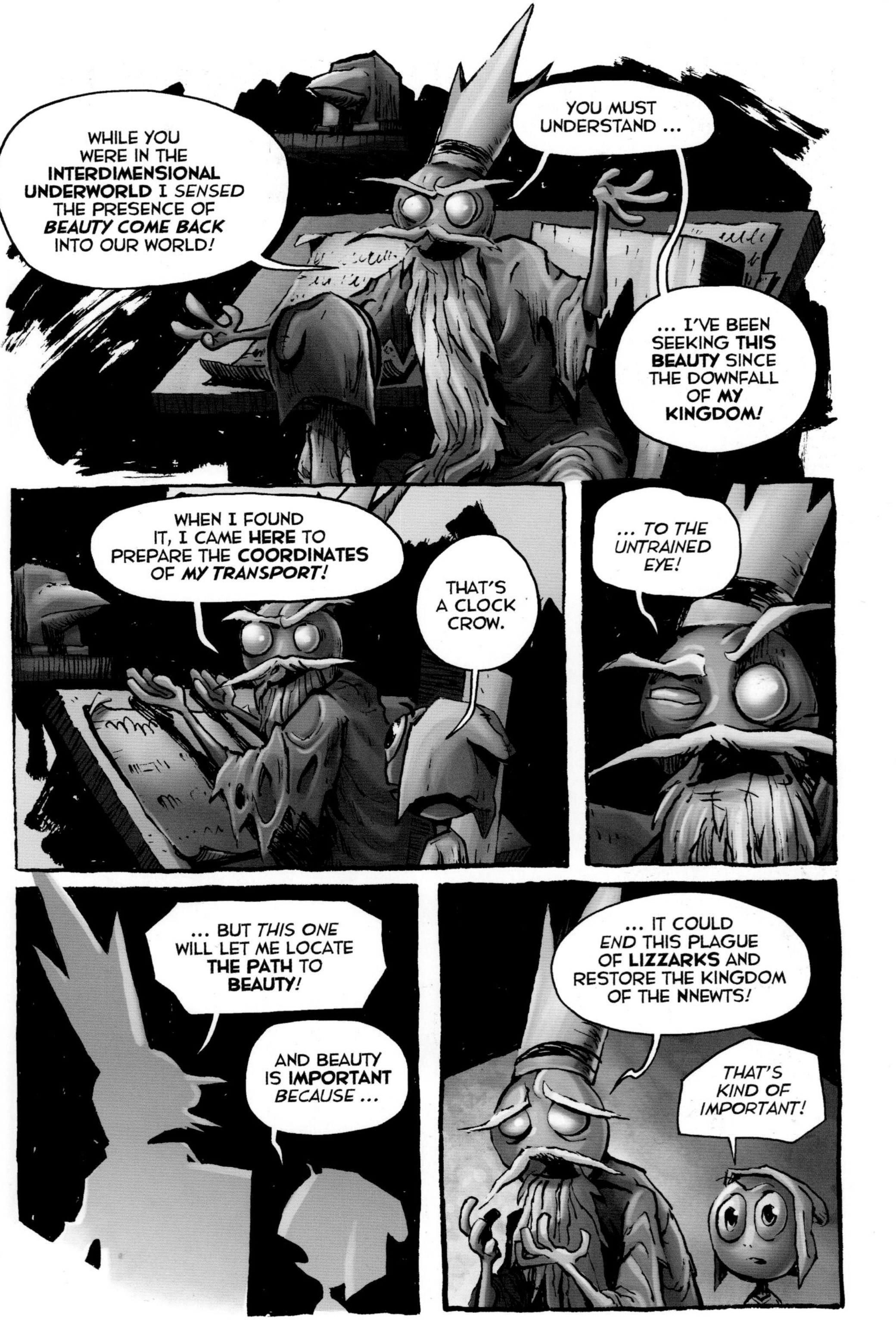
WHILE YOU WERE IN THE INTERDIMENSIONAL UNDERWORLD I SENSED THE PRESENCE OF BEAUTY COME BACK INTO OUR WORLD!
YOU MUST UNDERSTAND ...
... I'VE BEEN SEEKING THIS BEAUTY SINCE THE DOWNFALL OF MY KINGDOM!
WHEN I FOUND IT, I CAME HERE TO PREPARE THE COORDINATES OF MY TRANSPORT!
THAT'S A CLOCK CROW.
... TO THE UNTRAINED EYE!
... BUT THIS ONE WILL LET ME LOCATE THE PATH TO BEAUTY!
AND BEAUTY IS IMPORTANT BECAUSE ...
... IT COULD END THIS PLAGUE OF LIZZARKS AND RESTORE THE KINGDOM OF THE NNEWTS!
THAT'S KIND OF IMPORTANT!

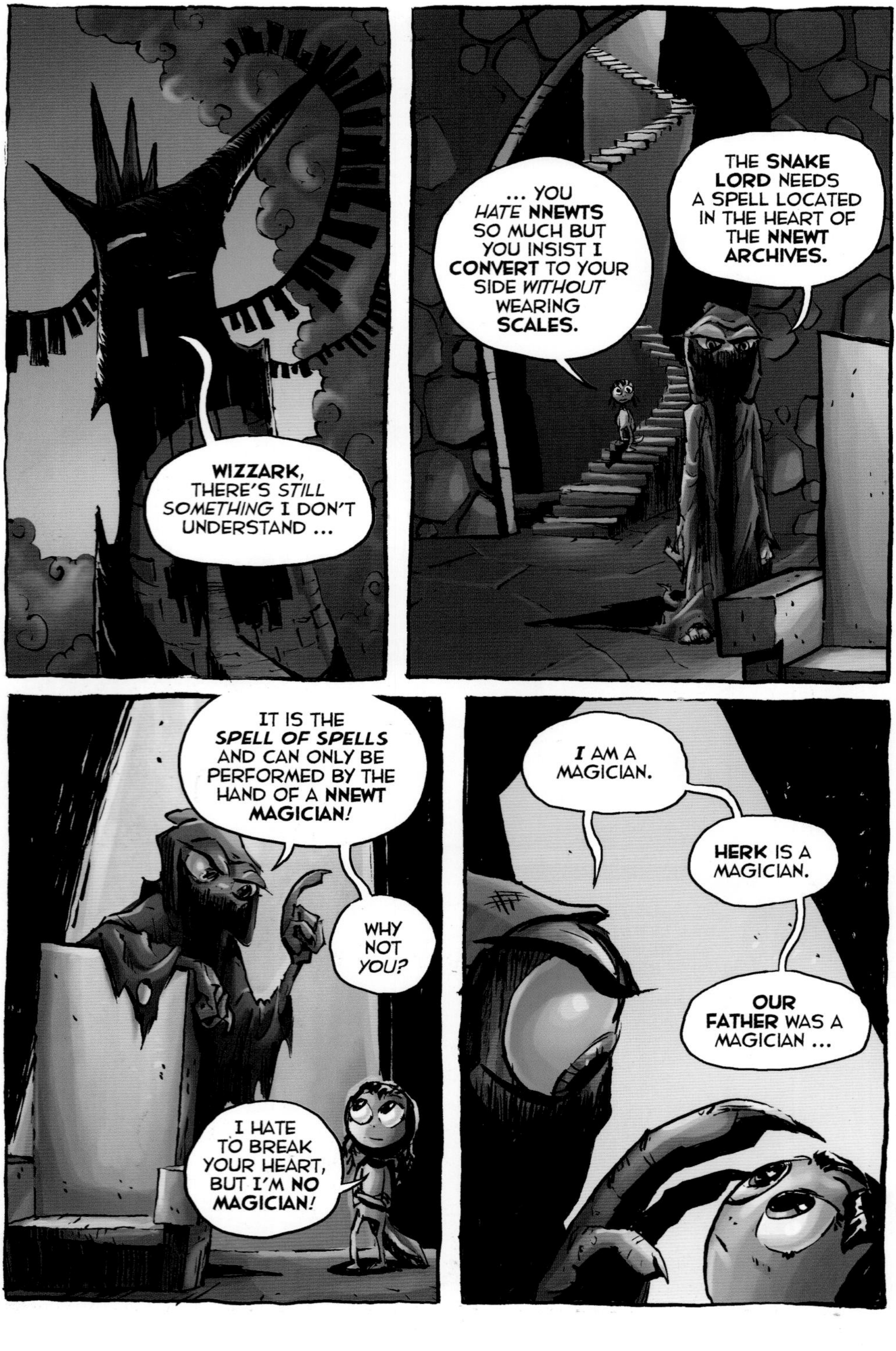
WIZZARK, THERE'S STILL SOMETHING I DON'T UNDERSTAND ...
... YOU HATE NNEWTS SO MUCH BUT YOU INSIST I CONVERT TO YOUR SIDE WITHOUT WEARING SCALES.
THE SNAKE LORD NEEDS A SPELL LOCATED IN THE HEART OF THE NNEWT ARCHIVES.
IT IS THE SPELL OF SPELLS AND CAN ONLY BE PERFORMED BY THE HAND OF A NNEWT MAGICIAN!
WHY NOT YOU?
I HATE TO BREAK YOUR HEART, BUT I'M NO MAGICIAN!
I AM A MAGICIAN.
HERK IS A MAGICIAN.
OUR FATHER WAS A MAGICIAN ...

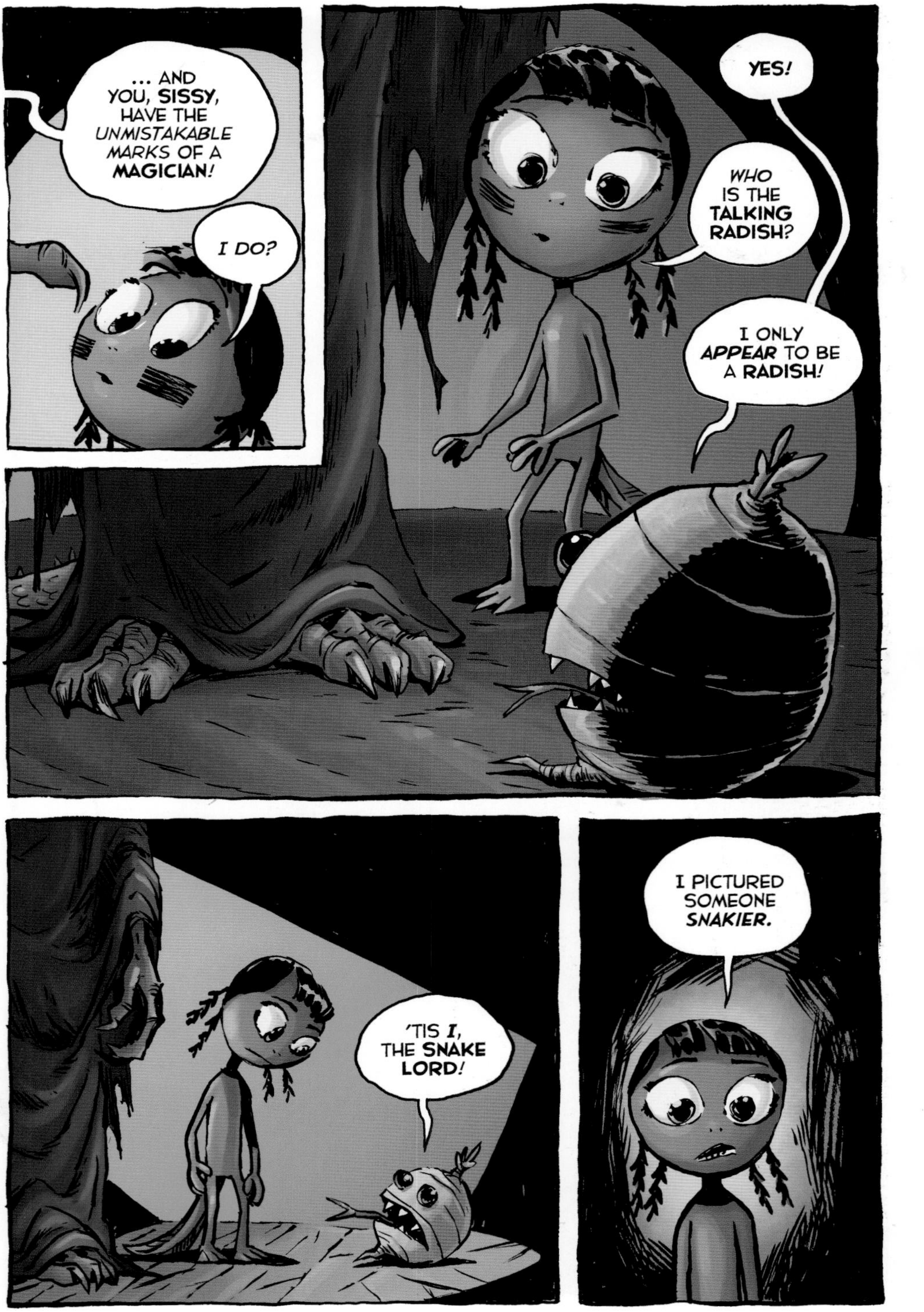
... AND YOU, SISSY, HAVE THE UNMISTAKABLE MARKS OF A MAGICIAN!
I DO?
YES!
WHO IS THE TALKING RADISH?
I ONLY APPEAR TO BE A RADISH!
'TIS I, THE SNAKE LORD!
I PICTURED SOMEONE SNAKIER.

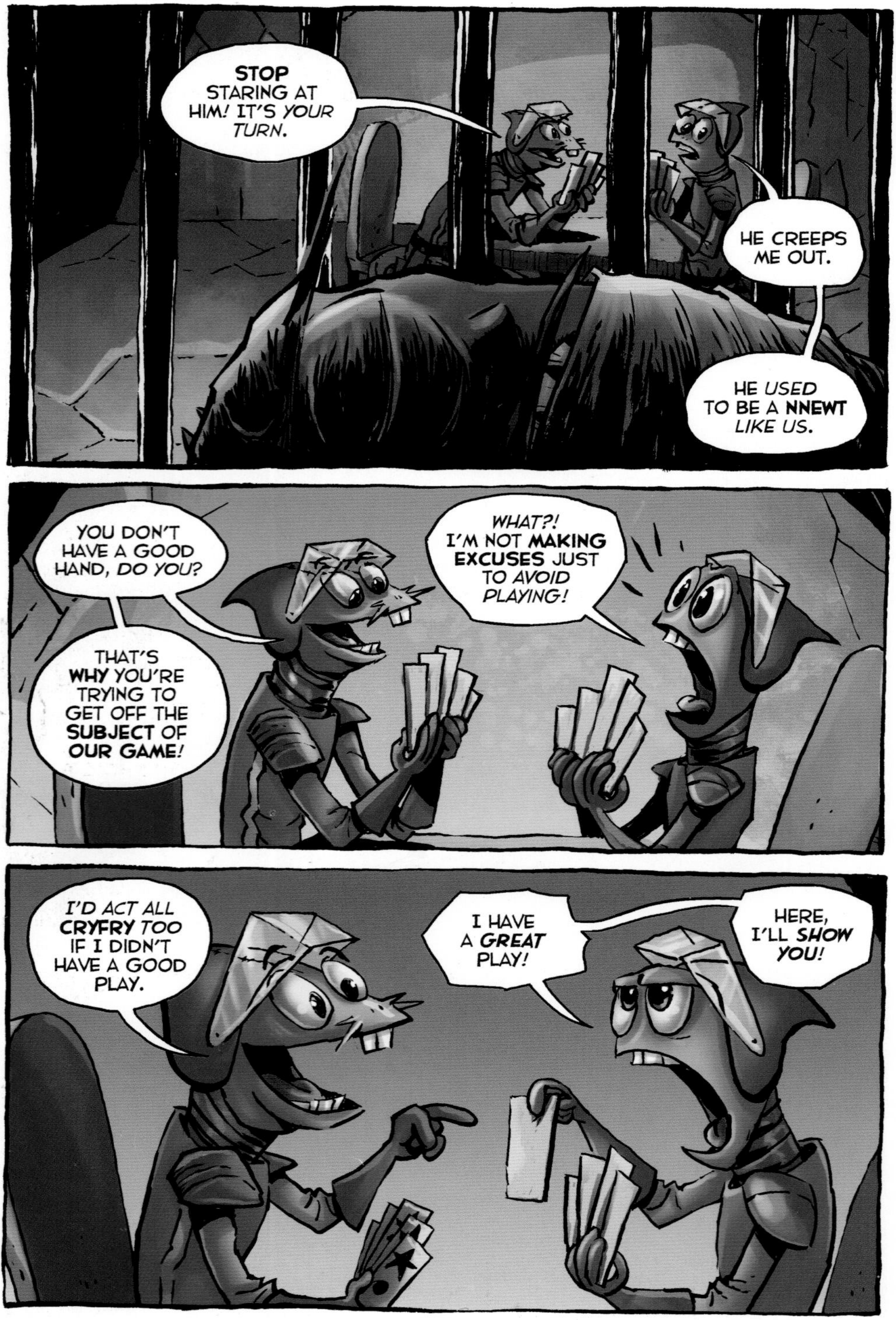

STOP STARING AT HIM! IT'S YOUR TURN.
HE CREEPS ME OUT.
HE USED TO BE A NNEWT LIKE US.
YOU DON'T HAVE A GOOD HAND, DO YOU?
THAT'S WHY YOU'RE TRYING TO GET OFF THE SUBJECT OF OUR GAME!
WHAT?! I'M NOT MAKING EXCUSES JUST TO AVOID PLAYING!
I'D ACT ALL CRYFRY TOO IF I DIDN'T HAVE A GOOD PLAY.
I HAVE A GREAT PLAY!
HERE, I'LL SHOW YOU!

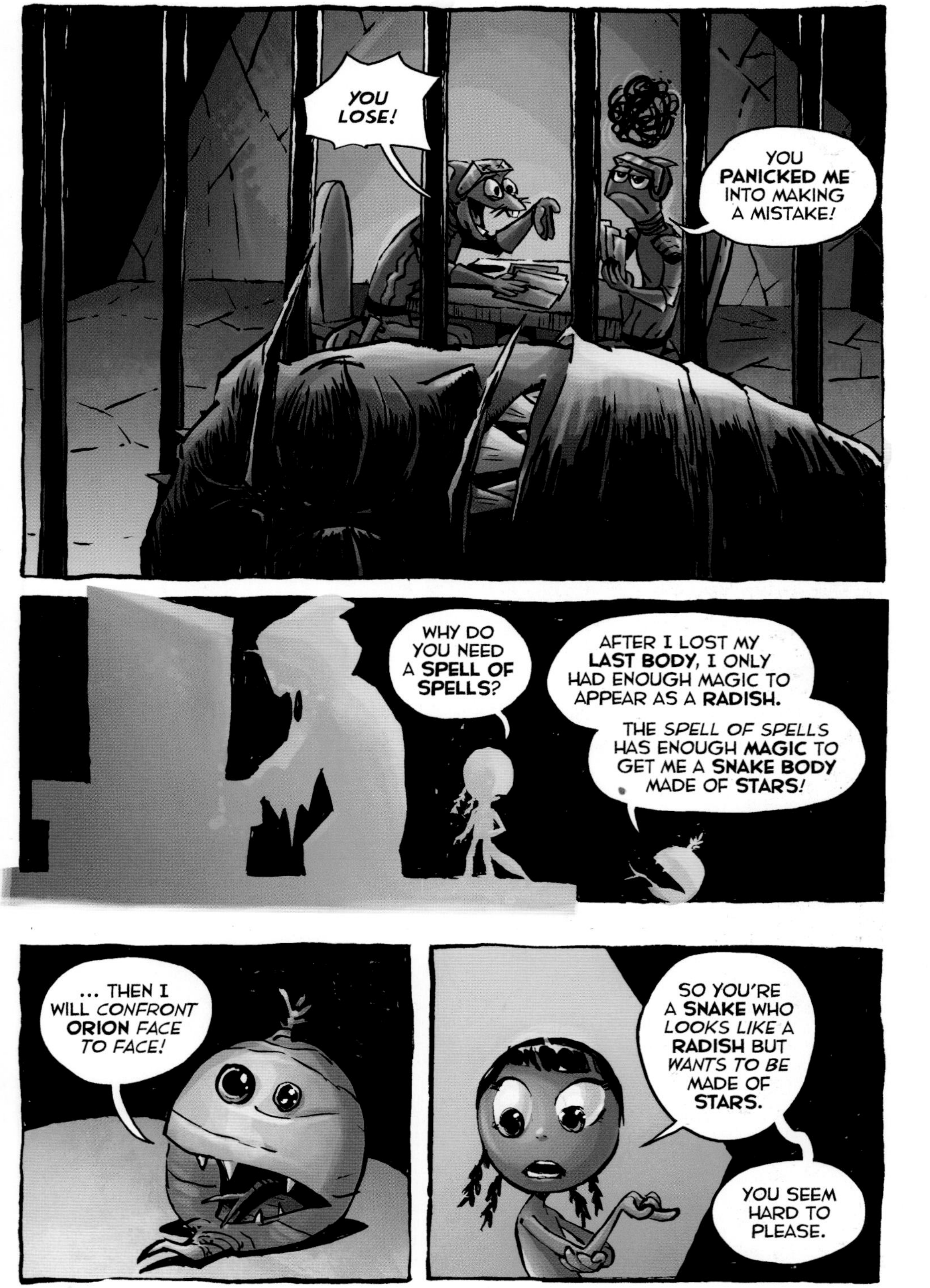
YOU LOSE!
YOU PANICKED ME INTO MAKING A MISTAKE!
WHY DO YOU NEED A SPELL OF SPELLS?
AFTER I LOST MY LAST BODY, I ONLY HAD ENOUGH MAGIC TO APPEAR AS A RADISH.
THE SPELL OF SPELLS HAS ENOUGH MAGIC TO GET ME A SNAKE BODY MADE OF STARS!
... THEN I WILL CONFRONT ORION FACE TO FACE!
SO YOU'RE A SNAKE WHO LOOKS LIKE A RADISH BUT WANTS TO BE MADE OF STARS.
YOU SEEM HARD TO PLEASE.

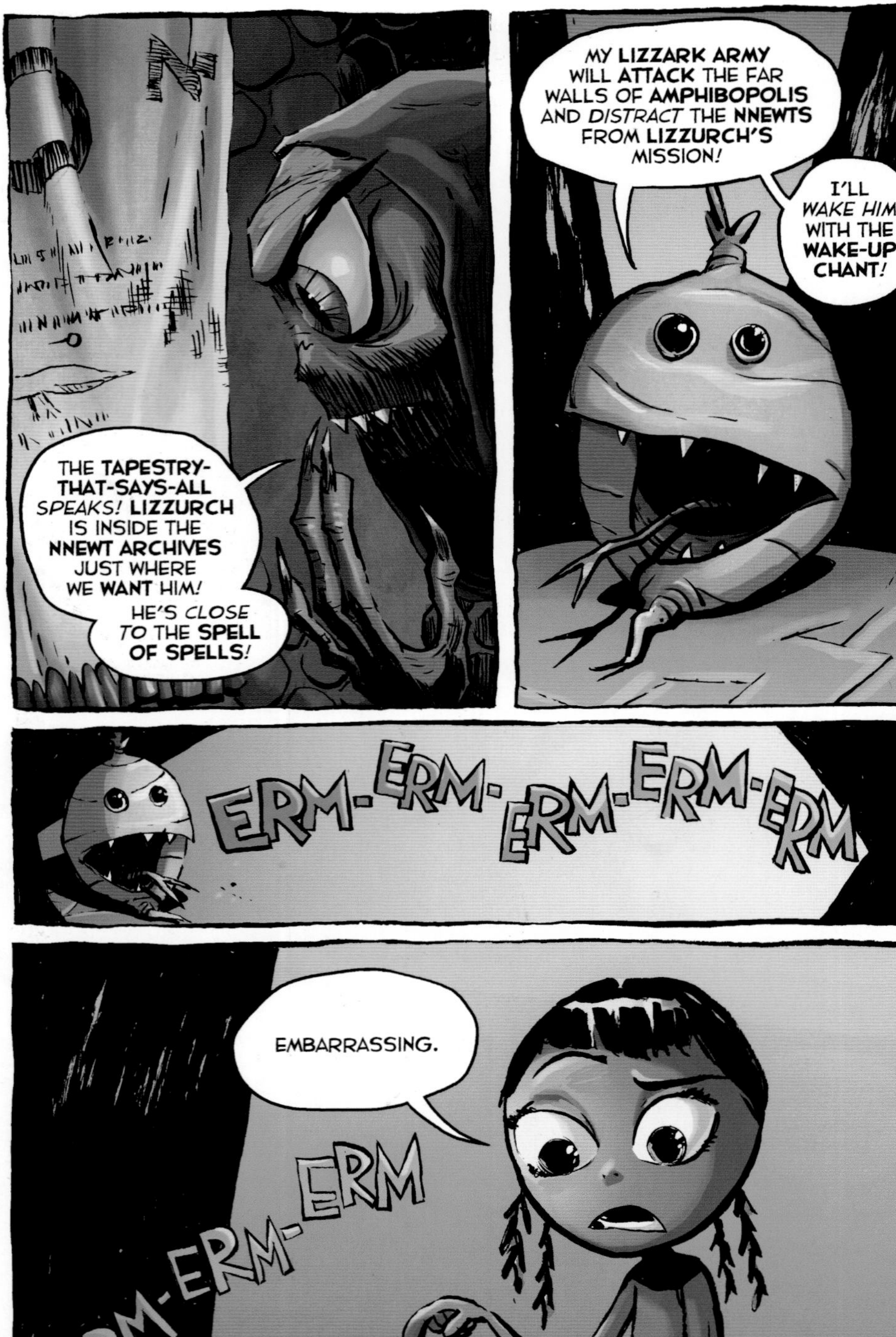
THE TAPESTRY-THAT-SAYS-ALL SPEAKS! LIZZURCH IS INSIDE THE NNEWT ARCHIVES JUST WHERE WE WANT HIM!
HE'S CLOSE TO THE SPELL OF SPELLS!
MY LIZZARK ARMY WILL ATTACK THE FAR WALLS OF AMPHIBOPOLIS AND DISTRACT THE NNEWTS FROM LIZZURCH'S MISSION!
I'LL WAKE HIM WITH THE WAKE-UP CHANT!
ERM-ERM-ERM-ERM-ERM
EMBARRASSING.
ERM-ERM-ERM

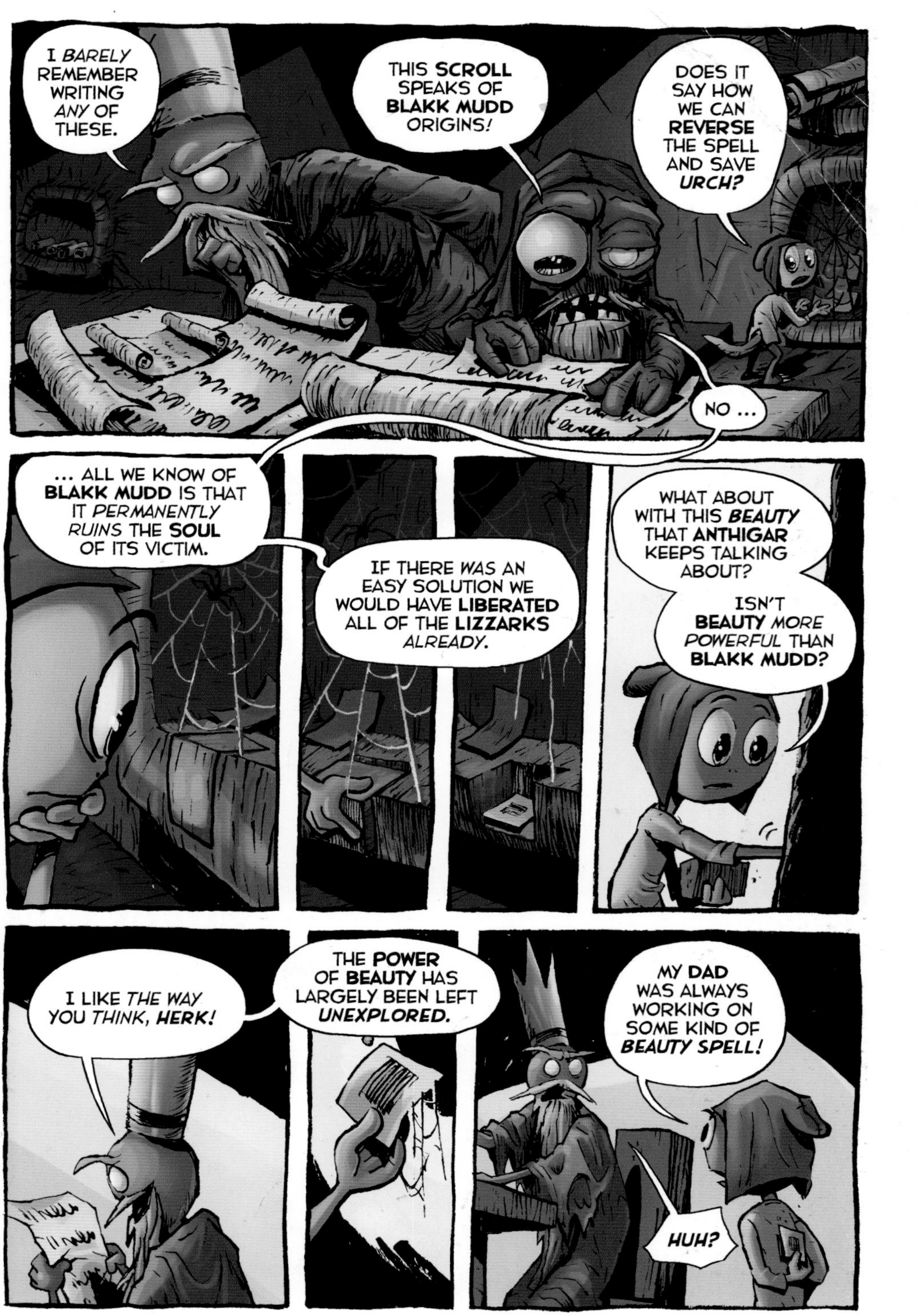
I BARELY REMEMBER WRITING ANY OF THESE.
THIS SCROLL SPEAKS OF BLAKK MUDD ORIGINS!
DOES IT SAY HOW WE CAN REVERSE THE SPELL AND SAVE URCH?
NO ...
... ALL WE KNOW OF BLAKK MUDD IS THAT IT PERMANENTLY RUINS THE SOUL OF ITS VICTIM.
IF THERE WAS AN EASY SOLUTION WE WOULD HAVE LIBERATED ALL OF THE LIZZARKS ALREADY.
WHAT ABOUT WITH THIS BEAUTY THAT ANTHIGAR KEEPS TALKING ABOUT?
ISN'T BEAUTY MORE POWERFUL THAN BLAKK MUDD?
I LIKE THE WAY YOU THINK, HERK!
THE POWER OF BEAUTY HAS LARGELY BEEN LEFT UNEXPLORED.
MY DAD WAS ALWAYS WORKING ON SOME KIND OF BEAUTY SPELL!
HUH?

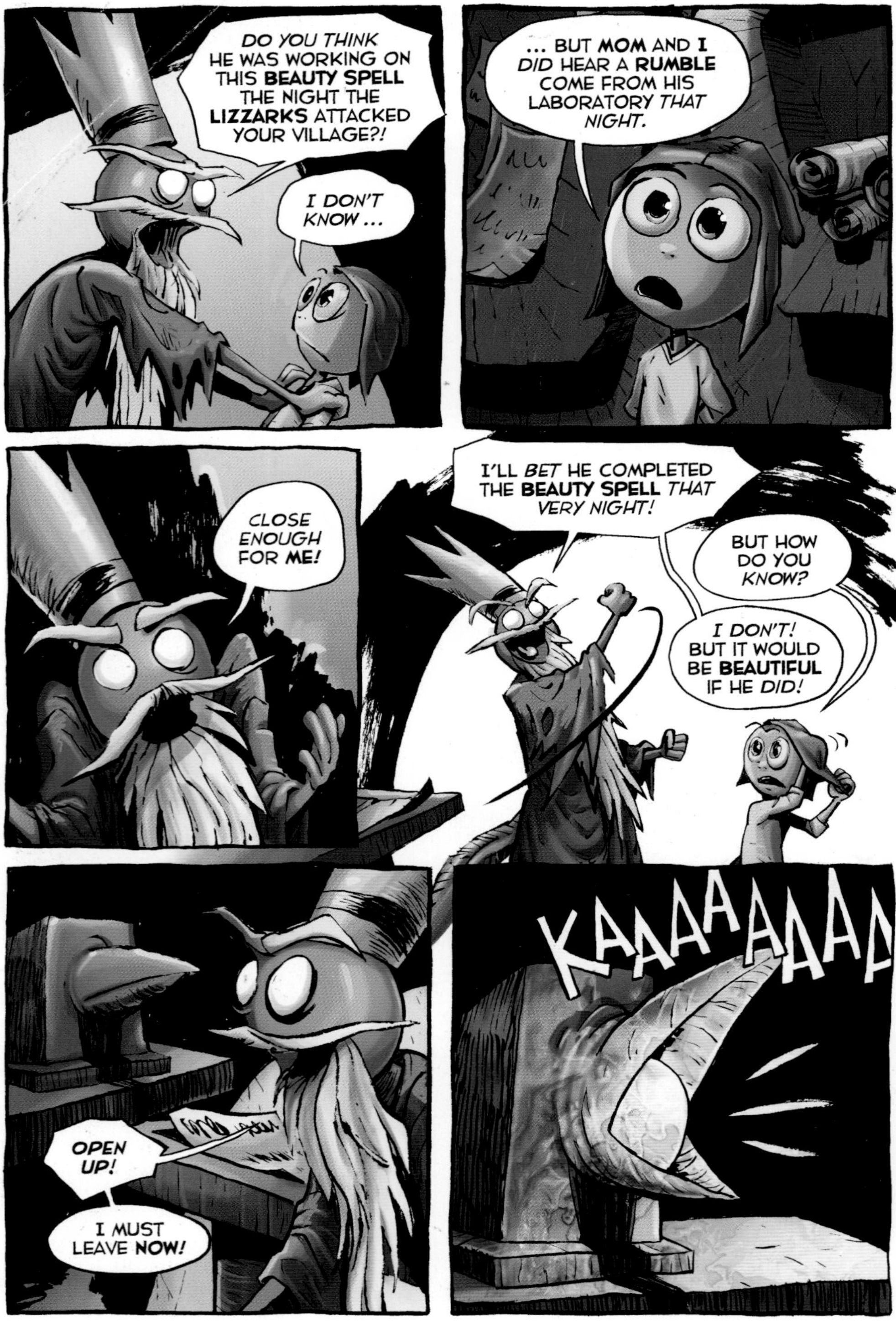
DO YOU THINK HE WAS WORKING ON THIS BEAUTY SPELL THE NIGHT THE LIZZARKS ATTACKED YOUR VILLAGE?!
I DON'T KNOW ...
... BUT MOM AND I DID HEAR A RUMBLE COME FROM HIS LABORATORY THAT NIGHT.
CLOSE ENOUGH FOR ME!
I'LL BET HE COMPLETED THE BEAUTY SPELL THAT VERY NIGHT!
BUT HOW DO YOU KNOW?
I DON'T! BUT IT WOULD BE BEAUTIFUL IF HE DID!
OPEN UP!
I MUST LEAVE NOW!
KAAAAAAAA

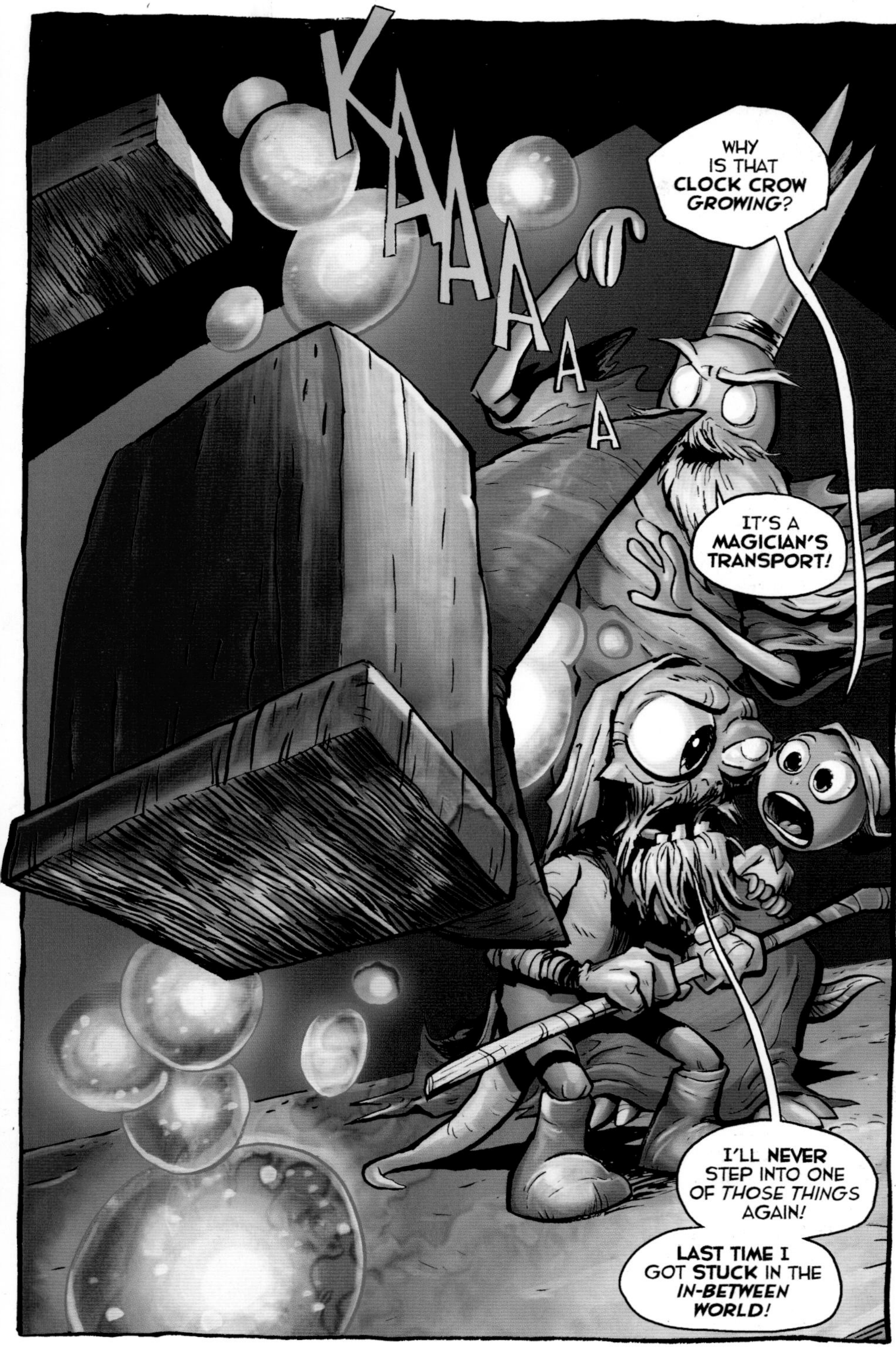
KAAAAAAA
WHY IS THAT **CLOCK CROW** *GROWING?*
IT'S A **MAGICIAN'S TRANSPORT!**
I'LL **NEVER** STEP INTO ONE OF *THOSE THINGS* AGAIN!
LAST TIME I GOT **STUCK** IN THE ***IN-BETWEEN* WORLD!**

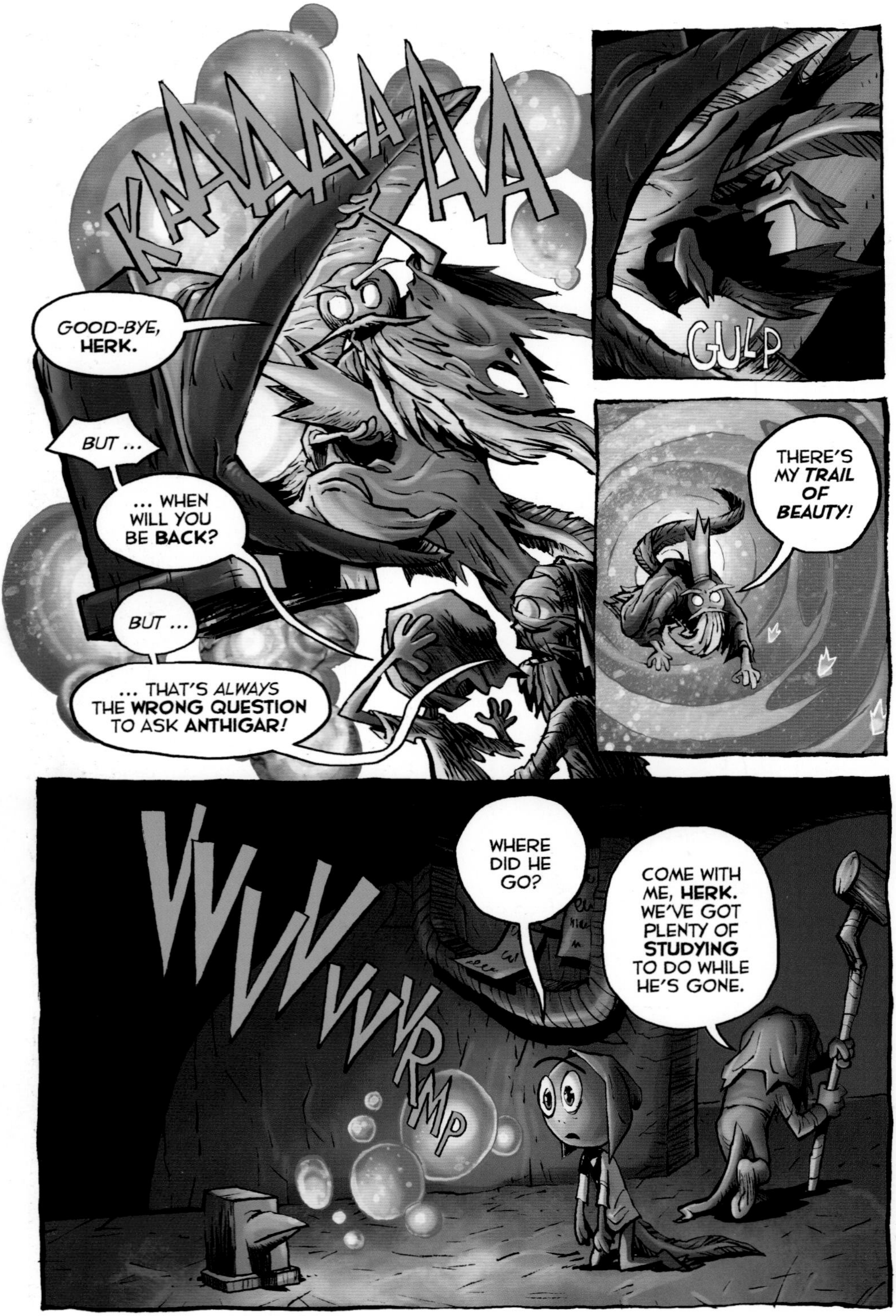
KAAAAAAAA
GOOD-BYE, HERK.
BUT ...
... WHEN WILL YOU BE BACK?
BUT ...
... THAT'S ALWAYS THE WRONG QUESTION TO ASK ANTHIGAR!
GULP
THERE'S MY TRAIL OF BEAUTY!
VVVVVVVVRMP
WHERE DID HE GO?
COME WITH ME, HERK. WE'VE GOT PLENTY OF STUDYING TO DO WHILE HE'S GONE.

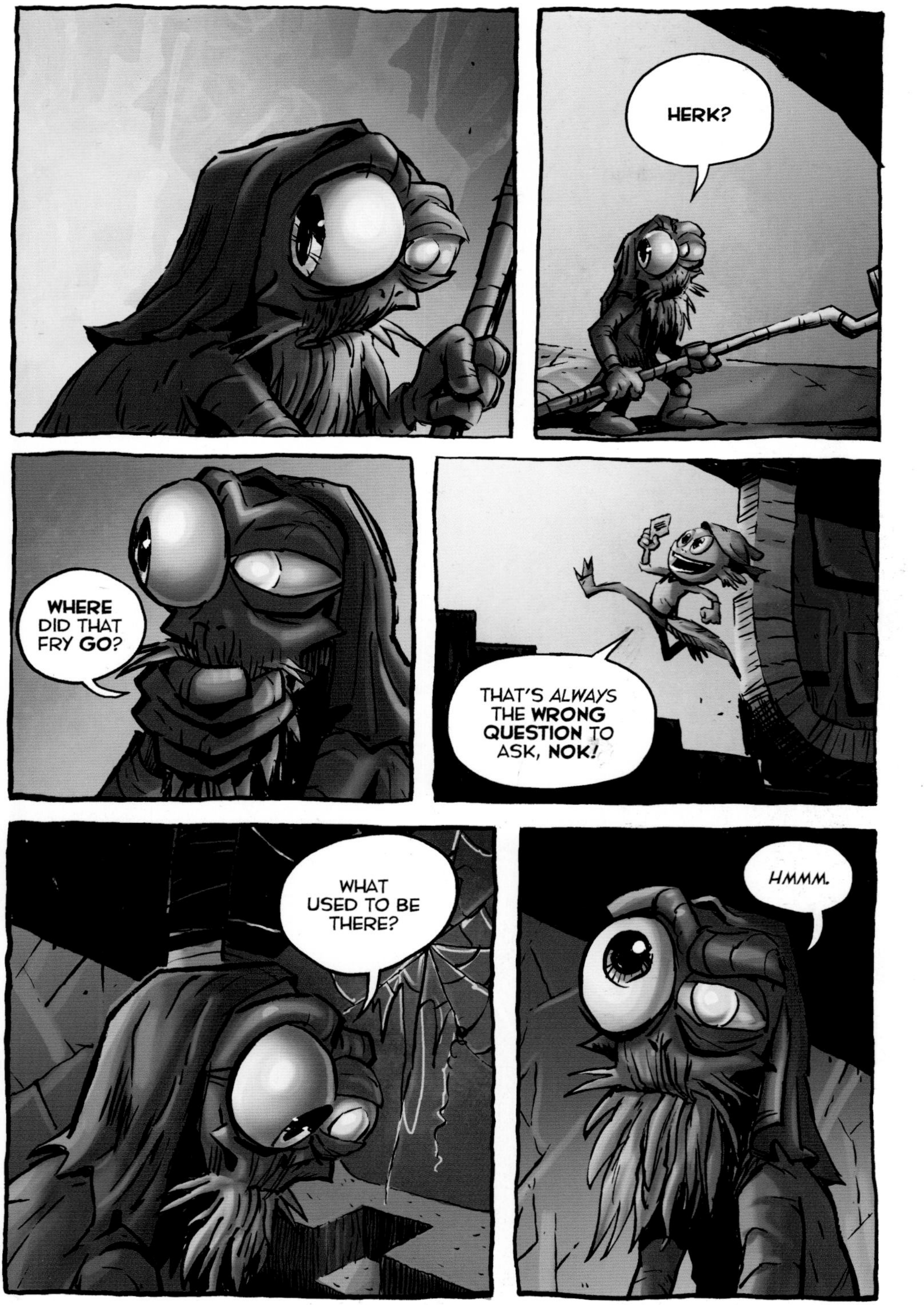
HERK?
WHERE DID THAT FRY GO?
THAT'S *ALWAYS* THE **WRONG QUESTION** TO ASK, **NOK!**
WHAT USED TO BE THERE?
HMMM.

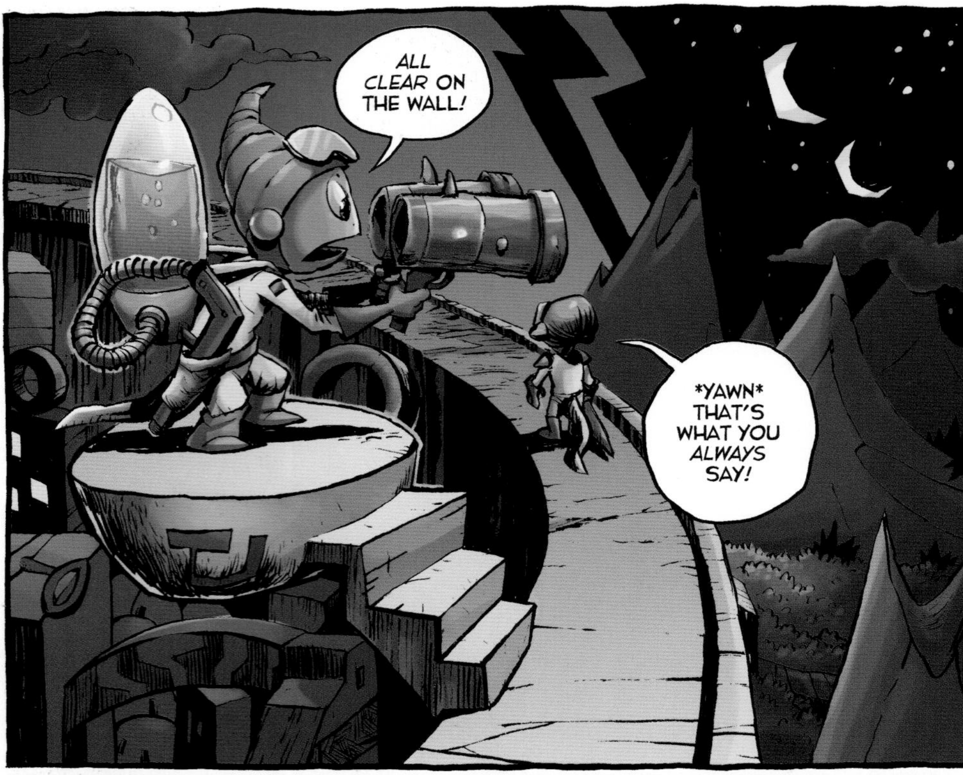
ALL CLEAR ON THE WALL!
YAWN THAT'S WHAT YOU ALWAYS SAY!

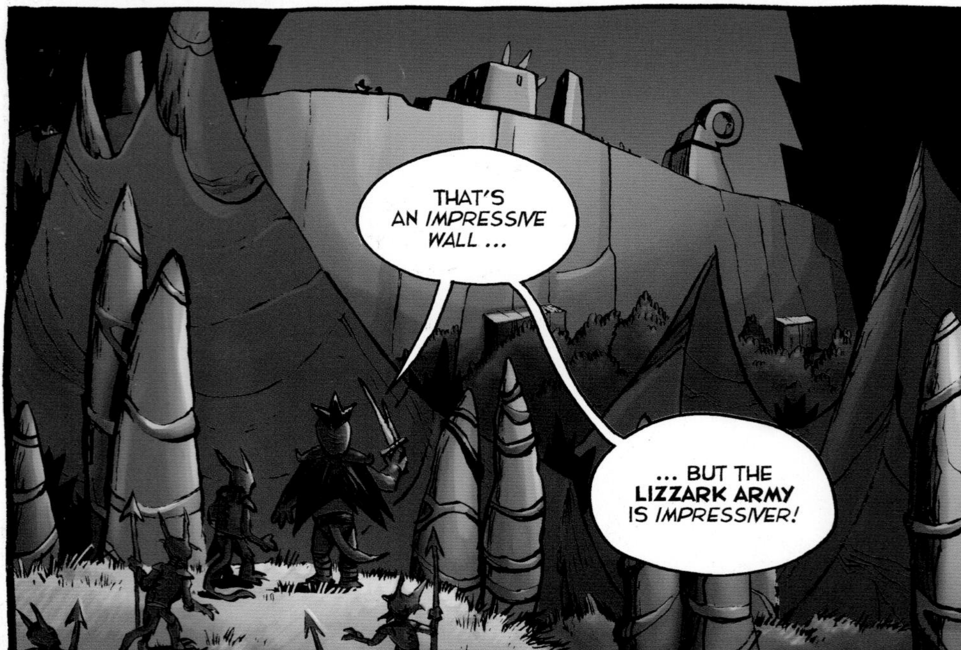
THAT'S AN IMPRESSIVE WALL ...
... BUT THE LIZZARK ARMY IS IMPRESSIVER!

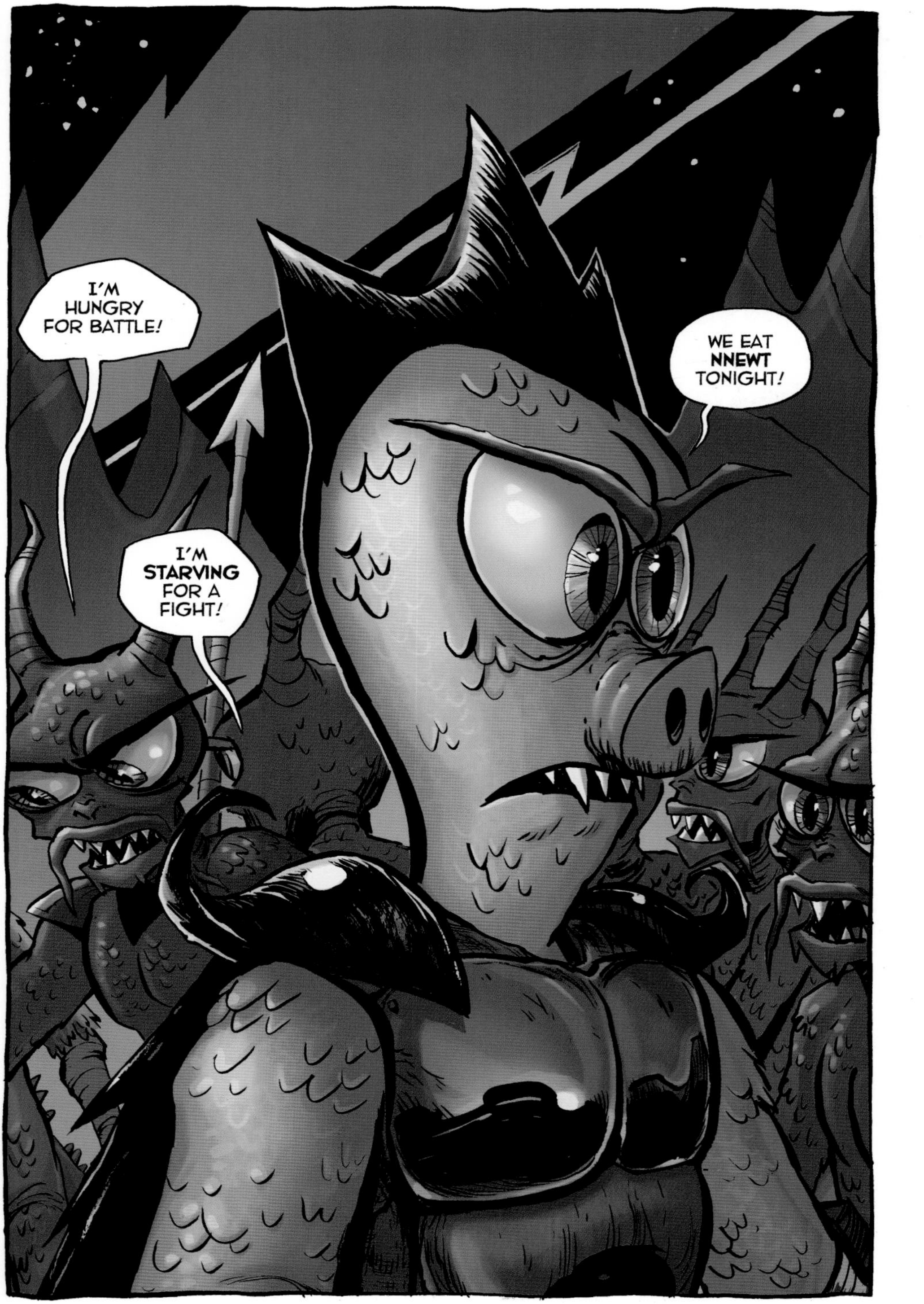
I'M HUNGRY FOR BATTLE!
WE EAT **NNEWT** TONIGHT!
I'M **STARVING** FOR A FIGHT!

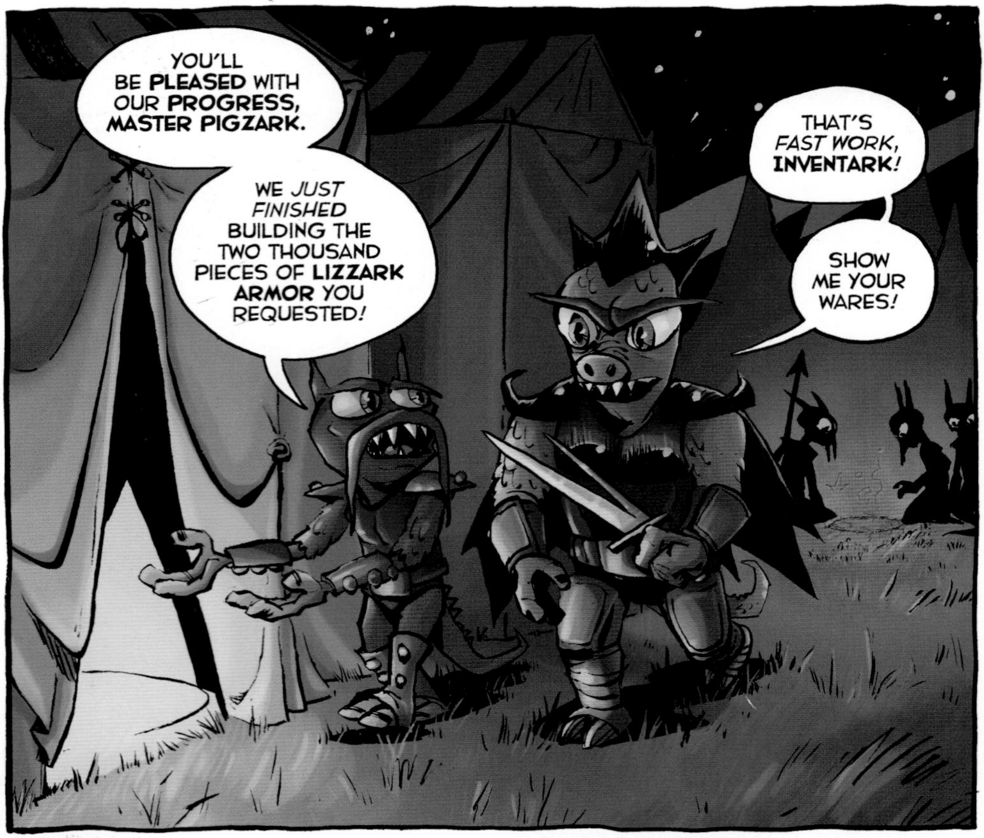
YOU'LL BE **PLEASED** WITH OUR **PROGRESS, MASTER PIGZARK.**
WE *JUST FINISHED* BUILDING THE TWO THOUSAND PIECES OF **LIZZARK ARMOR** YOU REQUESTED!
THAT'S *FAST WORK,* **INVENTARK!**
SHOW ME YOUR WARES!

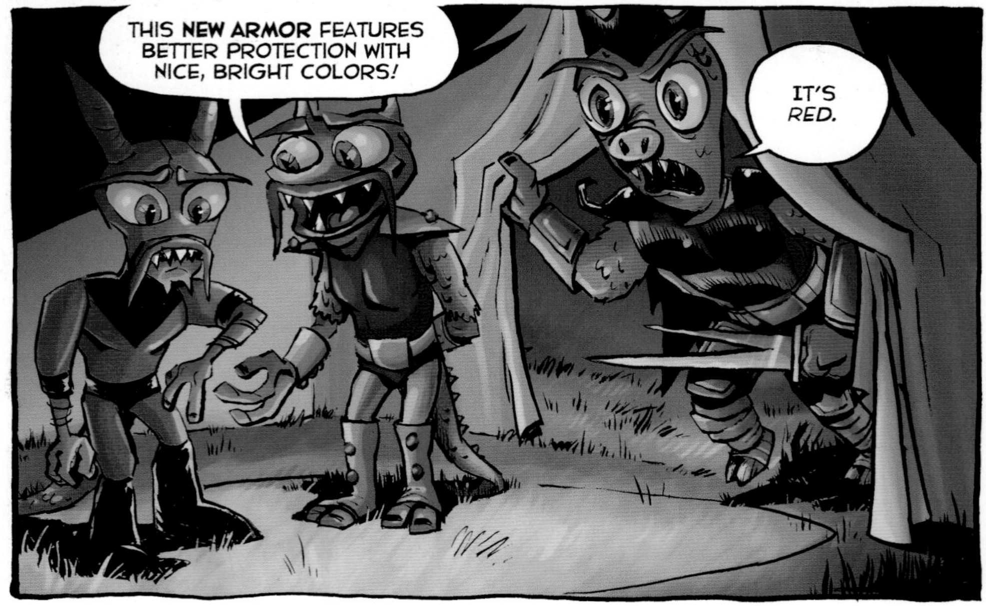
THIS **NEW ARMOR** FEATURES BETTER PROTECTION WITH NICE, BRIGHT COLORS!
IT'S *RED.*

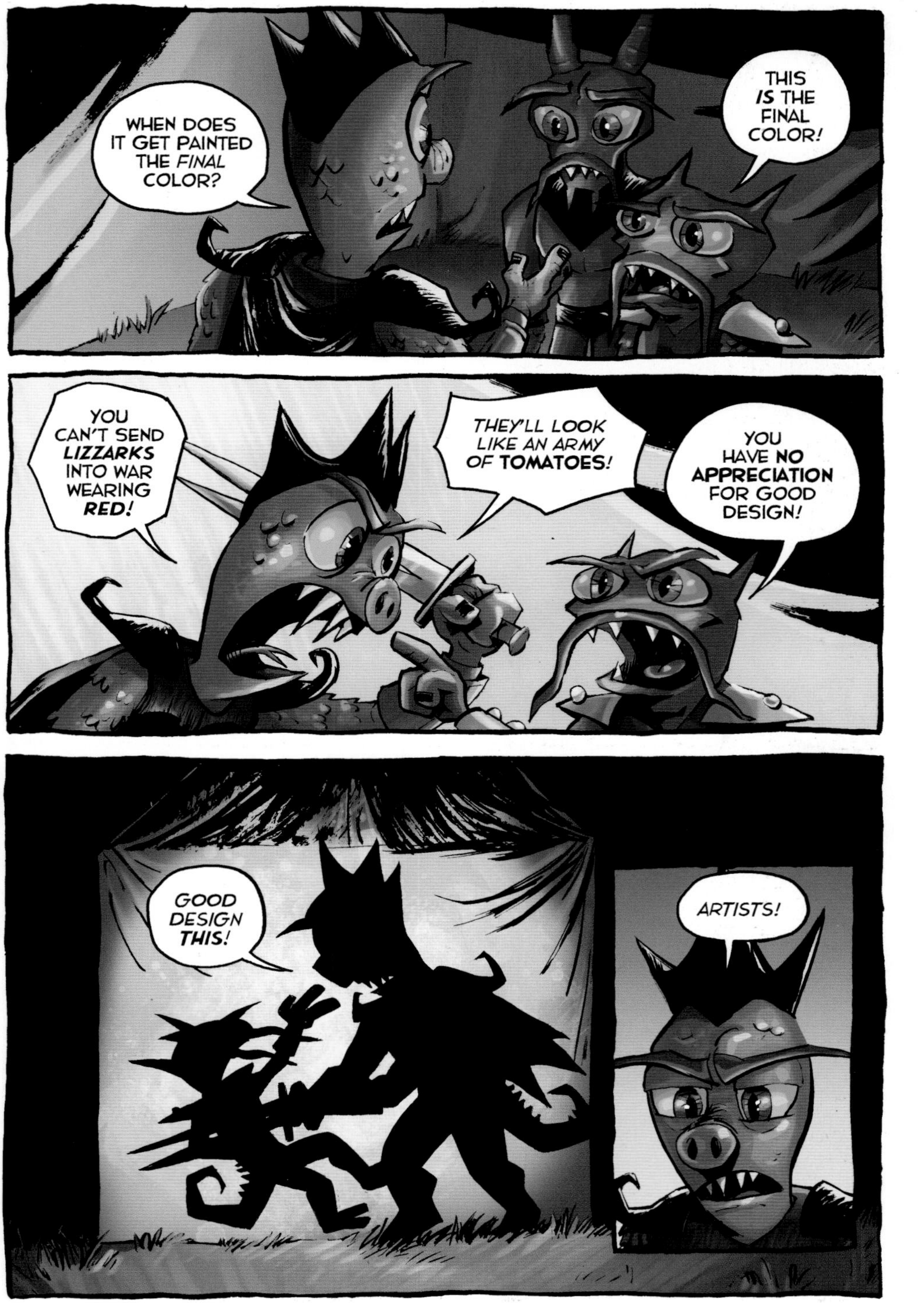
WHEN DOES IT GET PAINTED THE *FINAL* COLOR?
THIS *IS* THE FINAL COLOR!
YOU CAN'T SEND **LIZZARKS** INTO WAR WEARING ***RED!***
THEY'LL LOOK LIKE AN ARMY OF ***TOMATOES!***
YOU HAVE **NO APPRECIATION** FOR GOOD DESIGN!
GOOD DESIGN ***THIS!***
ARTISTS!

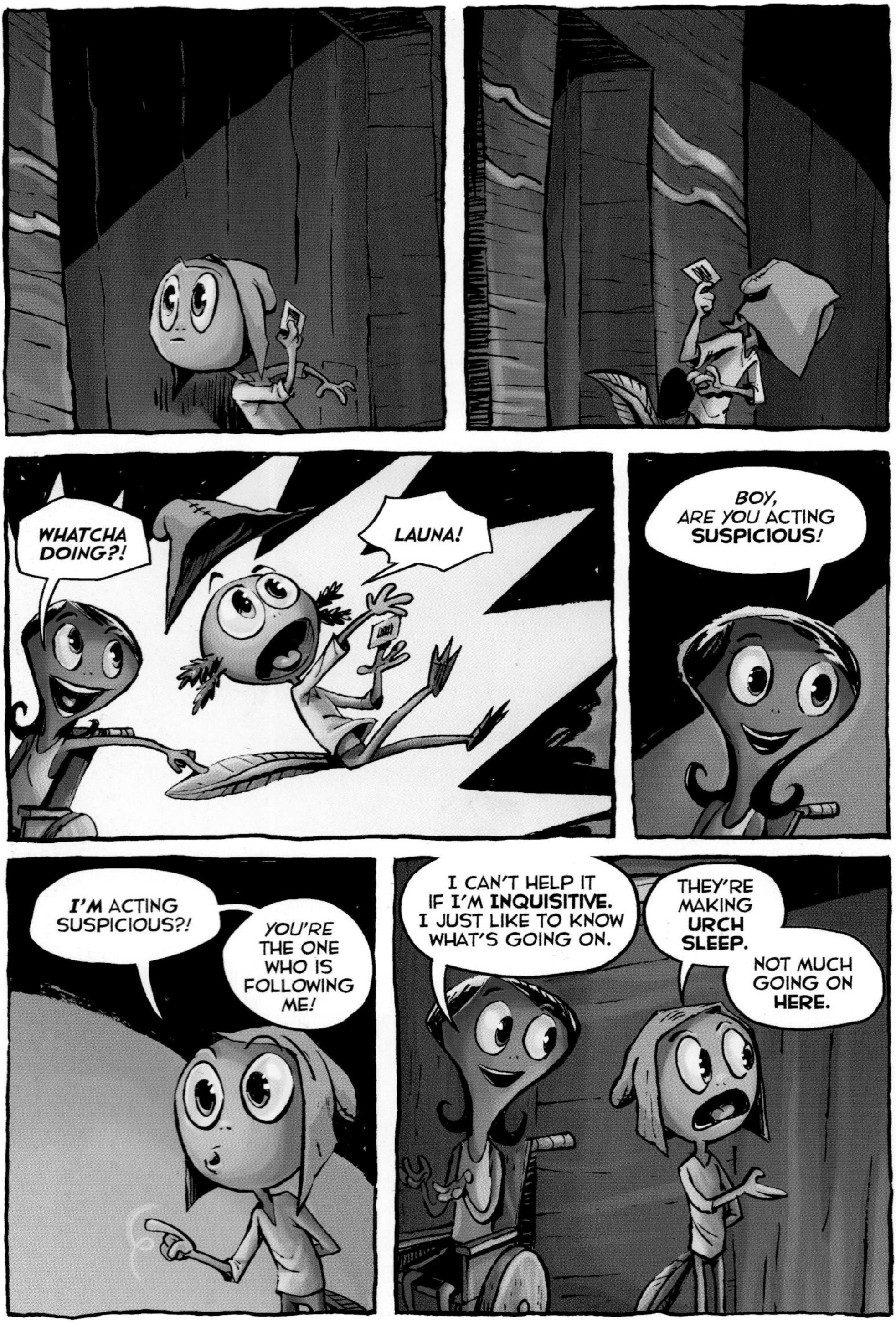
WHATCHA DOING?!
LAUNA!
BOY, ARE YOU ACTING SUSPICIOUS!
I'M ACTING SUSPICIOUS?!
YOU'RE THE ONE WHO IS FOLLOWING ME!
I CAN'T HELP IT IF I'M INQUISITIVE. I JUST LIKE TO KNOW WHAT'S GOING ON.
THEY'RE MAKING URCH SLEEP.
NOT MUCH GOING ON HERE.

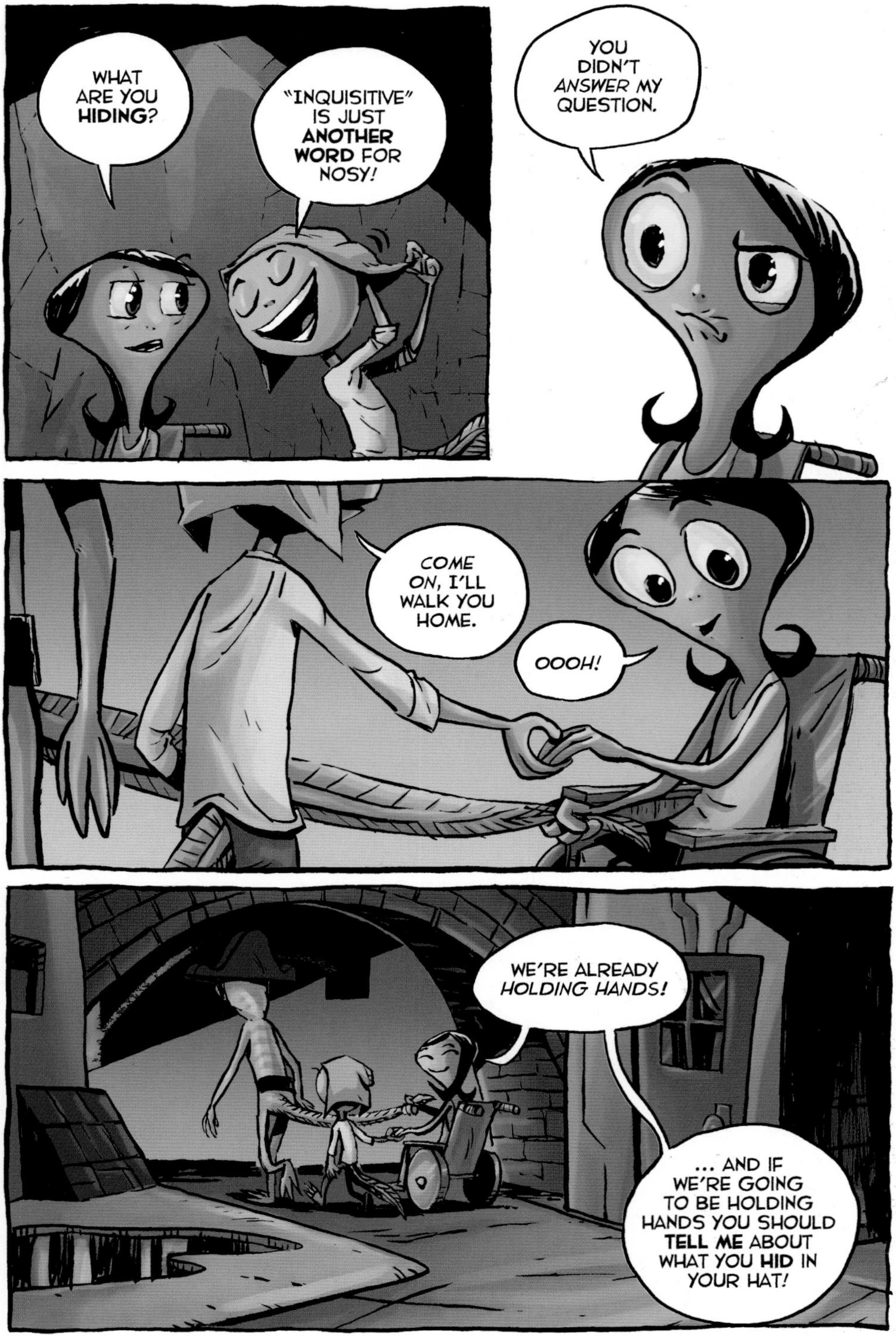
WHAT ARE YOU **HIDING**?
"INQUISITIVE" IS JUST **ANOTHER WORD** FOR NOSY!
YOU DIDN'T *ANSWER* MY QUESTION.
COME ON, I'LL WALK YOU HOME.
OOOH!
WE'RE ALREADY *HOLDING HANDS!*
... AND IF WE'RE GOING TO BE HOLDING HANDS YOU SHOULD **TELL ME** ABOUT WHAT YOU **HID** IN YOUR HAT!

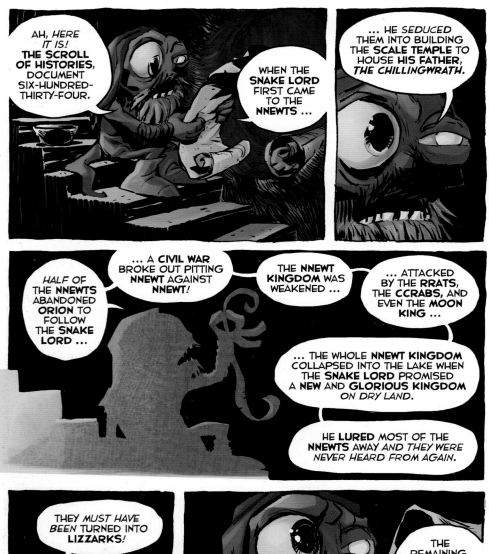

AH, *HERE IT IS!* **THE SCROLL OF HISTORIES,** DOCUMENT SIX-HUNDRED-THIRTY-FOUR.

WHEN THE **SNAKE LORD** FIRST CAME TO THE **NNEWTS** ...

... HE *SEDUCED* THEM INTO BUILDING THE **SCALE TEMPLE** TO HOUSE **HIS FATHER,** *THE CHILLINGWRATH.*

HALF OF THE **NNEWTS** ABANDONED **ORION** TO FOLLOW THE **SNAKE LORD** ...

... A **CIVIL WAR** BROKE OUT PITTING **NNEWT** AGAINST **NNEWT!**

THE **NNEWT KINGDOM** WAS WEAKENED ...

... ATTACKED BY THE **RRATS,** THE **CCRABS,** AND EVEN THE **MOON KING** ...

... THE WHOLE **NNEWT KINGDOM** COLLAPSED INTO THE LAKE WHEN THE **SNAKE LORD** PROMISED A **NEW** AND **GLORIOUS KINGDOM** *ON DRY LAND.*

HE **LURED** MOST OF THE **NNEWTS** AWAY *AND THEY WERE NEVER HEARD FROM AGAIN.*

THEY *MUST HAVE BEEN* TURNED INTO **LIZZARKS!**

THE REMAINING **NNEWTS** WERE FORBIDDEN FROM DELVING INTO MAGIC *EVER AGAIN.*

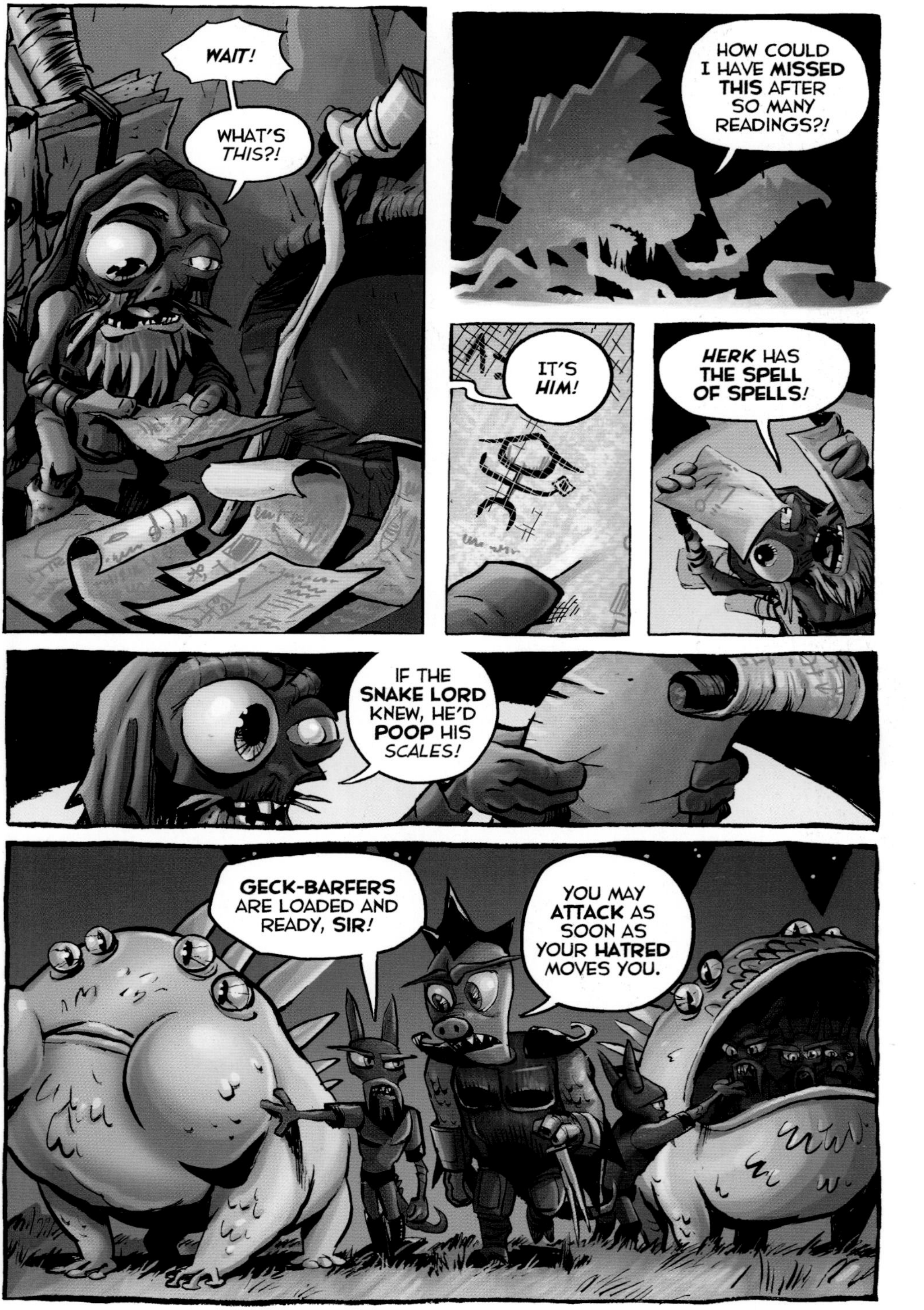
WAIT!
WHAT'S THIS?!
HOW COULD I HAVE MISSED THIS AFTER SO MANY READINGS?!
IT'S HIM!
HERK HAS THE SPELL OF SPELLS!
IF THE SNAKE LORD KNEW, HE'D POOP HIS SCALES!
GECK-BARFERS ARE LOADED AND READY, SIR!
YOU MAY ATTACK AS SOON AS YOUR HATRED MOVES YOU.

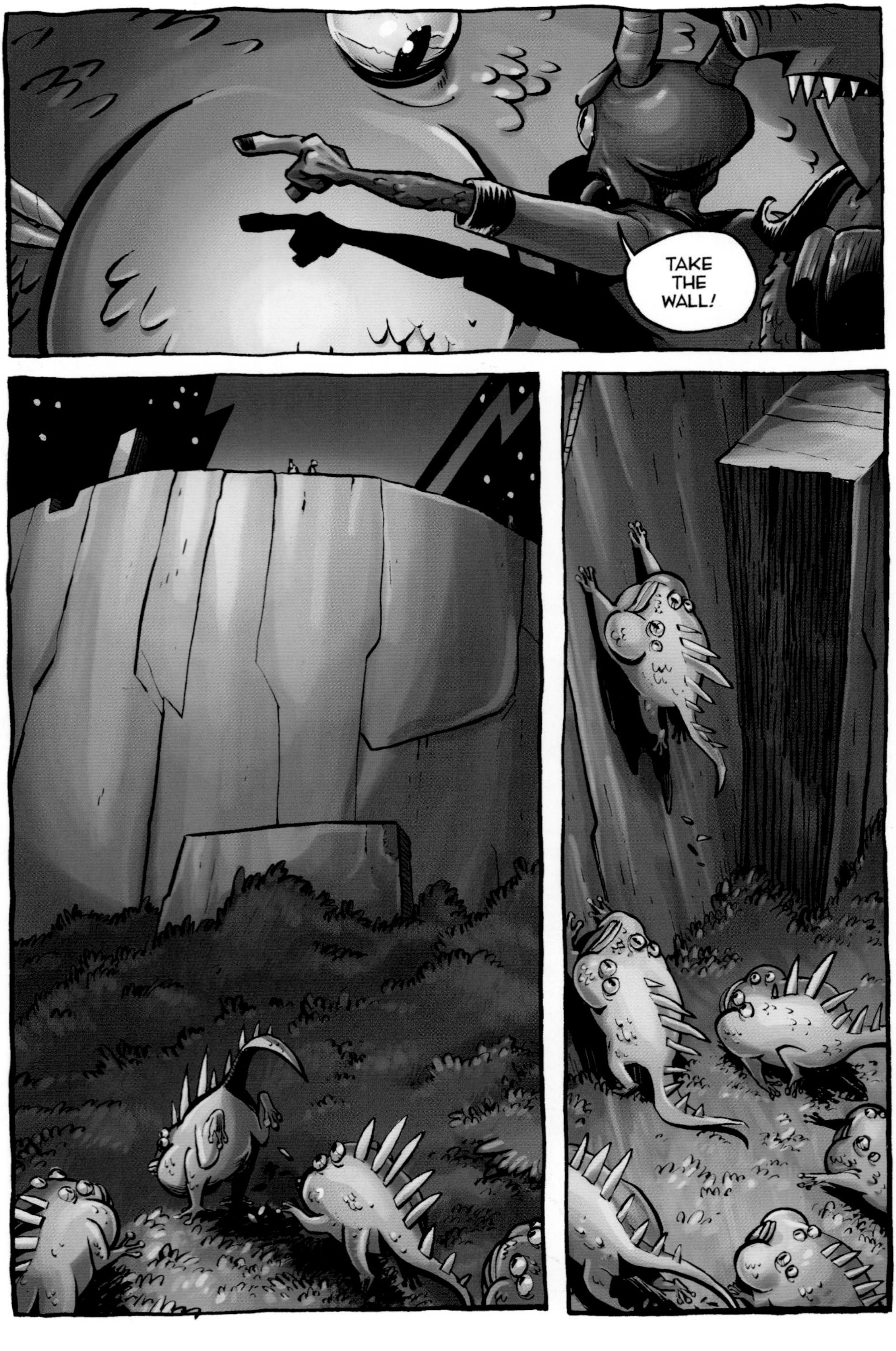
TAKE THE WALL!

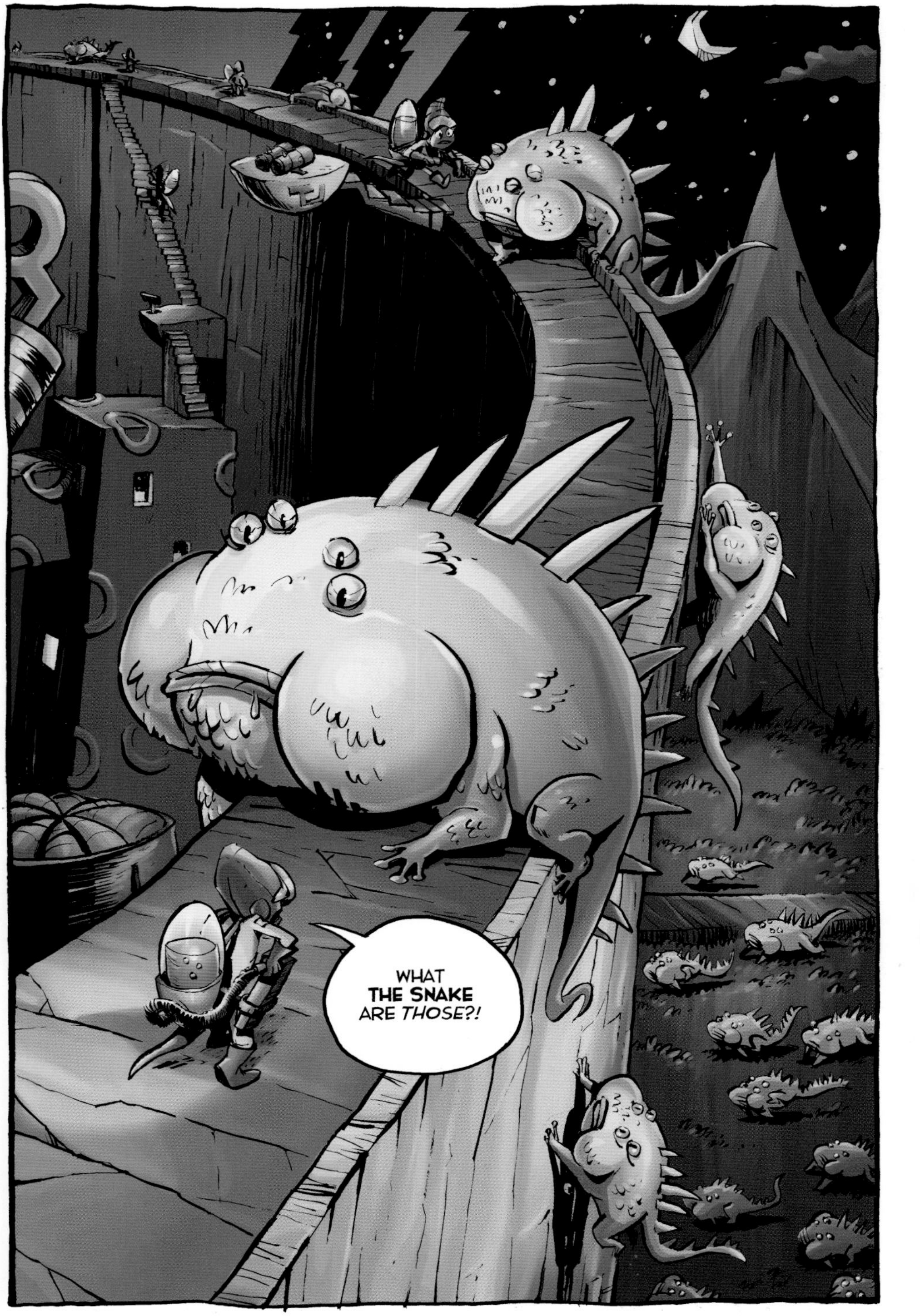
WHAT **THE SNAKE** ARE *THOSE?!*

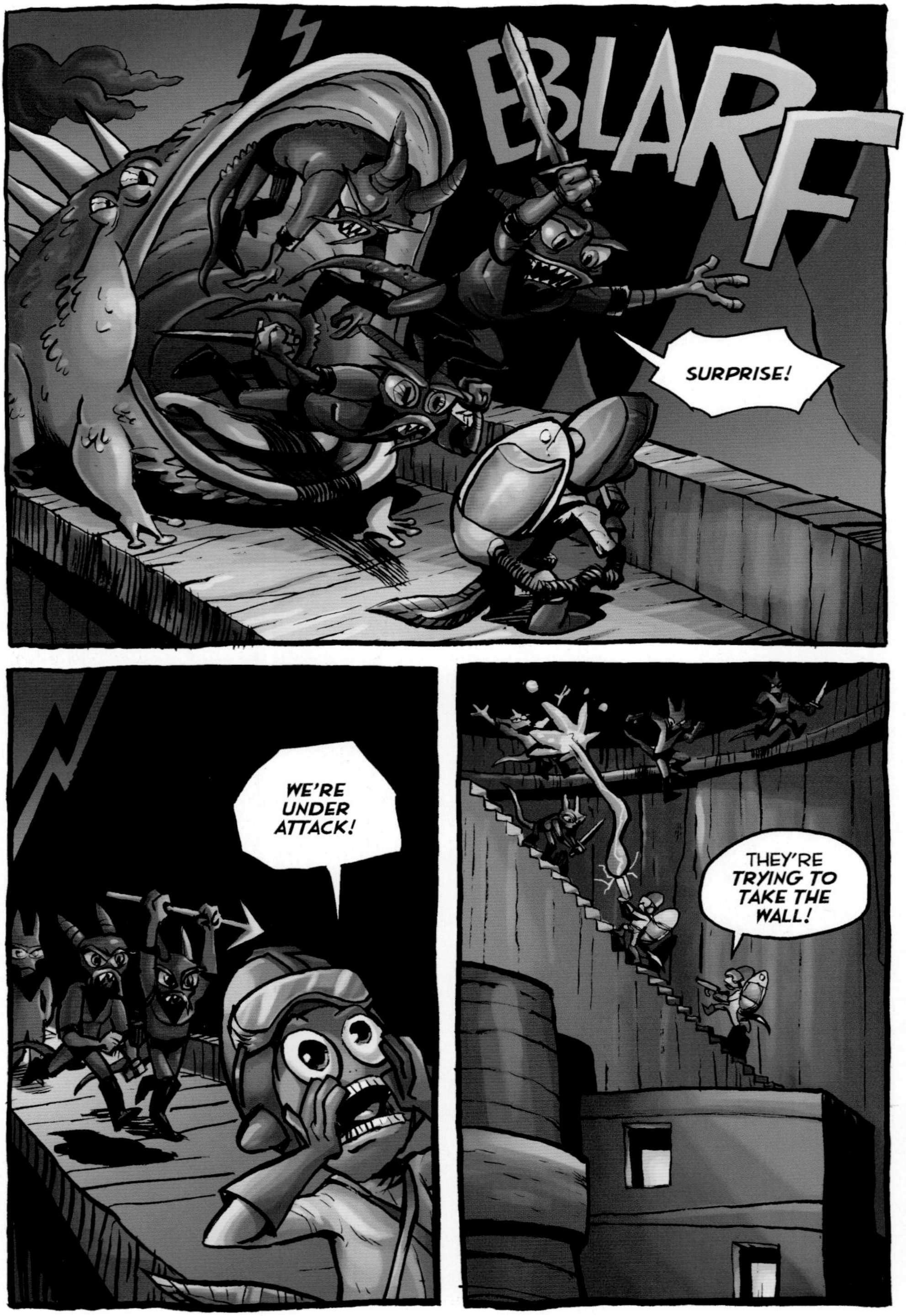

EBLARF
SURPRISE!
WE'RE UNDER ATTACK!
THEY'RE TRYING TO TAKE THE WALL!

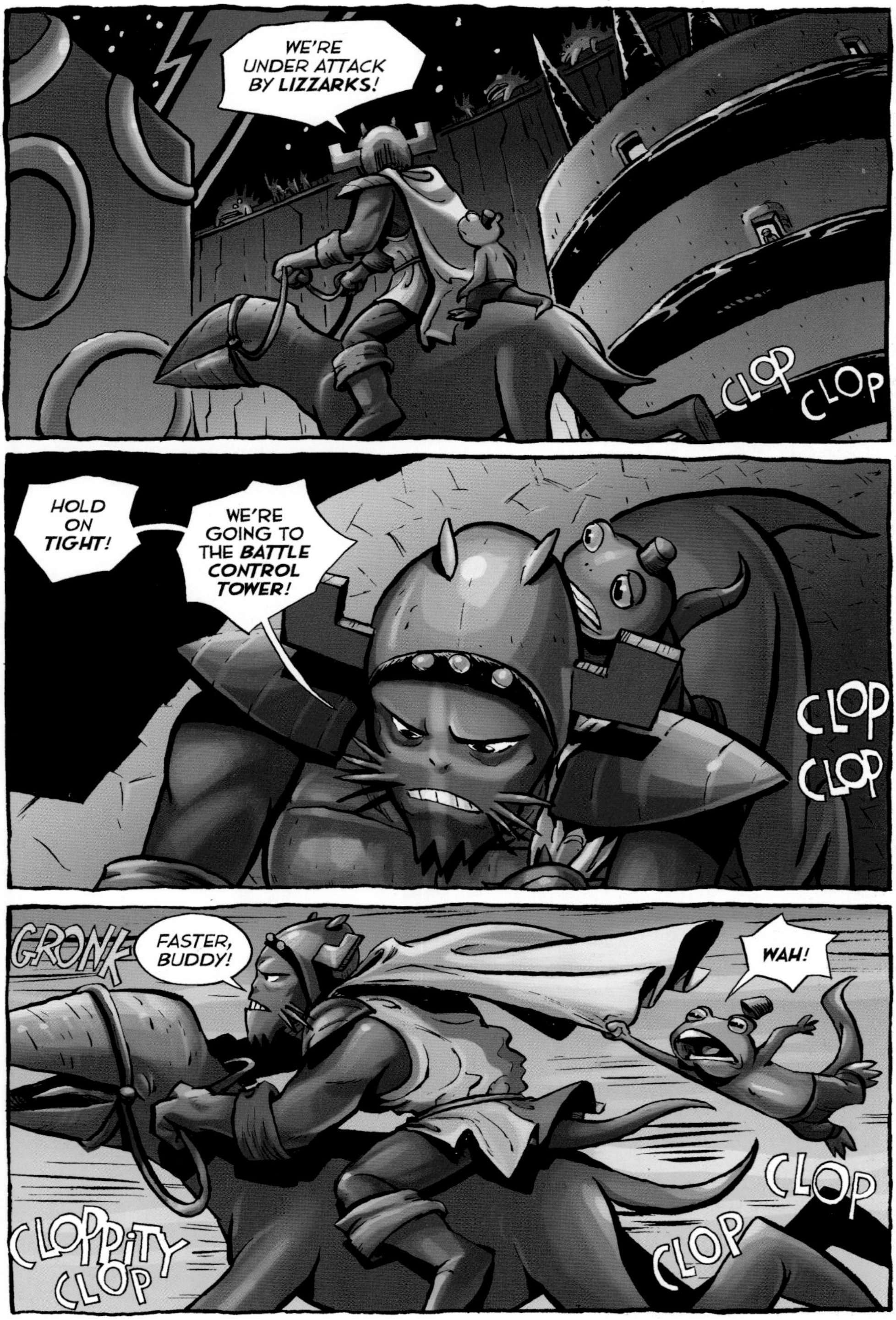
WE'RE UNDER ATTACK BY **LIZZARKS!**
CLOP CLOP
HOLD ON **TIGHT!**
WE'RE GOING TO THE **BATTLE CONTROL TOWER!**
CLOP CLOP
GRONK
FASTER, BUDDY!
WAH!
CLOPPITY CLOP
CLOP CLOP

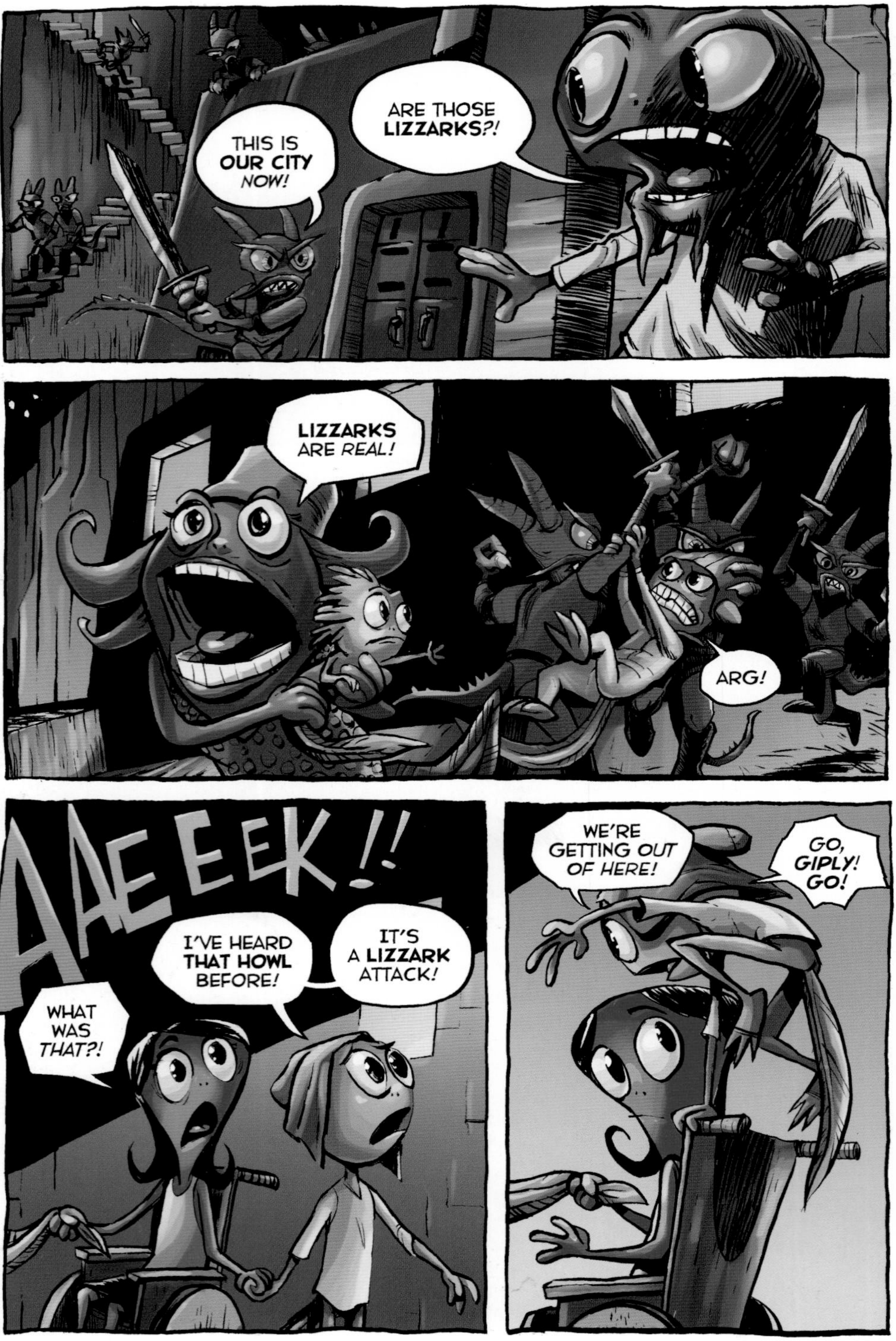
ARE THOSE LIZZARKS?!
THIS IS OUR CITY NOW!
LIZZARKS ARE REAL!
ARG!
AAEEEK!!
WHAT WAS THAT?!
I'VE HEARD THAT HOWL BEFORE!
IT'S A LIZZARK ATTACK!
WE'RE GETTING OUT OF HERE!
GO, GIPLY! GO!

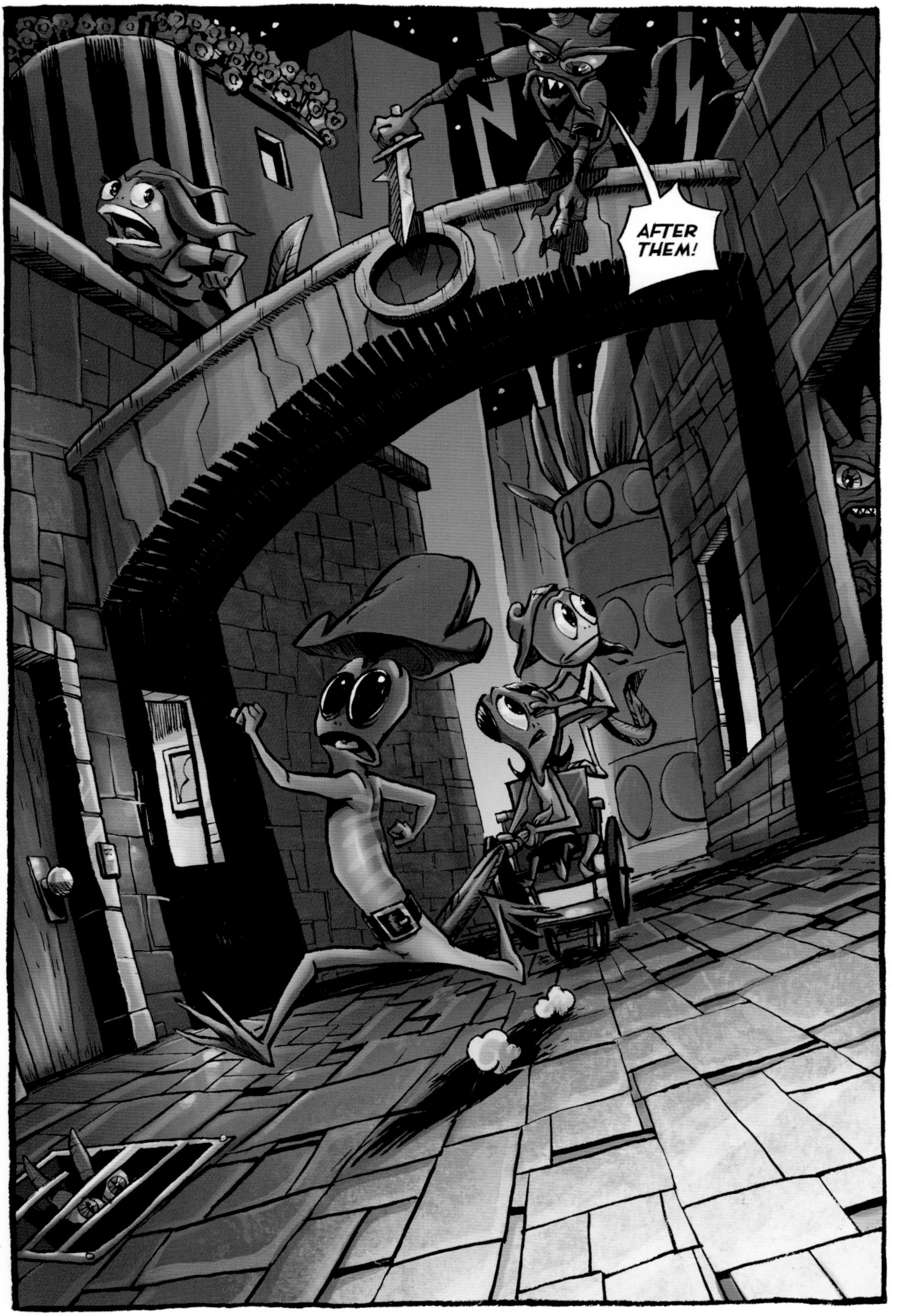
AFTER THEM!

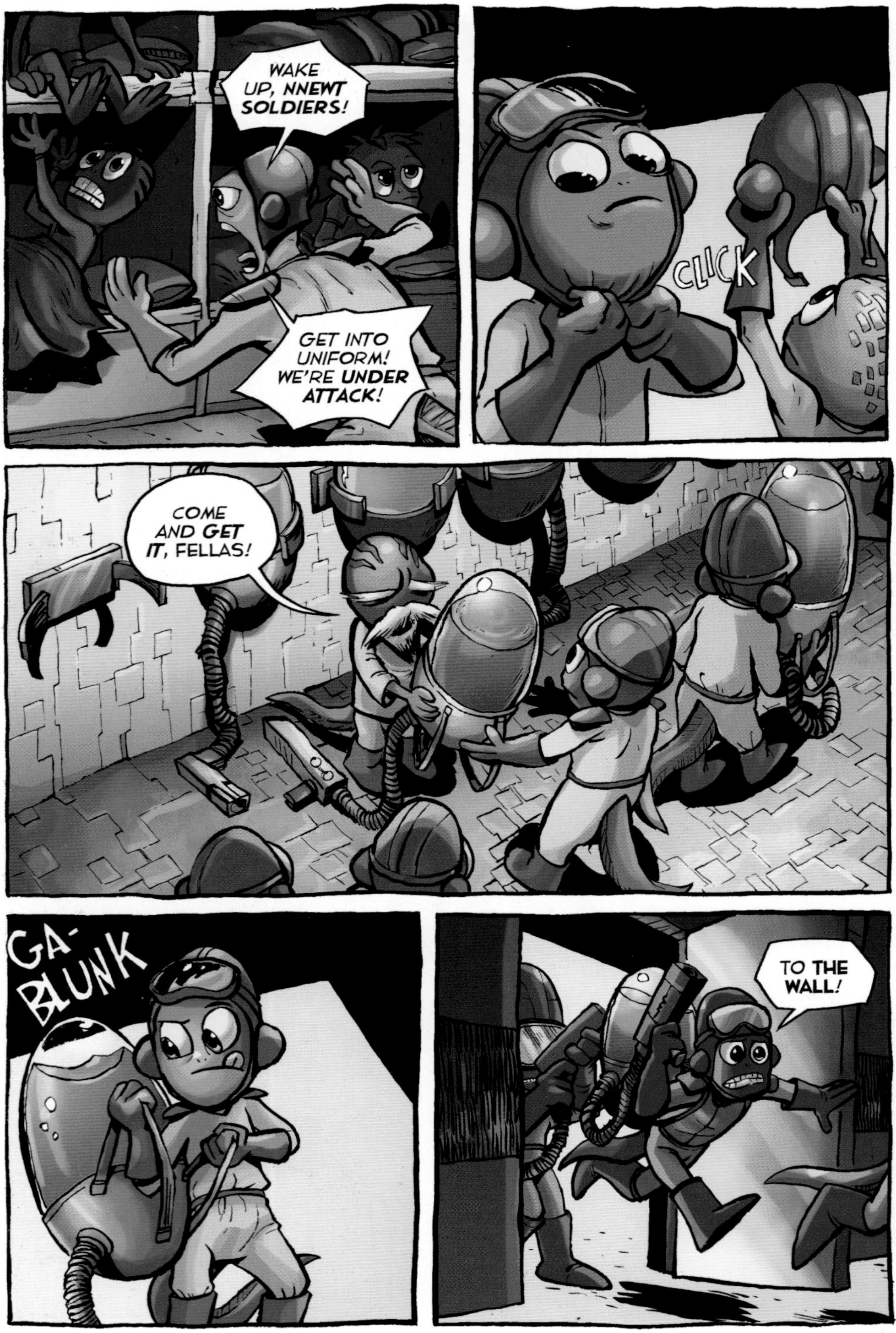
WAKE UP, NNEWT SOLDIERS!
GET INTO UNIFORM! WE'RE UNDER ATTACK!
CLICK
COME AND GET IT, FELLAS!
GA-BLUNK
TO THE WALL!

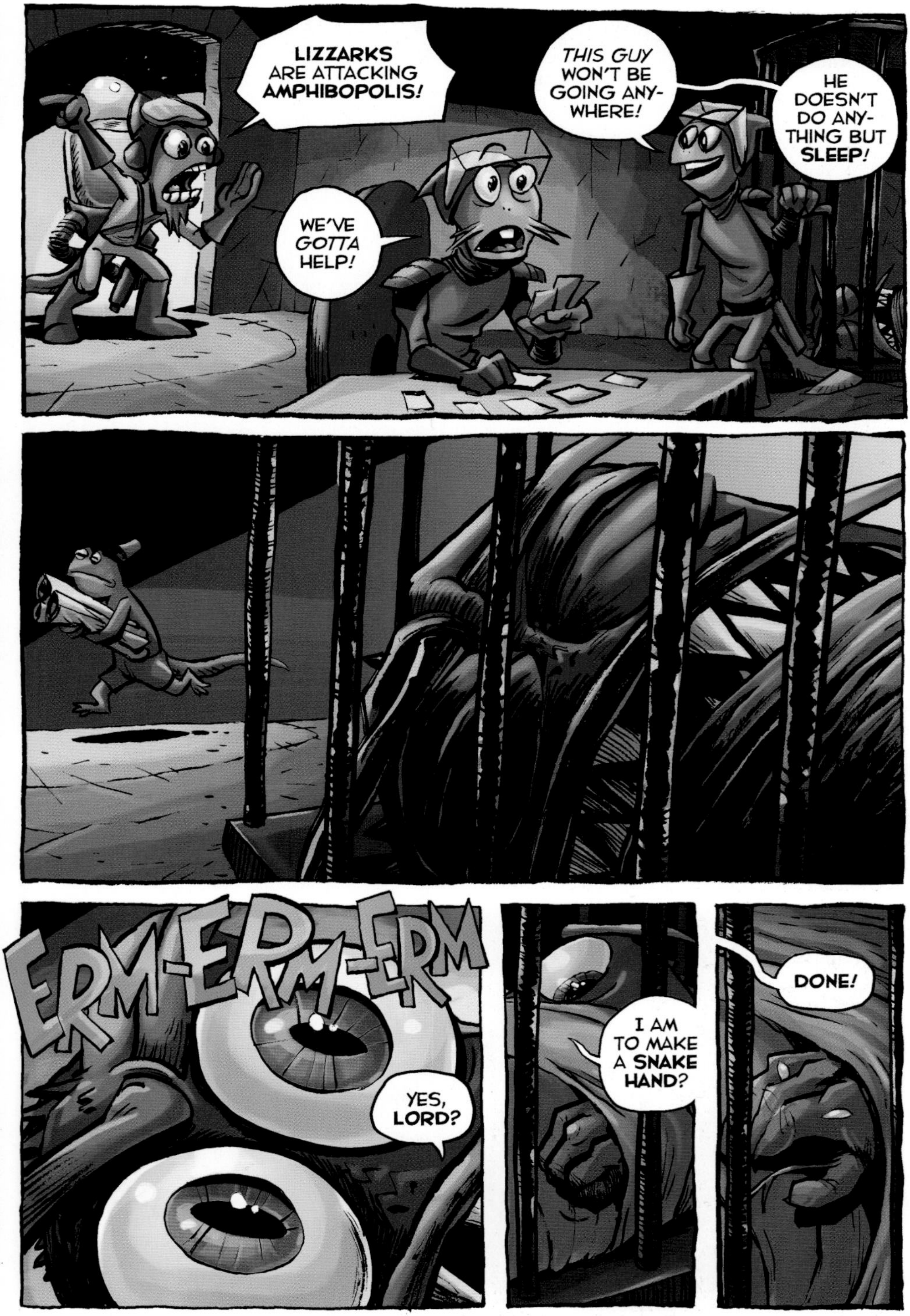
LIZZARKS ARE ATTACKING AMPHIBOPOLIS!
WE'VE GOTTA HELP!
THIS GUY WON'T BE GOING ANYWHERE!
HE DOESN'T DO ANYTHING BUT SLEEP!
ERM-ERM-ERM
YES, LORD?
I AM TO MAKE A SNAKE HAND?
DONE!

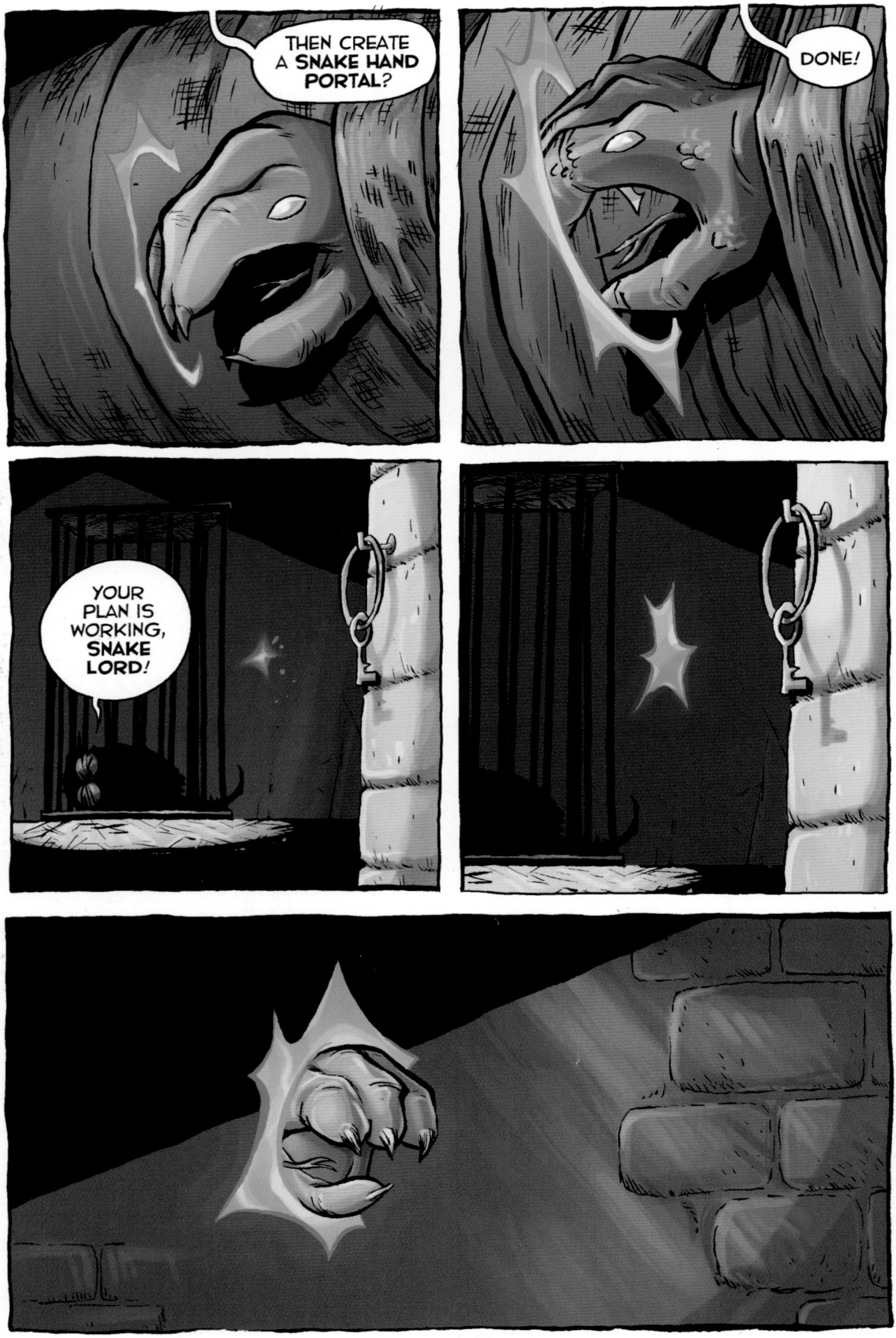
THEN CREATE A SNAKE HAND PORTAL?
DONE!
YOUR PLAN IS WORKING, SNAKE LORD!

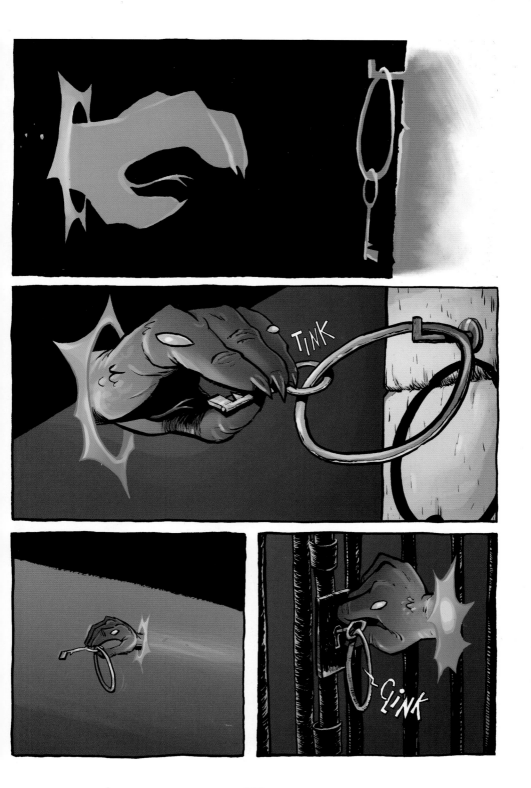

TINK

CLINK

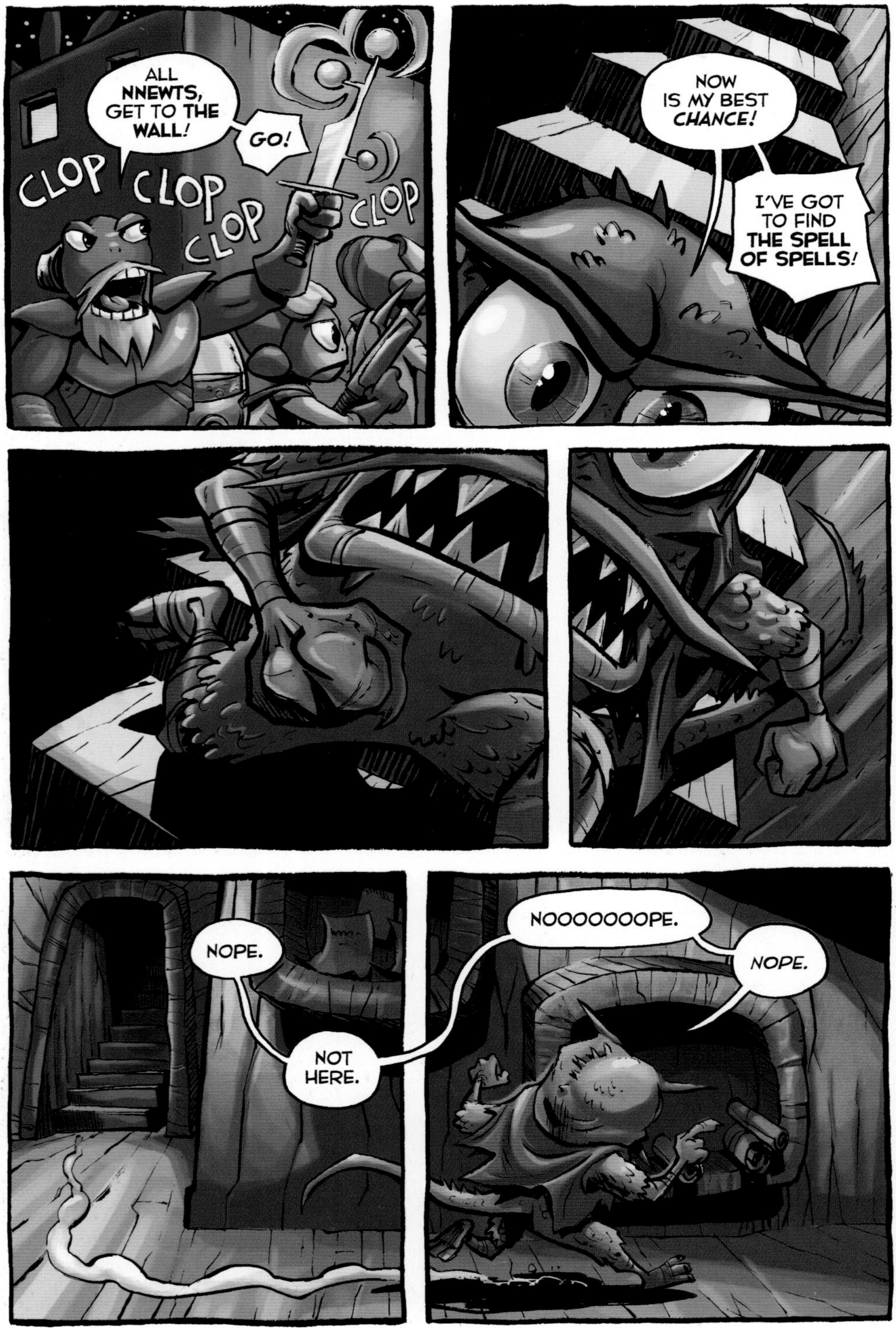
ALL NNEWTS, GET TO THE WALL!
GO!
CLOP CLOP CLOP CLOP
NOW IS MY BEST CHANCE!
I'VE GOT TO FIND THE SPELL OF SPELLS!
NOPE.
NOT HERE.
NOOOOOOOPE.
NOPE.

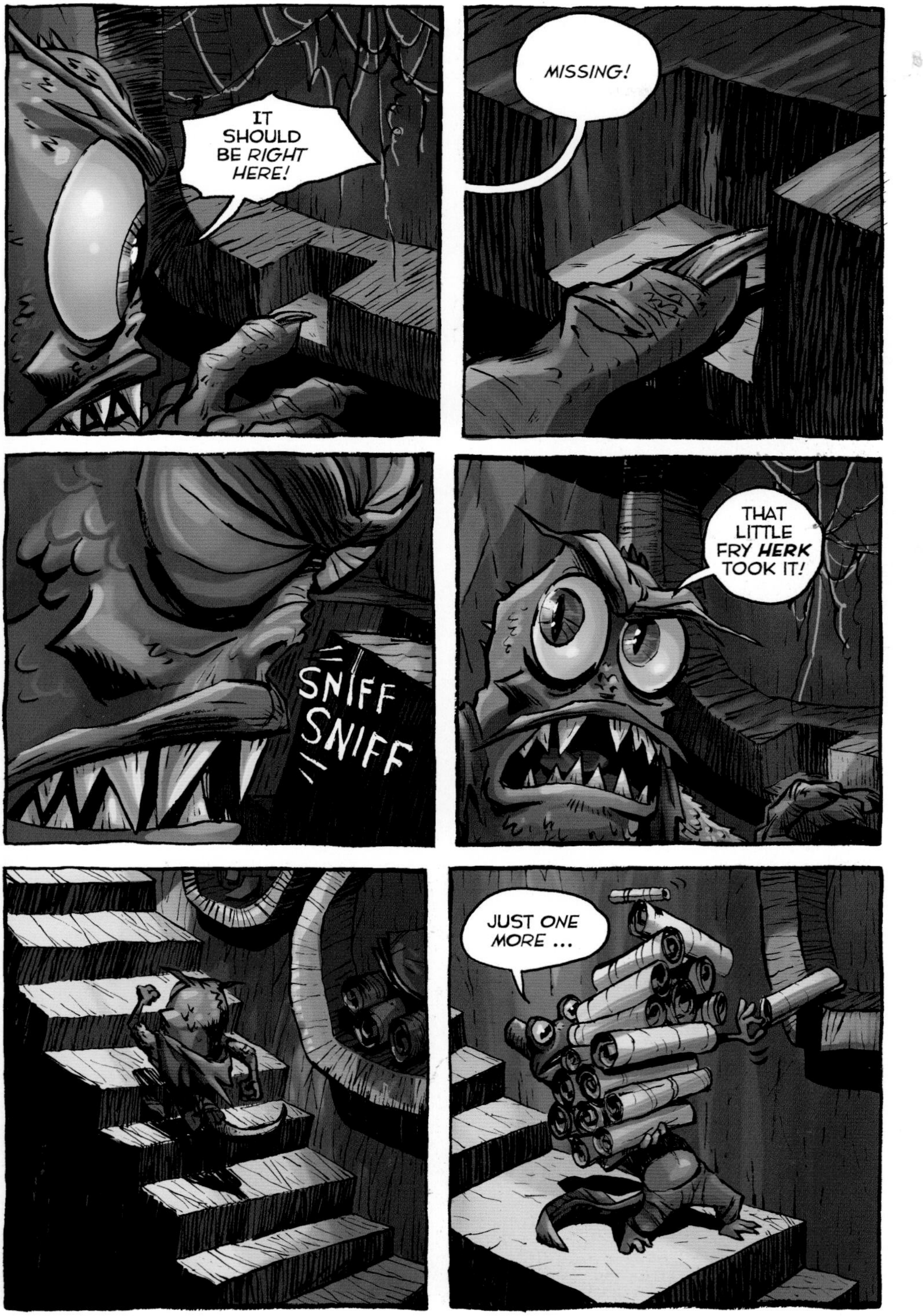
IT SHOULD BE RIGHT HERE!
MISSING!
SNIFF SNIFF
THAT LITTLE FRY **HERK** TOOK IT!
JUST ONE MORE ...

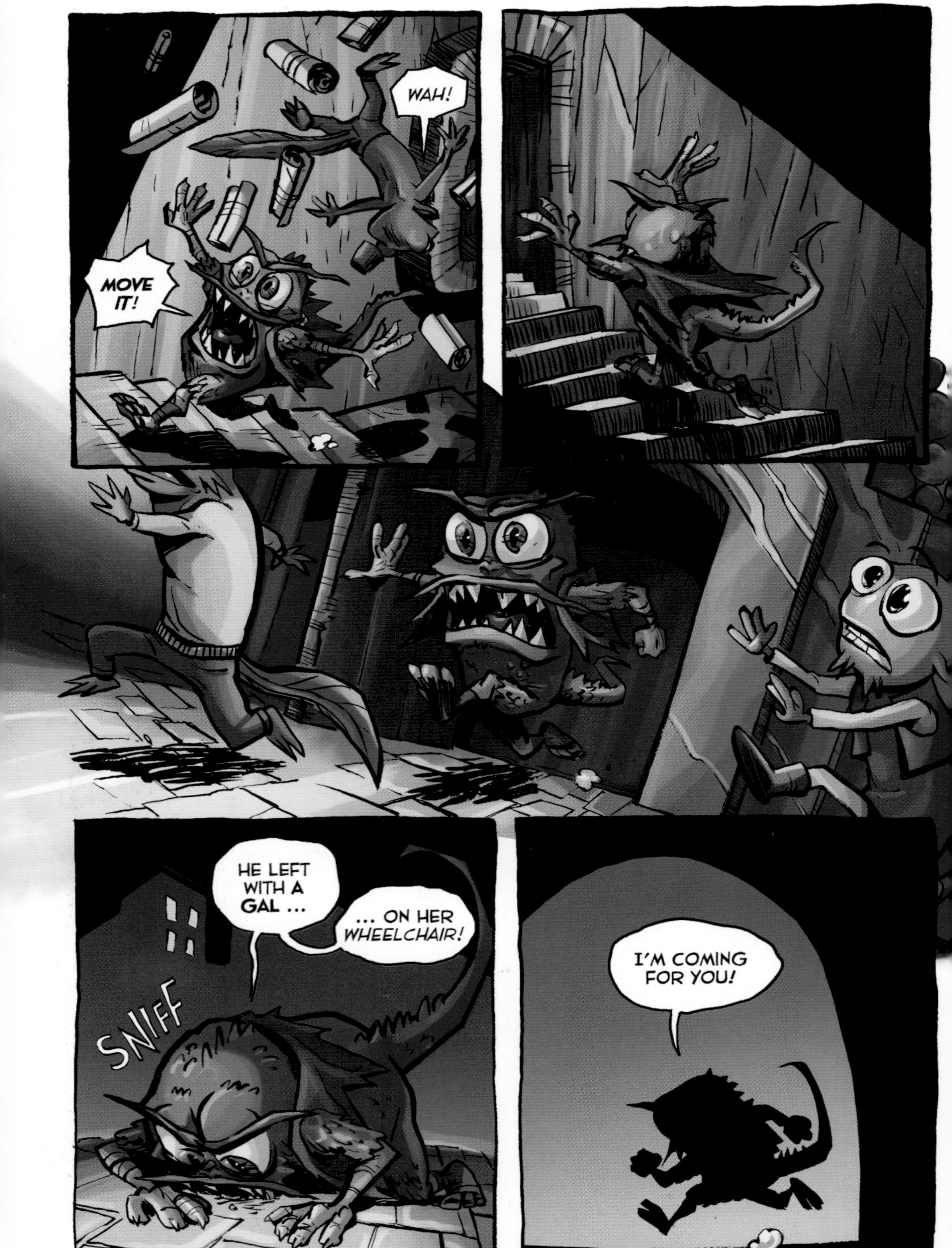
WAH!
MOVE IT!
HE LEFT WITH A GAL ...
... ON HER WHEELCHAIR!
SNIFF
I'M COMING FOR YOU!

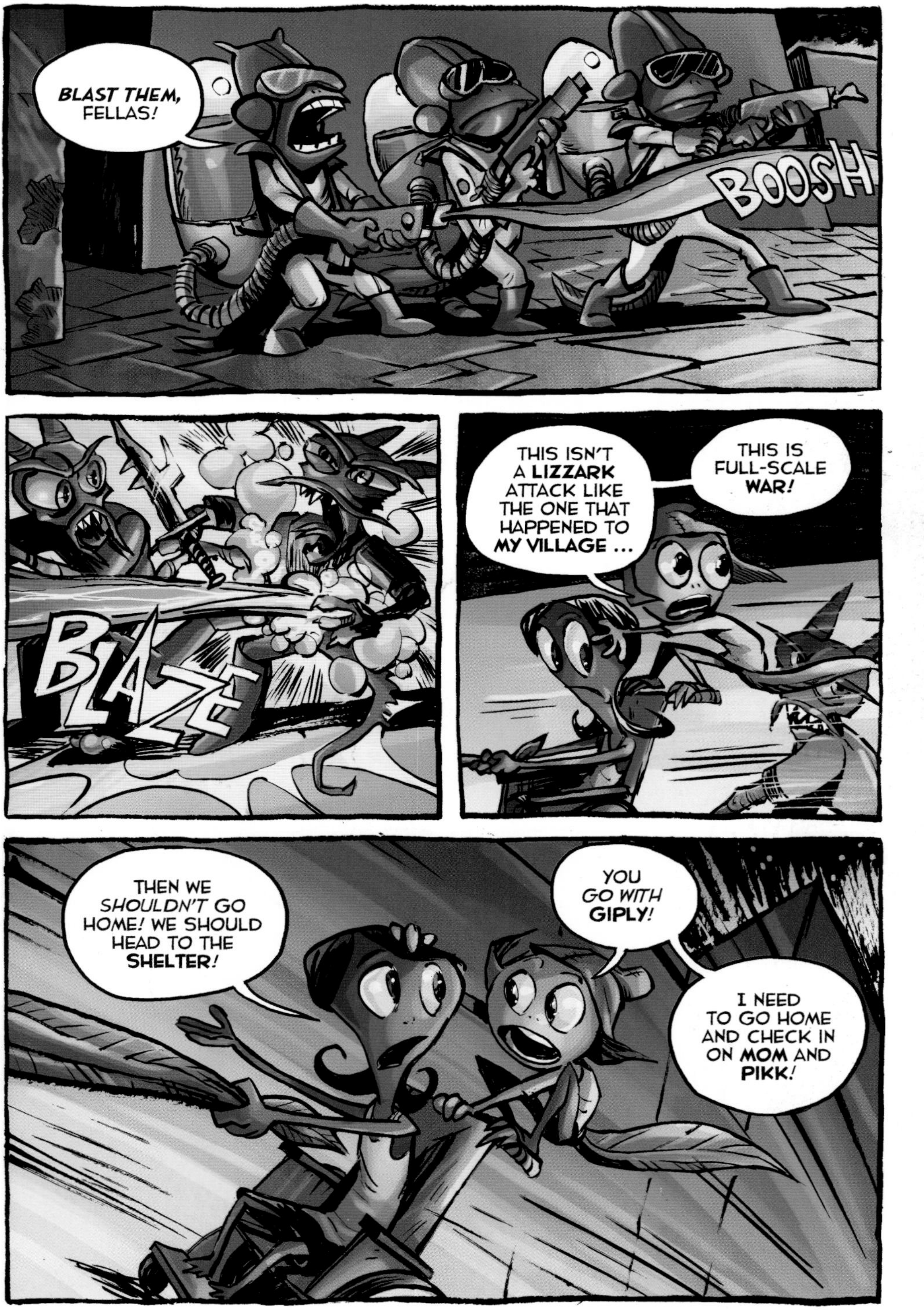
BLAST THEM, FELLAS!
BOOSH
BLAZE
THIS ISN'T A LIZZARK ATTACK LIKE THE ONE THAT HAPPENED TO MY VILLAGE ...
THIS IS FULL-SCALE WAR!
THEN WE SHOULDN'T GO HOME! WE SHOULD HEAD TO THE SHELTER!
YOU GO WITH GIPLY!
I NEED TO GO HOME AND CHECK IN ON MOM AND PIKK!

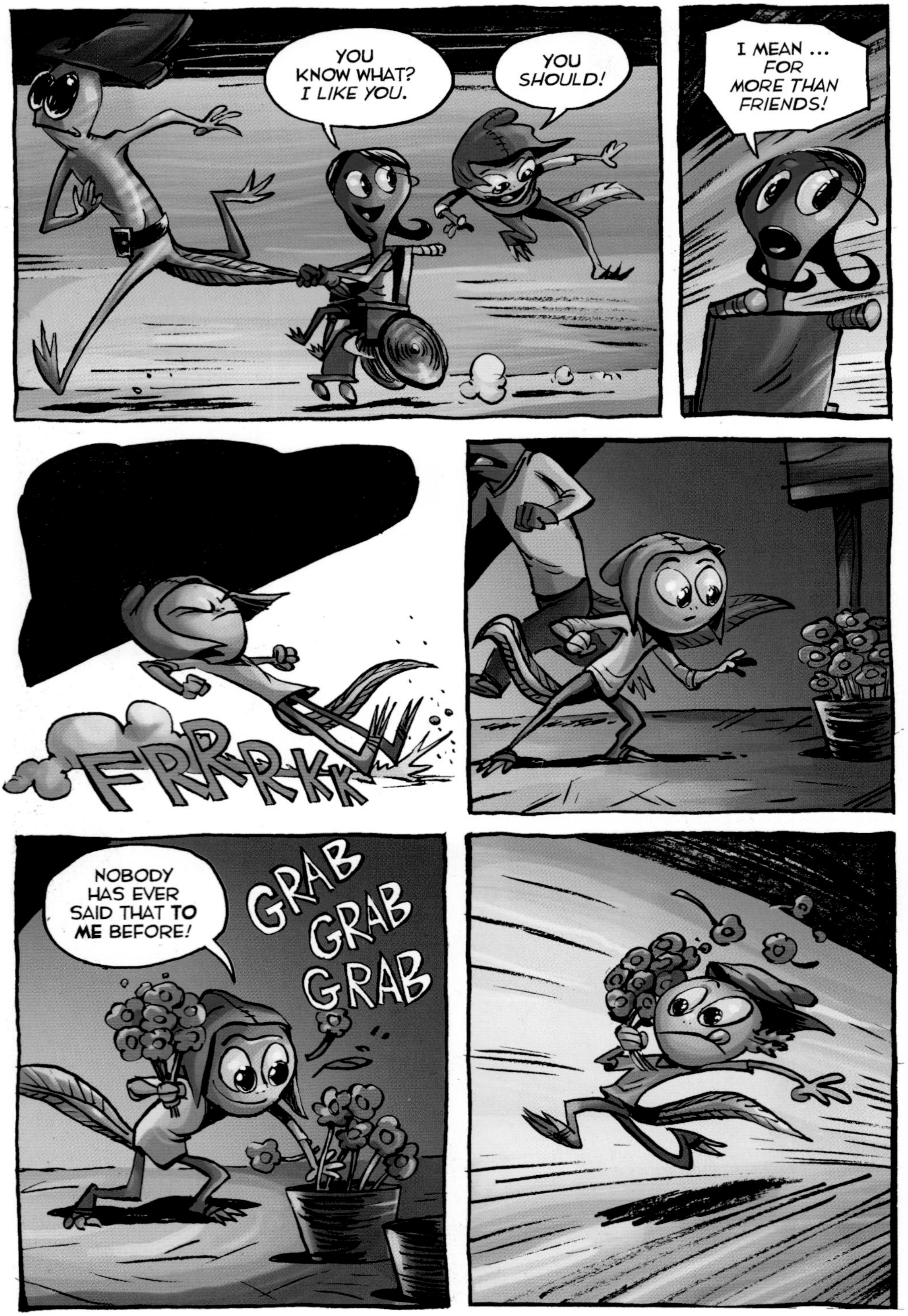
YOU KNOW WHAT? I LIKE YOU.
YOU SHOULD!
I MEAN ... FOR MORE THAN FRIENDS!
FRRRKK
NOBODY HAS EVER SAID THAT TO ME BEFORE!
GRAB GRAB GRAB

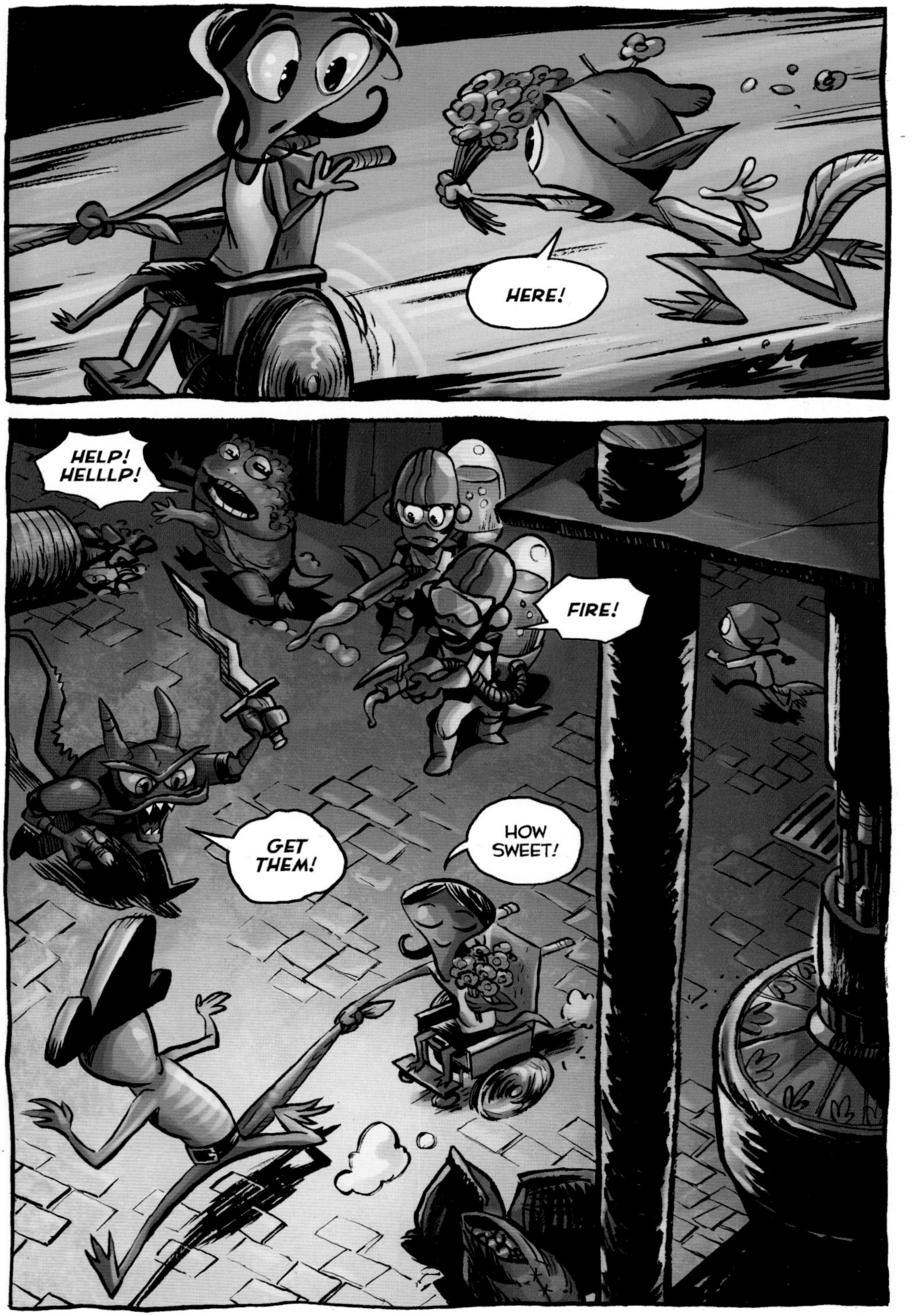
HERE!
HELP! HELLLP!
FIRE!
GET THEM!
HOW SWEET!

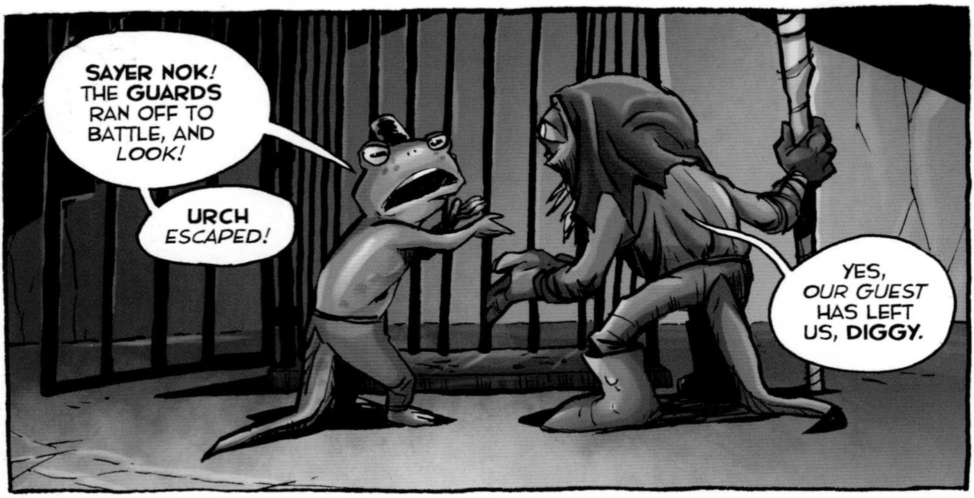
SAYER NOK! THE GUARDS RAN OFF TO BATTLE, AND LOOK!
URCH ESCAPED!
YES, OUR GUEST HAS LEFT US, DIGGY.

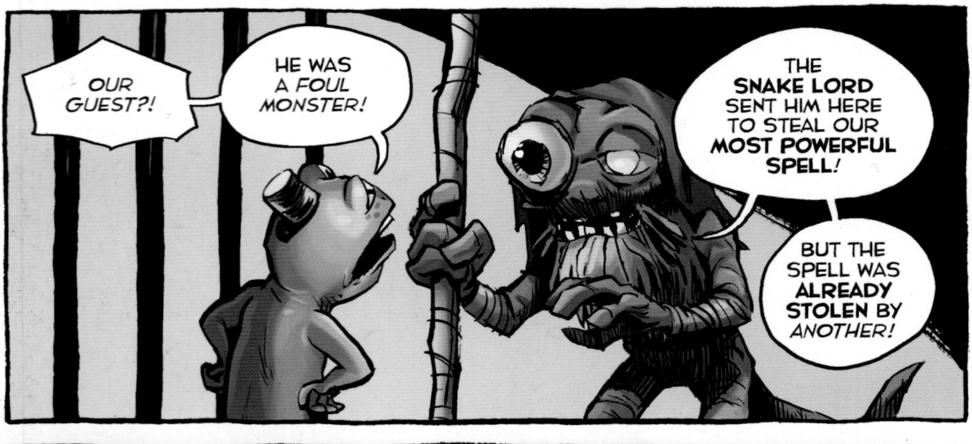
OUR GUEST?!
HE WAS A FOUL MONSTER!
THE SNAKE LORD SENT HIM HERE TO STEAL OUR MOST POWERFUL SPELL!
BUT THE SPELL WAS ALREADY STOLEN BY ANOTHER!

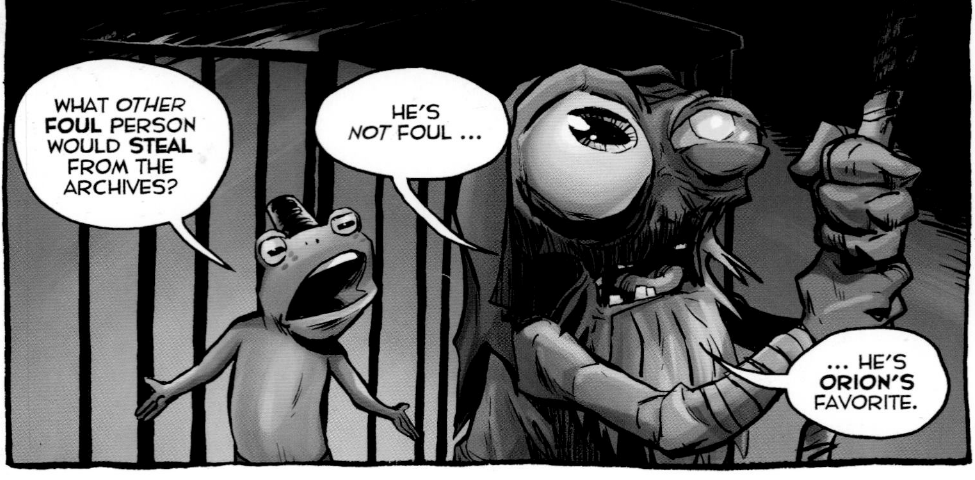
WHAT OTHER FOUL PERSON WOULD STEAL FROM THE ARCHIVES?
HE'S NOT FOUL ...
... HE'S ORION'S FAVORITE.

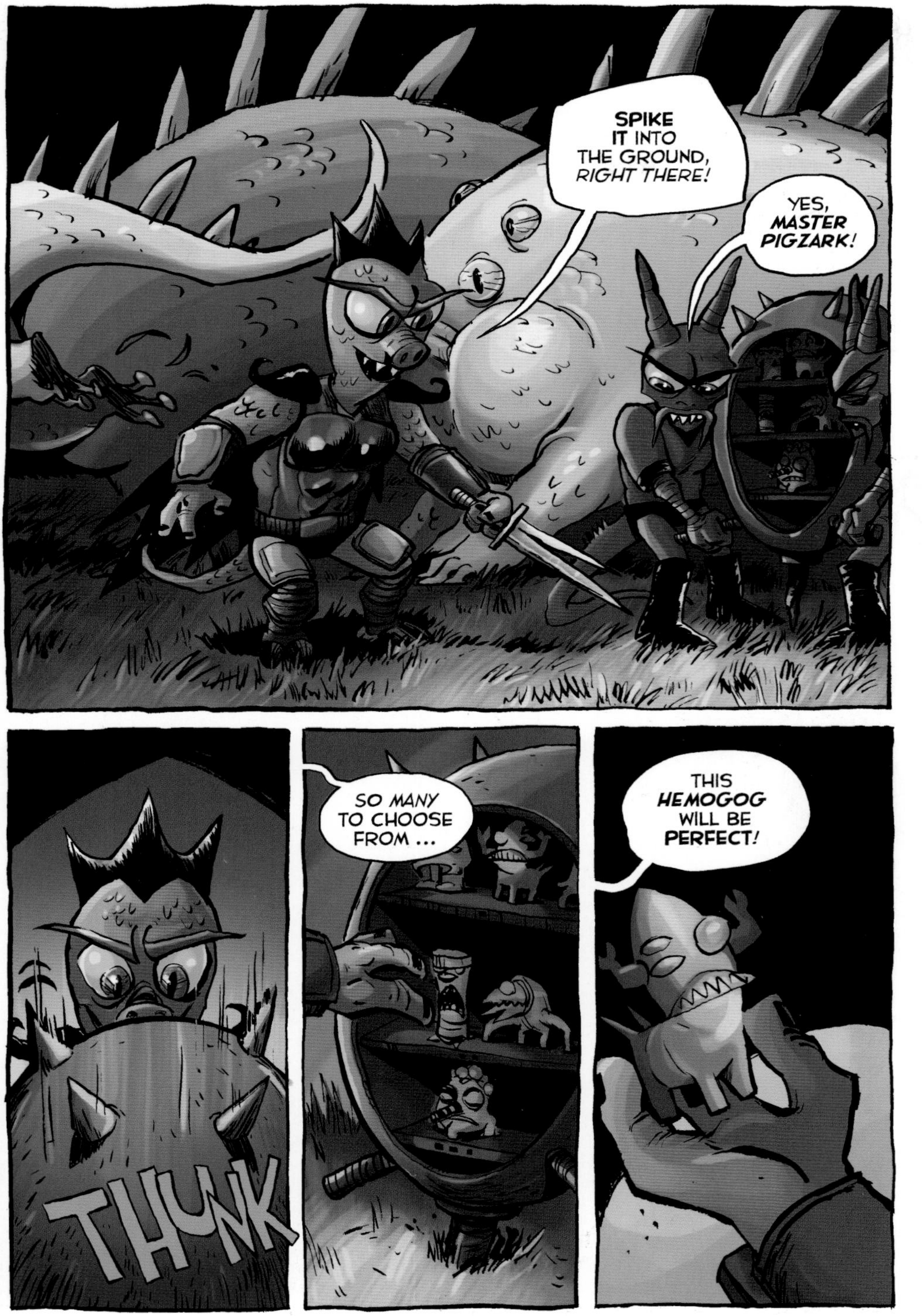
SPIKE IT INTO THE GROUND, RIGHT THERE!
YES, MASTER PIGZARK!
THUNK
SO MANY TO CHOOSE FROM ...
THIS HEMOGOG WILL BE PERFECT!

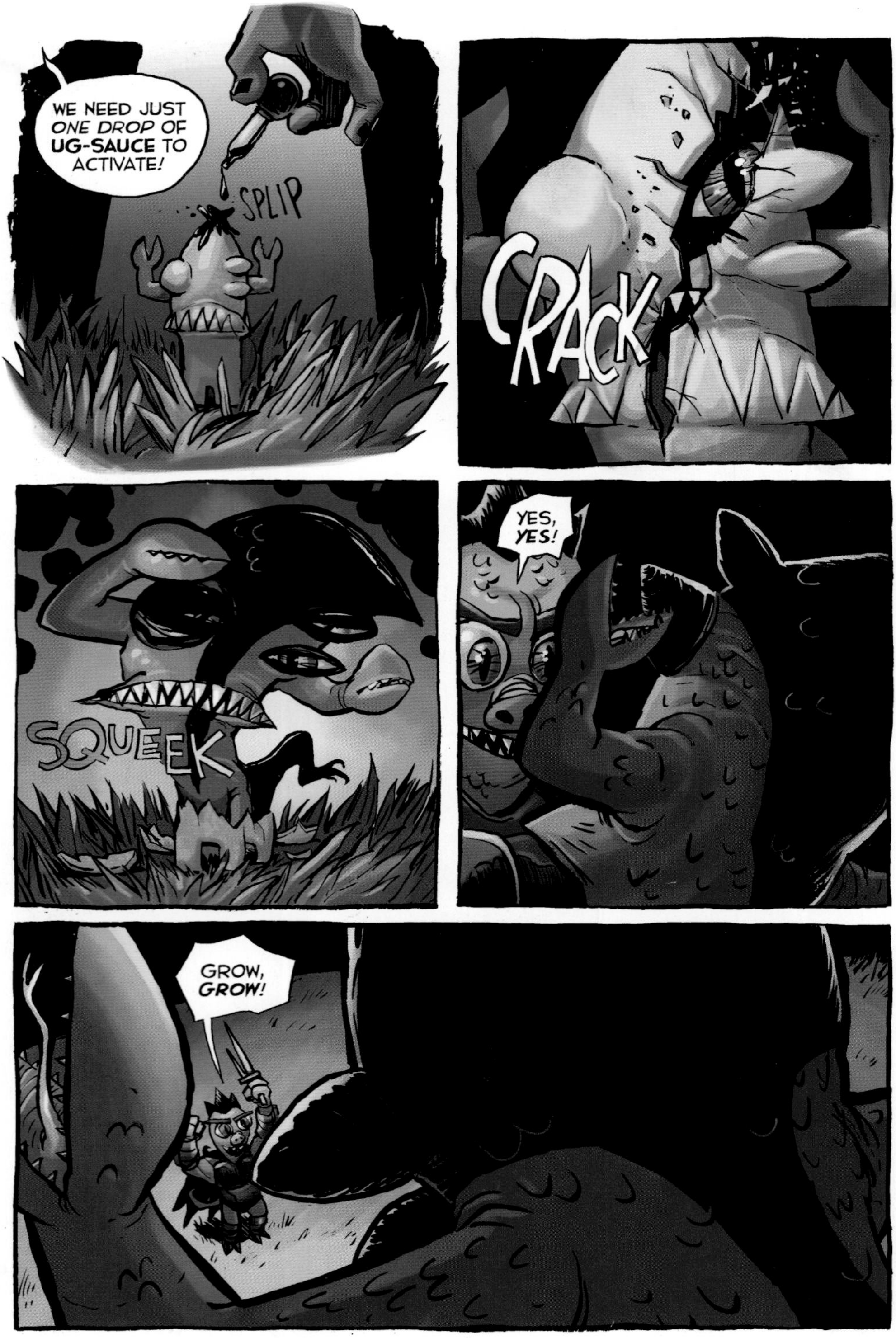
WE NEED JUST *ONE DROP* OF **UG-SAUCE** TO ACTIVATE!
SPLIP
CRACK
SQUEEK
YES, *YES!*
GROW, *GROW!*

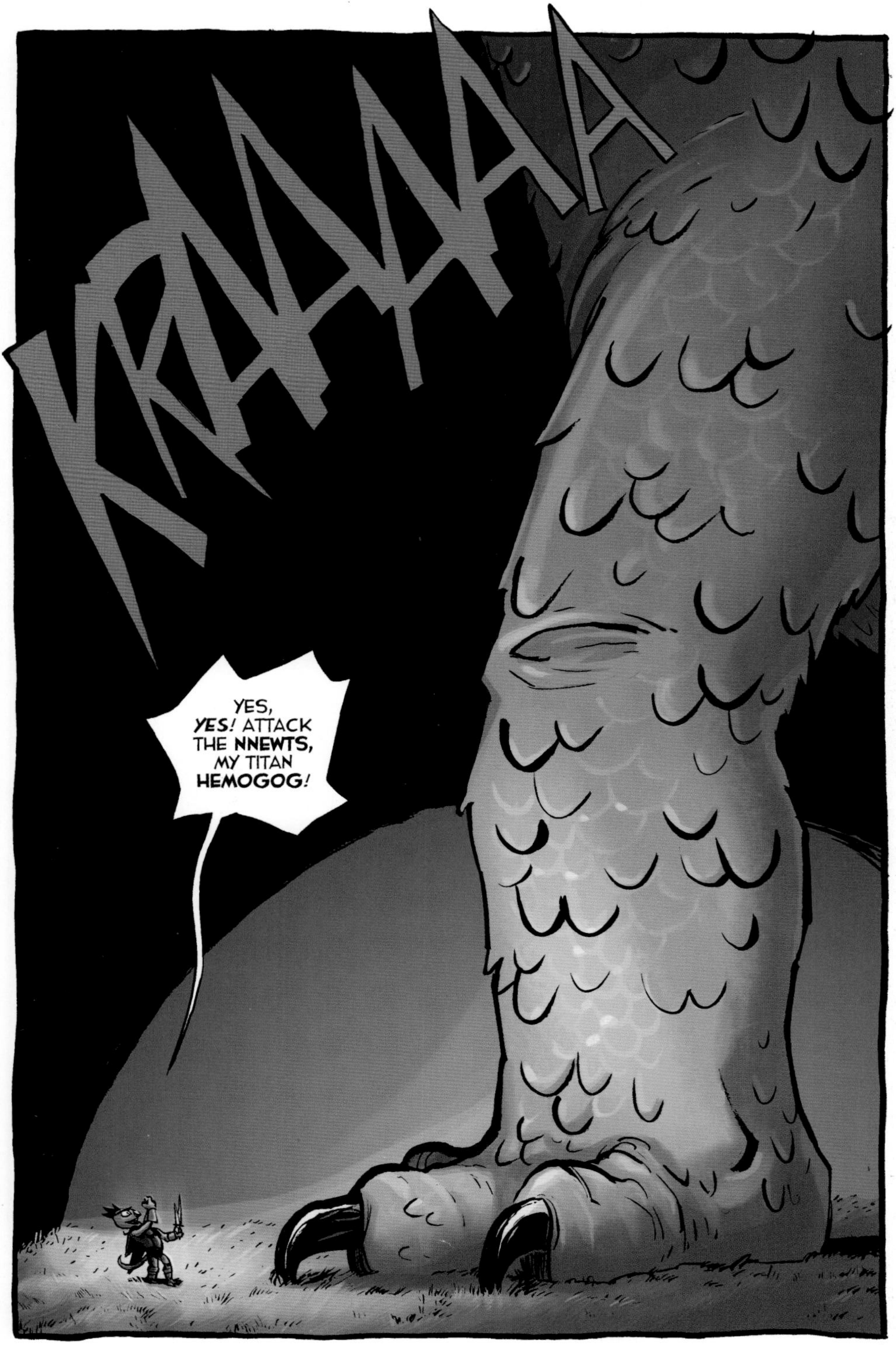
KRAAAA
YES, *YES!* ATTACK THE **NNEWTS,** MY TITAN **HEMOGOG!**

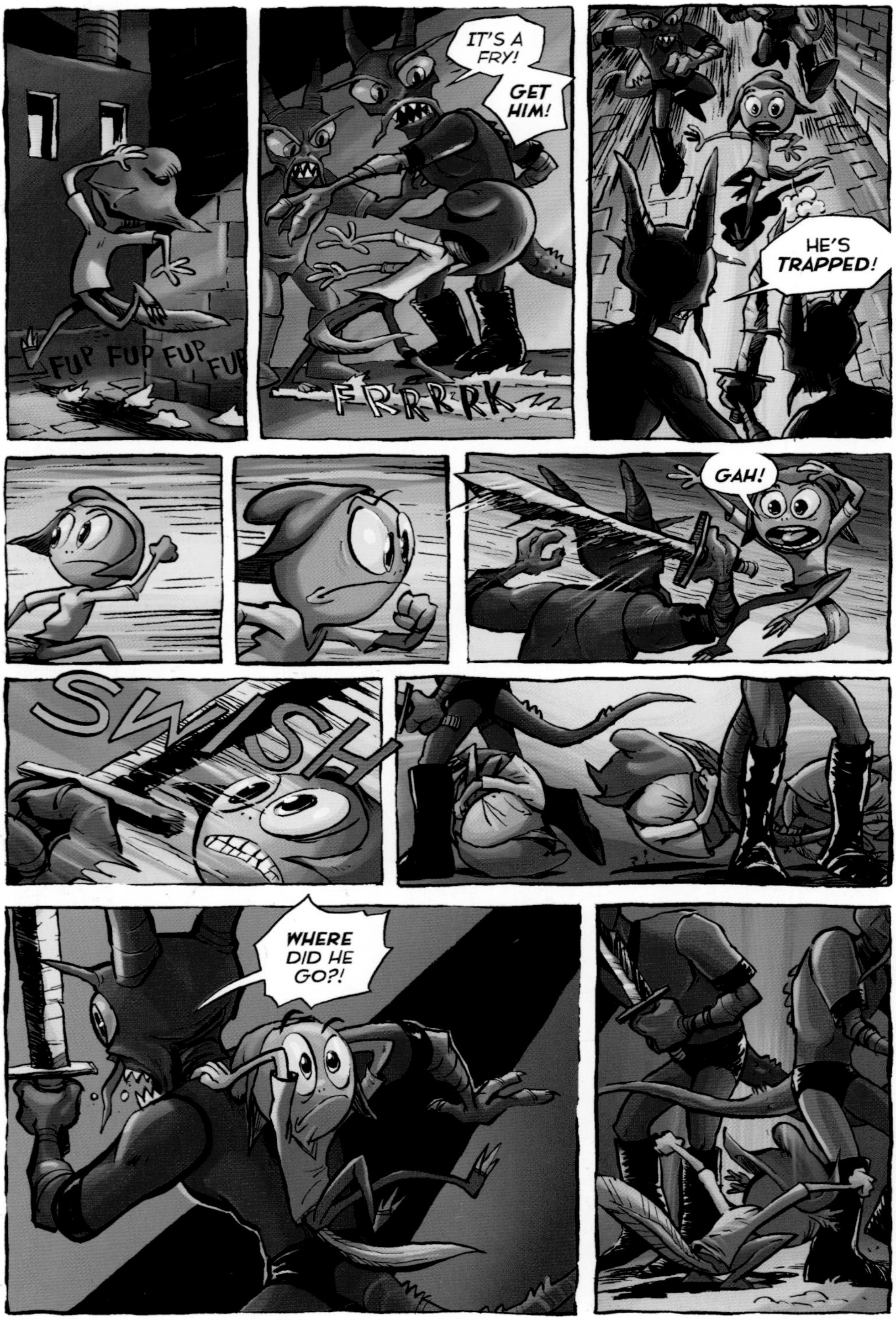
FUP FUP FUP FUP
IT'S A FRY!
GET HIM!
FRRRRRK
HE'S TRAPPED!
GAH!
SWISH
WHERE DID HE GO?!

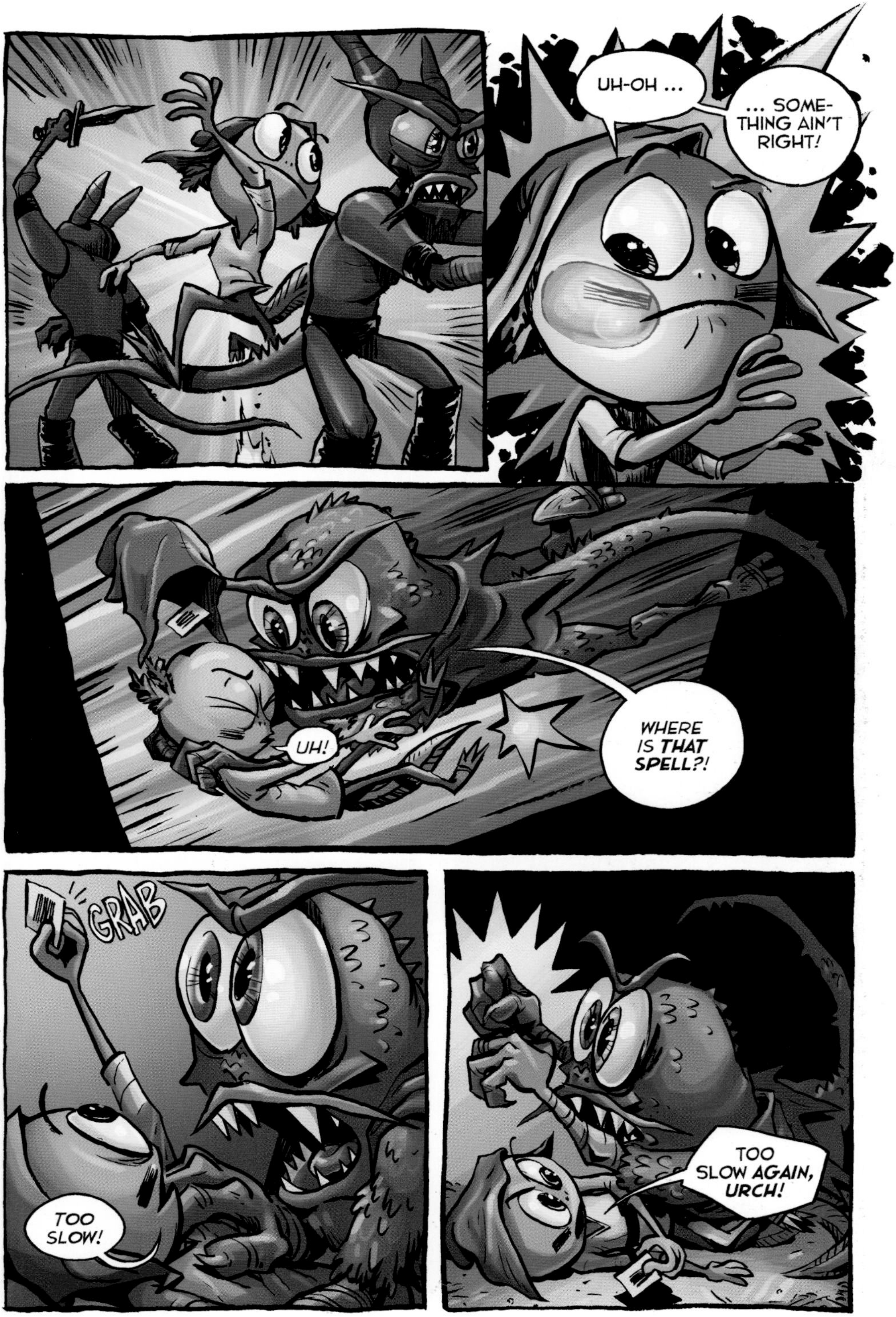
UH-OH ...
... SOME-THING AIN'T RIGHT!
UH!
WHERE IS **THAT SPELL?!**
GRAB
TOO SLOW!
TOO SLOW **AGAIN, URCH!**

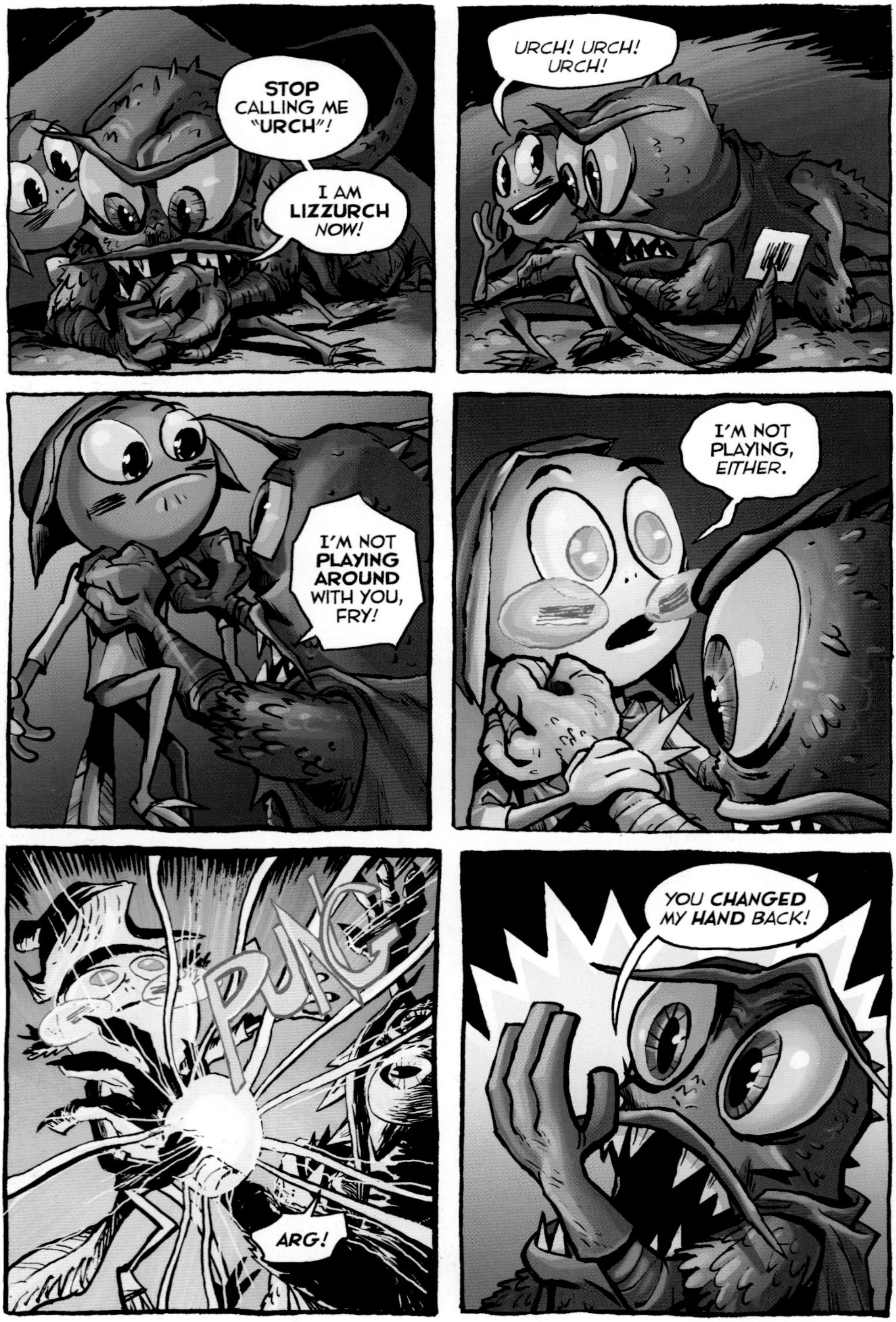
STOP CALLING ME "URCH"!
I AM LIZZURCH NOW!
URCH! URCH! URCH!
I'M NOT PLAYING AROUND WITH YOU, FRY!
I'M NOT PLAYING, EITHER.
PUNG
ARG!
YOU CHANGED MY HAND BACK!

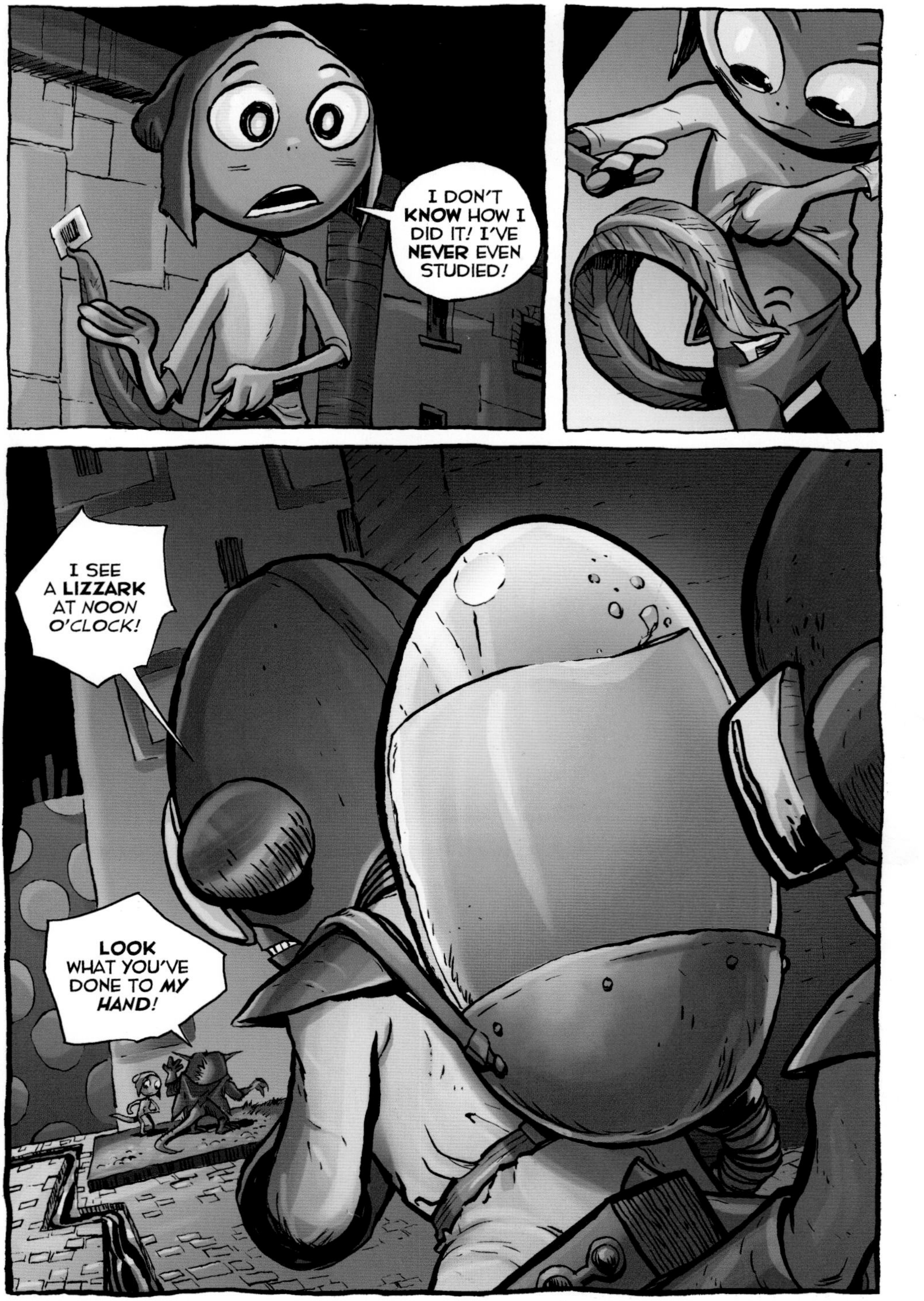
I DON'T **KNOW** HOW I DID IT! I'VE **NEVER** EVEN STUDIED!
I SEE A **LIZZARK** AT *NOON O'CLOCK!*
LOOK WHAT YOU'VE DONE TO ***MY HAND!***

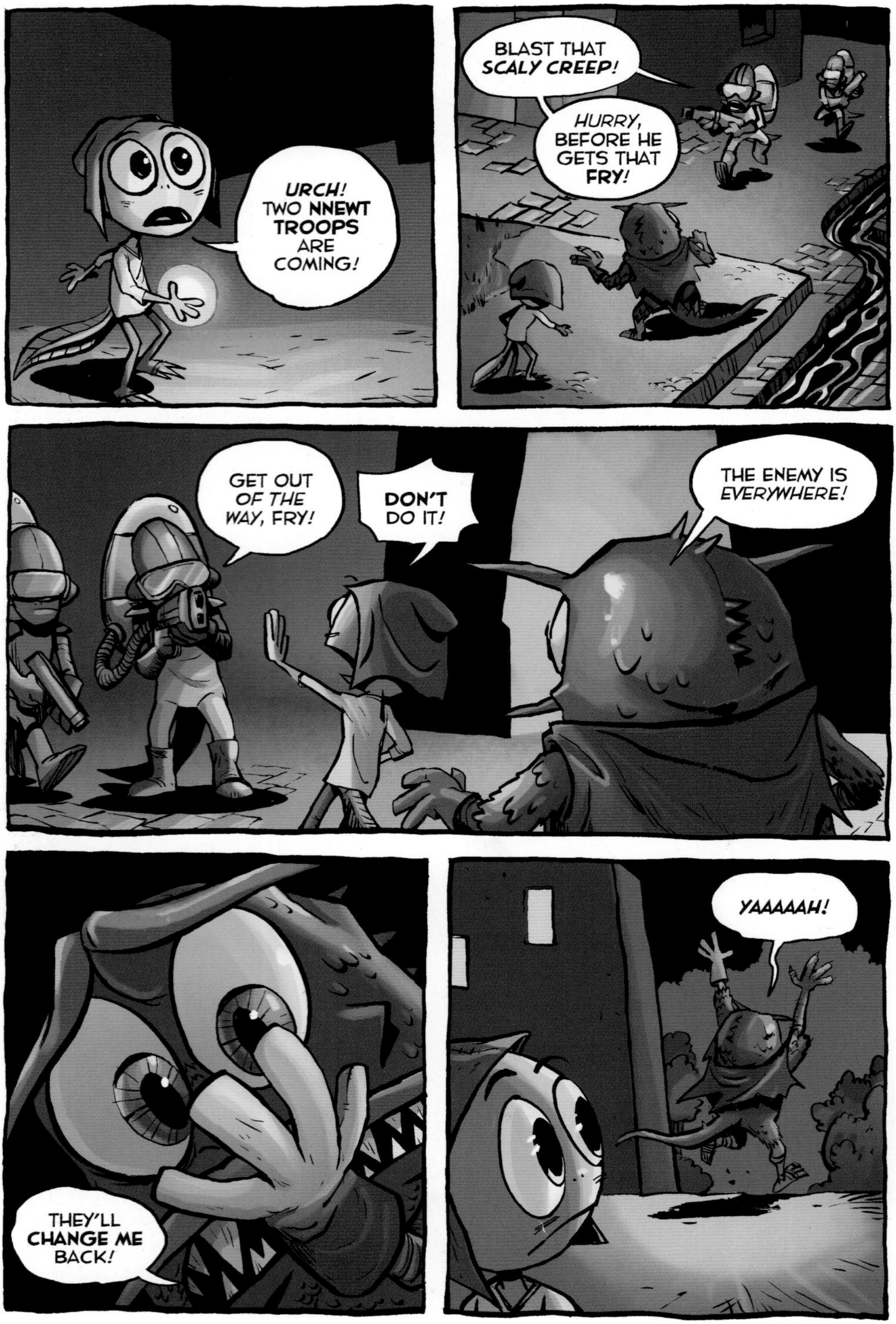
URCH! TWO NNEWT TROOPS ARE COMING!
BLAST THAT SCALY CREEP!
HURRY, BEFORE HE GETS THAT FRY!
GET OUT OF THE WAY, FRY!
DON'T DO IT!
THE ENEMY IS EVERYWHERE!
THEY'LL CHANGE ME BACK!
YAAAAAH!

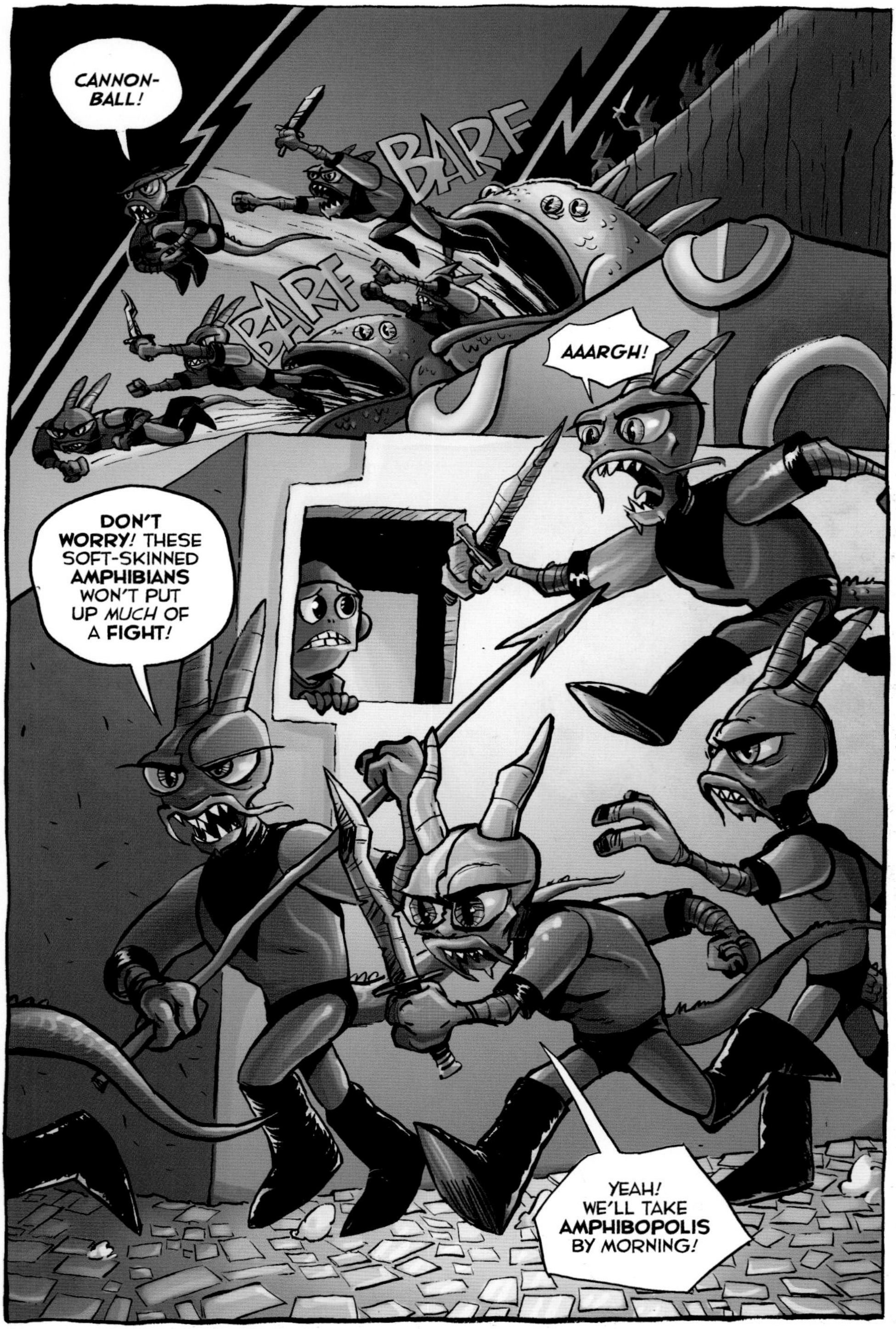
CANNON-BALL!
BARF
BARF
AAARGH!
DON'T WORRY! THESE SOFT-SKINNED AMPHIBIANS WON'T PUT UP MUCH OF A FIGHT!
YEAH! WE'LL TAKE AMPHIBOPOLIS BY MORNING!

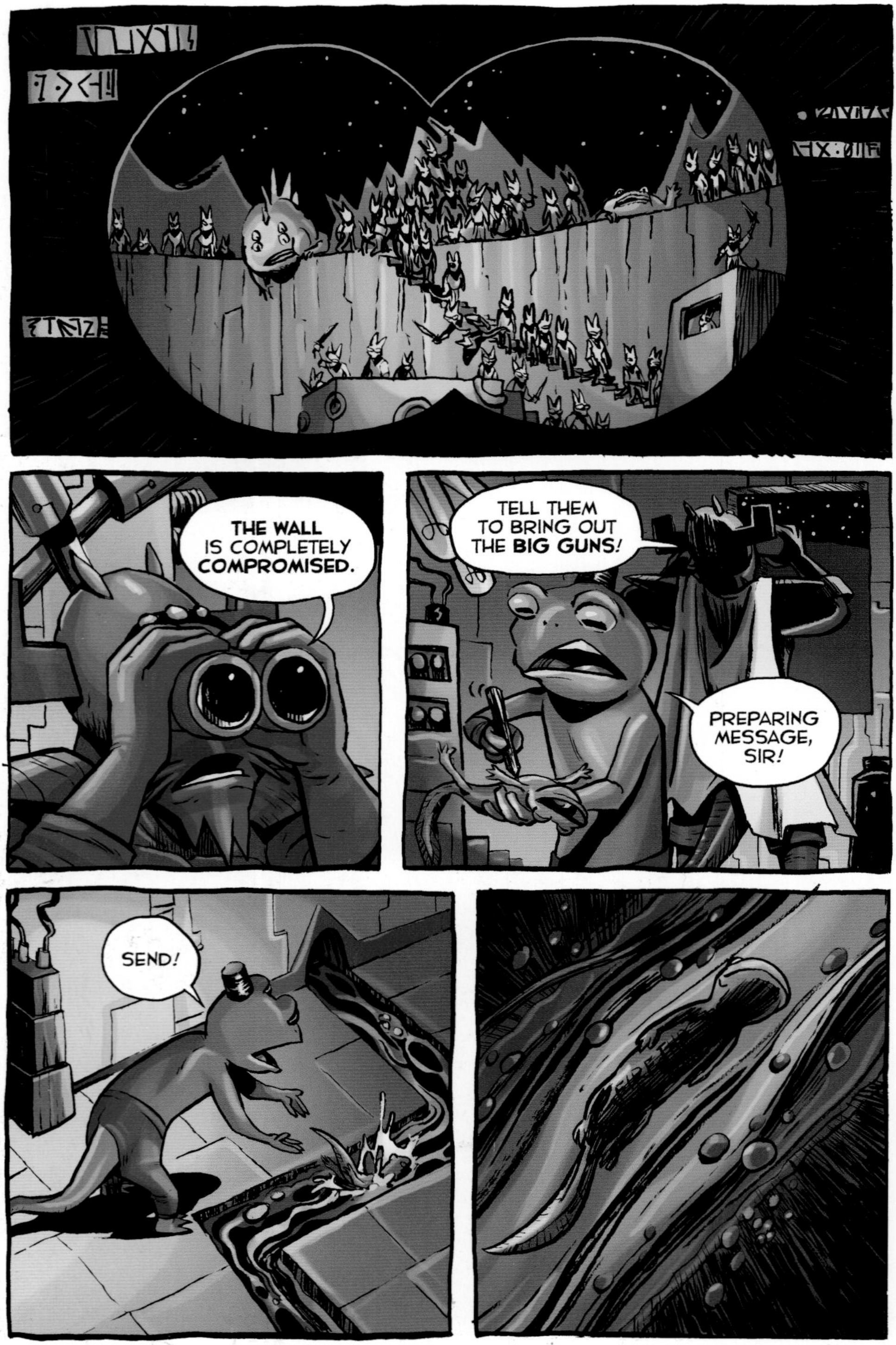
THE WALL IS COMPLETELY COMPROMISED.
TELL THEM TO BRING OUT THE BIG GUNS!
PREPARING MESSAGE, SIR!
SEND!

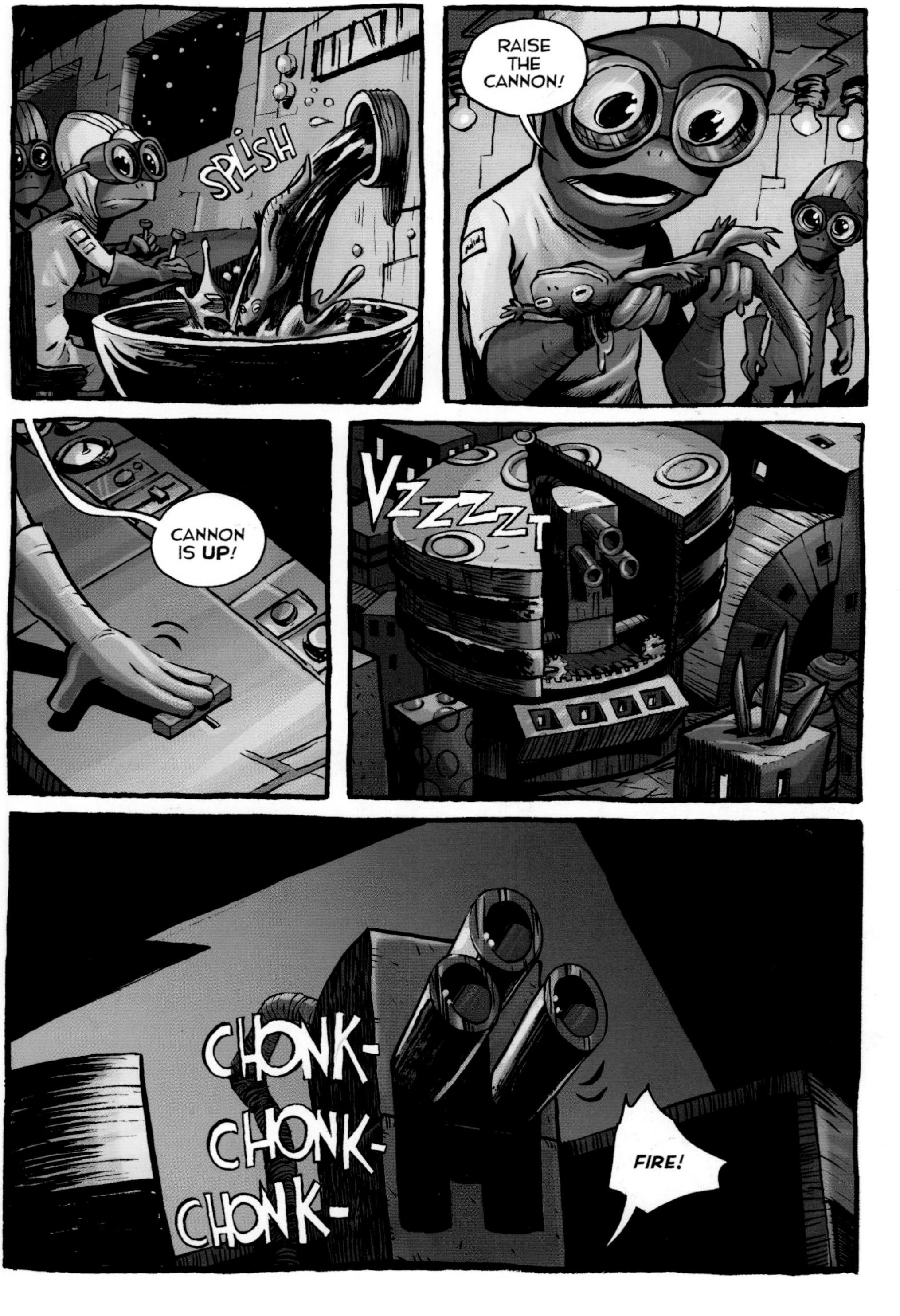
SPLISH
RAISE THE CANNON!
CANNON IS UP!
VZZZZZT
CHONK-
CHONK-
CHONK-
FIRE!

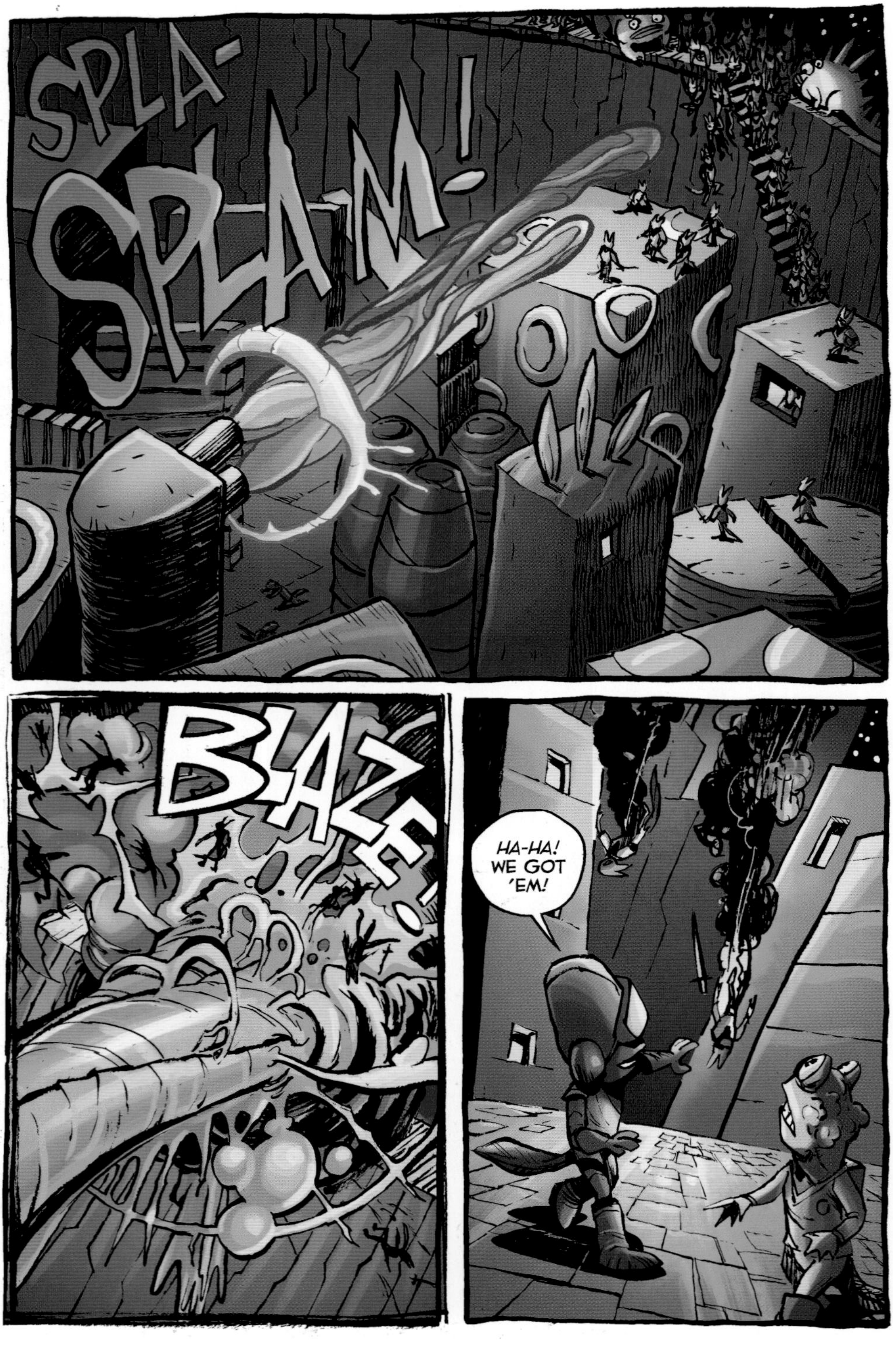
SPLA-
SPLAM!
BLAZE!
HA-HA! WE GOT 'EM!

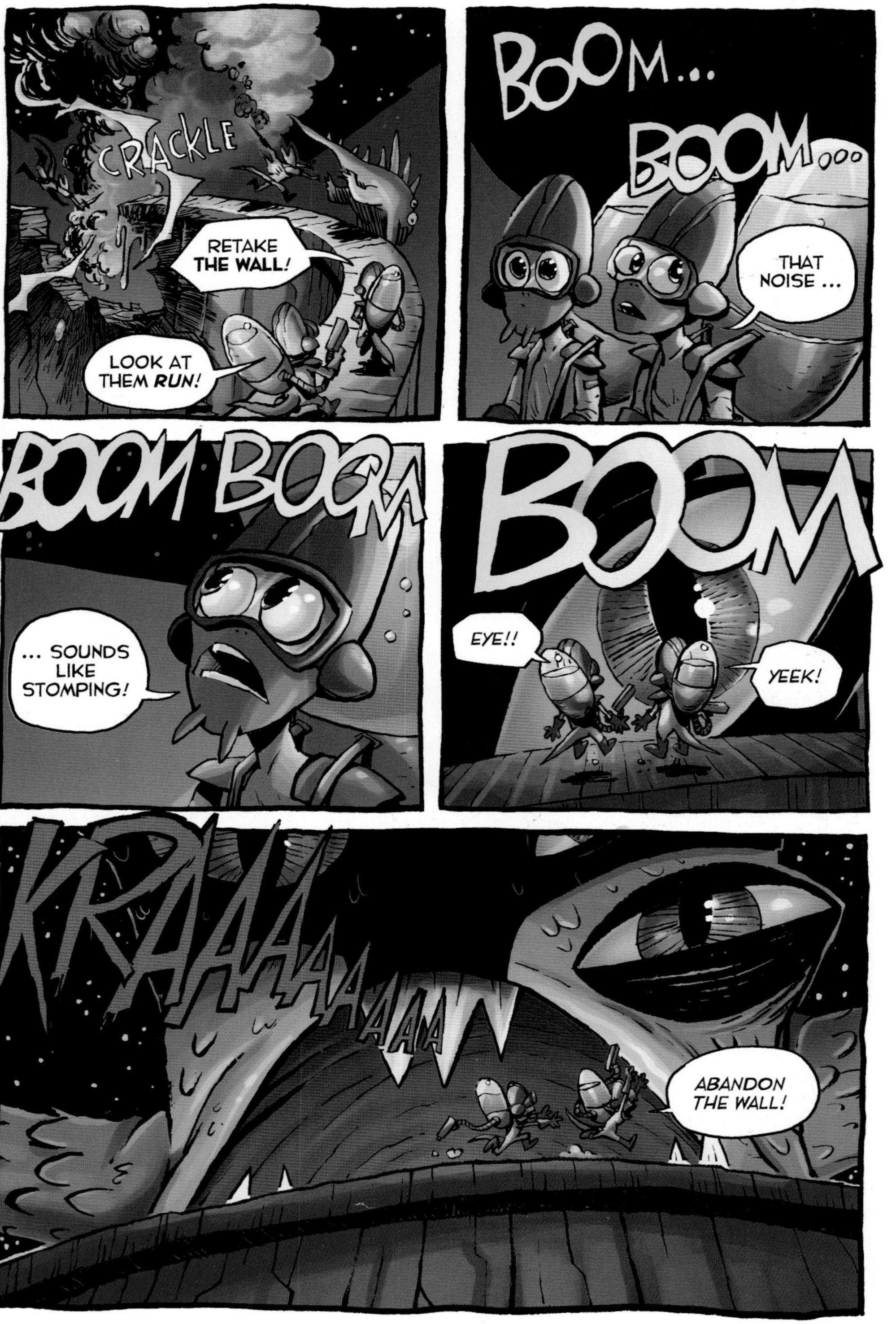
CRACKLE
RETAKE THE WALL!
LOOK AT THEM RUN!
BOOM...
BOOM...
THAT NOISE ...
BOOM BOOM
... SOUNDS LIKE STOMPING!
BOOM
EYE!!
YEEK!
KRAAAAAAAAAA
ABANDON THE WALL!

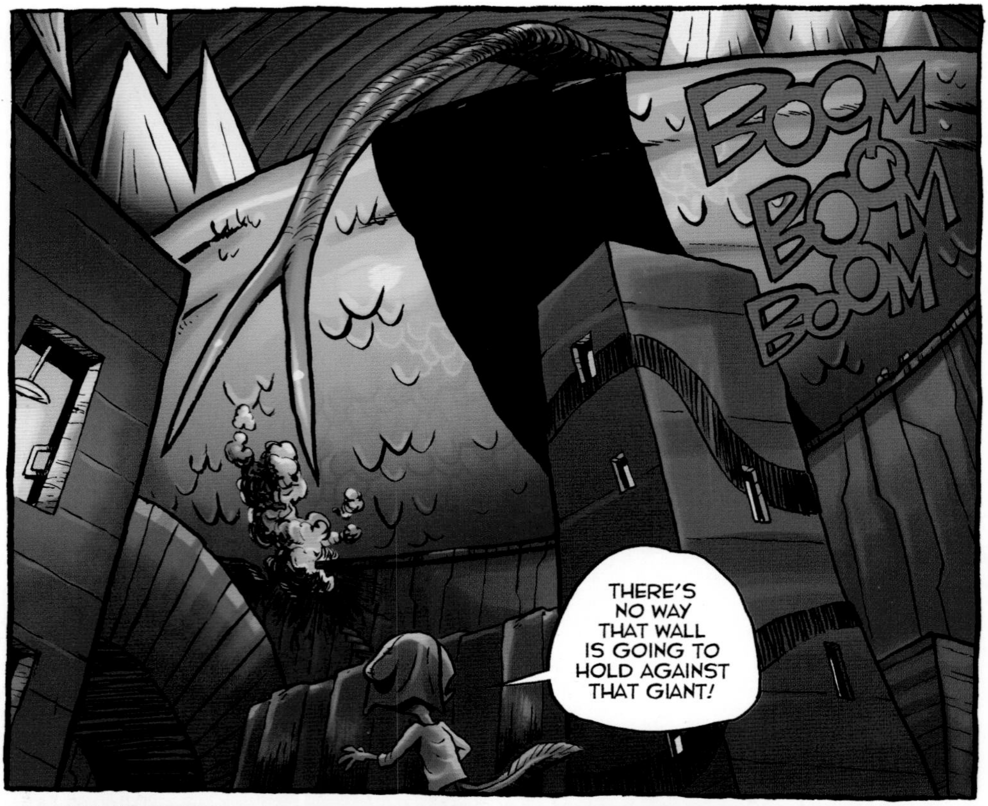
BOOM BOOM BOOM BOOM
THERE'S NO WAY THAT WALL IS GOING TO HOLD AGAINST THAT GIANT!

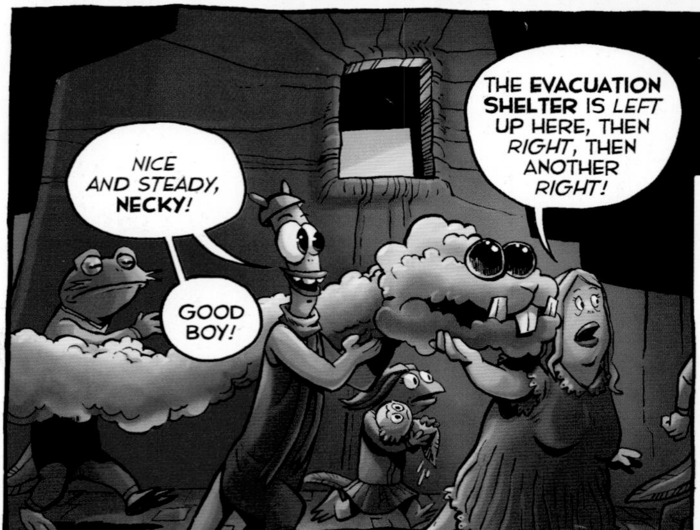
NICE AND STEADY, **NECKY**!
GOOD BOY!
THE **EVACUATION SHELTER** IS *LEFT* UP HERE, THEN *RIGHT*, THEN ANOTHER *RIGHT*!

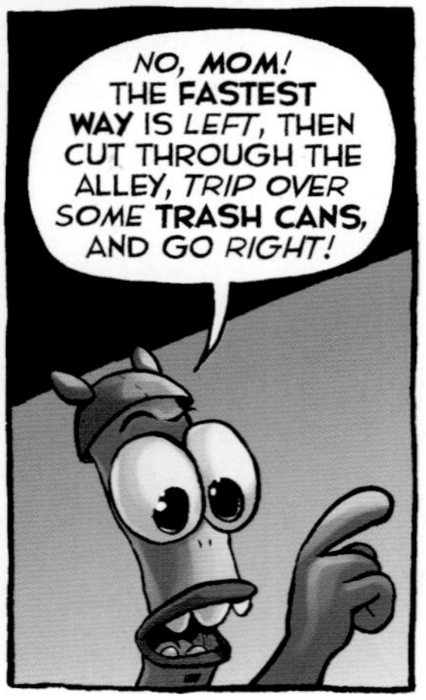
NO, **MOM**! THE **FASTEST WAY** IS *LEFT*, THEN CUT THROUGH THE ALLEY, *TRIP OVER SOME* **TRASH CANS**, AND GO *RIGHT*!

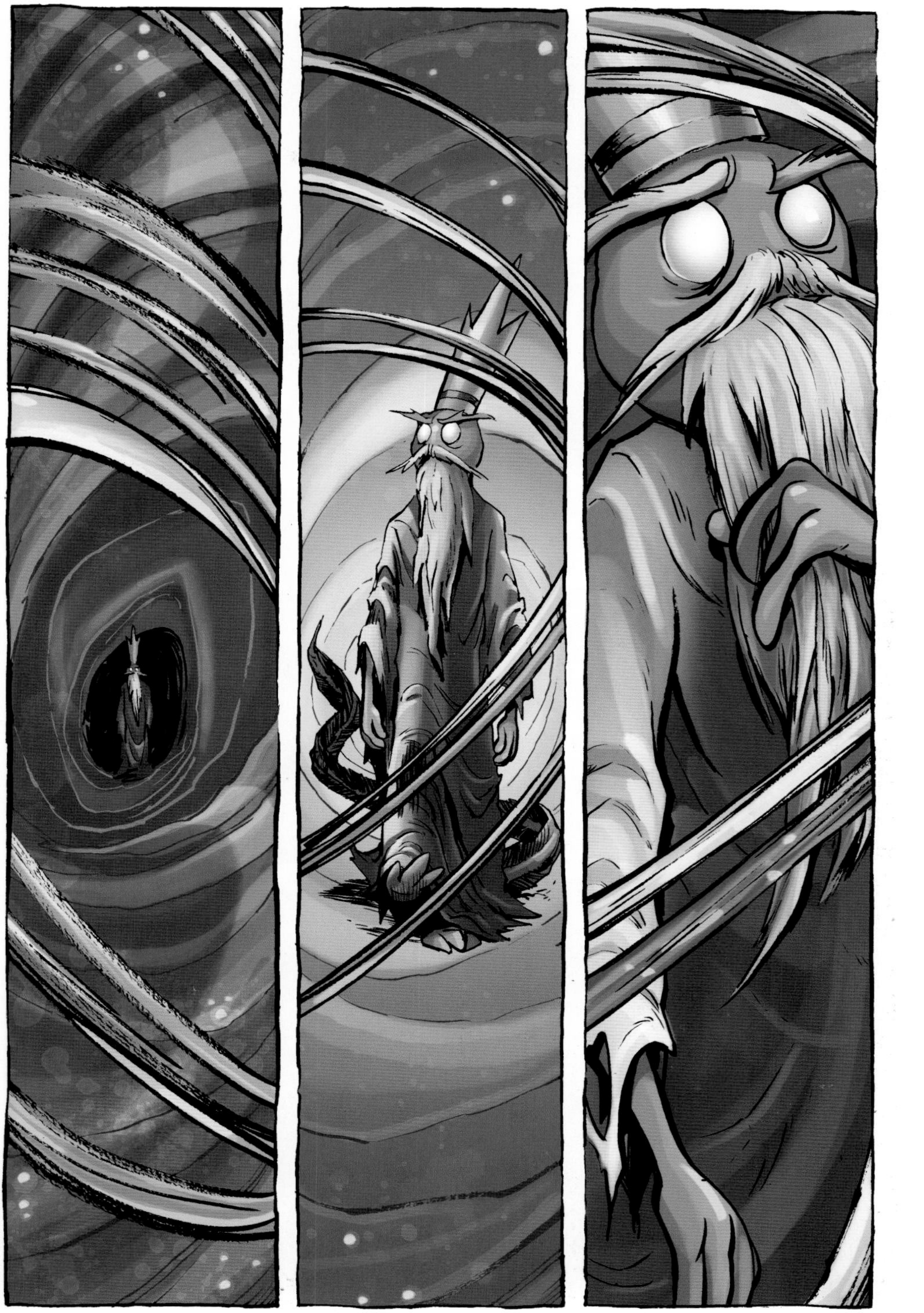

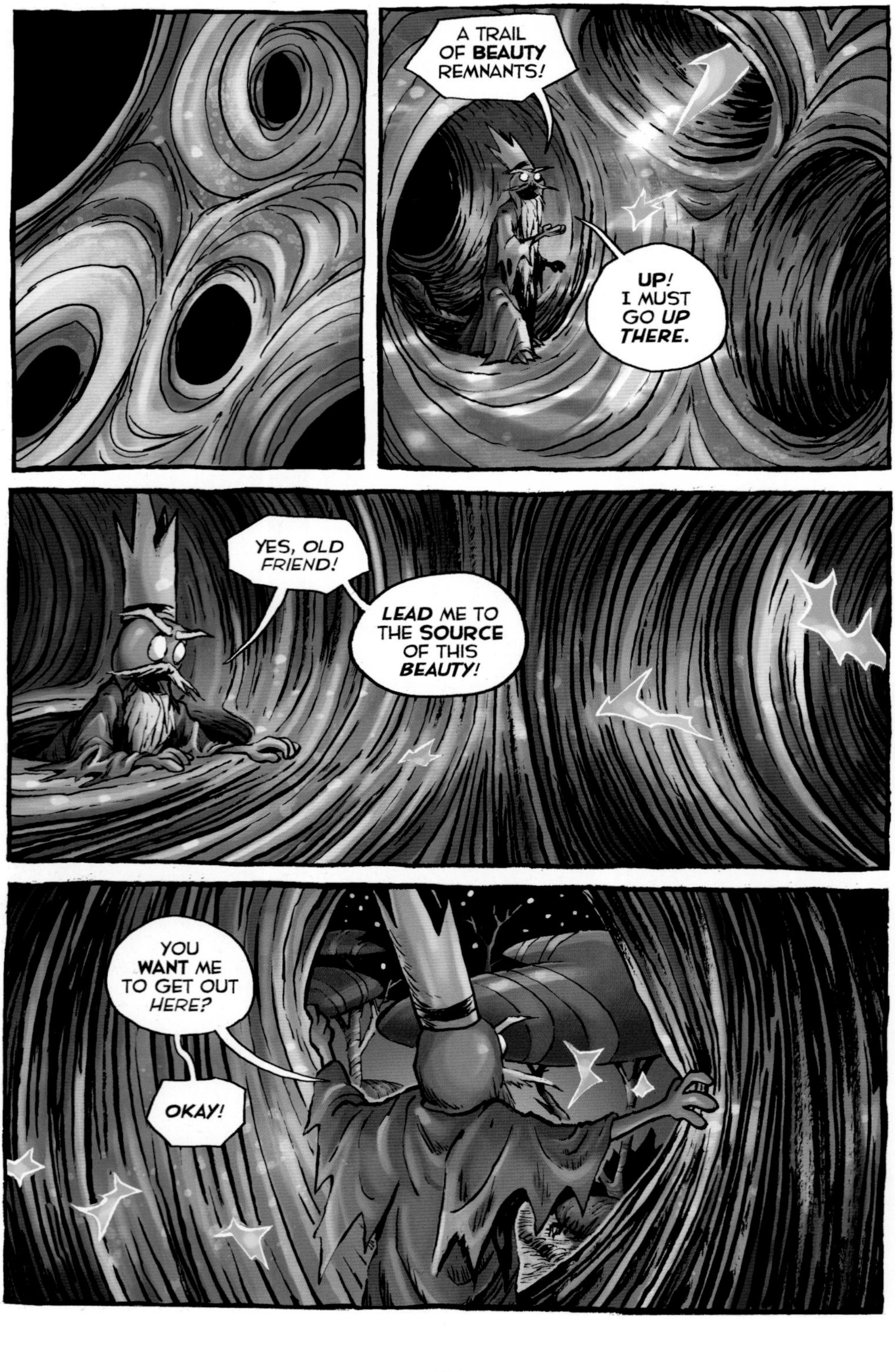
A TRAIL OF **BEAUTY** REMNANTS!
UP! I MUST GO ***UP THERE***.
YES, OLD FRIEND!
LEAD ME TO THE **SOURCE** OF THIS ***BEAUTY***!
YOU **WANT** ME TO GET OUT *HERE?*
OKAY!

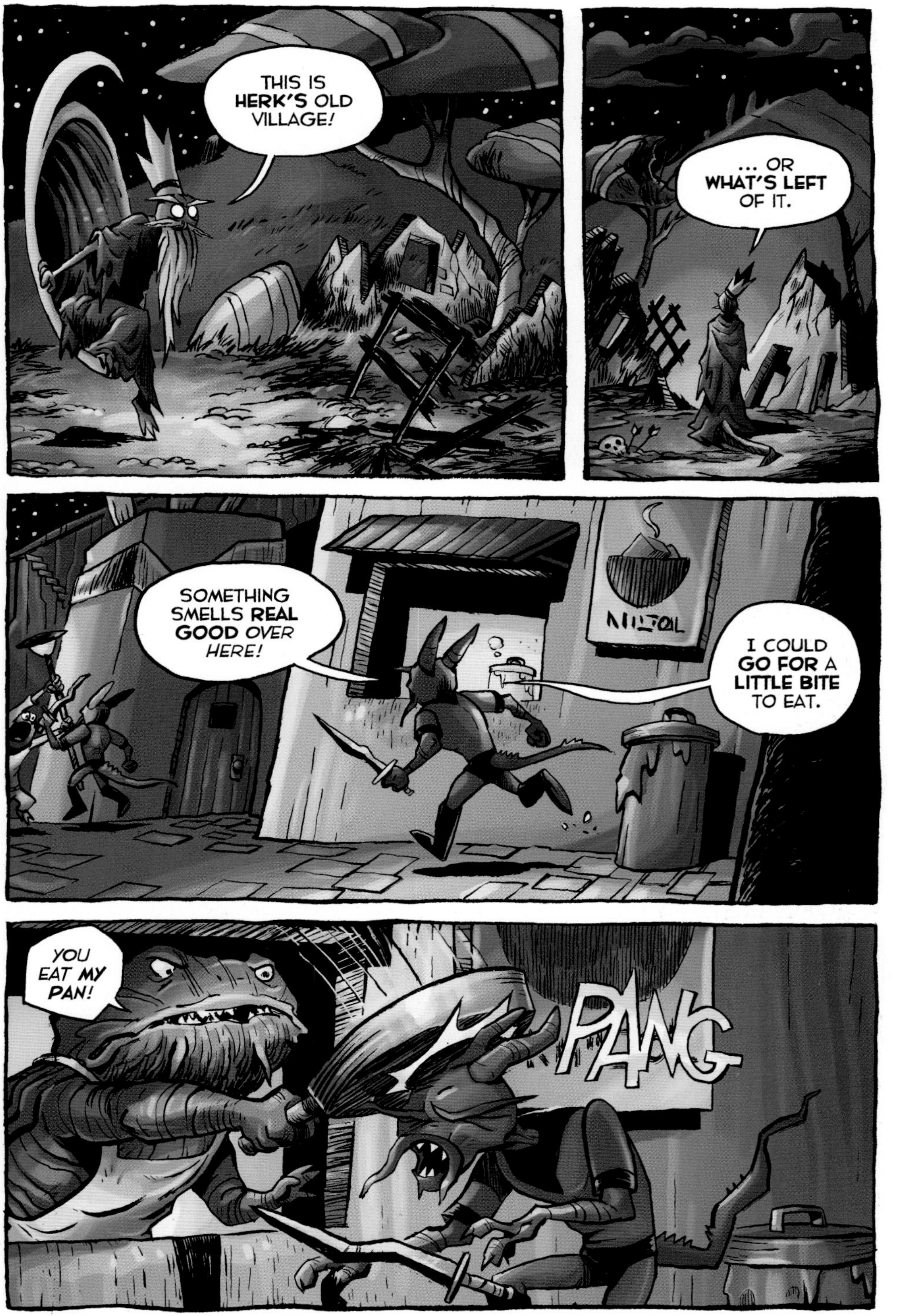
THIS IS HERK'S OLD VILLAGE!
... OR WHAT'S LEFT OF IT.
SOMETHING SMELLS REAL GOOD OVER HERE!
I COULD GO FOR A LITTLE BITE TO EAT.
YOU EAT MY PAN!
PANG

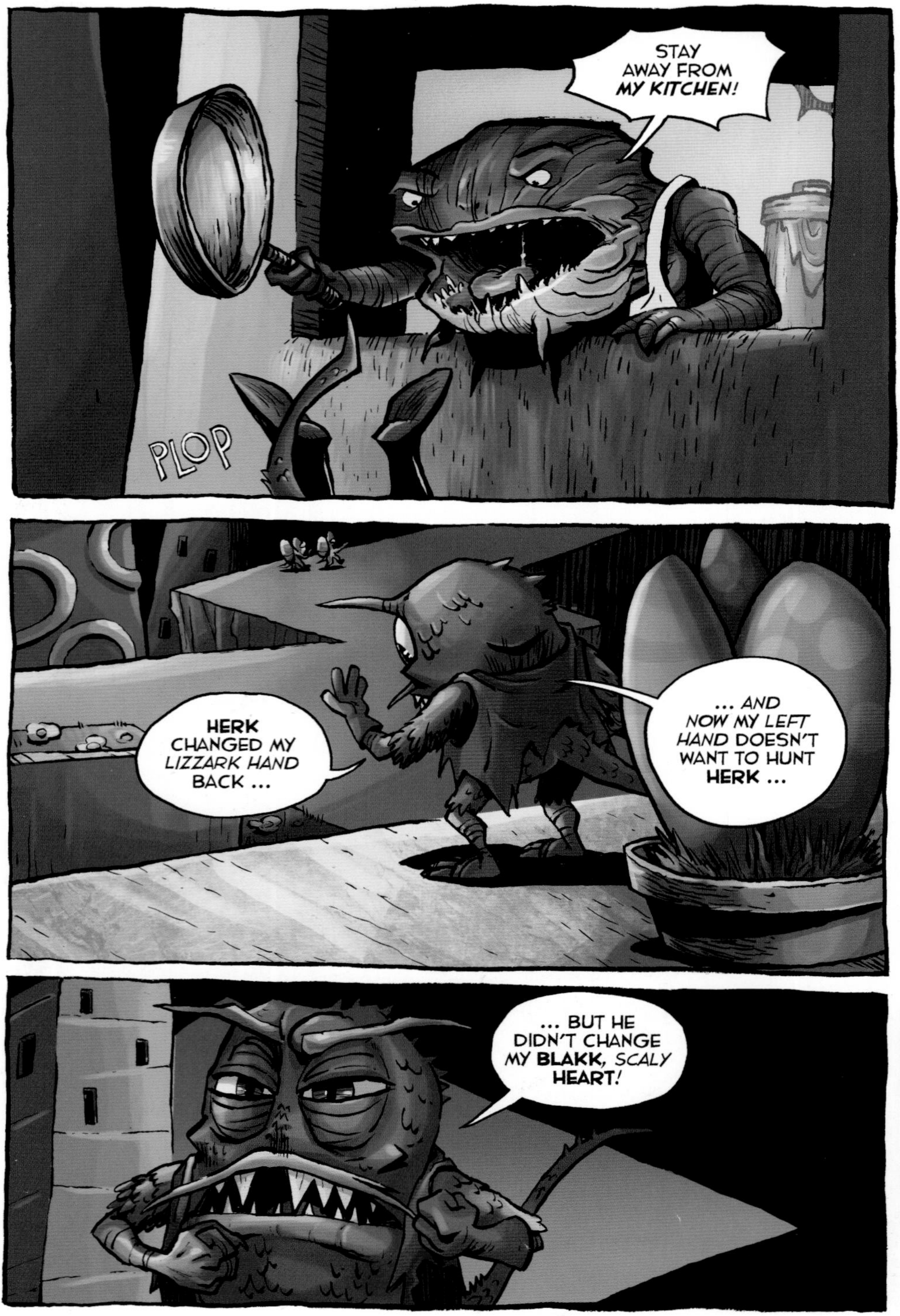
STAY AWAY FROM MY KITCHEN!
PLOP
HERK CHANGED MY LIZZARK HAND BACK ...
... AND NOW MY LEFT HAND DOESN'T WANT TO HUNT HERK ...
... BUT HE DIDN'T CHANGE MY BLAKK, SCALY HEART!

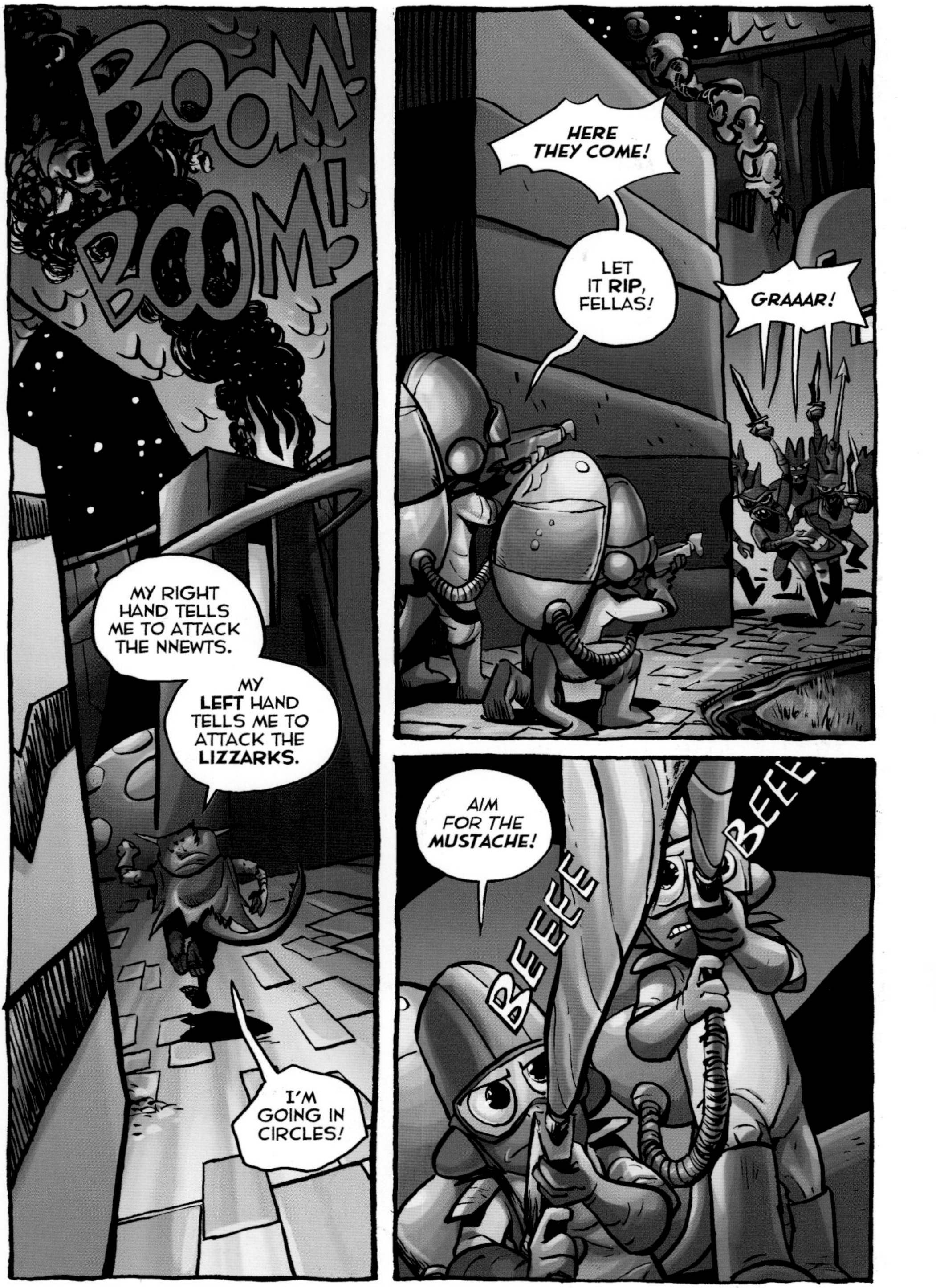
BOOM!
BOOM!
MY RIGHT HAND TELLS ME TO ATTACK THE NNEWTS.
MY LEFT HAND TELLS ME TO ATTACK THE LIZZARKS.
I'M GOING IN CIRCLES!
HERE THEY COME!
LET IT RIP, FELLAS!
GRAAAR!
AIM FOR THE MUSTACHE!
BEEEE
BEEEE

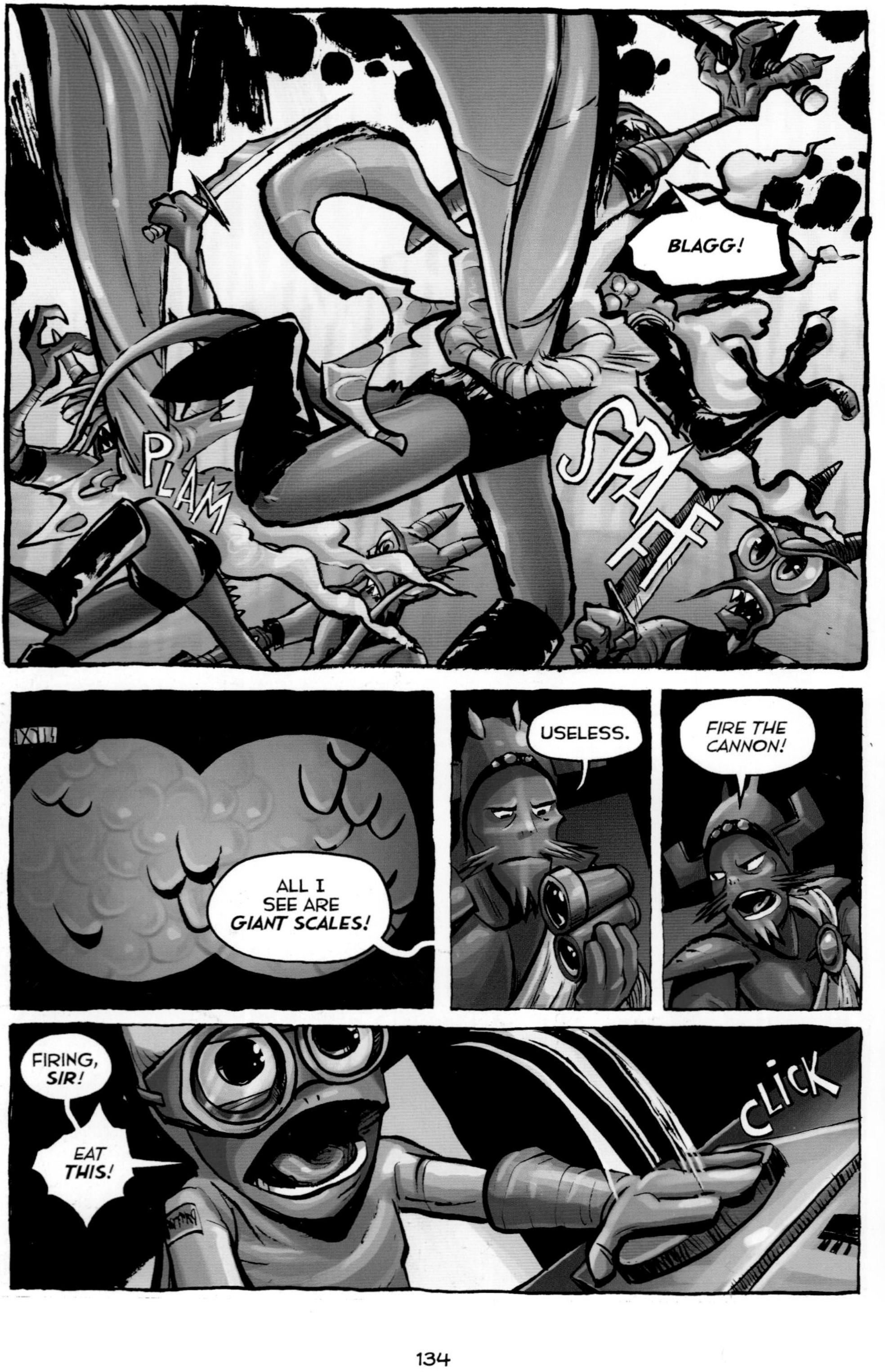

BLAGG!
PLAM
SPAFF
ALL I SEE ARE GIANT SCALES!
USELESS.
FIRE THE CANNON!
FIRING, SIR!
EAT THIS!
CLICK

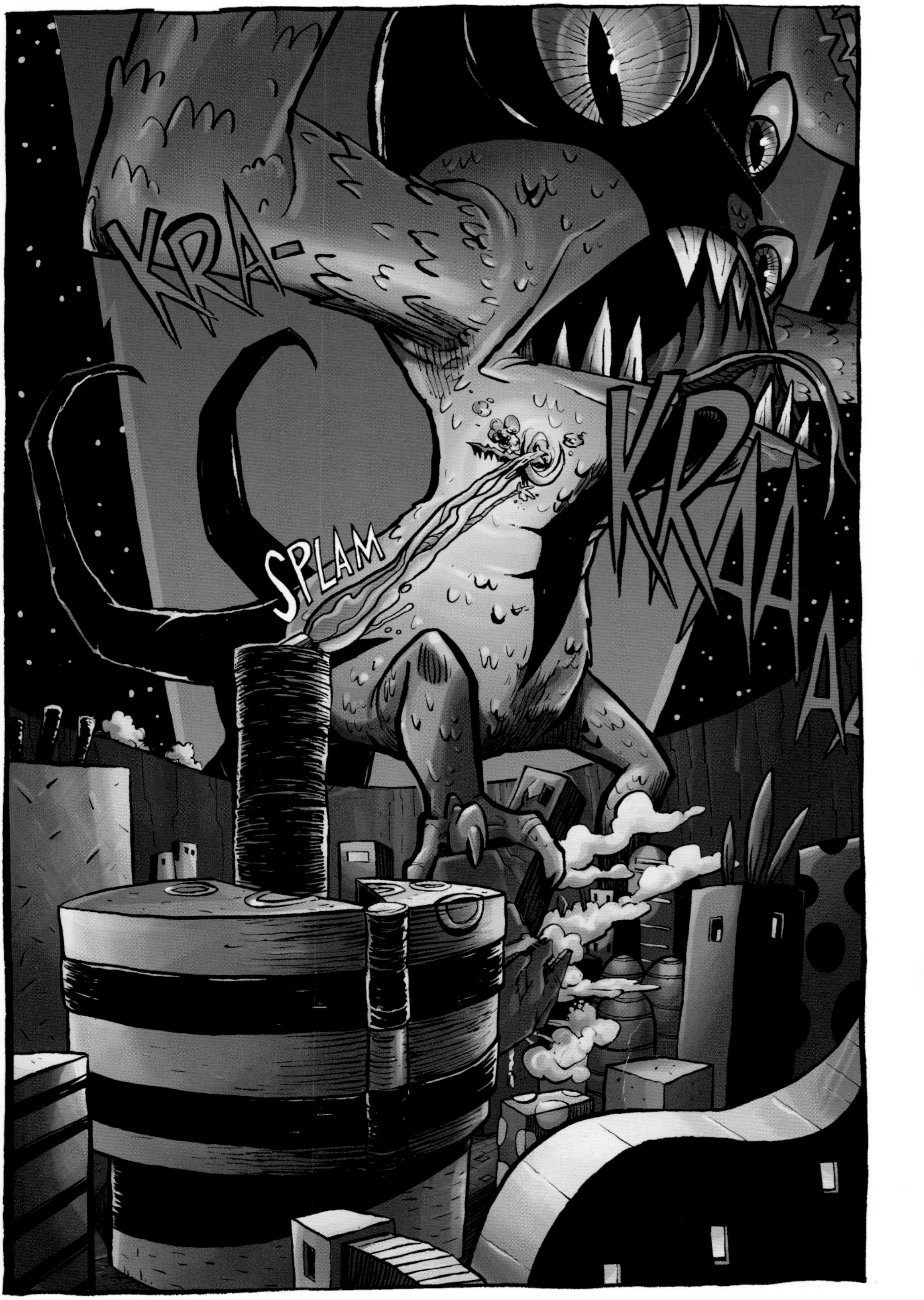
KRA-
KRAAAA
SPLAM

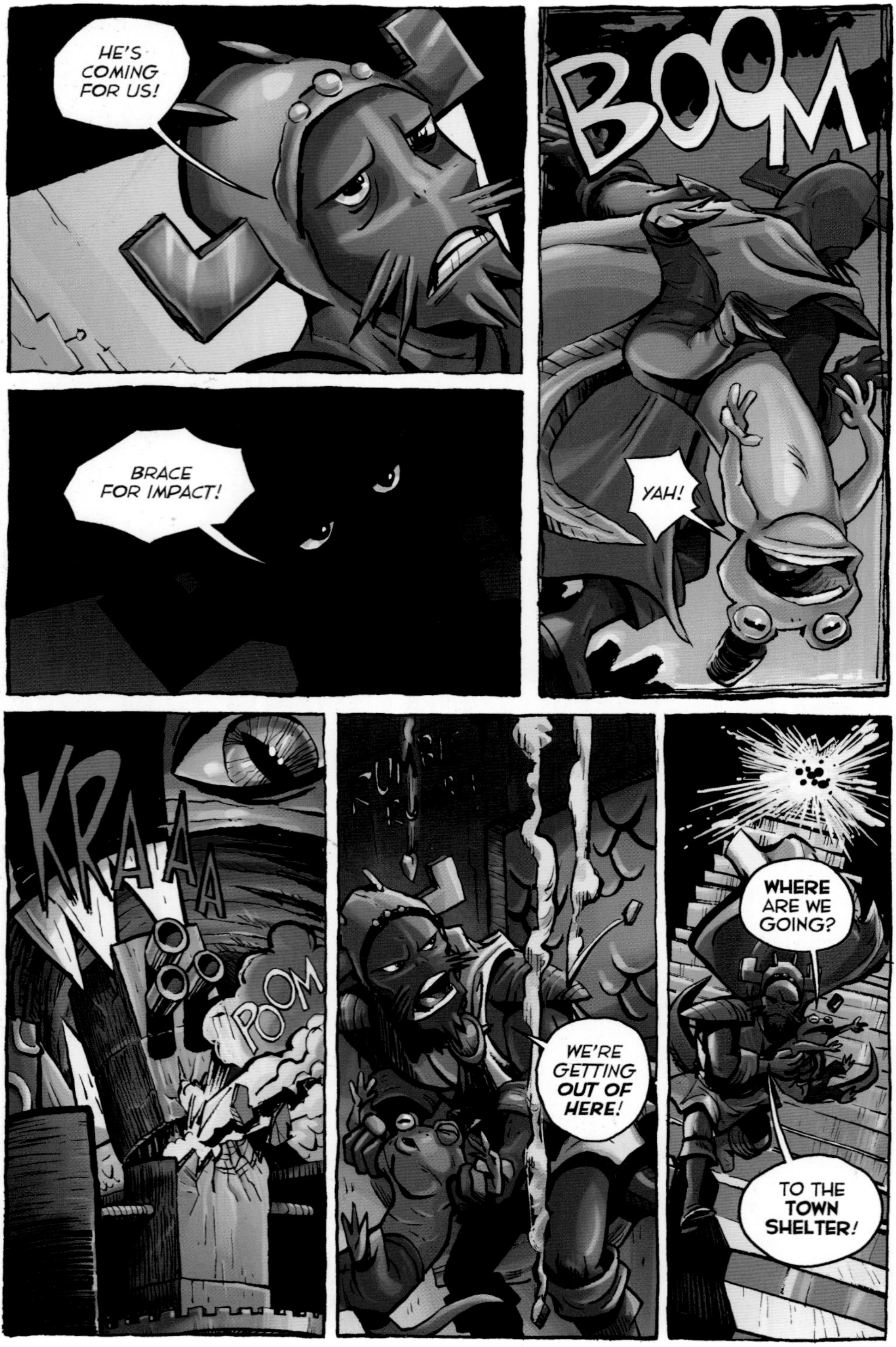
HE'S COMING FOR US!
BRACE FOR IMPACT!
BOOM
YAH!
KRAAAA
POOM
WE'RE GETTING OUT OF HERE!
WHERE ARE WE GOING?
TO THE TOWN SHELTER!

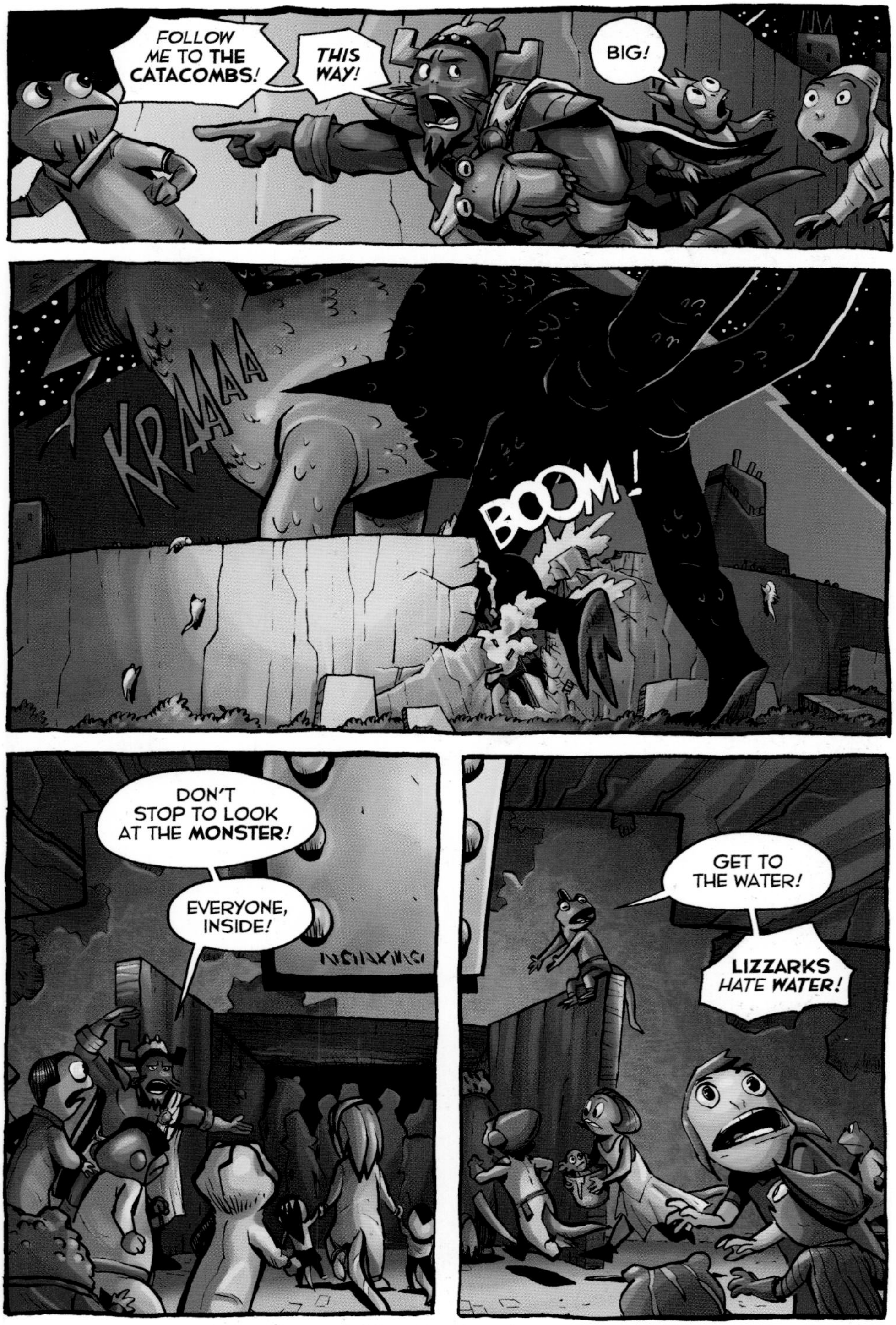
FOLLOW ME TO THE CATACOMBS!
THIS WAY!
BIG!
KRAAAA
BOOM!
DON'T STOP TO LOOK AT THE MONSTER!
EVERYONE, INSIDE!
GET TO THE WATER!
LIZZARKS HATE WATER!

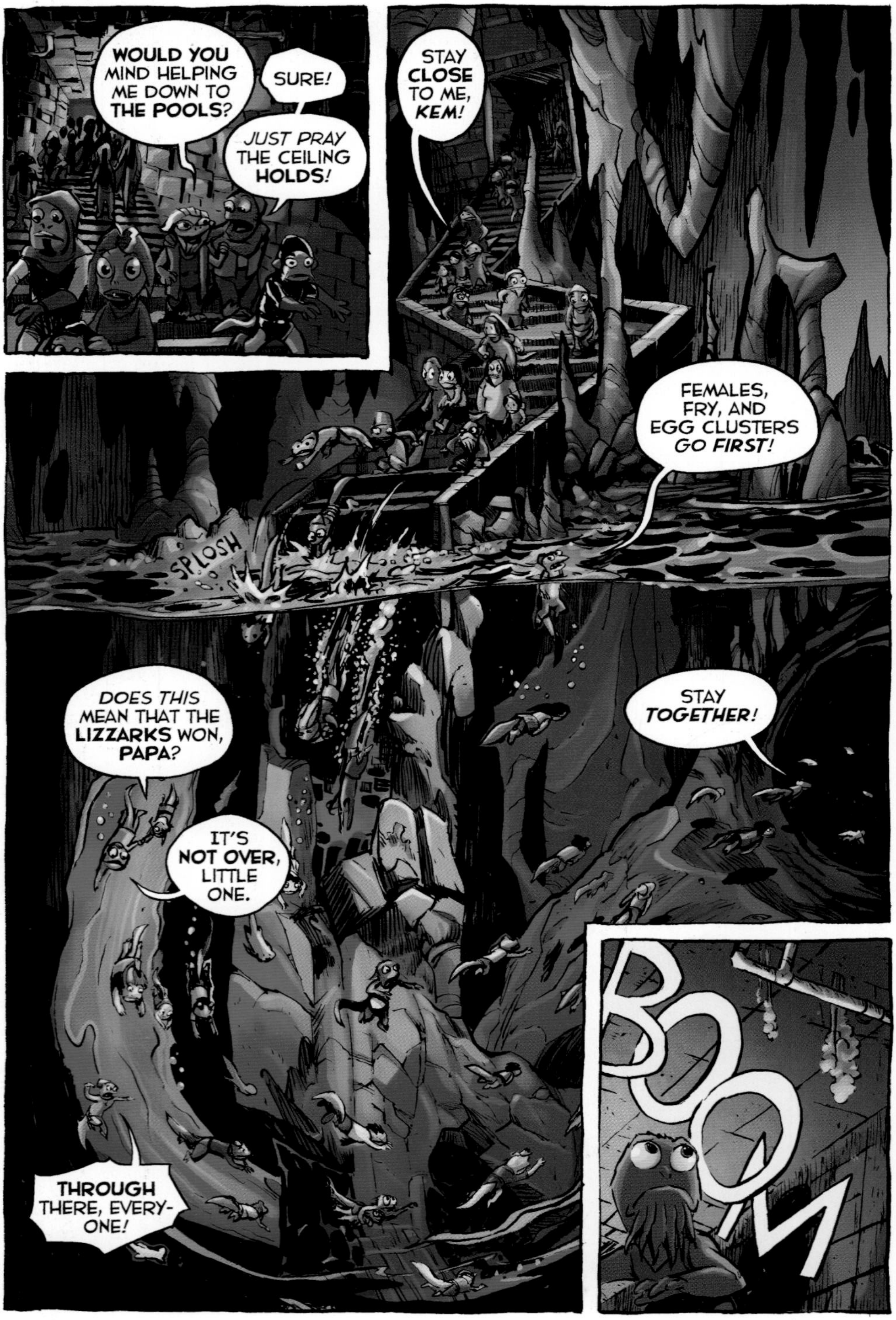
WOULD YOU MIND HELPING ME DOWN TO THE POOLS?
SURE!
JUST PRAY THE CEILING HOLDS!
STAY CLOSE TO ME, KEM!
FEMALES, FRY, AND EGG CLUSTERS GO FIRST!
SPLOSH
DOES THIS MEAN THAT THE LIZZARKS WON, PAPA?
IT'S NOT OVER, LITTLE ONE.
STAY TOGETHER!
THROUGH THERE, EVERY-ONE!
BOOM

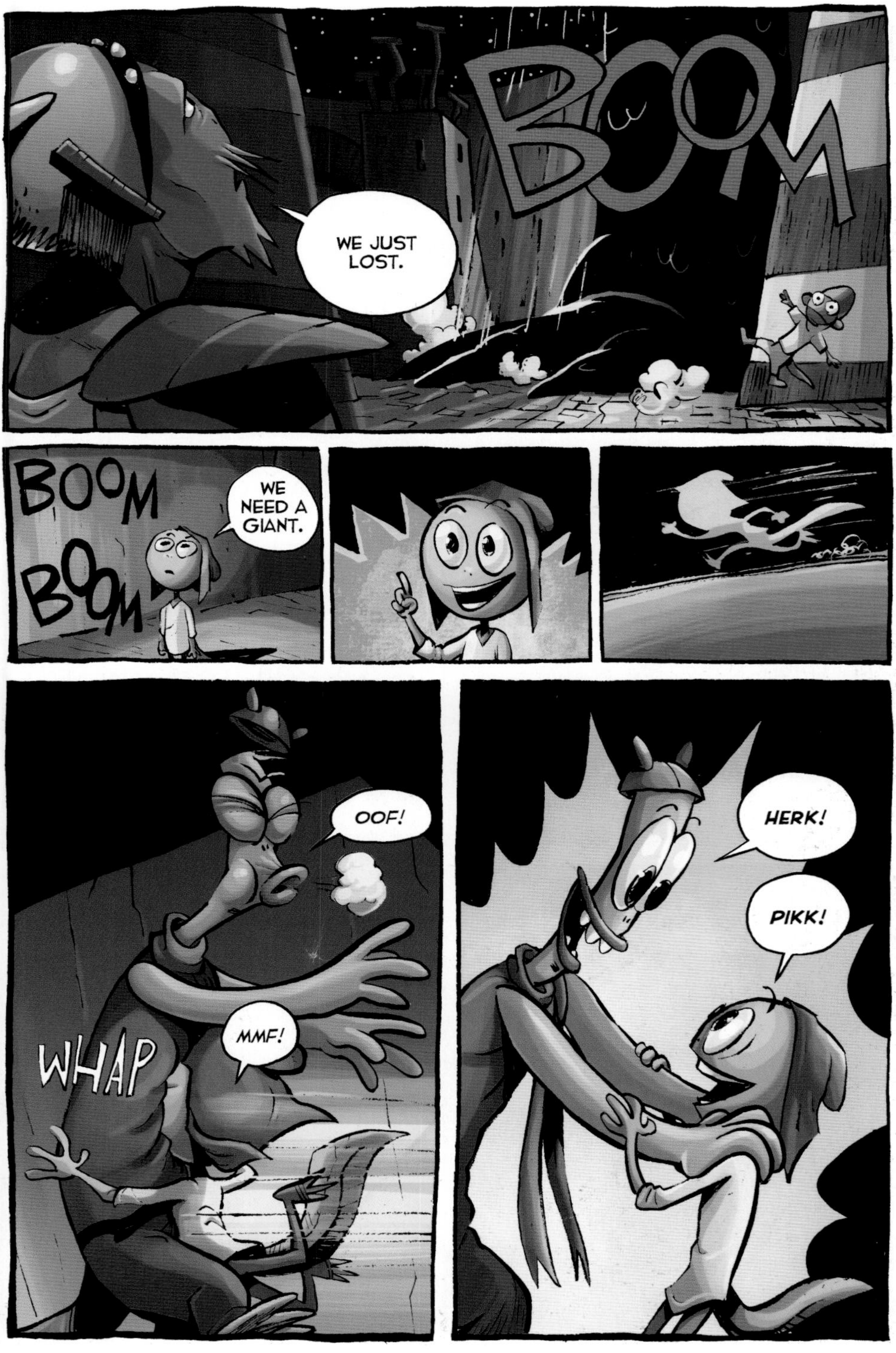
BOOM
WE JUST LOST.
BOOM
BOOM
WE NEED A GIANT.
OOF!
WHAP
MMF!
HERK!
PIKK!

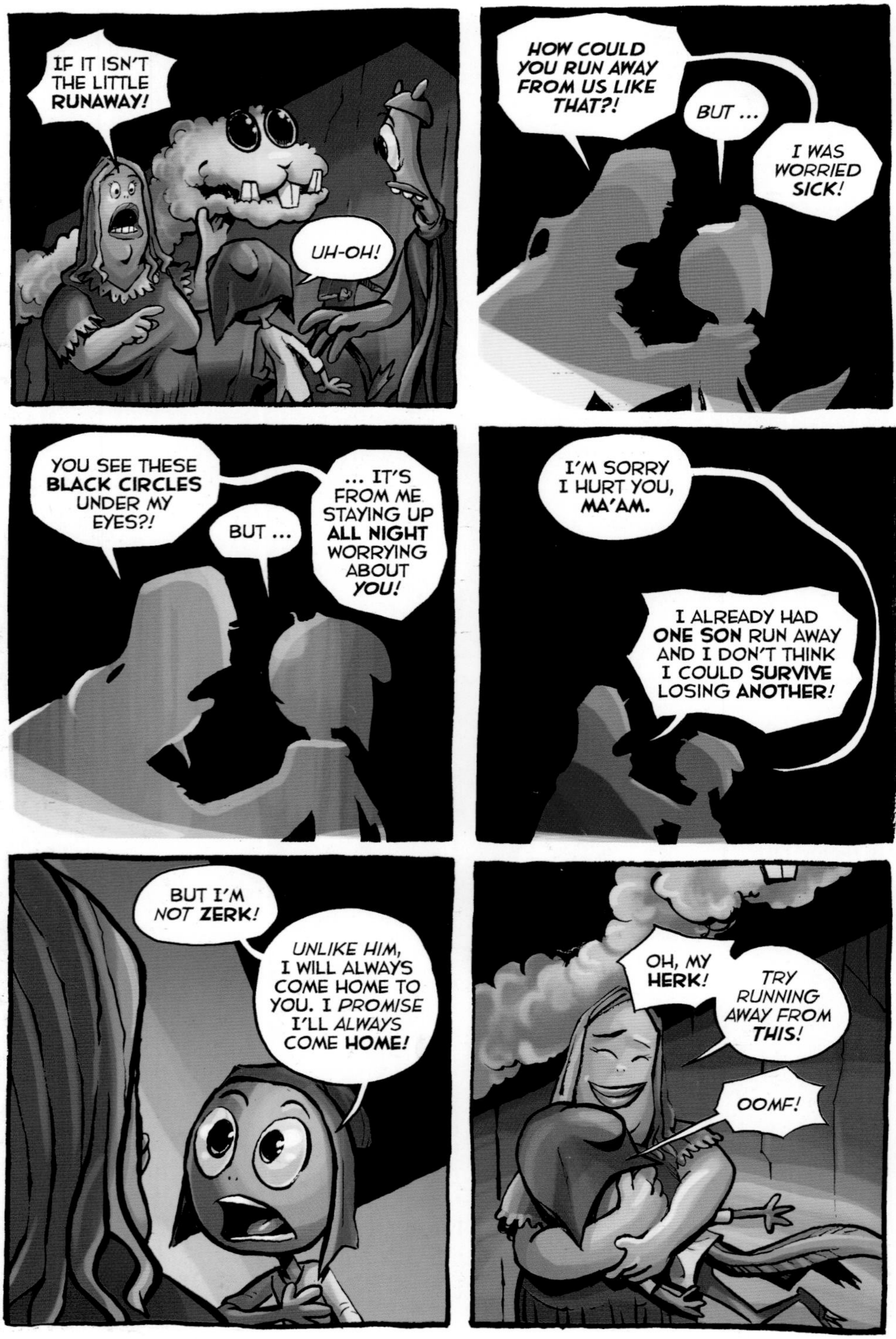
IF IT ISN'T THE LITTLE RUNAWAY!
UH-OH!
HOW COULD YOU RUN AWAY FROM US LIKE THAT?!
BUT ...
I WAS WORRIED SICK!
YOU SEE THESE BLACK CIRCLES UNDER MY EYES?!
BUT ...
... IT'S FROM ME STAYING UP ALL NIGHT WORRYING ABOUT YOU!
I'M SORRY I HURT YOU, MA'AM.
I ALREADY HAD ONE SON RUN AWAY AND I DON'T THINK I COULD SURVIVE LOSING ANOTHER!
BUT I'M NOT ZERK!
UNLIKE HIM, I WILL ALWAYS COME HOME TO YOU. I PROMISE I'LL ALWAYS COME HOME!
OH, MY HERK!
TRY RUNNING AWAY FROM THIS!
OOMF!

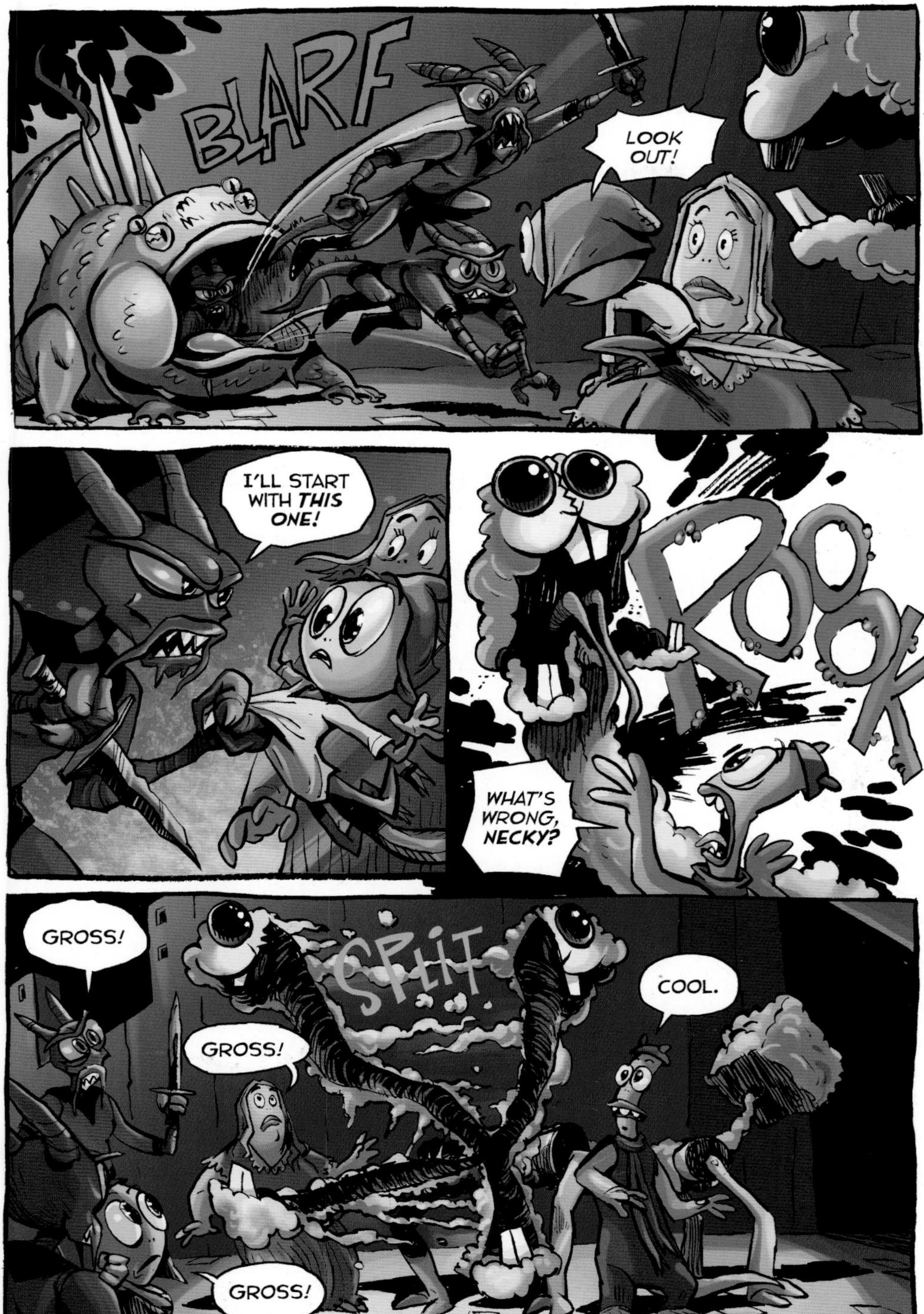
BLARF
LOOK OUT!
I'LL START WITH THIS ONE!
ROOOK
WHAT'S WRONG, NECKY?
GROSS!
SPLIT
GROSS!
COOL.
GROSS!

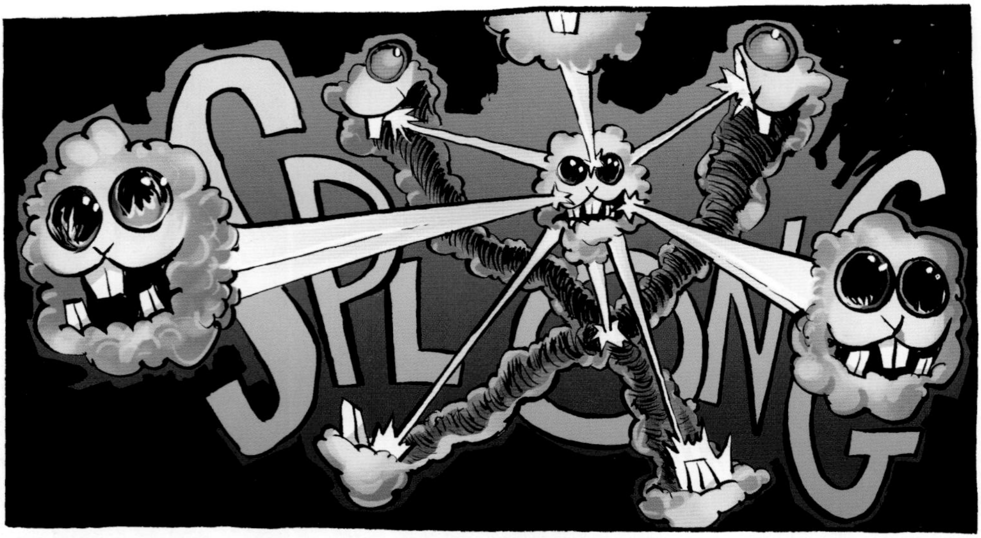
SPLOONG

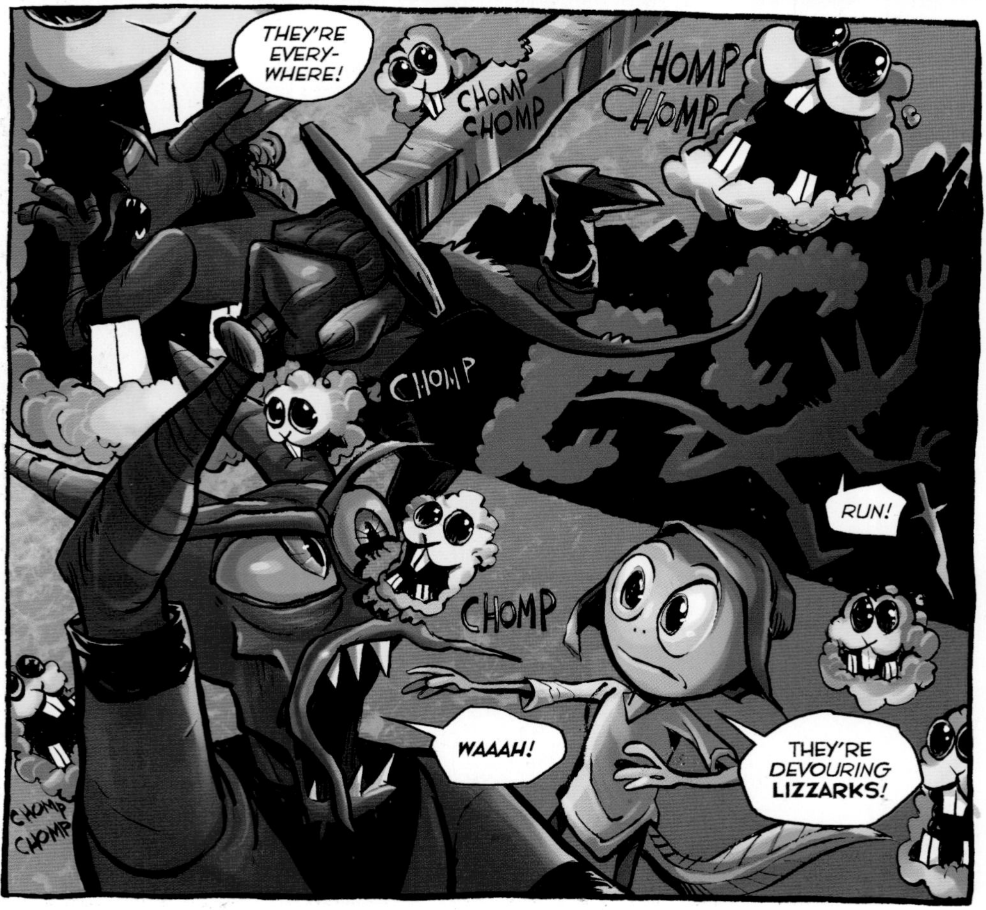
THEY'RE EVERY-WHERE!
CHOMP CHOMP
CHOMP CHOMP
CHOMP
RUN!
CHOMP
WAAAH!
THEY'RE DEVOURING LIZZARKS!
CHOMP CHOMP

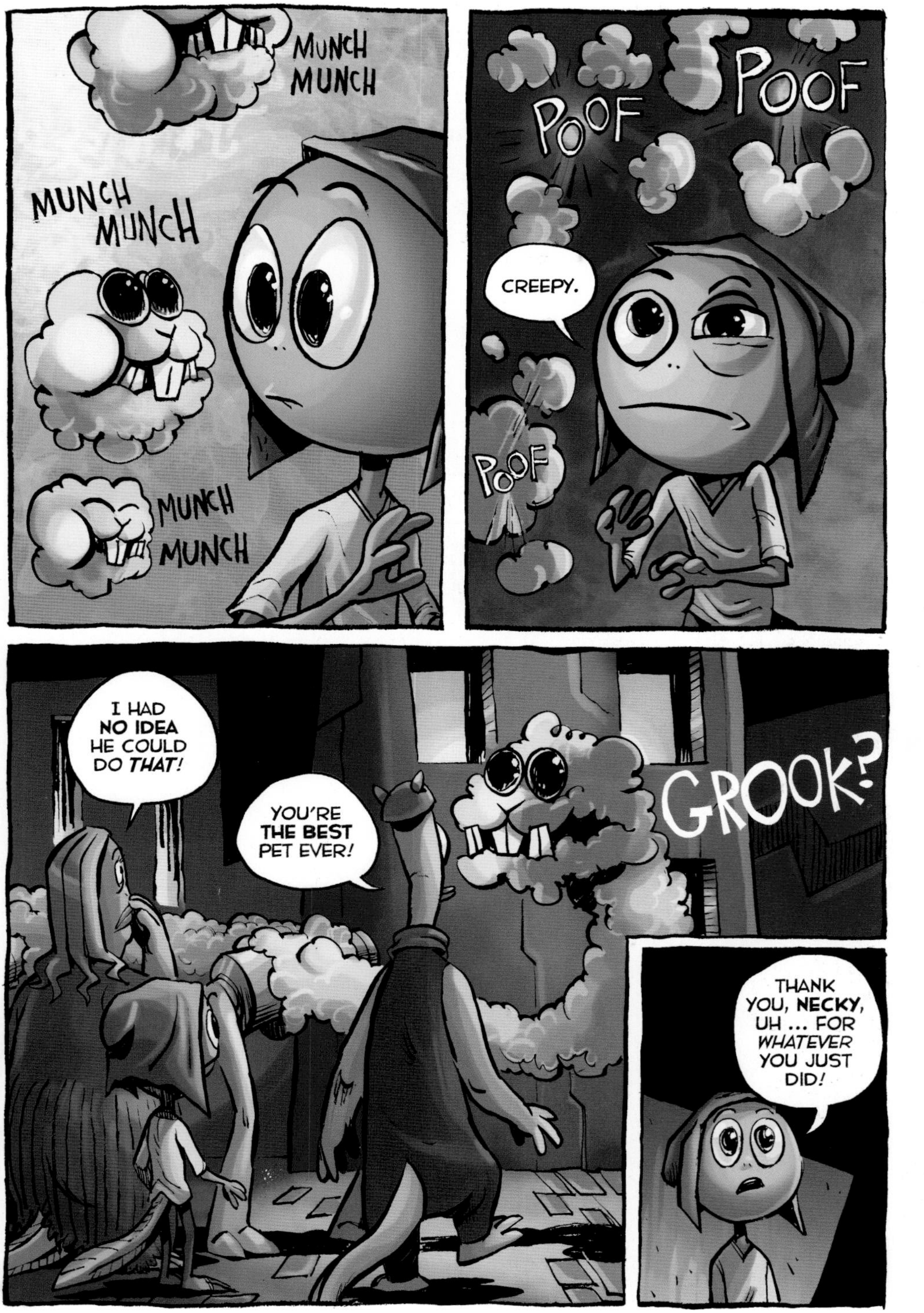
MUNCH MUNCH
MUNCH MUNCH
MUNCH MUNCH
POOF
POOF
CREEPY.
POOF
I HAD NO IDEA HE COULD DO THAT!
YOU'RE THE BEST PET EVER!
GROOK?
THANK YOU, NECKY, UH ... FOR WHATEVER YOU JUST DID!

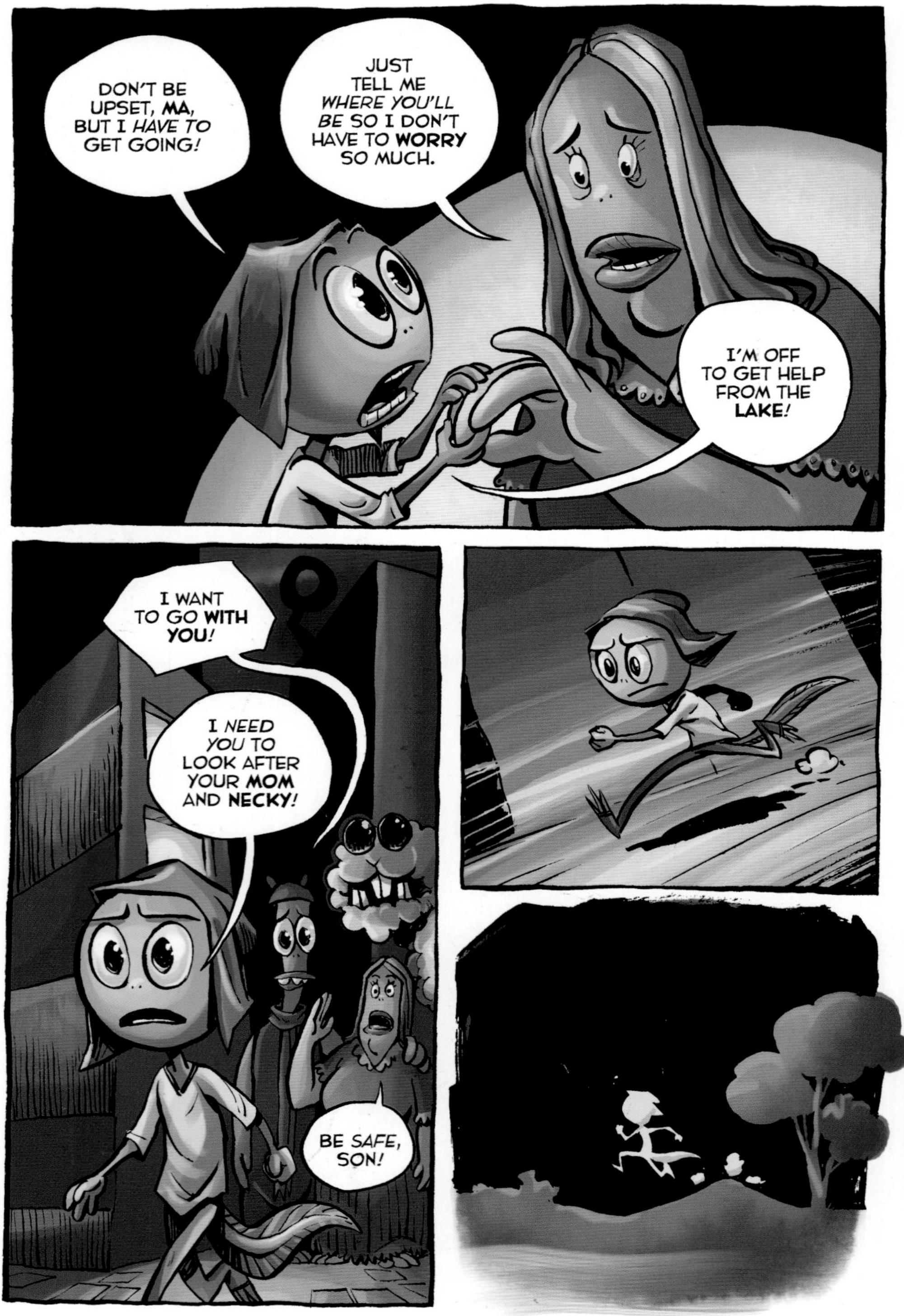
DON'T BE UPSET, MA, BUT I HAVE TO GET GOING!
JUST TELL ME WHERE YOU'LL BE SO I DON'T HAVE TO WORRY SO MUCH.
I'M OFF TO GET HELP FROM THE LAKE!
I WANT TO GO WITH YOU!
I NEED YOU TO LOOK AFTER YOUR MOM AND NECKY!
BE SAFE, SON!

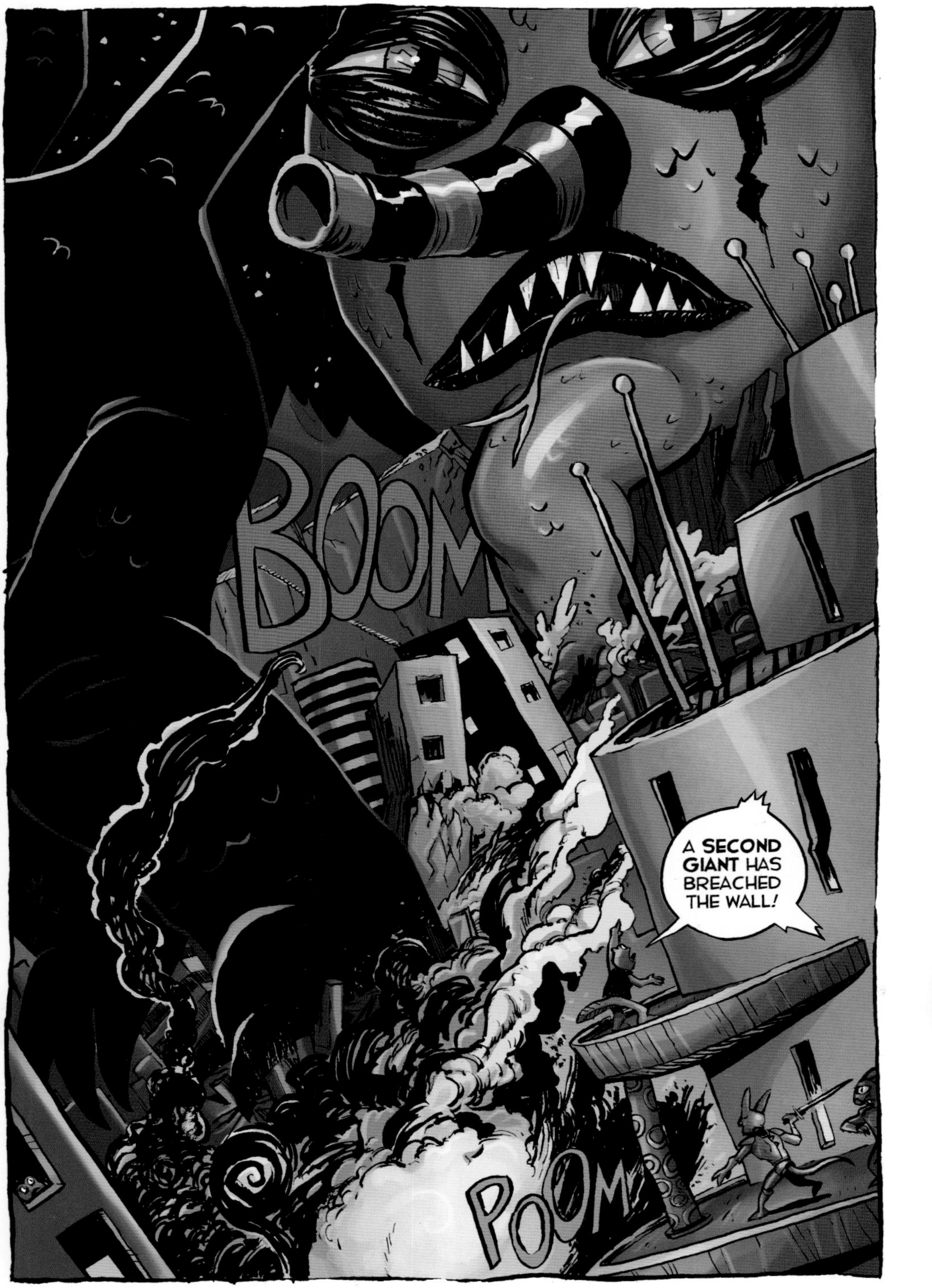
BOOM
A SECOND GIANT HAS BREACHED THE WALL!
POOM

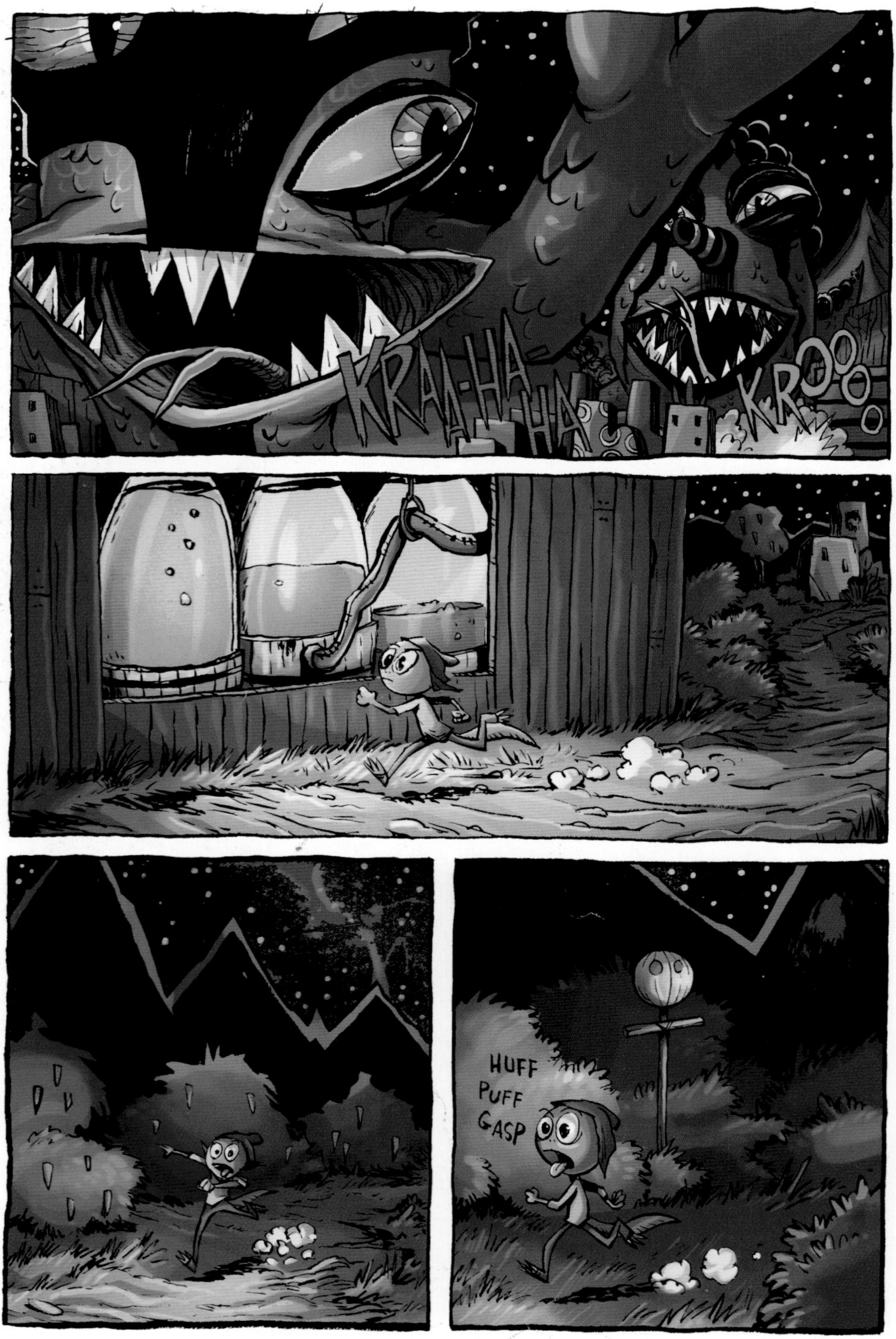
KRAA-HA-HA-HA
KROOOO
HUFF
PUFF
GASP

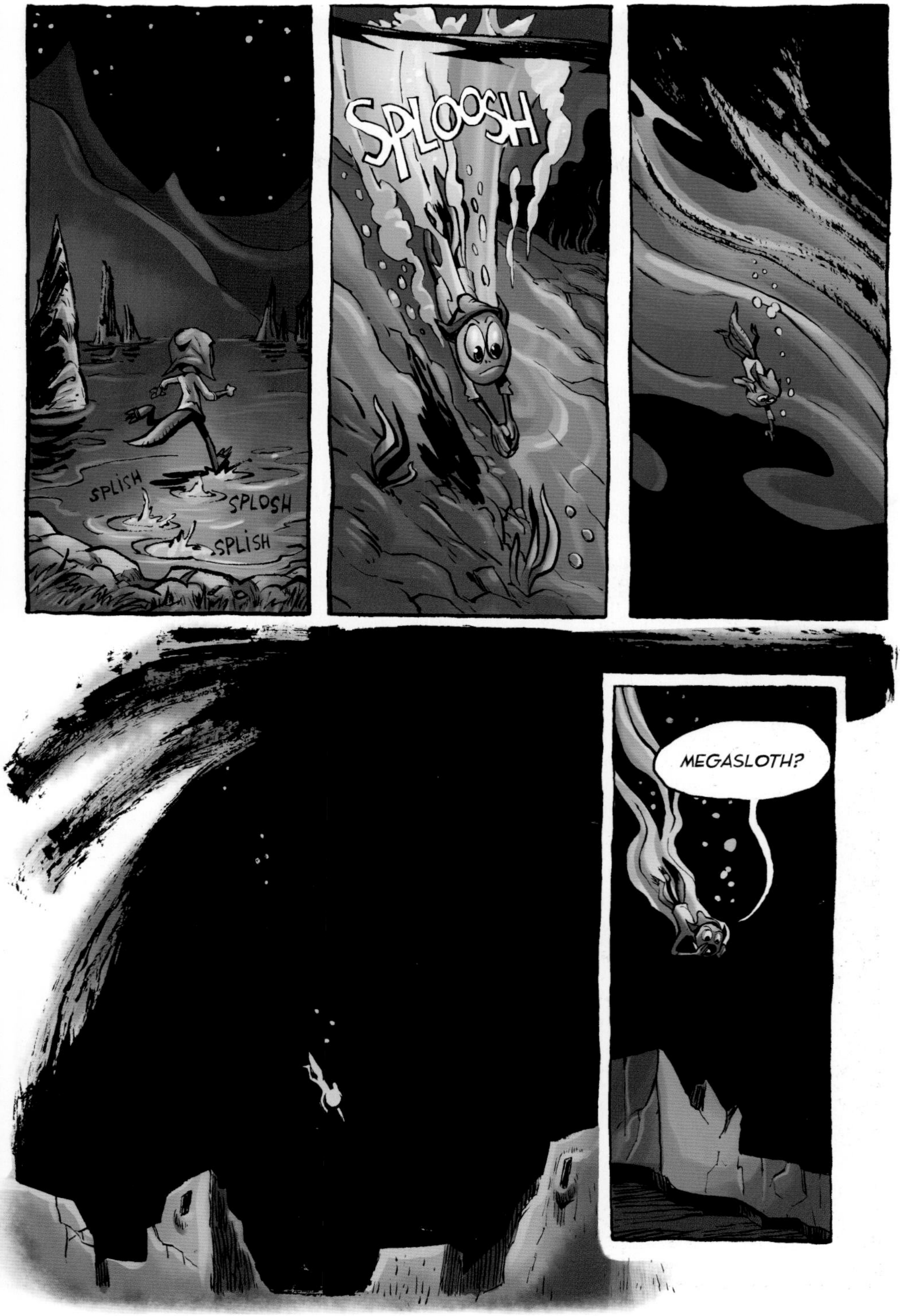
SPLISH
SPLOSH
SPLISH
SPLOOSH
MEGASLOTH?

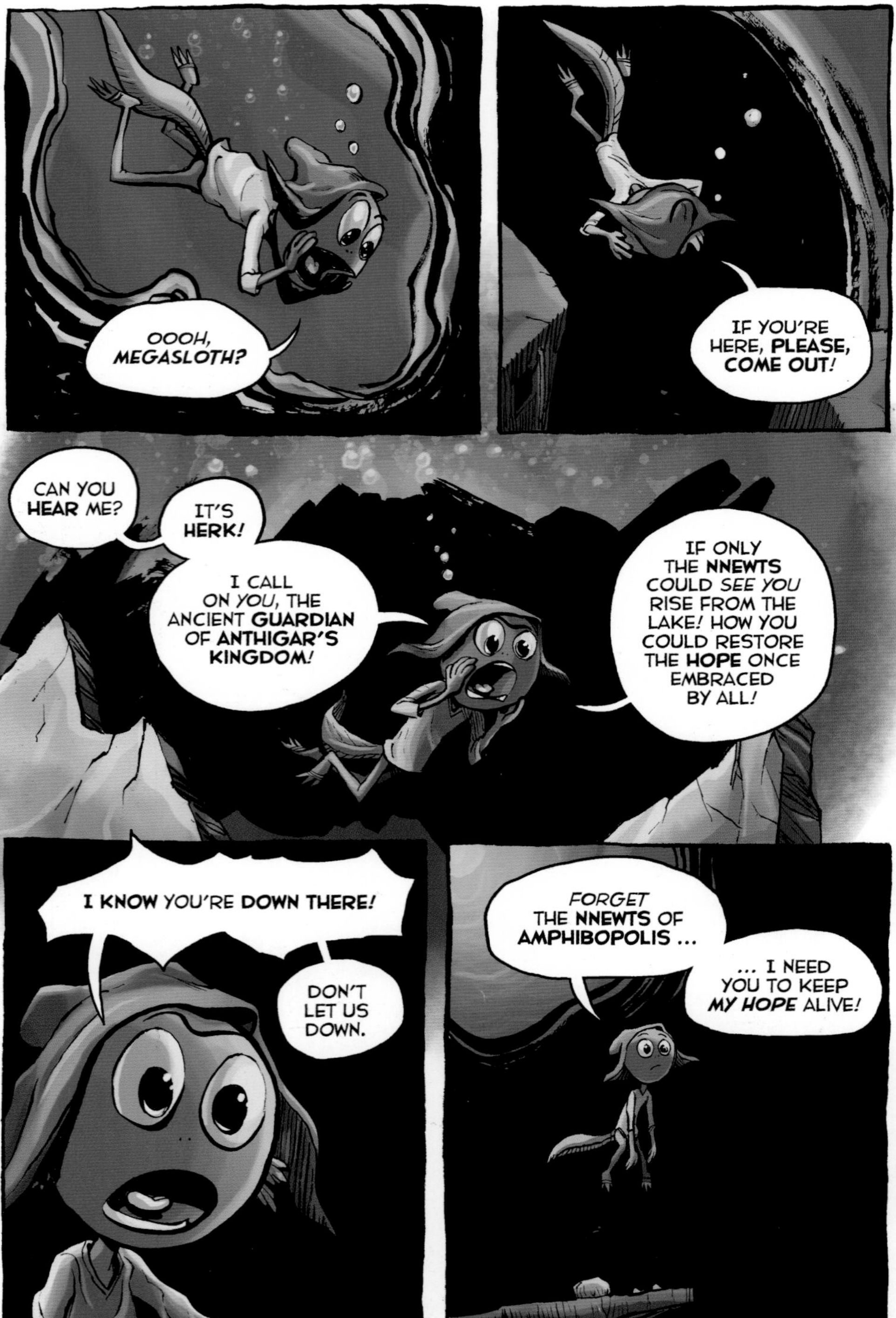
OOOH, MEGASLOTH?
IF YOU'RE HERE, PLEASE, COME OUT!
CAN YOU HEAR ME?
IT'S HERK!
I CALL ON YOU, THE ANCIENT GUARDIAN OF ANTHIGAR'S KINGDOM!
IF ONLY THE NNEWTS COULD SEE YOU RISE FROM THE LAKE! HOW YOU COULD RESTORE THE HOPE ONCE EMBRACED BY ALL!
I KNOW YOU'RE DOWN THERE!
DON'T LET US DOWN.
FORGET THE NNEWTS OF AMPHIBOPOLIS ...
... I NEED YOU TO KEEP MY HOPE ALIVE!

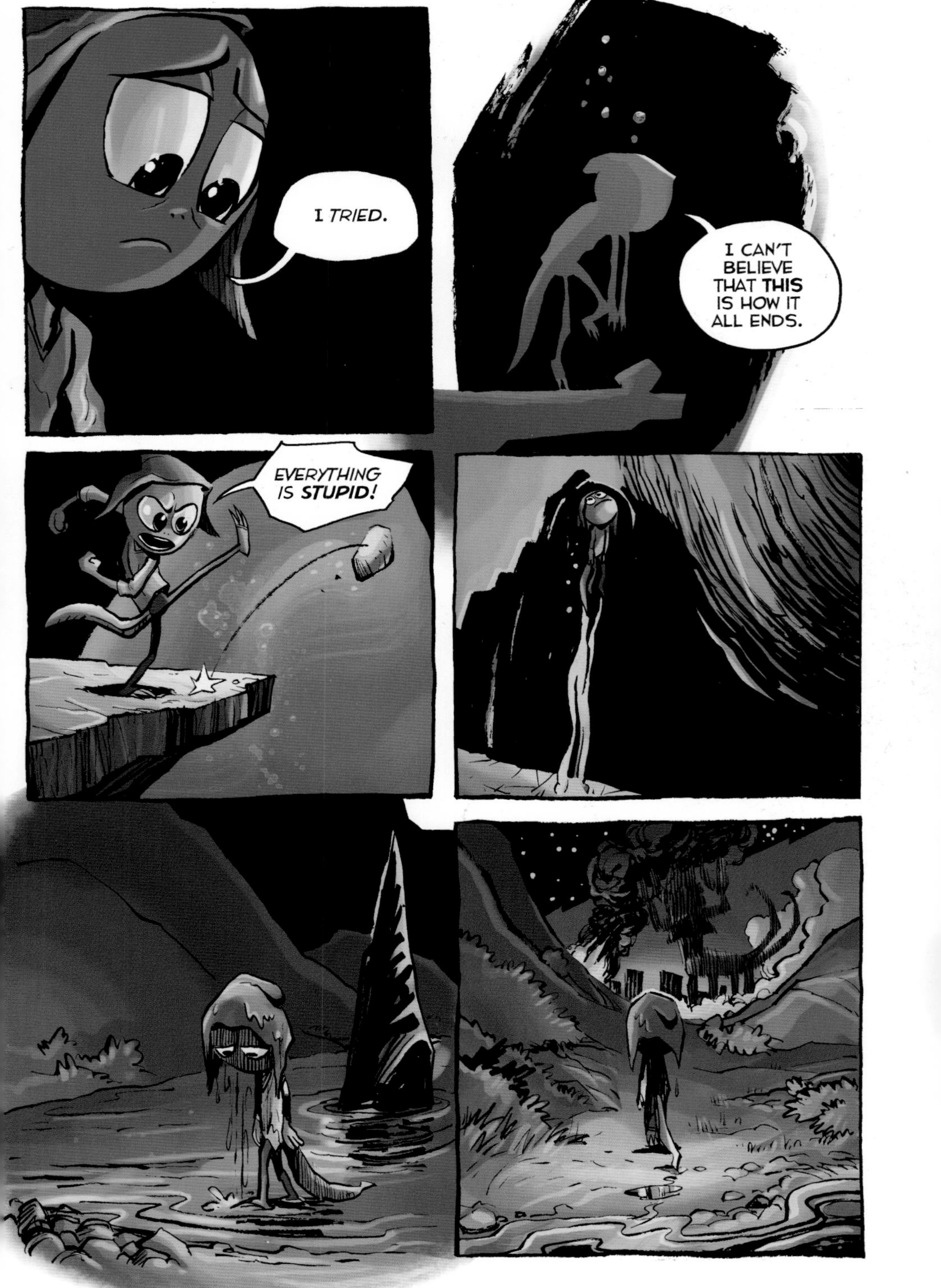
I *TRIED.*
I CAN'T BELIEVE THAT **THIS** IS HOW IT ALL ENDS.
EVERYTHING IS ***STUPID!***

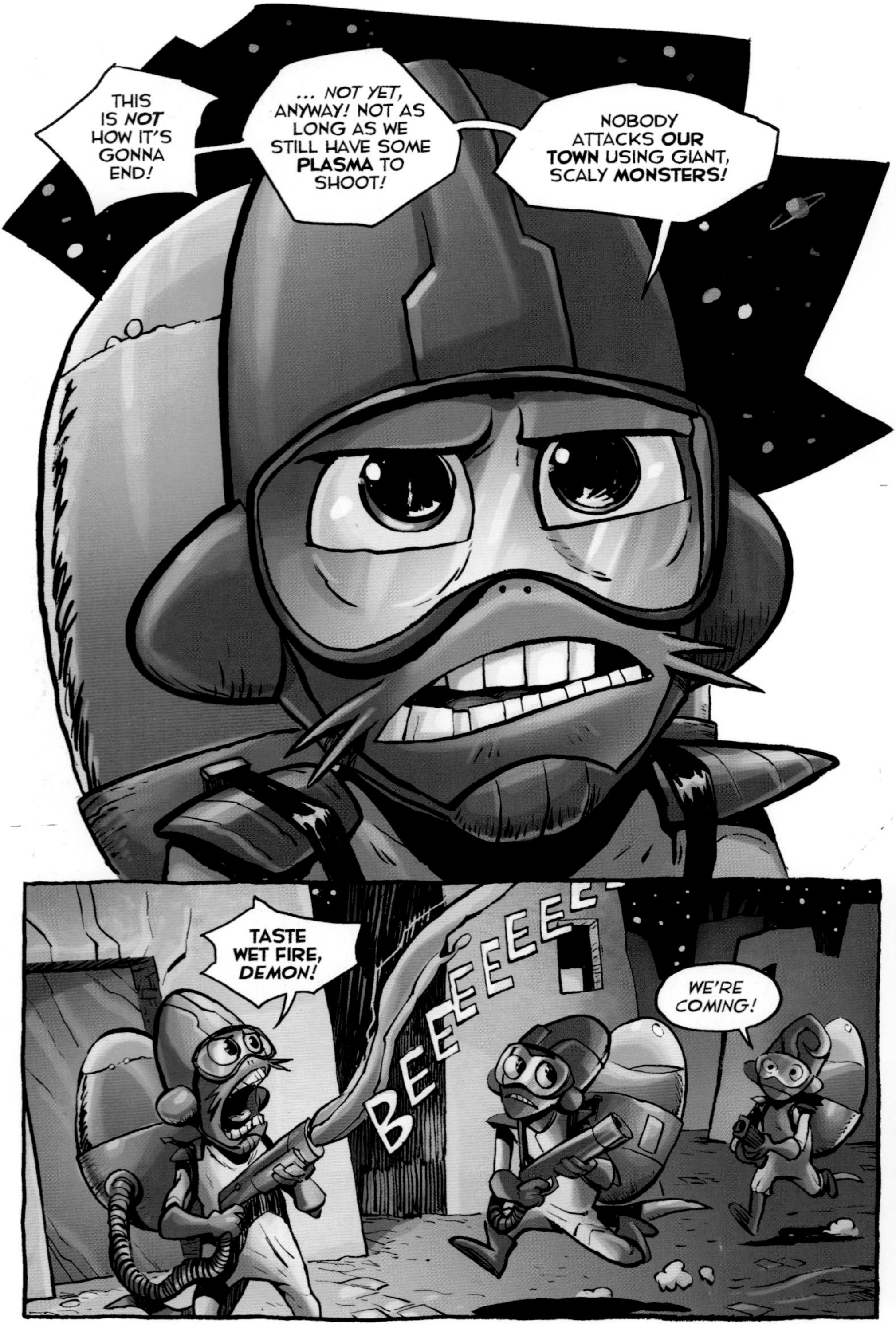
THIS IS *NOT* HOW IT'S GONNA END!
... *NOT YET,* ANYWAY! NOT AS LONG AS WE STILL HAVE SOME **PLASMA** TO SHOOT!
NOBODY ATTACKS **OUR TOWN** USING GIANT, SCALY **MONSTERS!**
TASTE WET FIRE, *DEMON!*
BEEEEEEEEE
WE'RE COMING!

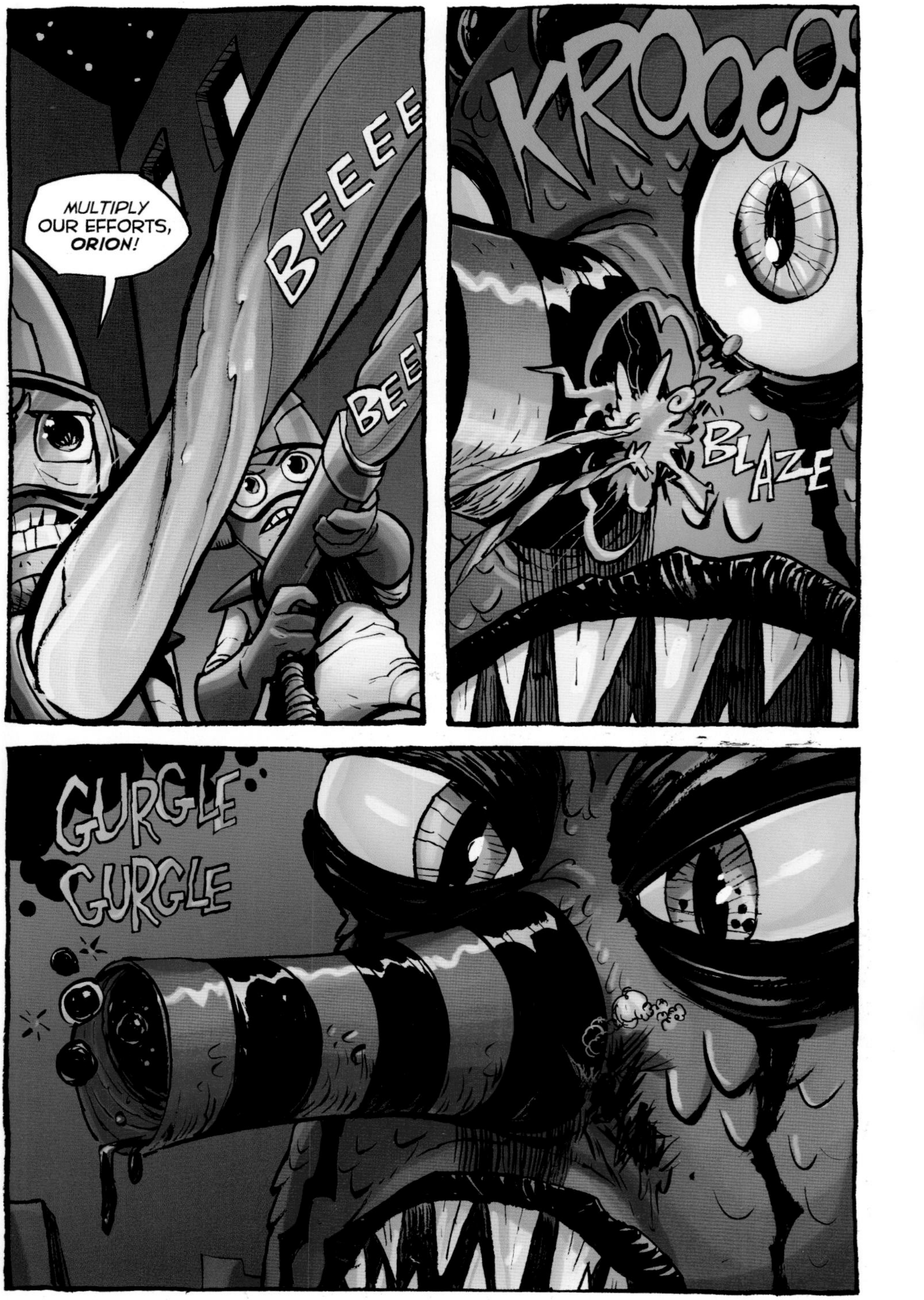
MULTIPLY OUR EFFORTS, ORION!
BEEEE
BEE
KROOOO
BLAZE
GURGLE GURGLE

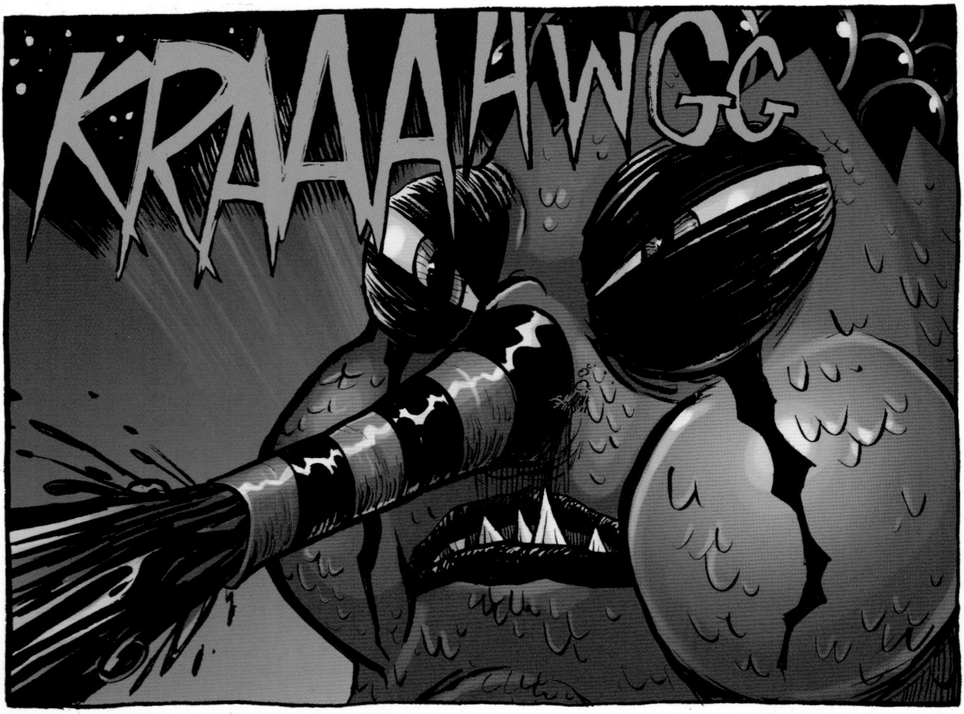
KRAAAHWGG

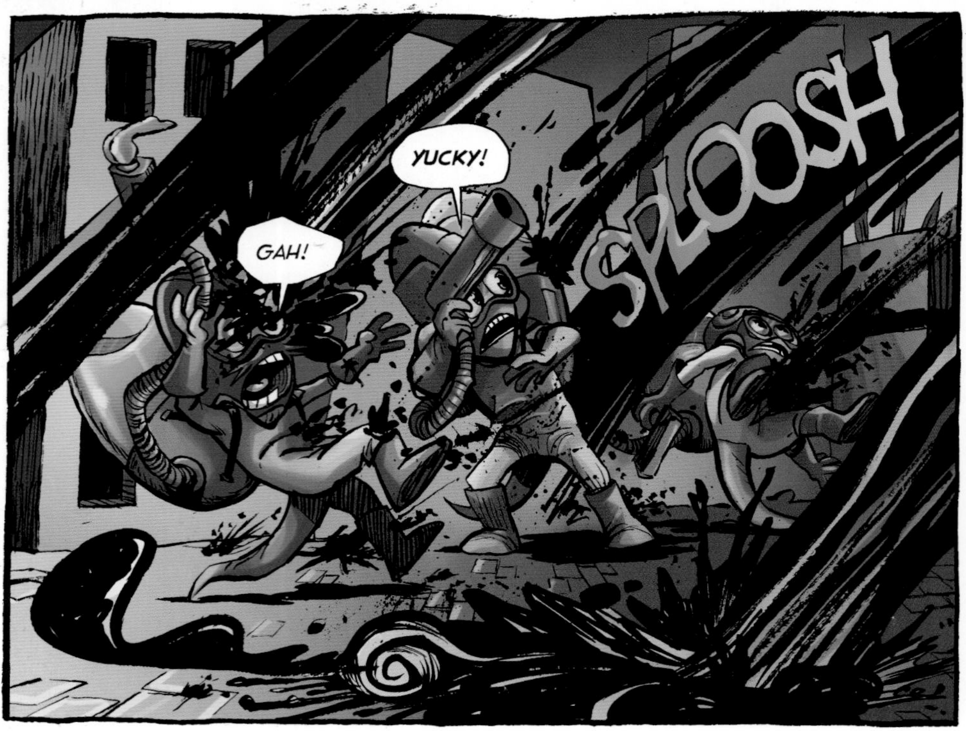
GAH!
YUCKY!
SPLOOSH

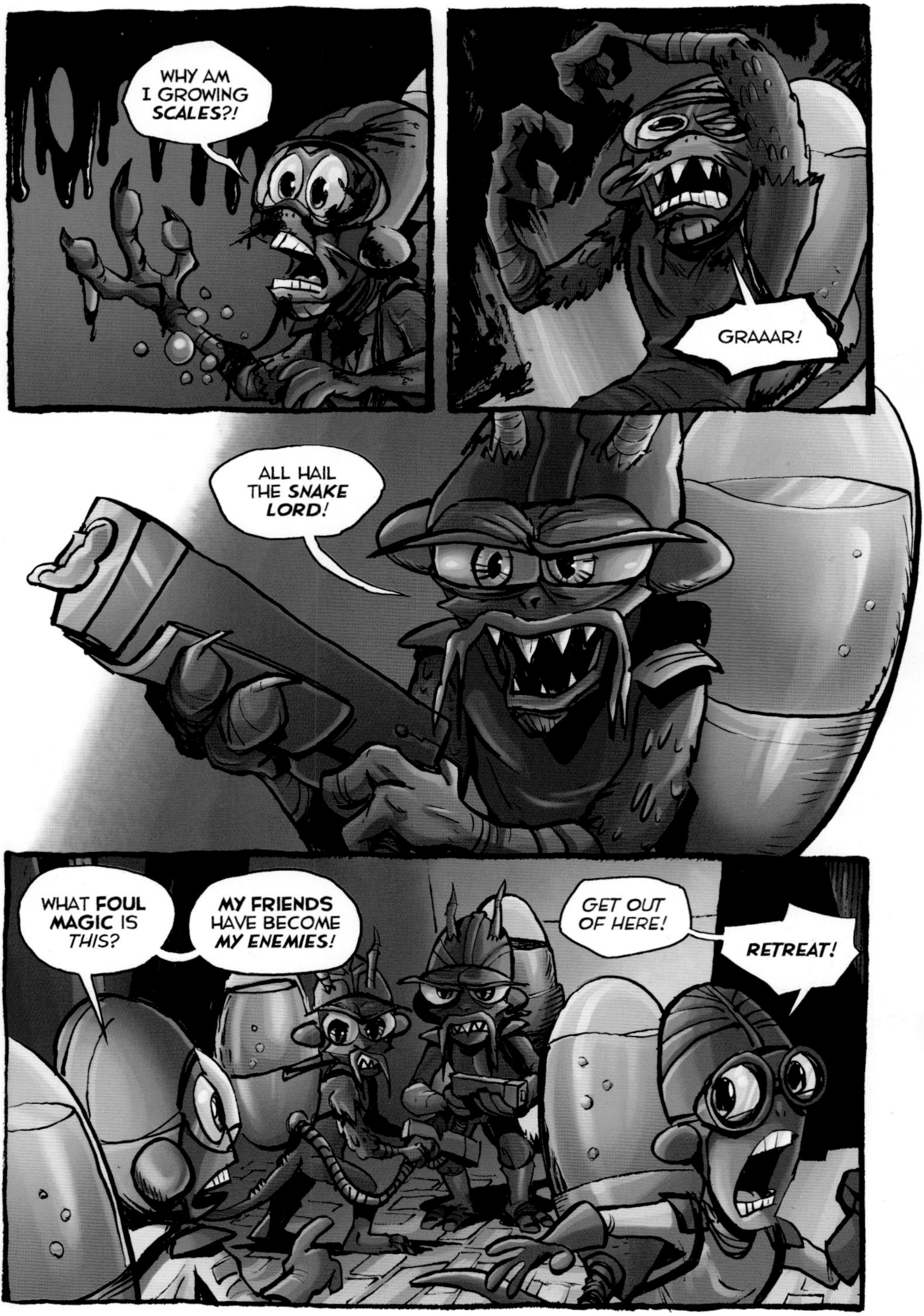
WHY AM I GROWING **SCALES?!**
GRAAAR!
ALL HAIL THE **SNAKE LORD!**
WHAT **FOUL MAGIC** IS *THIS?*
MY FRIENDS HAVE BECOME **MY ENEMIES!**
GET OUT OF HERE!
RETREAT!

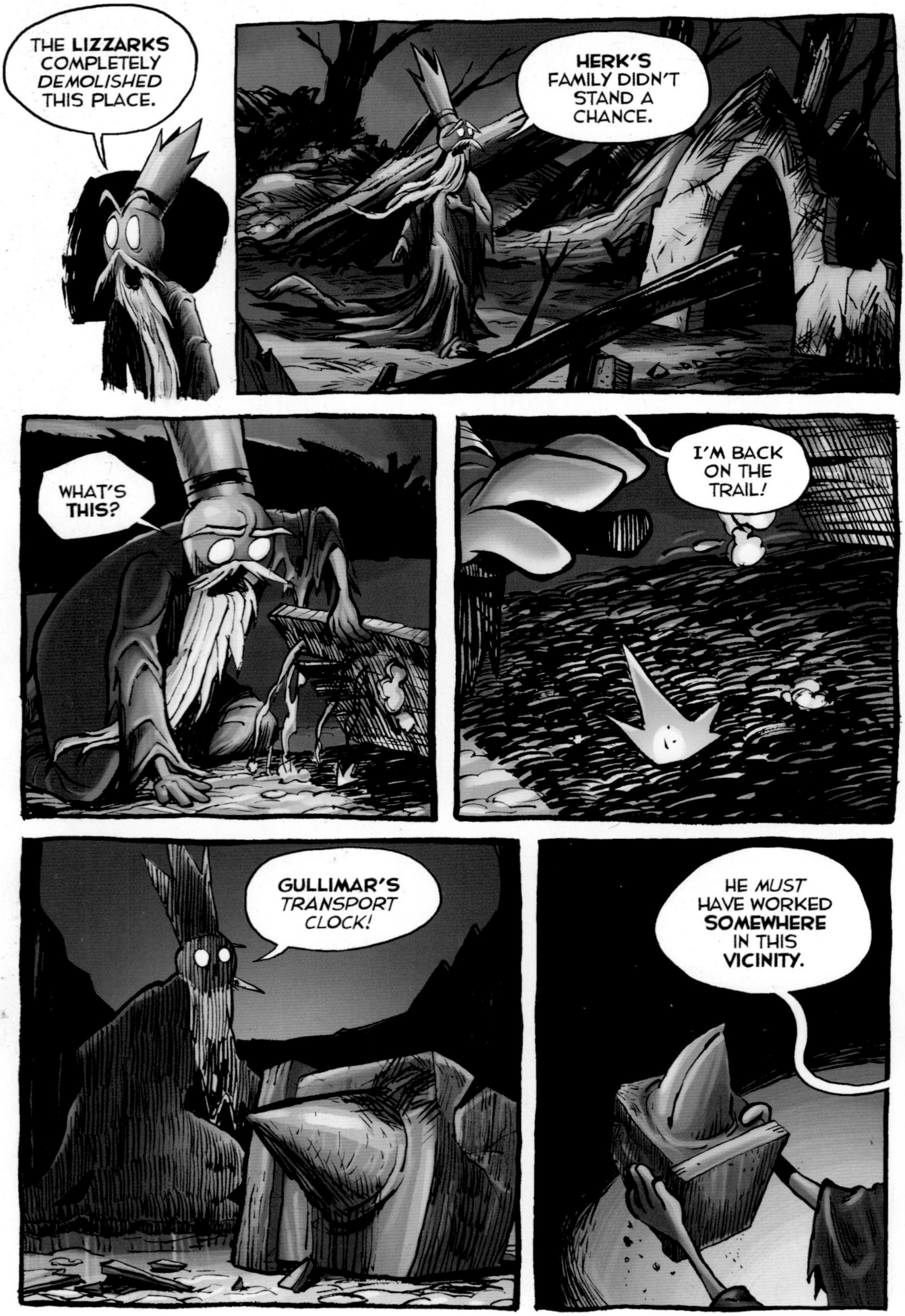

THE **LIZZARKS** COMPLETELY *DEMOLISHED* THIS PLACE.
HERK'S FAMILY DIDN'T STAND A CHANCE.
WHAT'S **THIS?**
I'M BACK ON THE TRAIL!
GULLIMAR'S *TRANSPORT* *CLOCK!*
HE *MUST* HAVE WORKED **SOMEWHERE** IN THIS **VICINITY.**

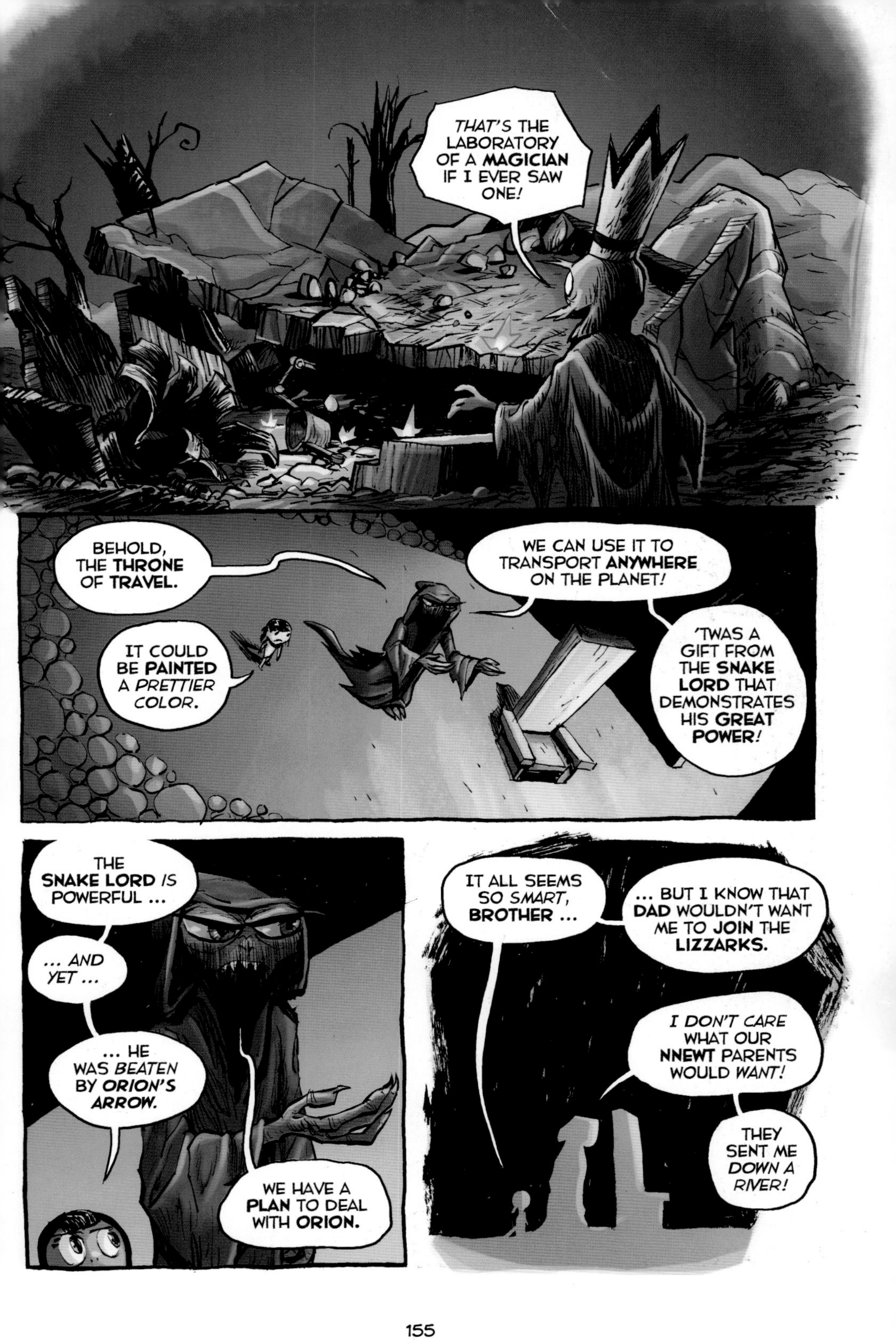
THAT'S THE LABORATORY OF A MAGICIAN IF I EVER SAW ONE!
BEHOLD, THE THRONE OF TRAVEL.
WE CAN USE IT TO TRANSPORT ANYWHERE ON THE PLANET!
IT COULD BE PAINTED A PRETTIER COLOR.
'TWAS A GIFT FROM THE SNAKE LORD THAT DEMONSTRATES HIS GREAT POWER!
THE SNAKE LORD IS POWERFUL ...
... AND YET ...
... HE WAS BEATEN BY ORION'S ARROW.
WE HAVE A PLAN TO DEAL WITH ORION.
IT ALL SEEMS SO SMART, BROTHER ...
... BUT I KNOW THAT DAD WOULDN'T WANT ME TO JOIN THE LIZZARKS.
I DON'T CARE WHAT OUR NNEWT PARENTS WOULD WANT!
THEY SENT ME DOWN A RIVER!

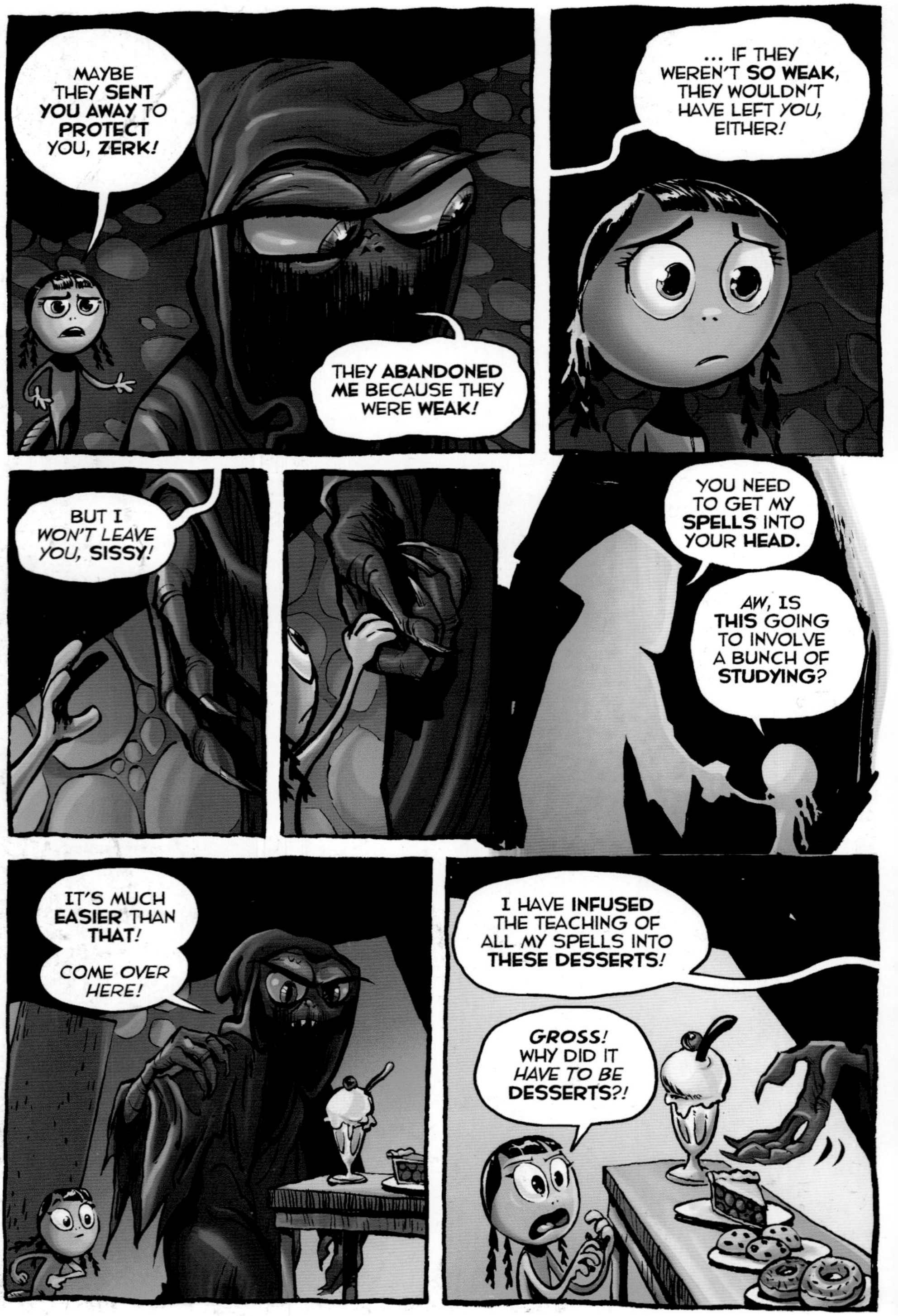
MAYBE THEY SENT YOU AWAY TO PROTECT YOU, ZERK!
THEY ABANDONED ME BECAUSE THEY WERE WEAK!
... IF THEY WEREN'T SO WEAK, THEY WOULDN'T HAVE LEFT YOU, EITHER!
BUT I WON'T LEAVE YOU, SISSY!
YOU NEED TO GET MY SPELLS INTO YOUR HEAD.
AW, IS THIS GOING TO INVOLVE A BUNCH OF STUDYING?
IT'S MUCH EASIER THAN THAT!
COME OVER HERE!
I HAVE INFUSED THE TEACHING OF ALL MY SPELLS INTO THESE DESSERTS!
GROSS! WHY DID IT HAVE TO BE DESSERTS?!

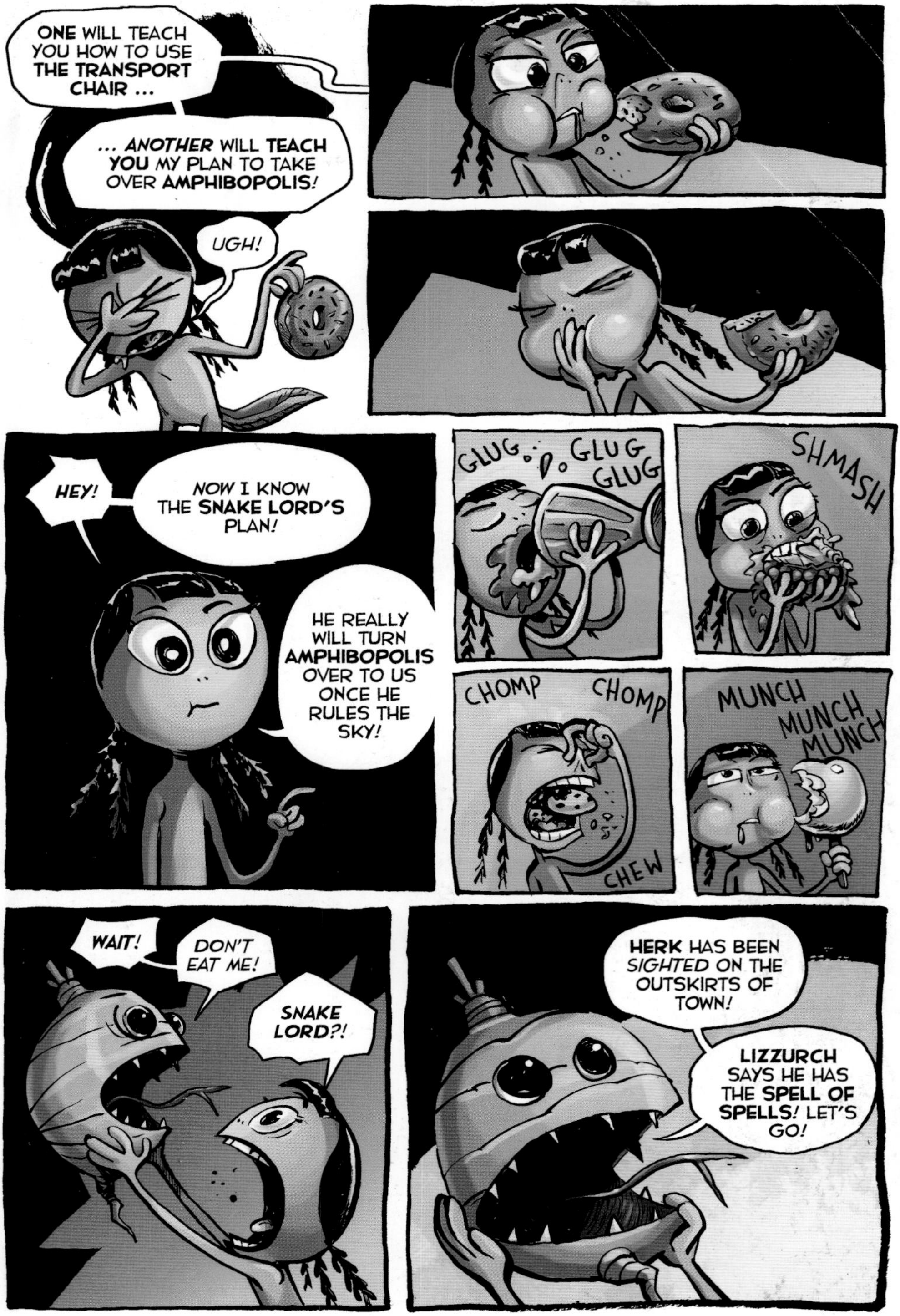

ONE WILL TEACH YOU HOW TO USE THE TRANSPORT CHAIR ...
... ANOTHER WILL TEACH YOU MY PLAN TO TAKE OVER AMPHIBOPOLIS!
UGH!
HEY!
NOW I KNOW THE SNAKE LORD'S PLAN!
HE REALLY WILL TURN AMPHIBOPOLIS OVER TO US ONCE HE RULES THE SKY!
GLUG GLUG GLUG
SHMASH
CHOMP CHOMP
CHEW
MUNCH MUNCH MUNCH
WAIT!
DON'T EAT ME!
SNAKE LORD?!
HERK HAS BEEN SIGHTED ON THE OUTSKIRTS OF TOWN!
LIZZURCH SAYS HE HAS THE SPELL OF SPELLS! LET'S GO!

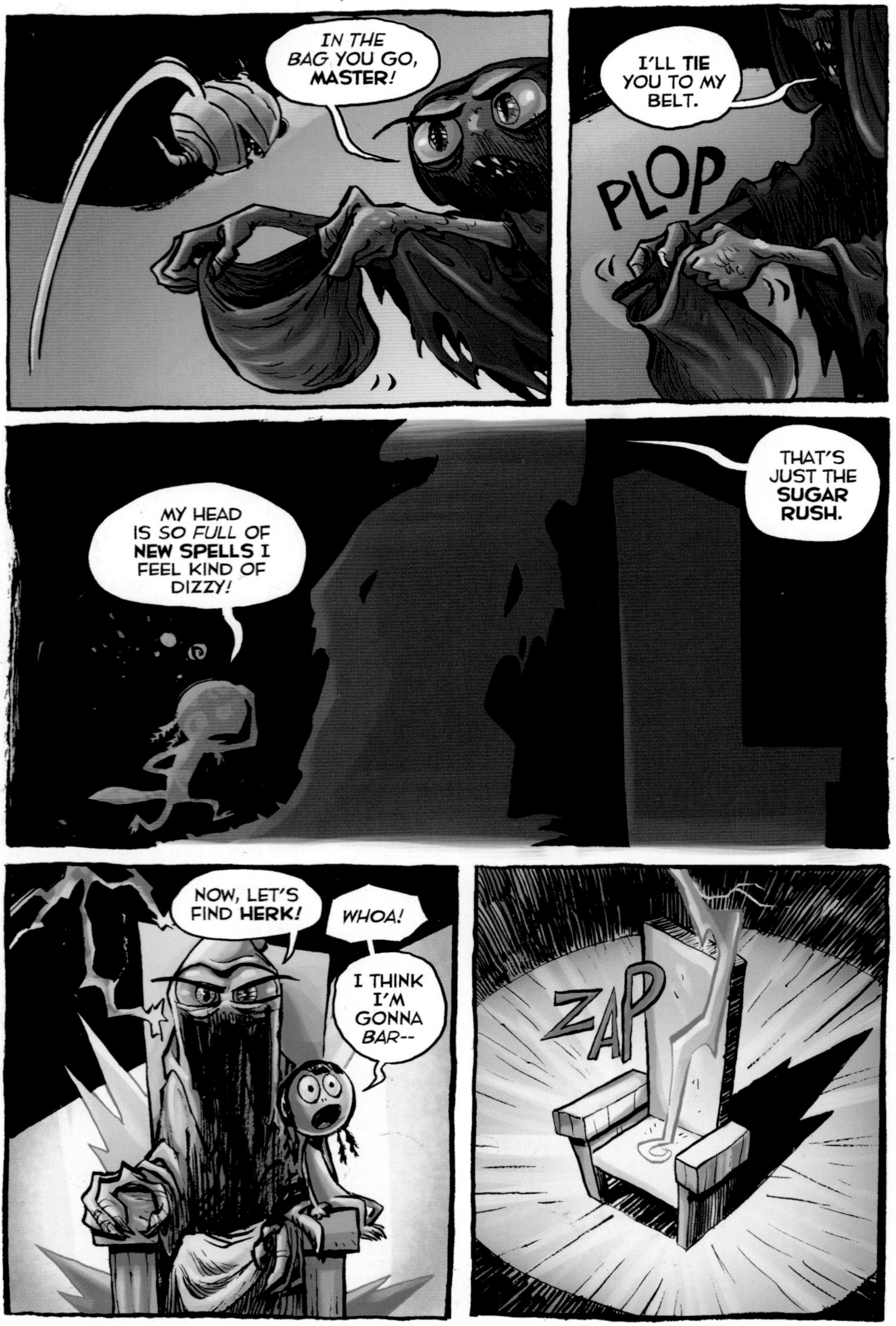
IN THE BAG YOU GO, MASTER!
I'LL TIE YOU TO MY BELT.
PLOP
MY HEAD IS SO FULL OF NEW SPELLS I FEEL KIND OF DIZZY!
THAT'S JUST THE SUGAR RUSH.
NOW, LET'S FIND HERK!
WHOA!
I THINK I'M GONNA BAR--
ZAP

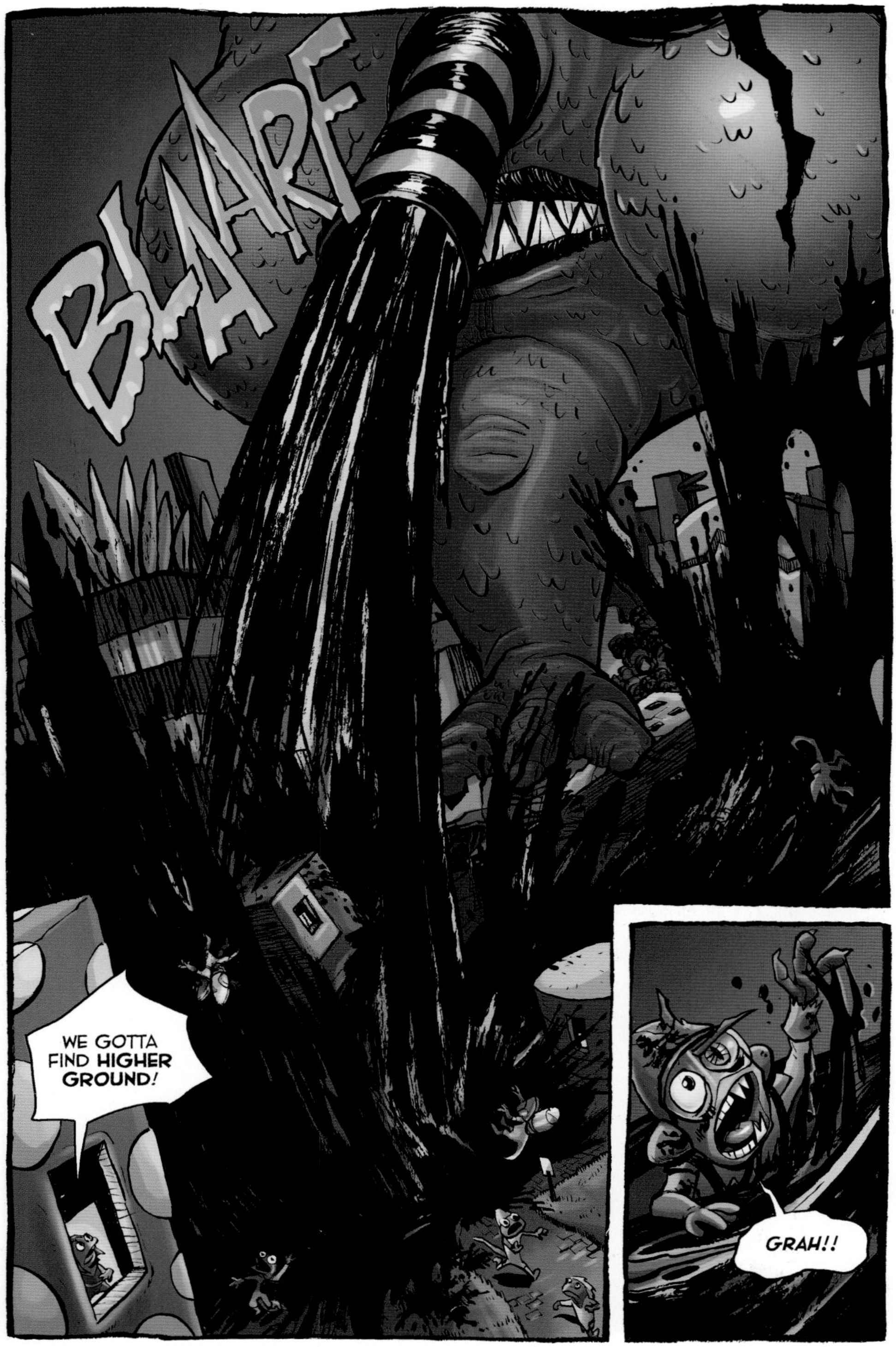
BLAARF
WE GOTTA FIND **HIGHER GROUND**!
GRAH!!

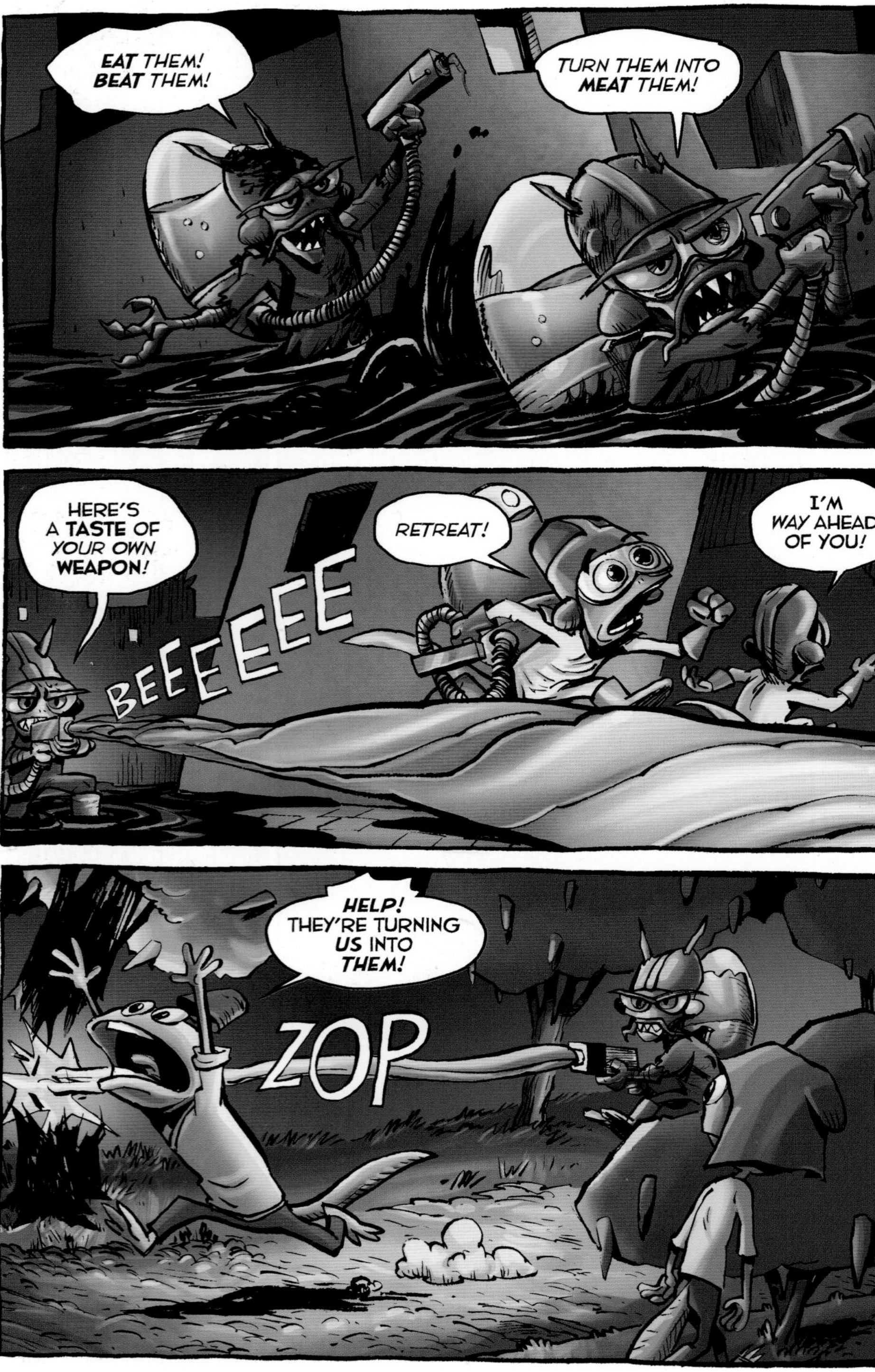
EAT THEM! BEAT THEM!
TURN THEM INTO MEAT THEM!
HERE'S A TASTE OF YOUR OWN WEAPON!
RETREAT!
I'M WAY AHEAD OF YOU!
BEEEEEEE
HELP! THEY'RE TURNING US INTO THEM!
ZOP

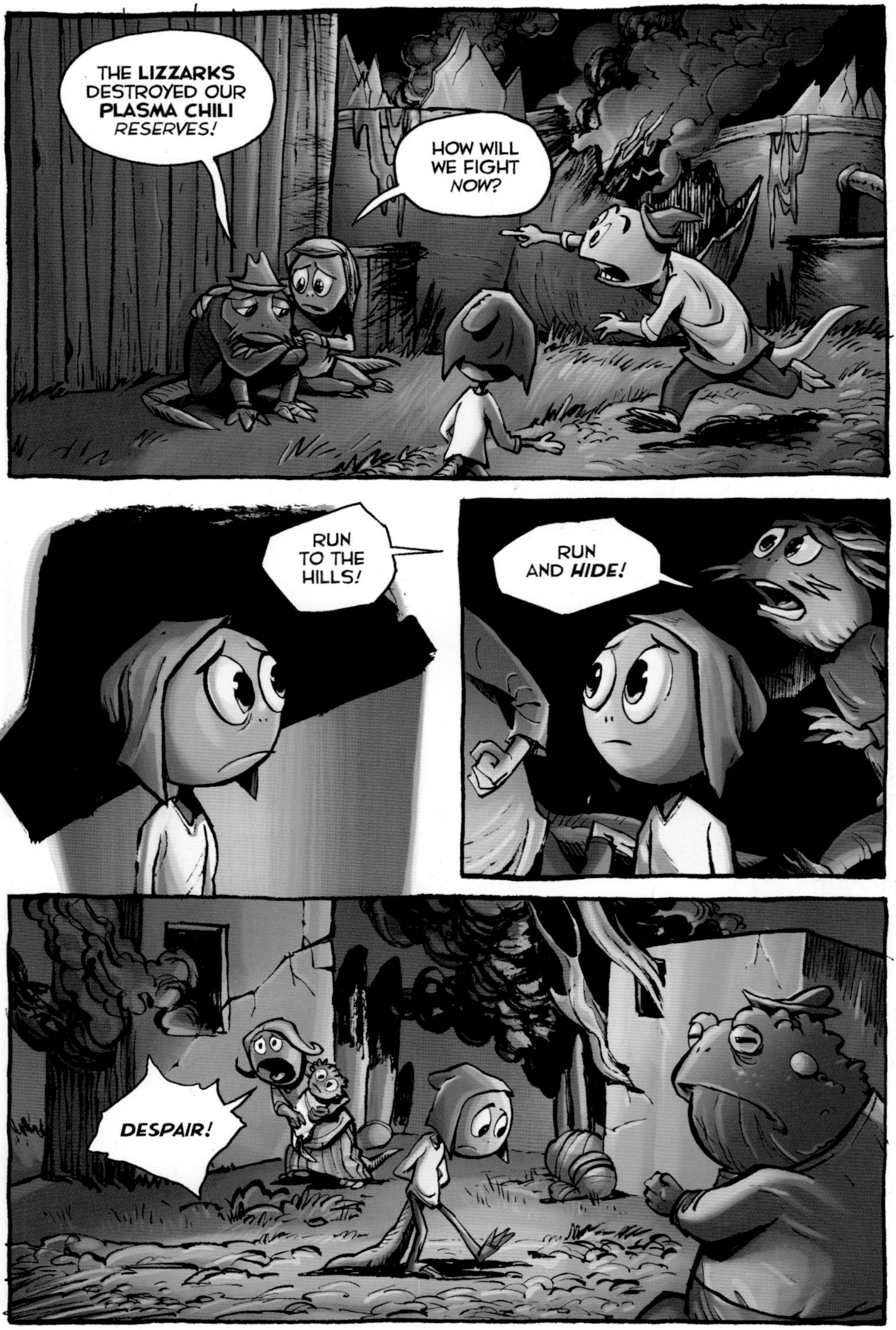
THE **LIZZARKS** DESTROYED OUR **PLASMA CHILI** *RESERVES!*
HOW WILL WE FIGHT *NOW?*
RUN TO THE HILLS!
RUN AND ***HIDE!***
DESPAIR!

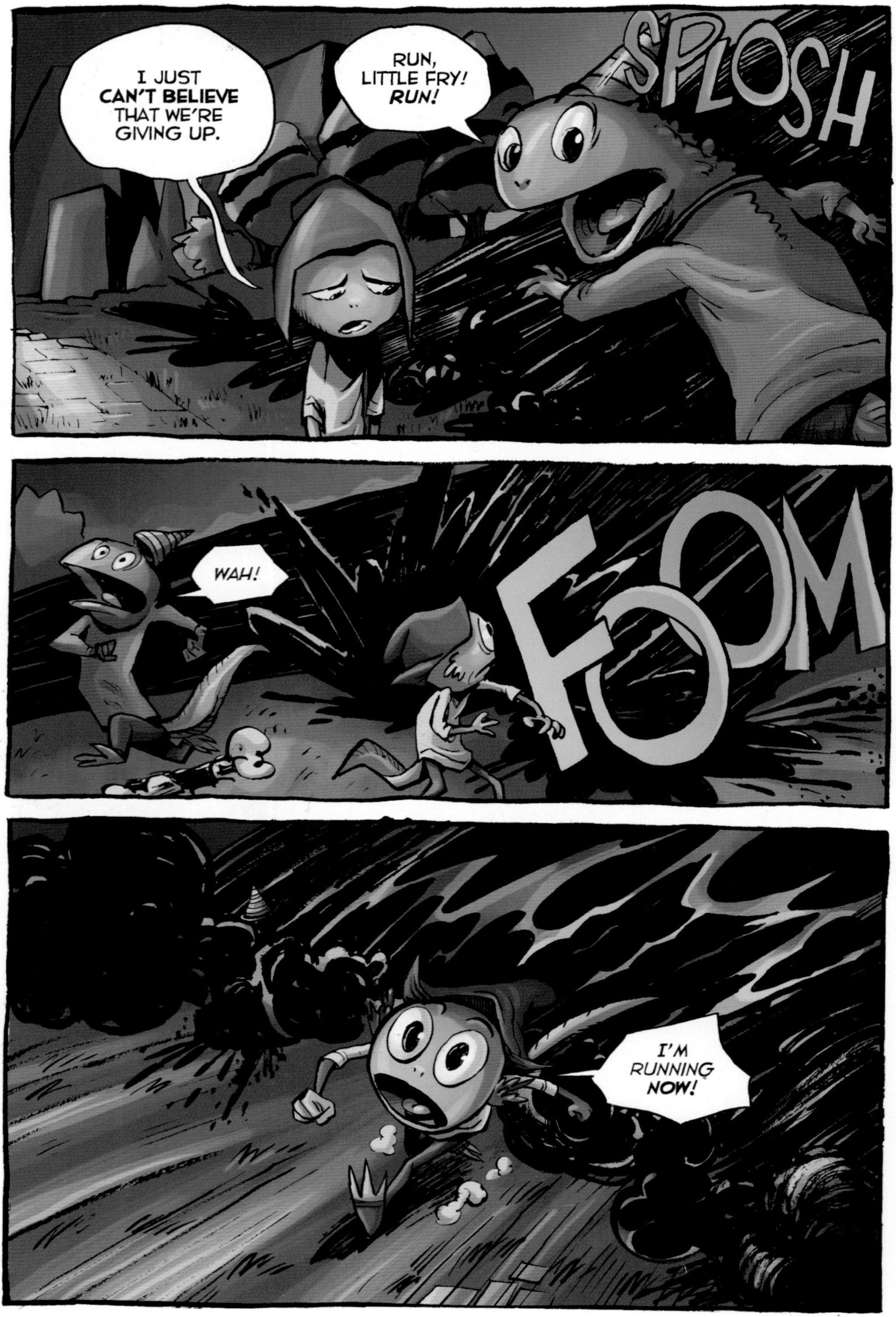
I JUST **CAN'T BELIEVE** THAT WE'RE GIVING UP.
RUN, LITTLE FRY! ***RUN!***
SPLOSH
WAH!
FOOM
I'M RUNNING ***NOW!***

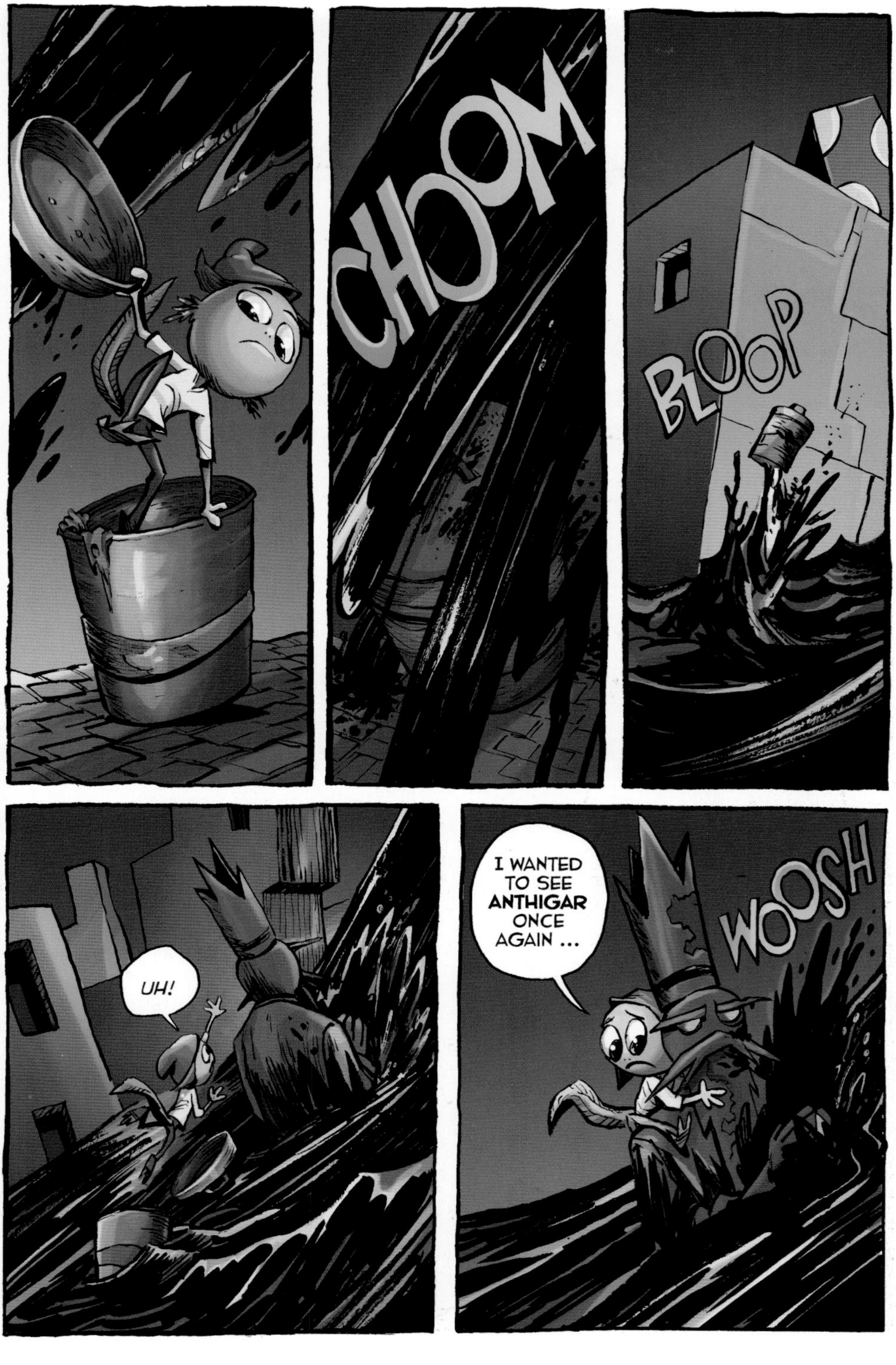
CHOOM
BLOOP
UH!
I WANTED TO SEE **ANTHIGAR** ONCE AGAIN ...
WOOSH

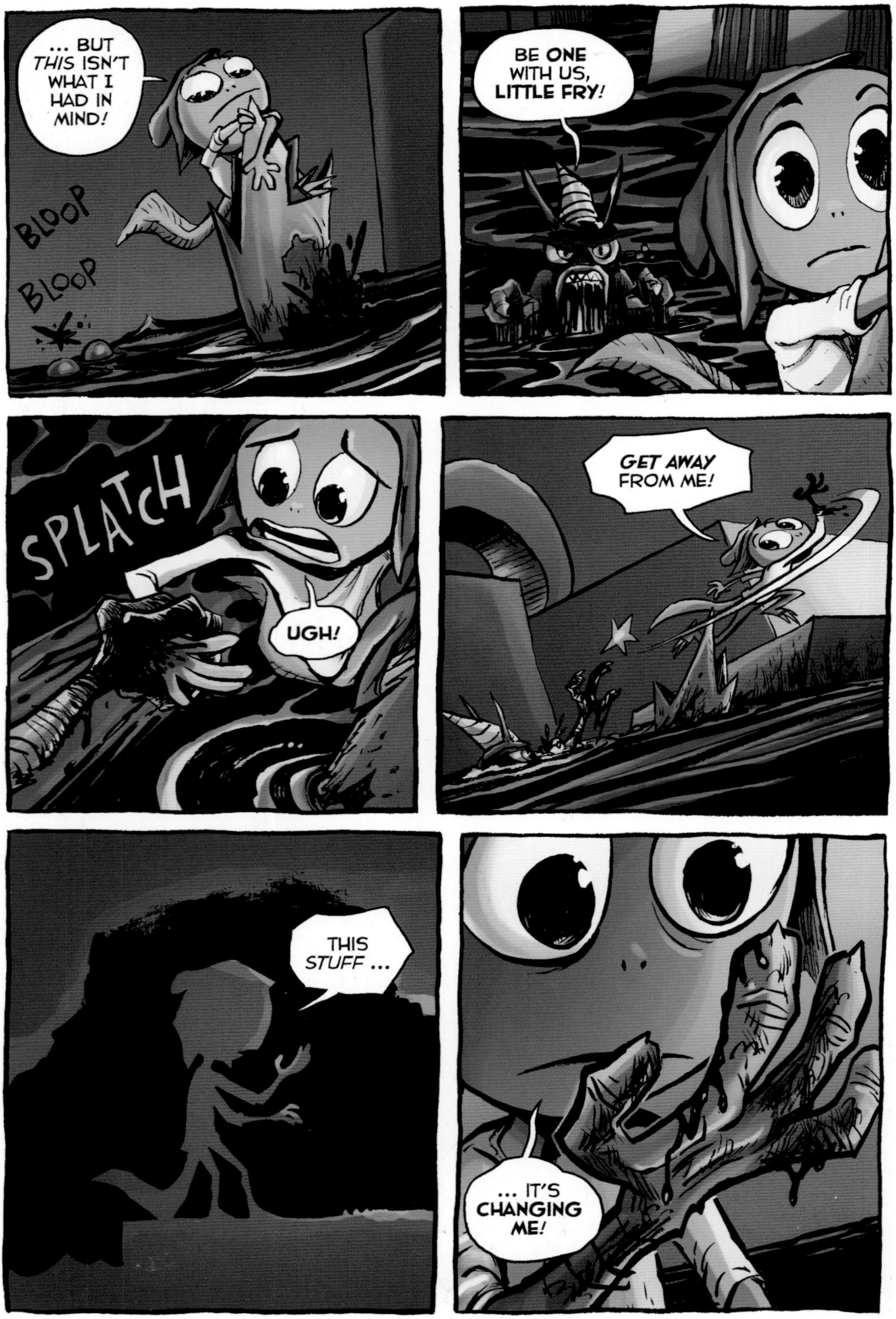
... BUT *THIS* ISN'T WHAT I HAD IN MIND!
BLOOP
BLOOP
BE **ONE** WITH US, **LITTLE FRY!**
SPLATCH
UGH!
GET AWAY FROM ME!
THIS *STUFF* ...
... IT'S **CHANGING** ME!

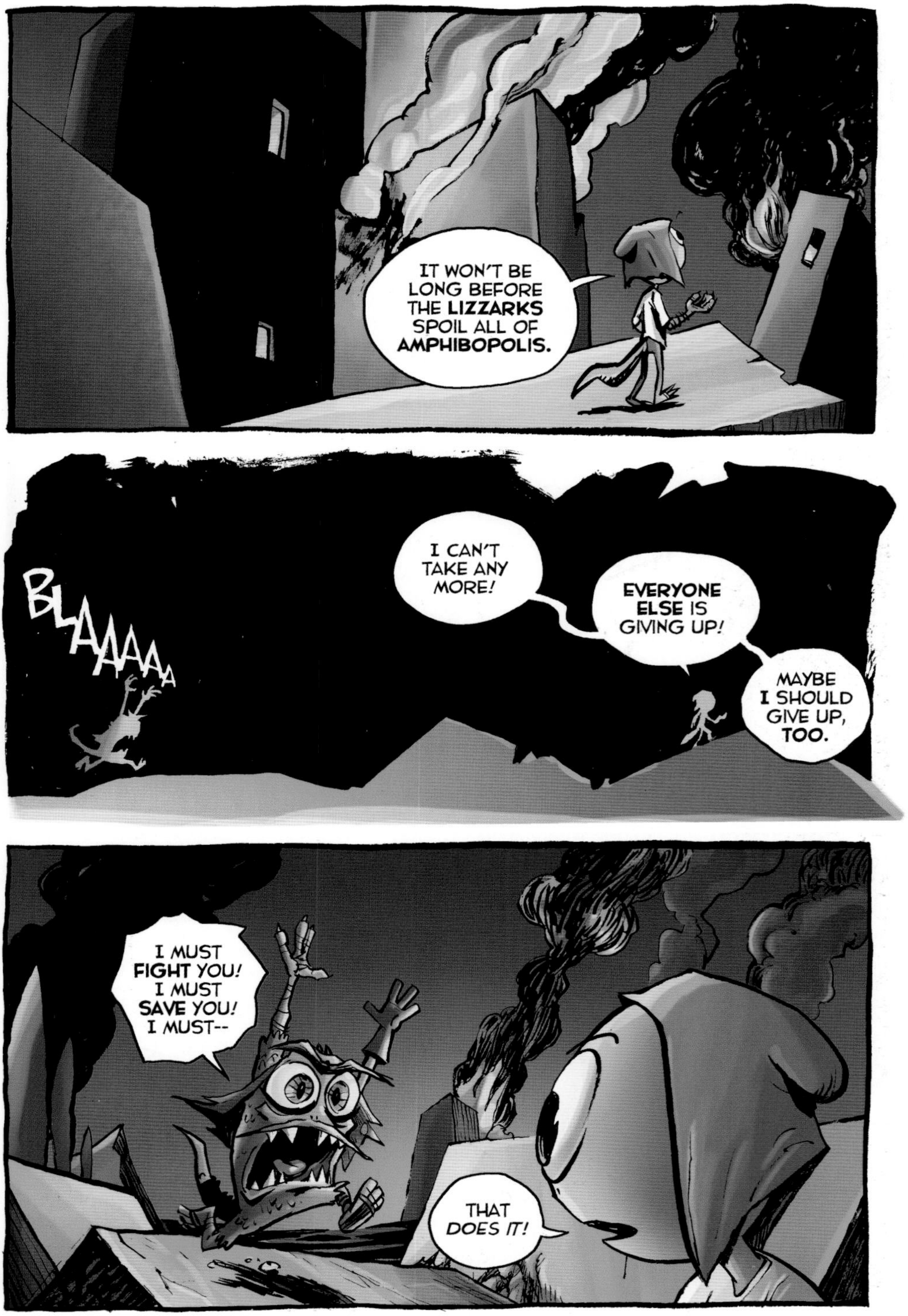
IT WON'T BE LONG BEFORE THE **LIZZARKS** SPOIL ALL OF **AMPHIBOPOLIS.**
BLAAAAAA
I CAN'T TAKE ANY MORE!
EVERYONE ELSE IS GIVING UP!
MAYBE **I** SHOULD GIVE UP, **TOO.**
I MUST **FIGHT** *YOU!* I MUST **SAVE** *YOU!* I MUST--
THAT *DOES IT!*

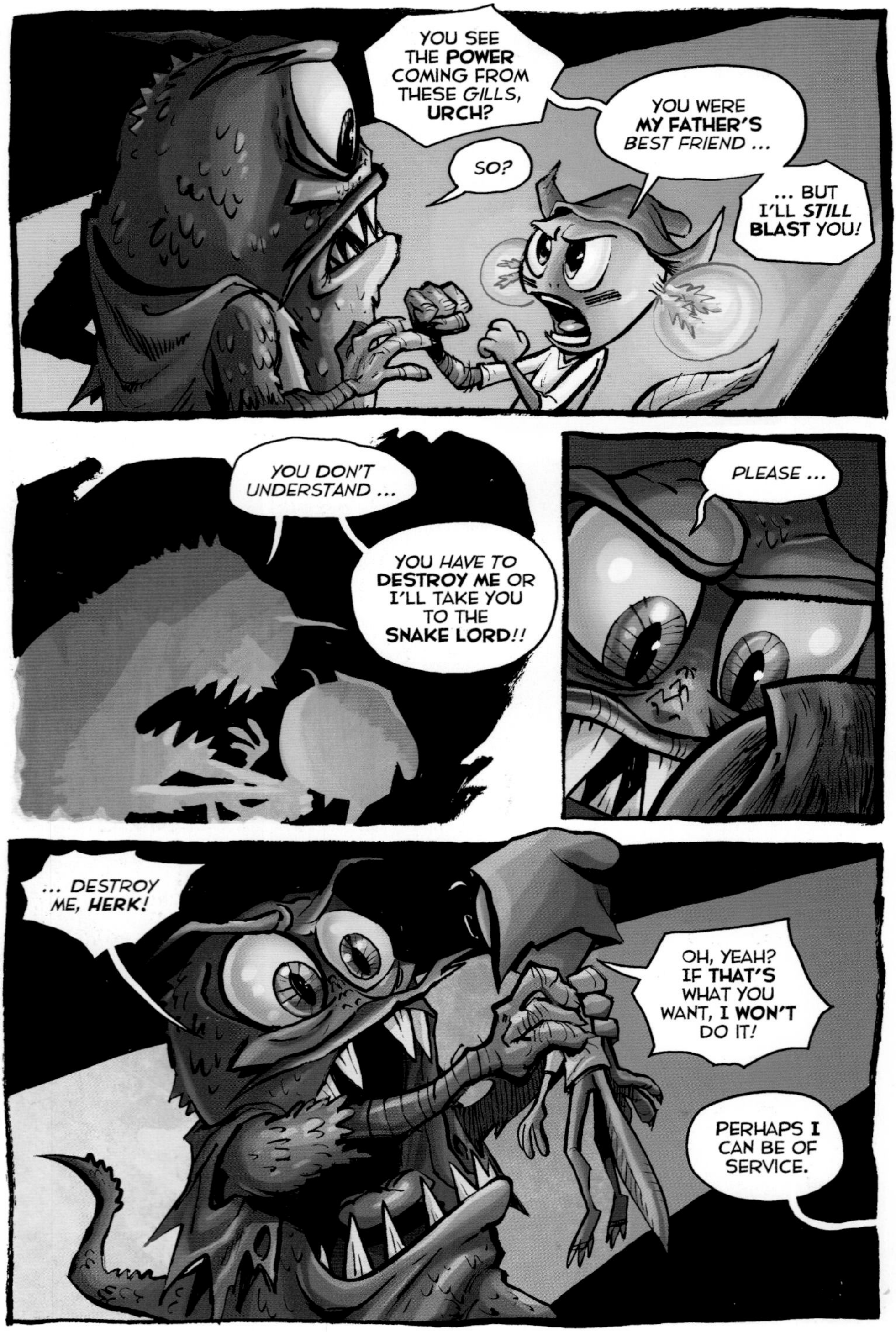
YOU SEE THE POWER COMING FROM THESE GILLS, URCH?
SO?
YOU WERE MY FATHER'S BEST FRIEND ...
... BUT I'LL STILL BLAST YOU!
YOU DON'T UNDERSTAND ...
YOU HAVE TO DESTROY ME OR I'LL TAKE YOU TO THE SNAKE LORD!!
PLEASE ...
... DESTROY ME, HERK!
OH, YEAH? IF THAT'S WHAT YOU WANT, I WON'T DO IT!
PERHAPS I CAN BE OF SERVICE.

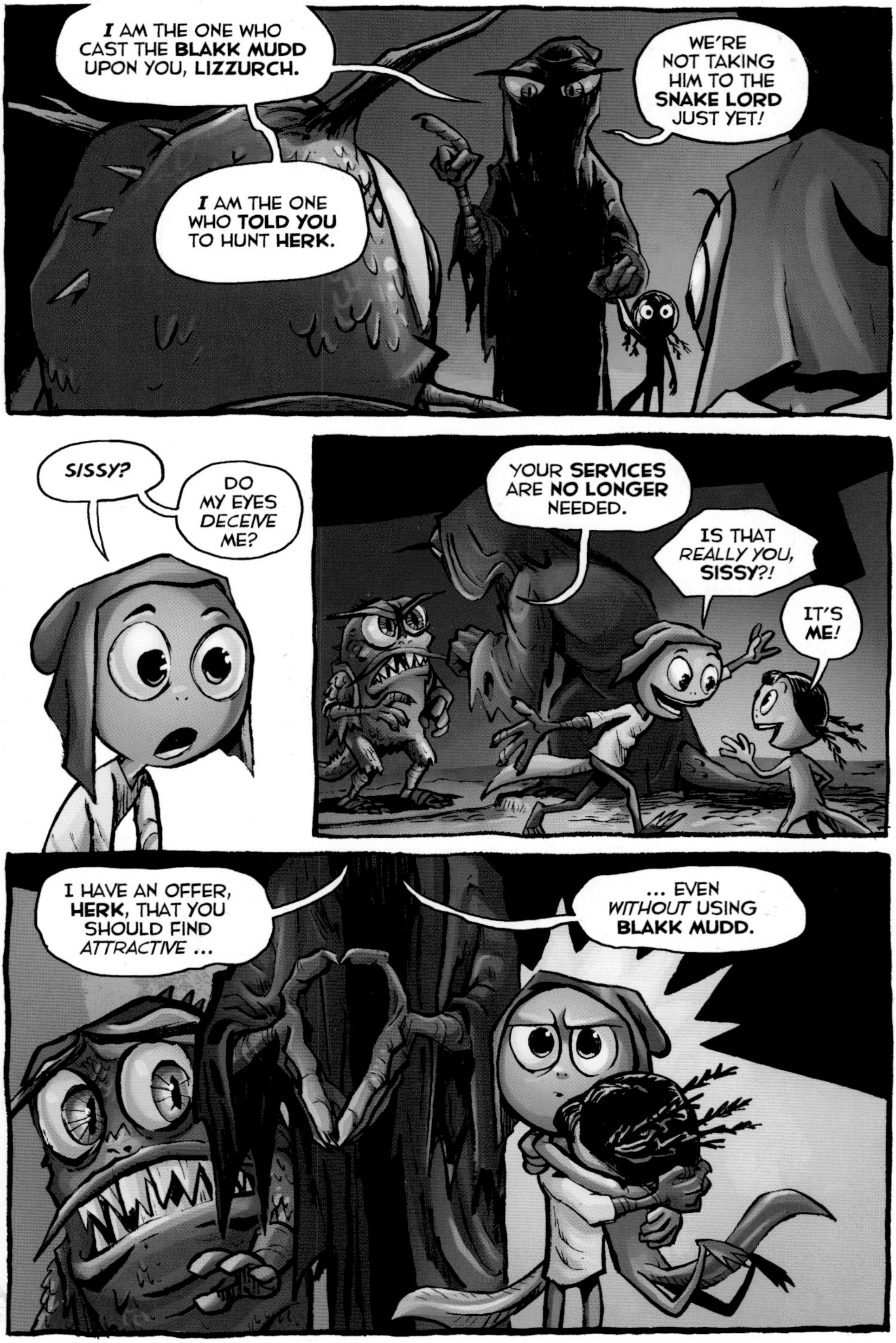
I AM THE ONE WHO CAST THE BLAKK MUDD UPON YOU, LIZZURCH.
I AM THE ONE WHO TOLD YOU TO HUNT HERK.
WE'RE NOT TAKING HIM TO THE SNAKE LORD JUST YET!
SISSY?
DO MY EYES DECEIVE ME?
YOUR SERVICES ARE NO LONGER NEEDED.
IS THAT REALLY YOU, SISSY?!
IT'S ME!
I HAVE AN OFFER, HERK, THAT YOU SHOULD FIND ATTRACTIVE ...
... EVEN WITHOUT USING BLAKK MUDD.

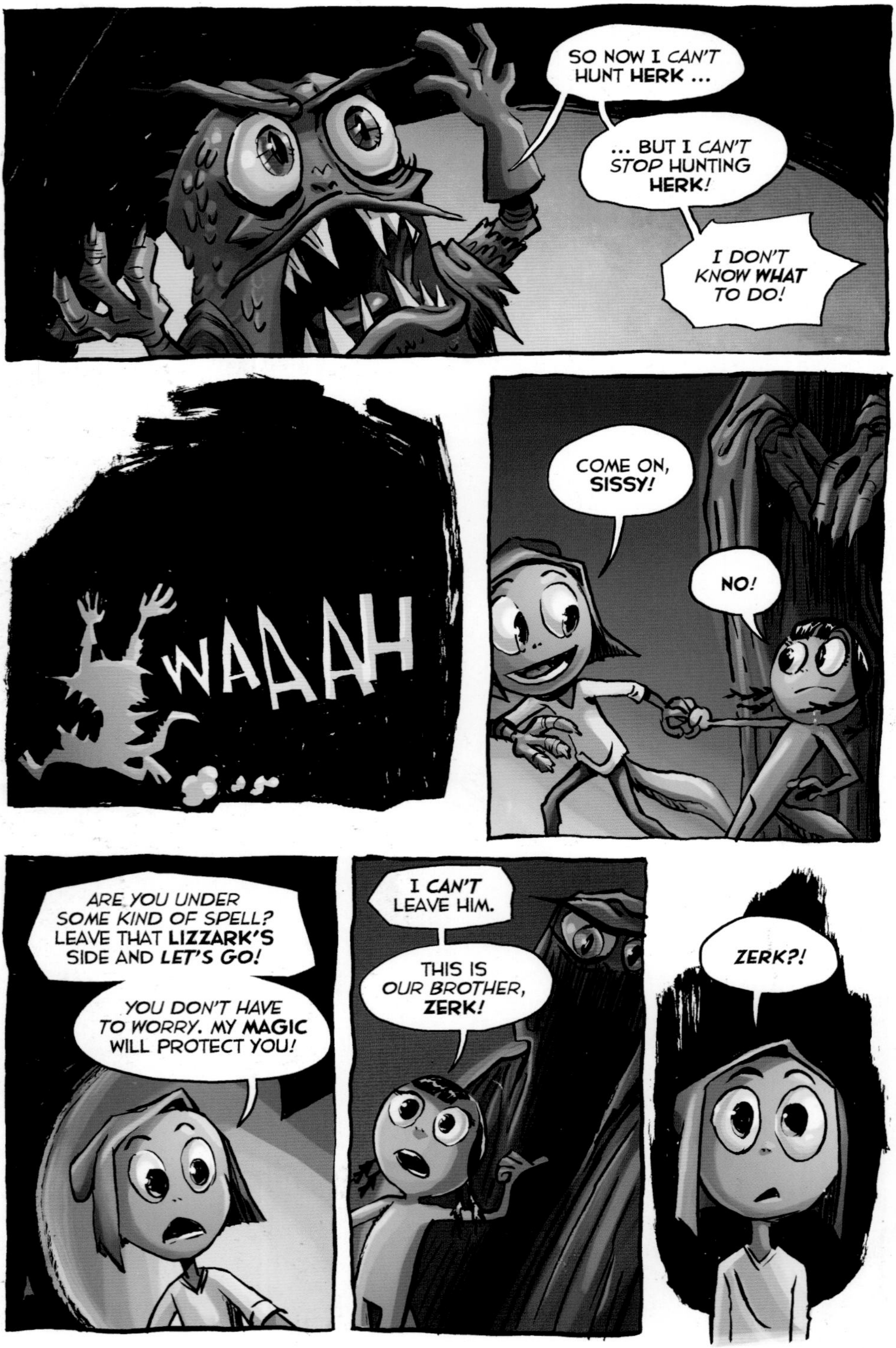
SO NOW I CAN'T HUNT HERK ...
... BUT I CAN'T STOP HUNTING HERK!
I DON'T KNOW WHAT TO DO!
WAAAH
COME ON, SISSY!
NO!
ARE YOU UNDER SOME KIND OF SPELL? LEAVE THAT LIZZARK'S SIDE AND LET'S GO!
YOU DON'T HAVE TO WORRY. MY MAGIC WILL PROTECT YOU!
I CAN'T LEAVE HIM.
THIS IS OUR BROTHER, ZERK!
ZERK?!

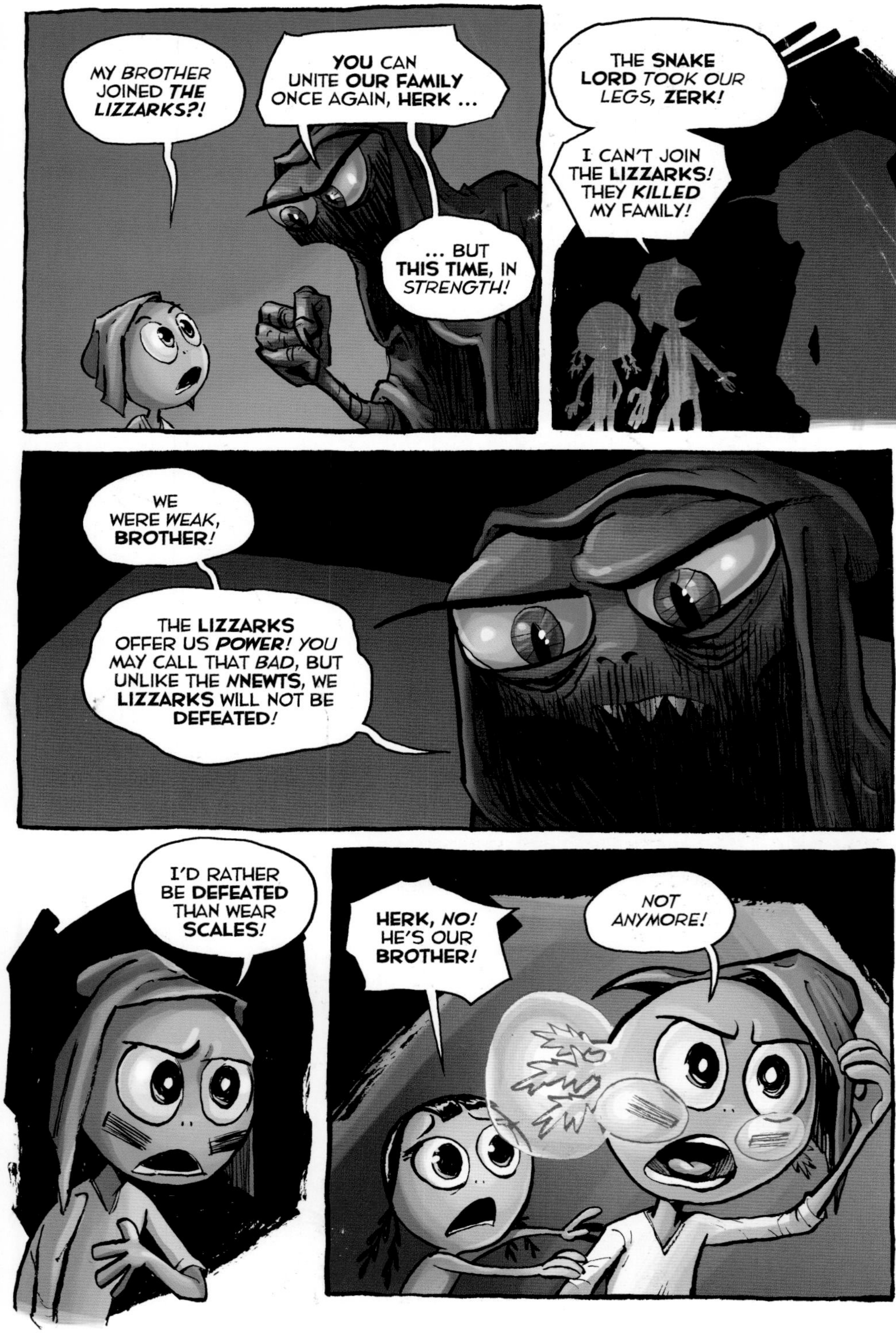

MY BROTHER JOINED THE LIZZARKS?!
YOU CAN UNITE OUR FAMILY ONCE AGAIN, HERK ...
... BUT THIS TIME, IN STRENGTH!
THE SNAKE LORD TOOK OUR LEGS, ZERK!
I CAN'T JOIN THE LIZZARKS! THEY KILLED MY FAMILY!
WE WERE WEAK, BROTHER!
THE LIZZARKS OFFER US POWER! YOU MAY CALL THAT BAD, BUT UNLIKE THE NNEWTS, WE LIZZARKS WILL NOT BE DEFEATED!
I'D RATHER BE DEFEATED THAN WEAR SCALES!
HERK, NO! HE'S OUR BROTHER!
NOT ANYMORE!

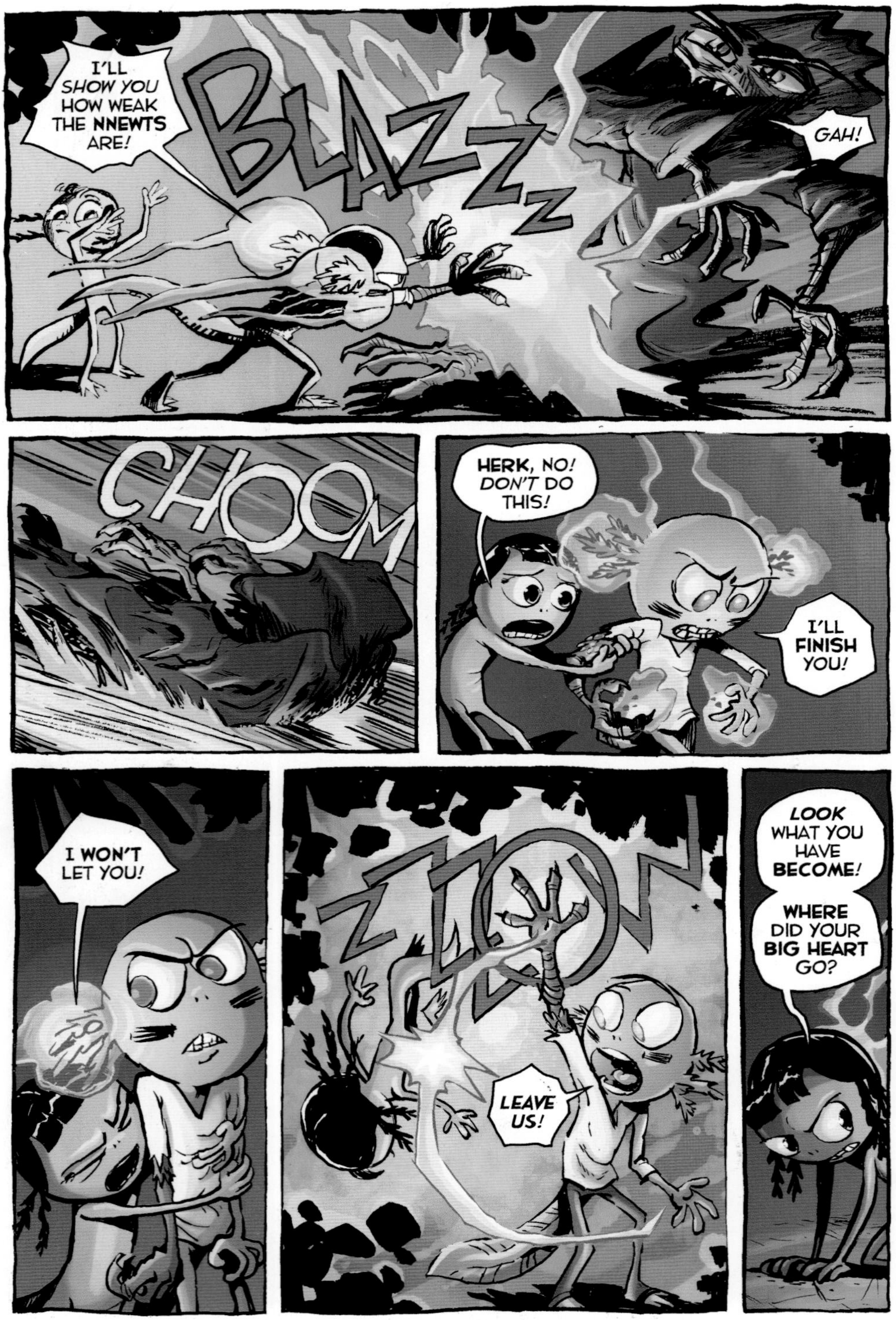
I'LL SHOW YOU HOW WEAK THE NNEWTS ARE!
BLAZZzz
GAH!
CHOOM
HERK, NO! DON'T DO THIS!
I'LL FINISH YOU!
I WON'T LET YOU!
ZZZOW
LEAVE US!
LOOK WHAT YOU HAVE BECOME!
WHERE DID YOUR BIG HEART GO?

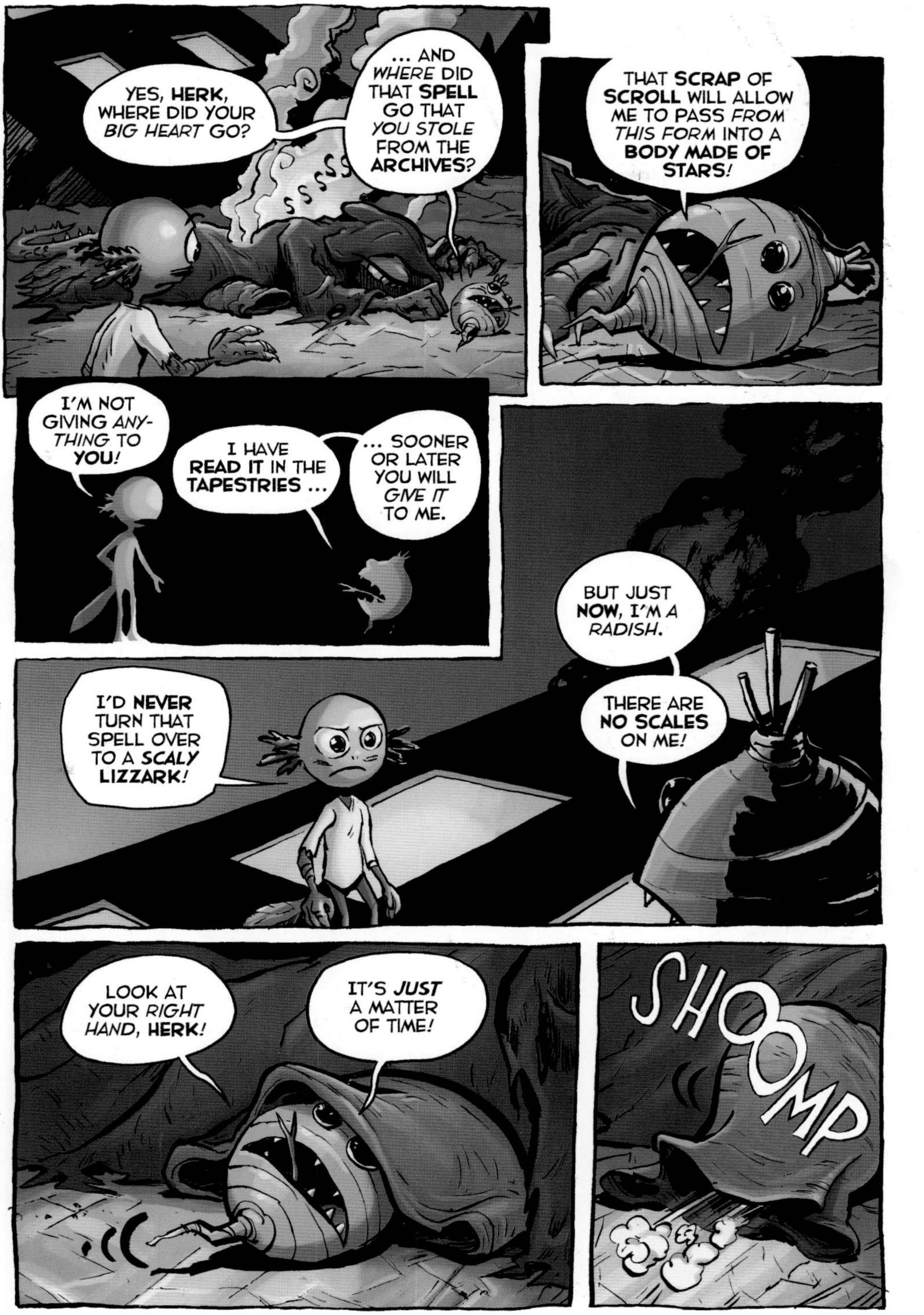

YES, HERK, WHERE DID YOUR BIG HEART GO?
... AND WHERE DID THAT SPELL GO THAT YOU STOLE FROM THE ARCHIVES?
SSSSS
THAT SCRAP OF SCROLL WILL ALLOW ME TO PASS FROM THIS FORM INTO A BODY MADE OF STARS!
I'M NOT GIVING ANY-THING TO YOU!
I HAVE READ IT IN THE TAPESTRIES ...
... SOONER OR LATER YOU WILL GIVE IT TO ME.
I'D NEVER TURN THAT SPELL OVER TO A SCALY LIZZARK!
BUT JUST NOW, I'M A RADISH.
THERE ARE NO SCALES ON ME!
LOOK AT YOUR RIGHT HAND, HERK!
IT'S JUST A MATTER OF TIME!
SHOOMP

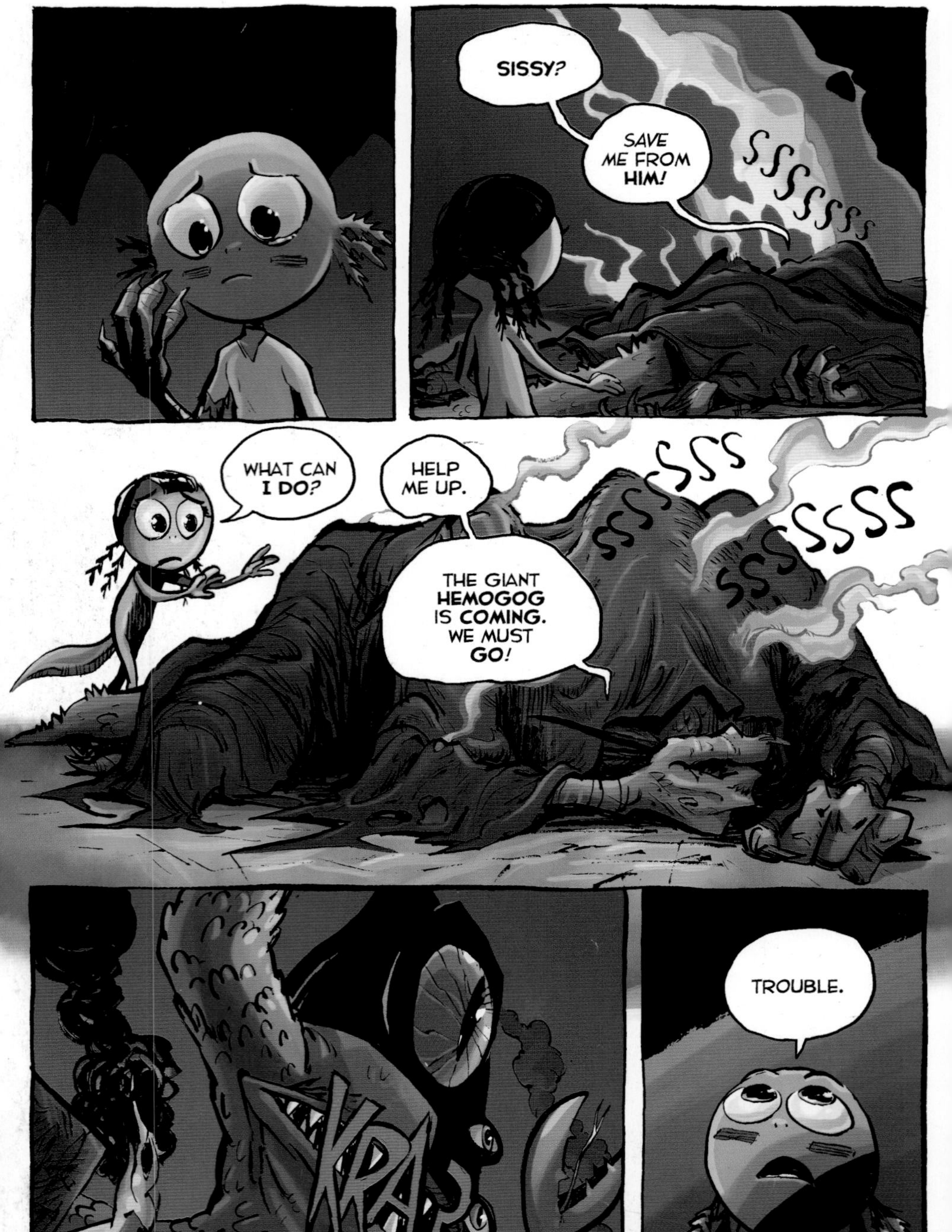
SISSY?
SAVE ME FROM HIM!
SSSSSSSS
WHAT CAN I DO?
HELP ME UP.
SSSSSS
SSSSSSSS
THE GIANT HEMOGOG IS COMING. WE MUST GO!
KRAP
TROUBLE.

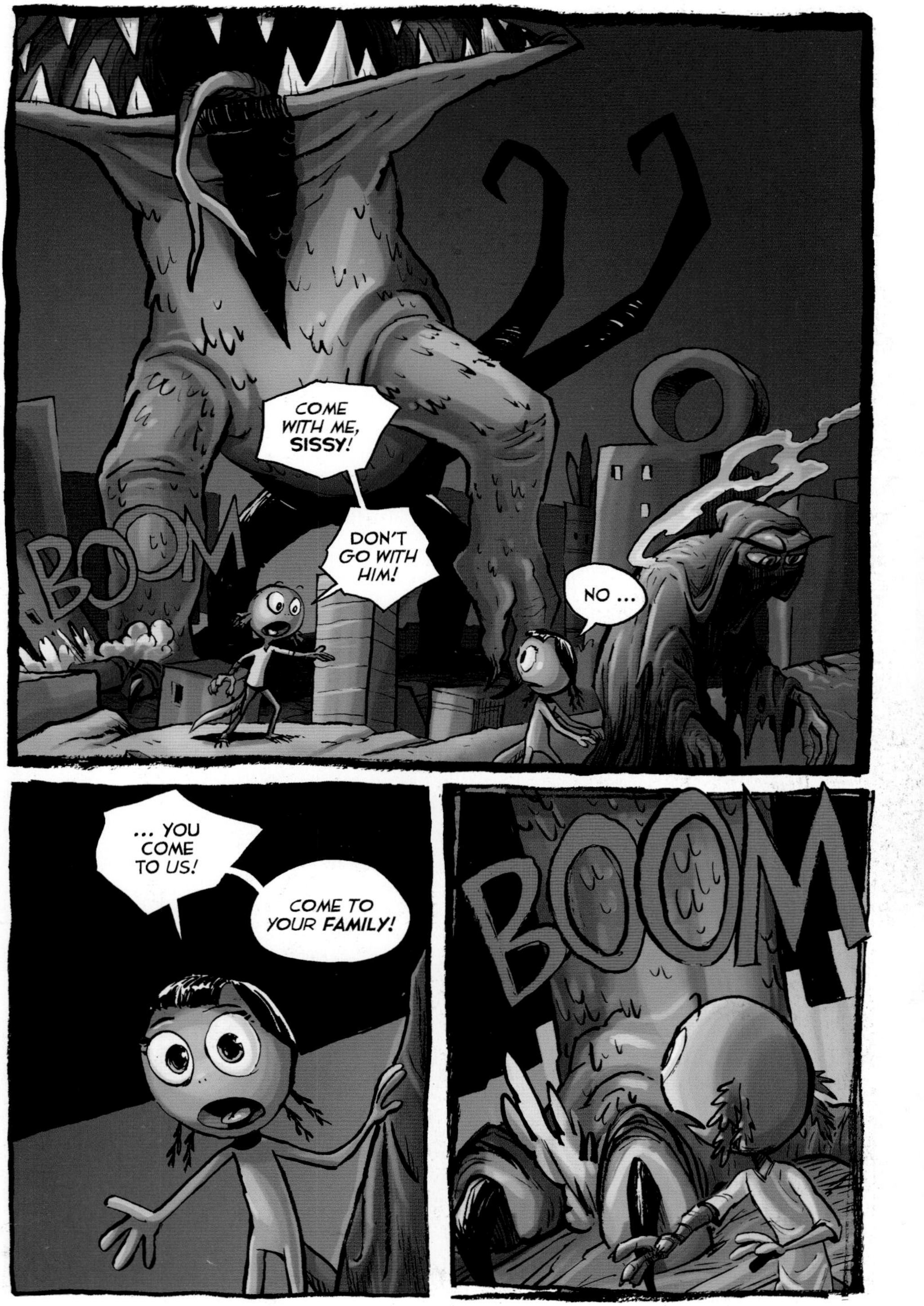
BOOM
COME WITH ME, SISSY!
DON'T GO WITH HIM!
NO ...
... YOU COME TO US!
COME TO YOUR FAMILY!
BOOM

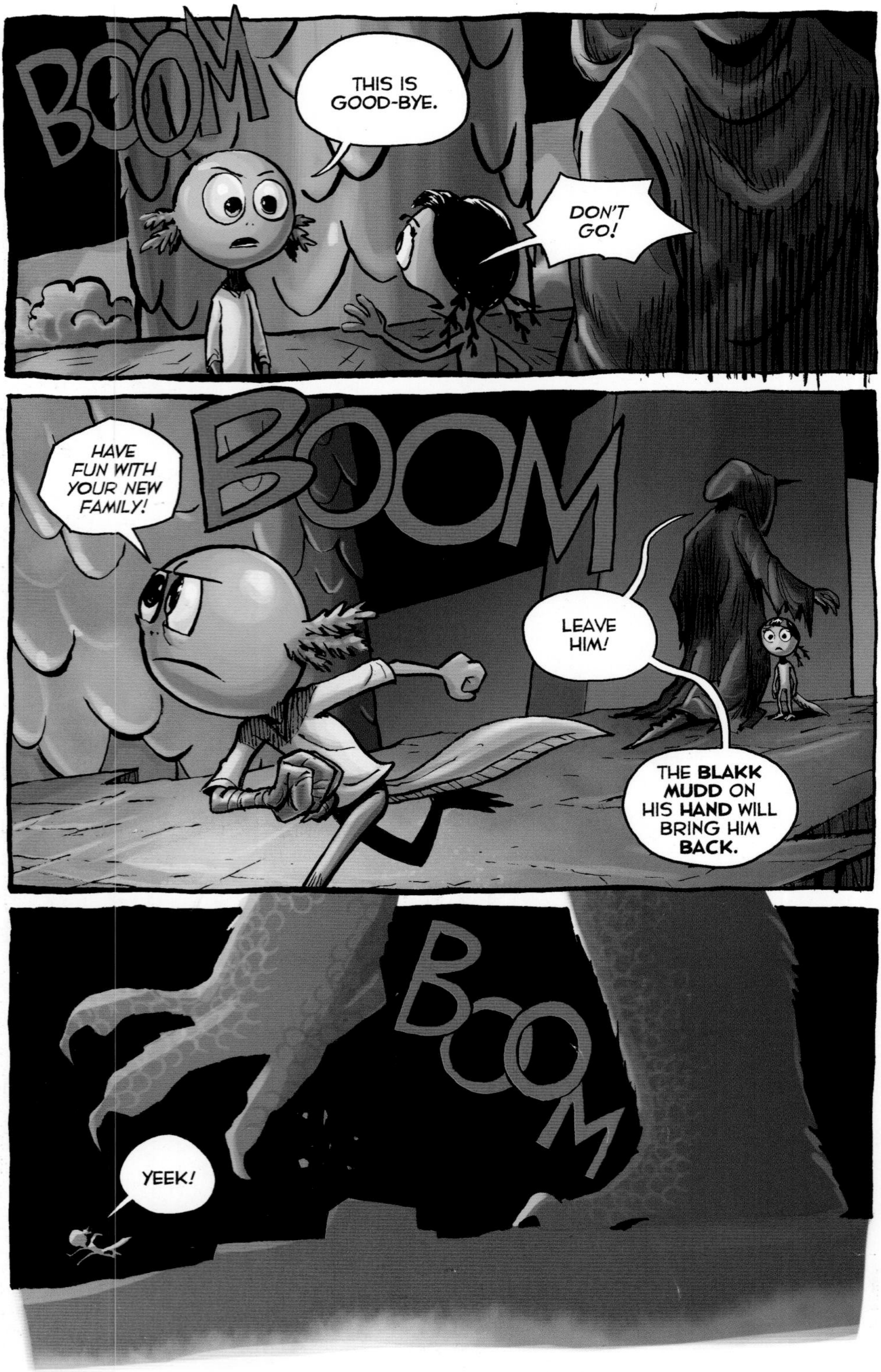
BOOM
THIS IS GOOD-BYE.
DON'T GO!
HAVE FUN WITH YOUR NEW FAMILY!
BOOM
LEAVE HIM!
THE BLAKK MUDD ON HIS HAND WILL BRING HIM BACK.
BOOM
YEEK!

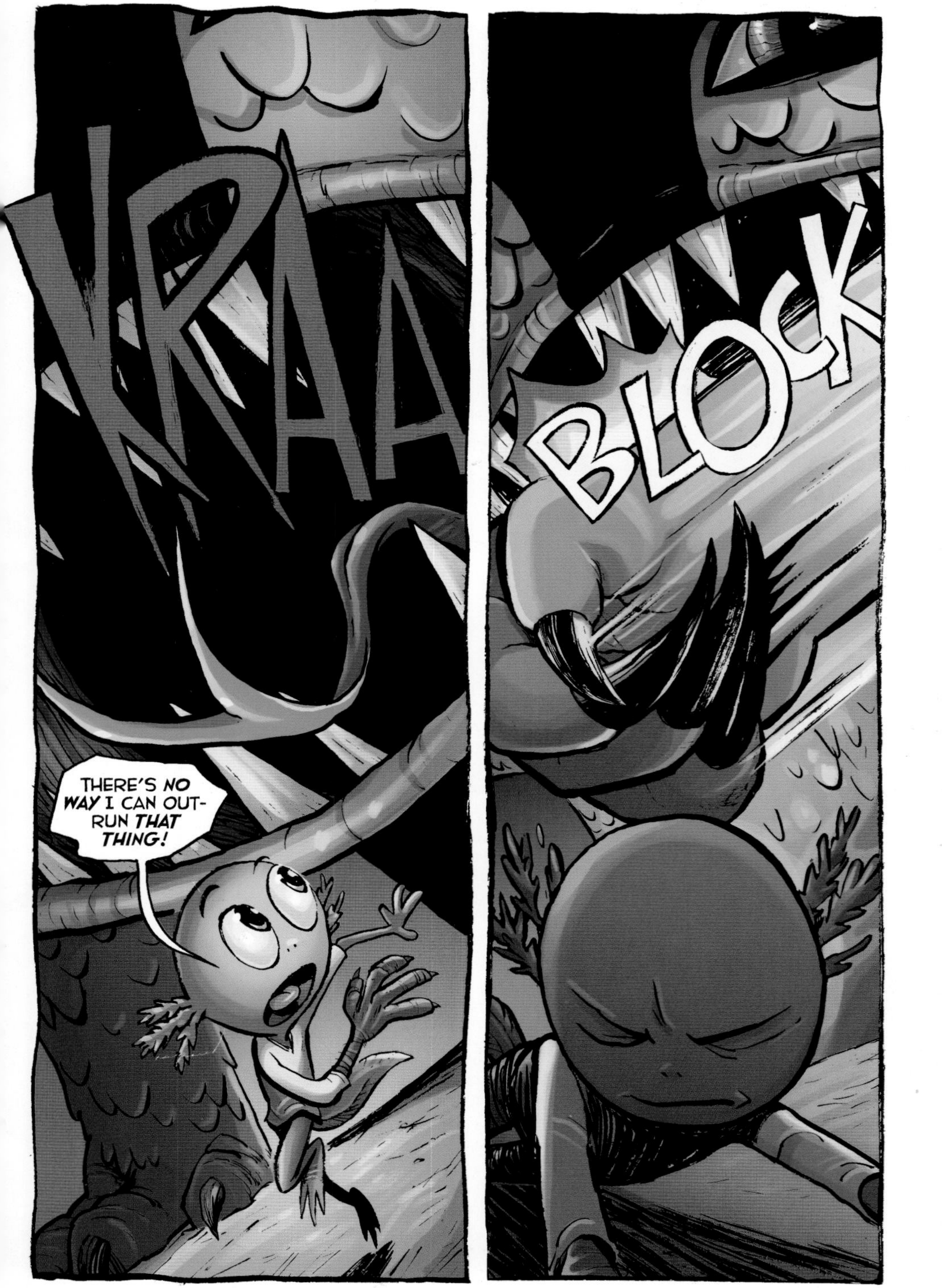
KRAA
THERE'S NO WAY I CAN OUT-RUN THAT THING!
BLOCK

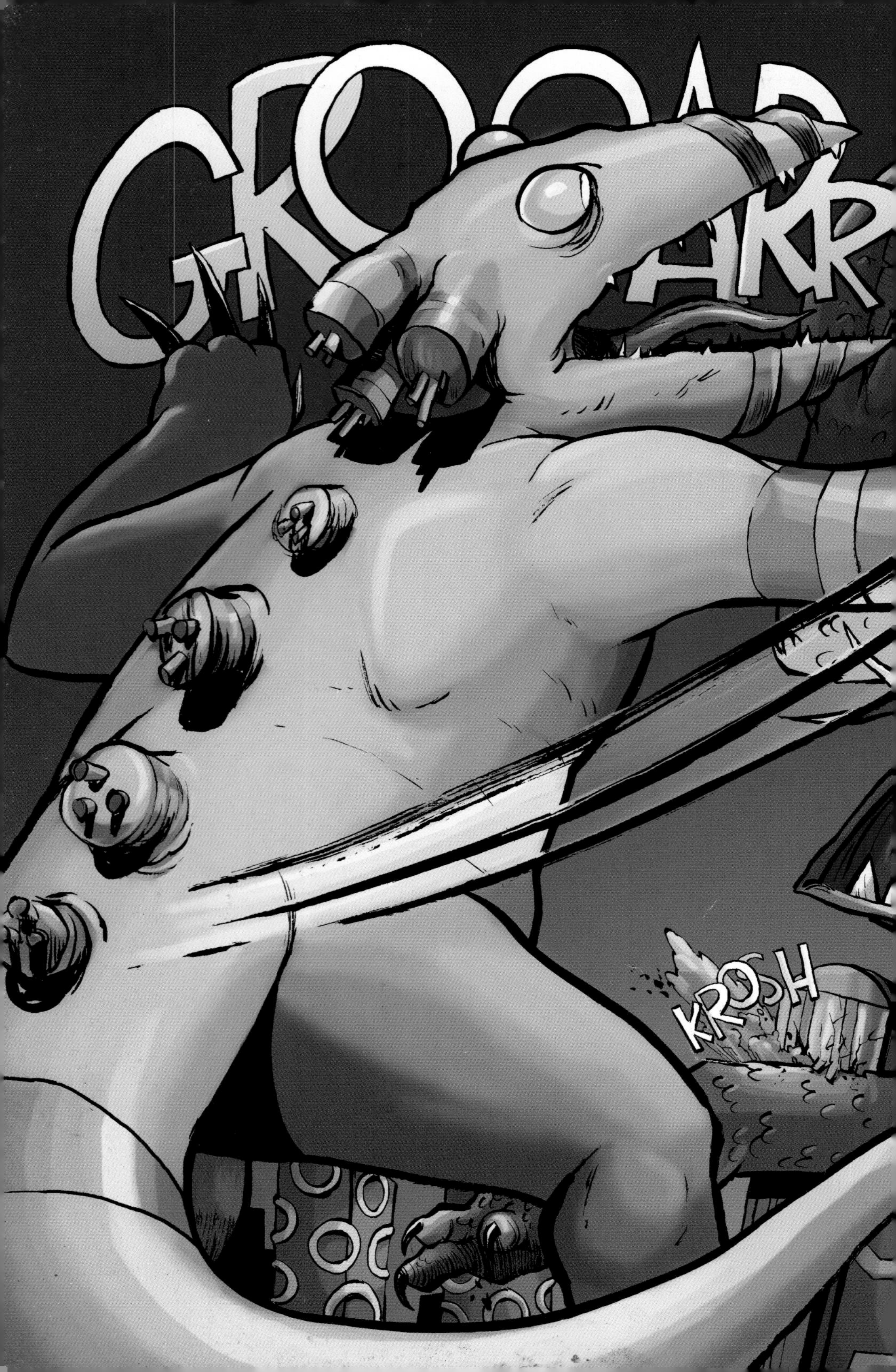
GROOOARRR
KROSH

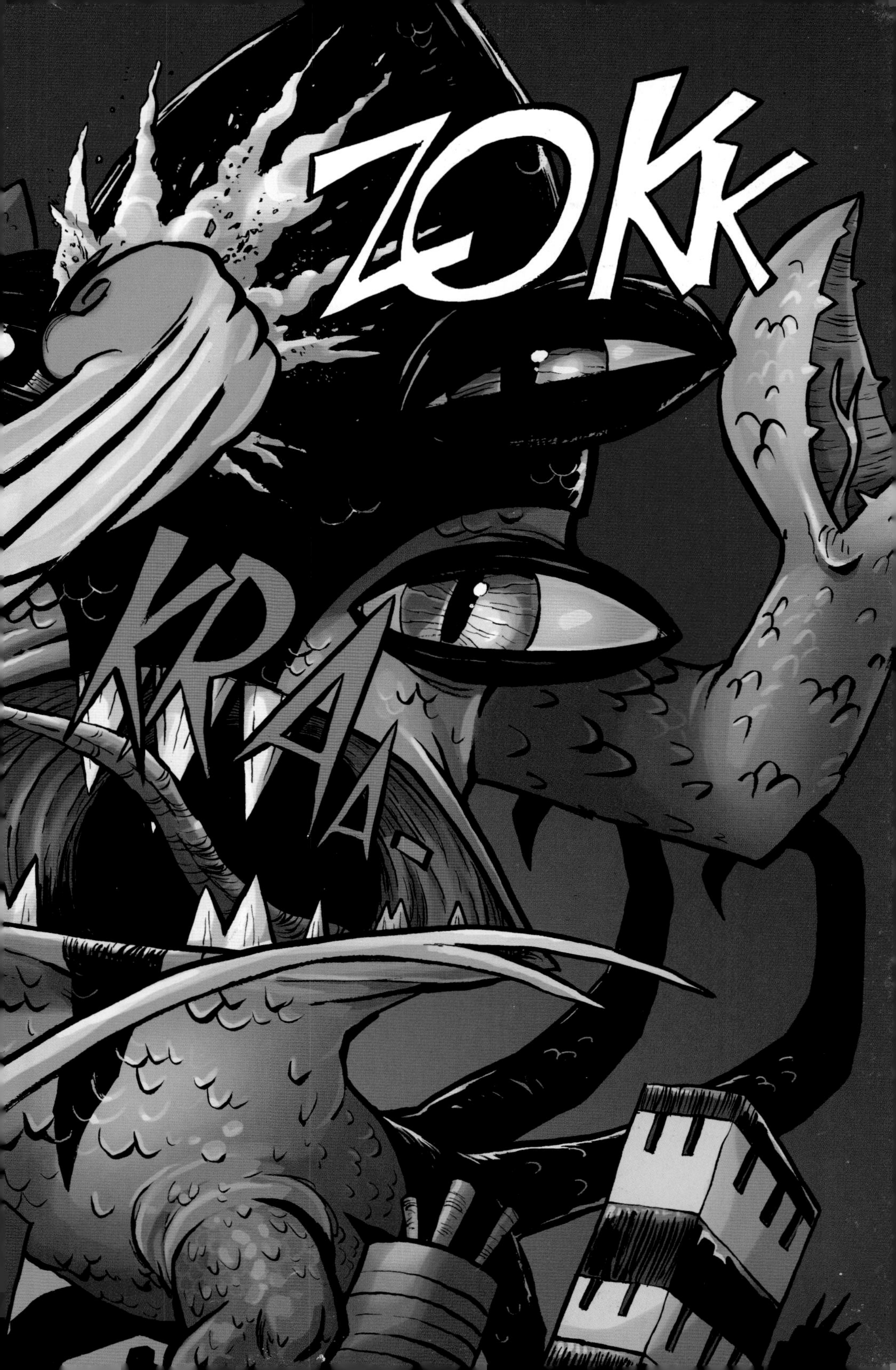
ZOKK
KRAA-

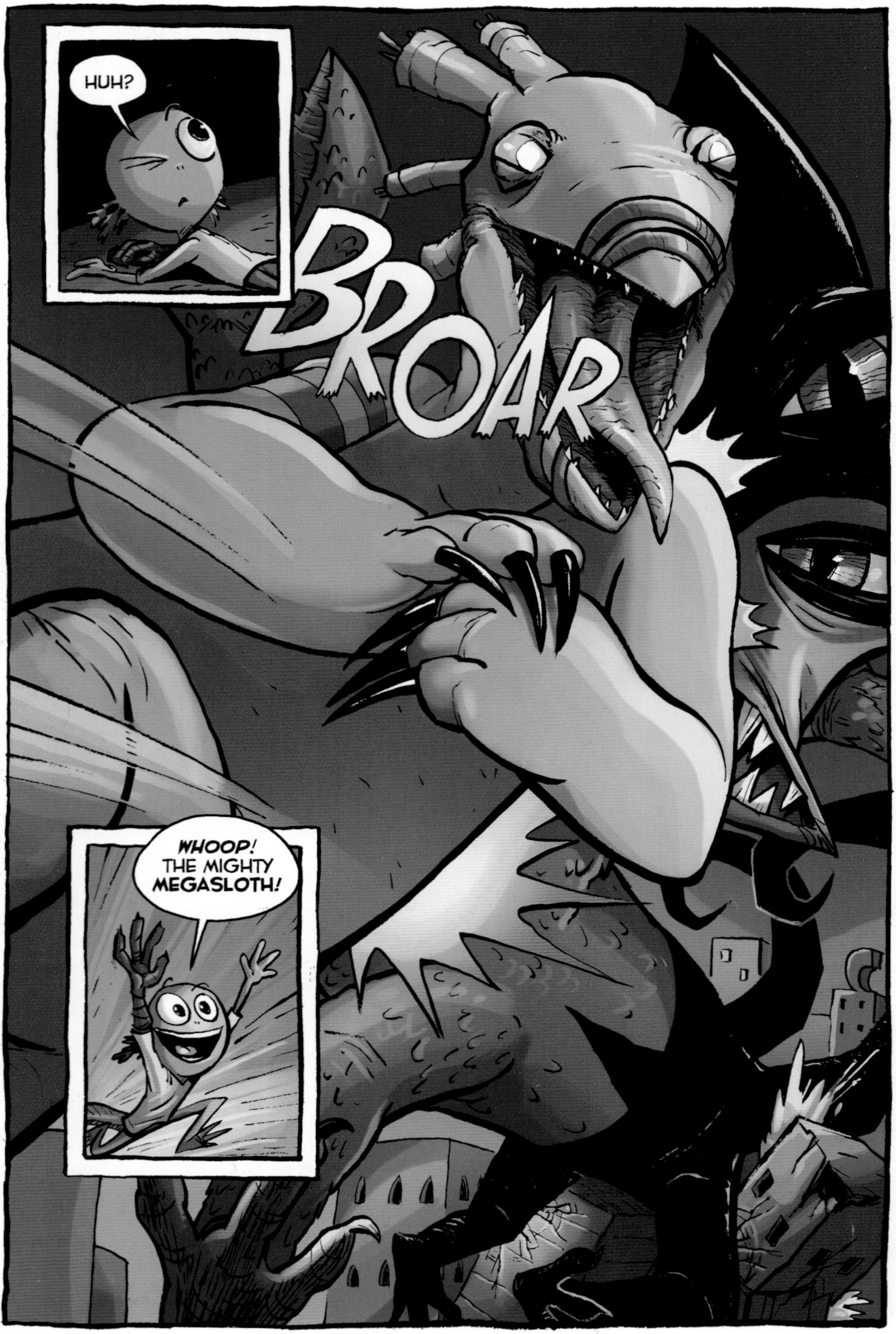
HUH?
BROAR
WHOOP! THE MIGHTY MEGASLOTH!

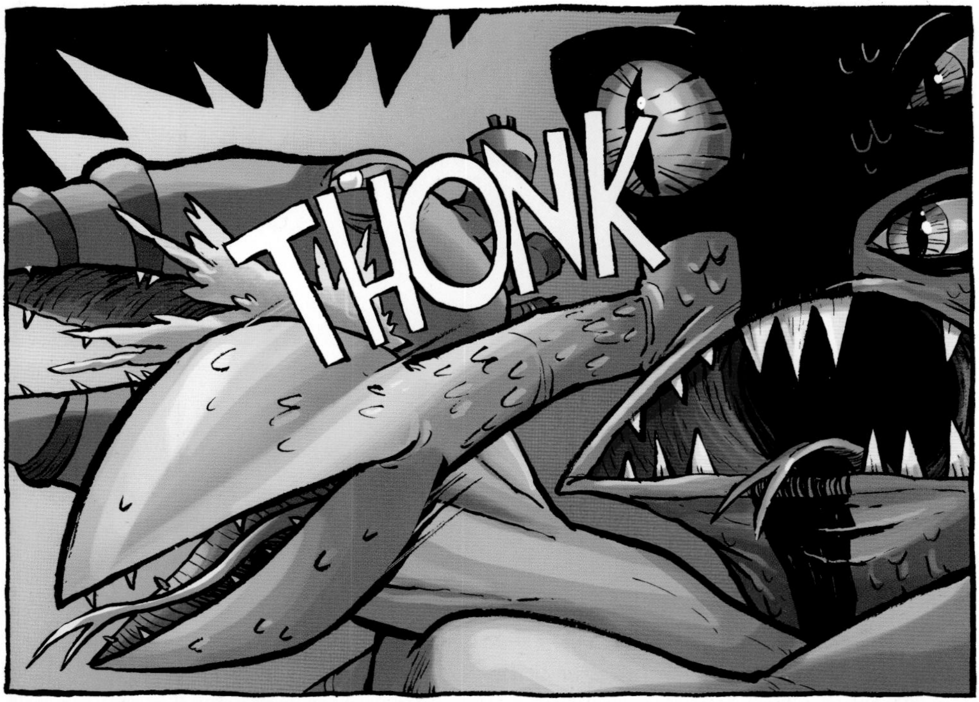
THONK

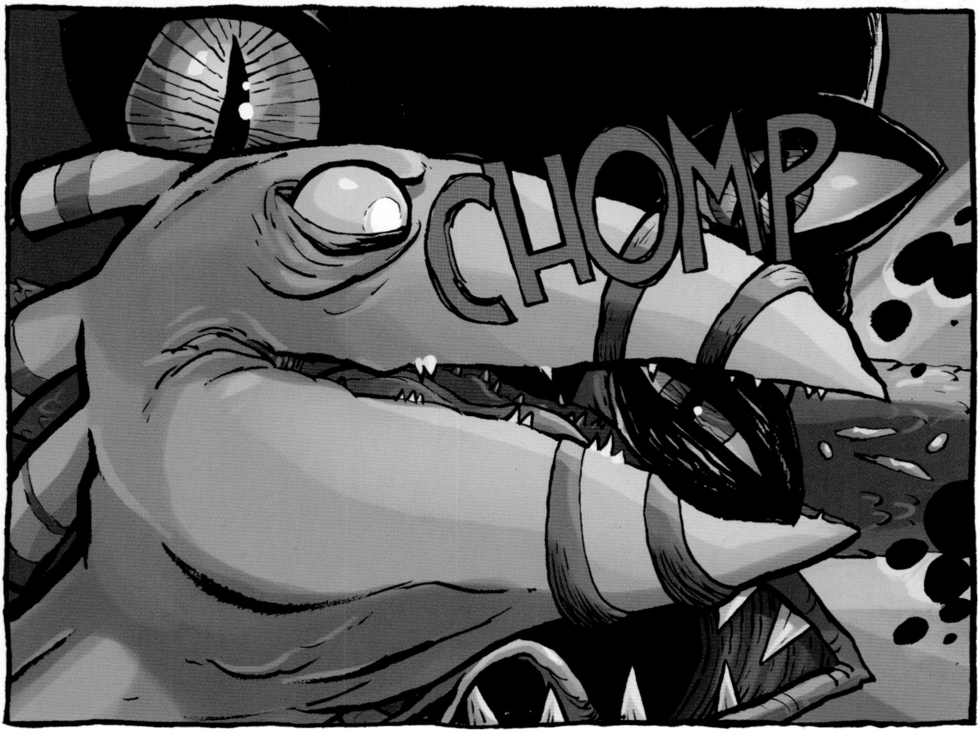
CHOMP

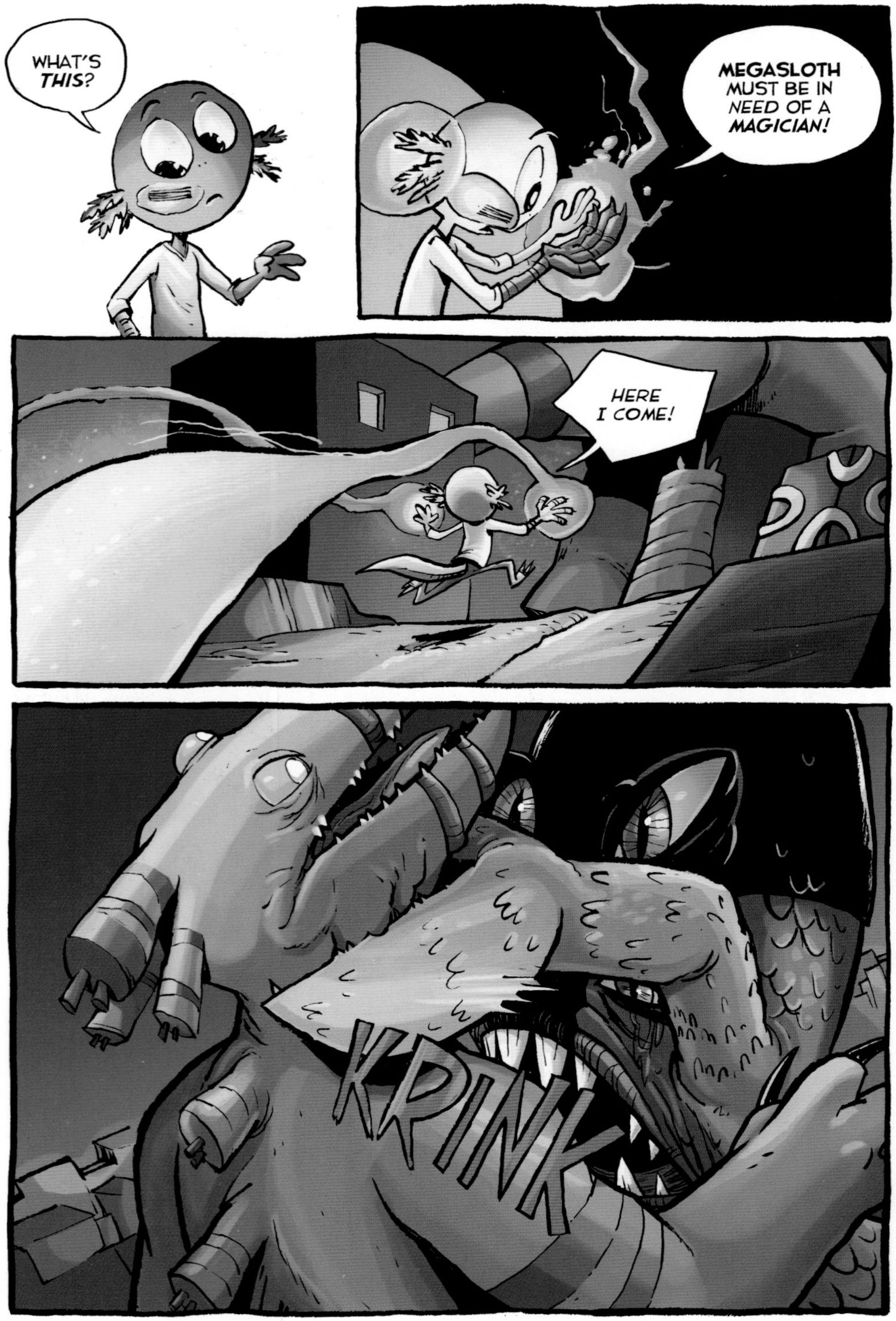
WHAT'S THIS?
MEGASLOTH MUST BE IN NEED OF A MAGICIAN!
HERE I COME!
KRINK

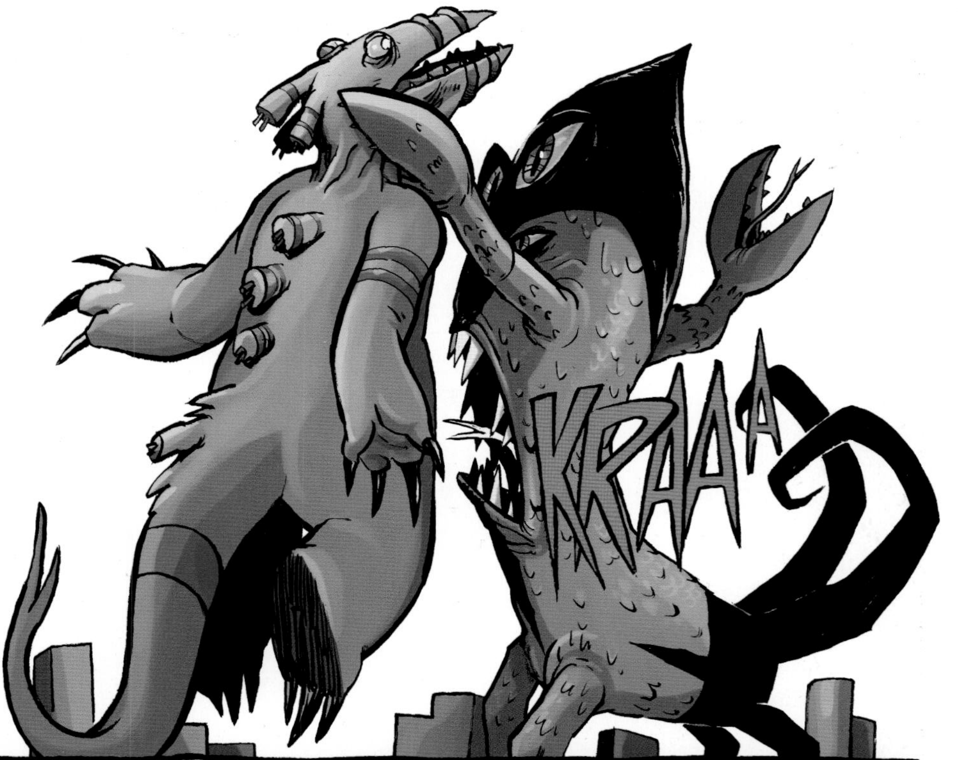
KRAAA

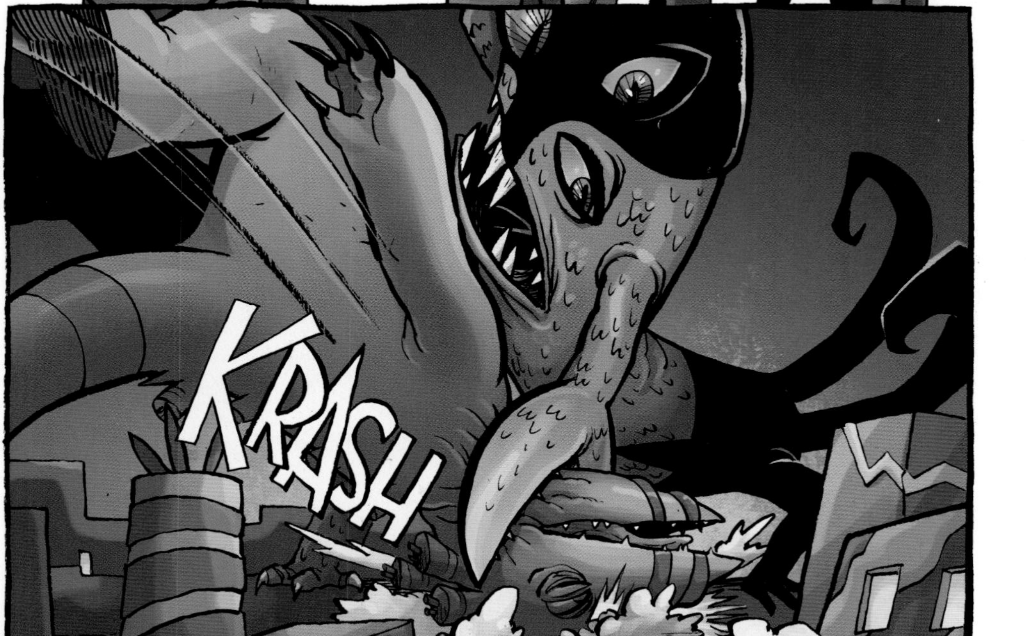
KRASH

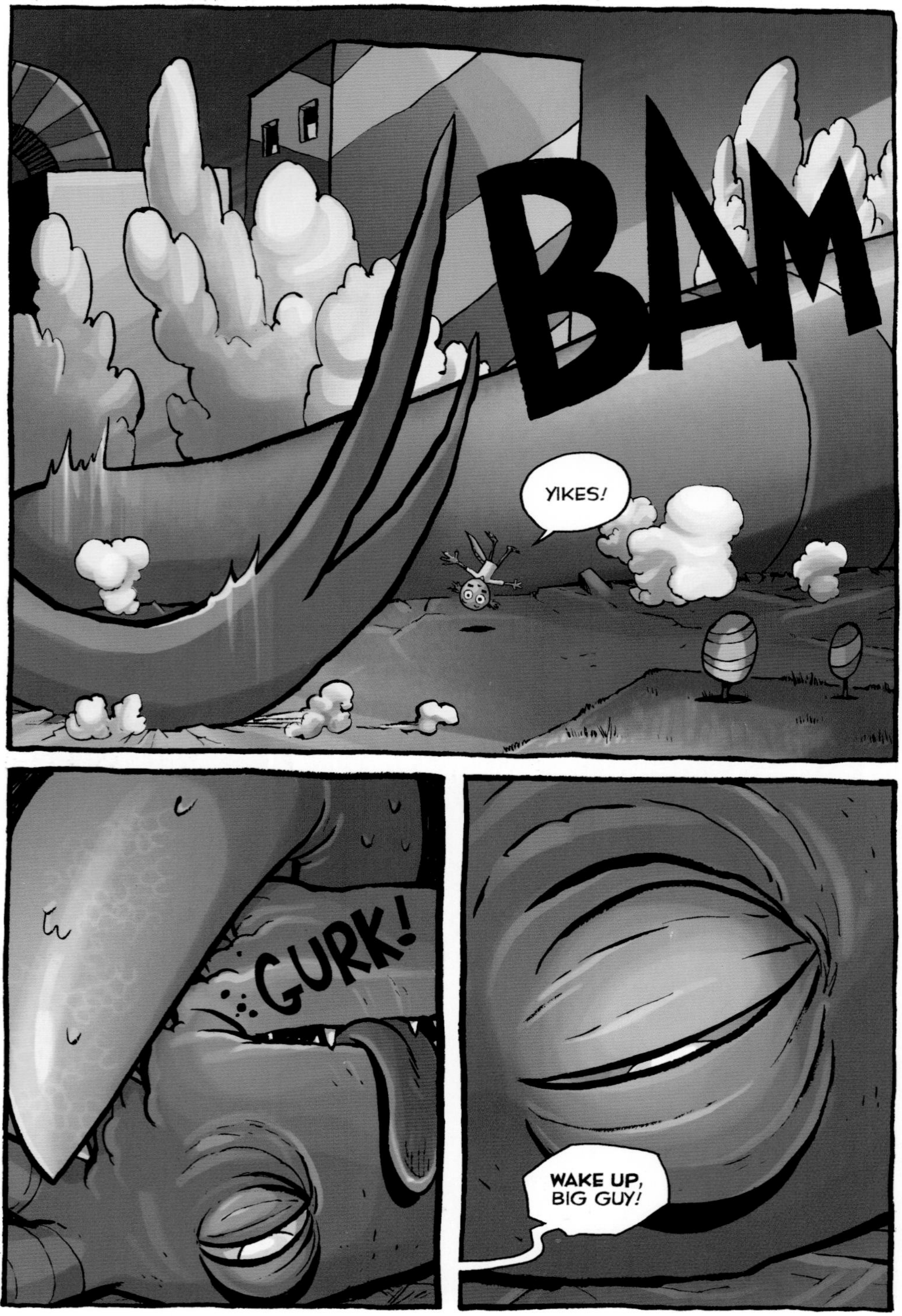
BAM
YIKES!
GURK!
WAKE UP, BIG GUY!

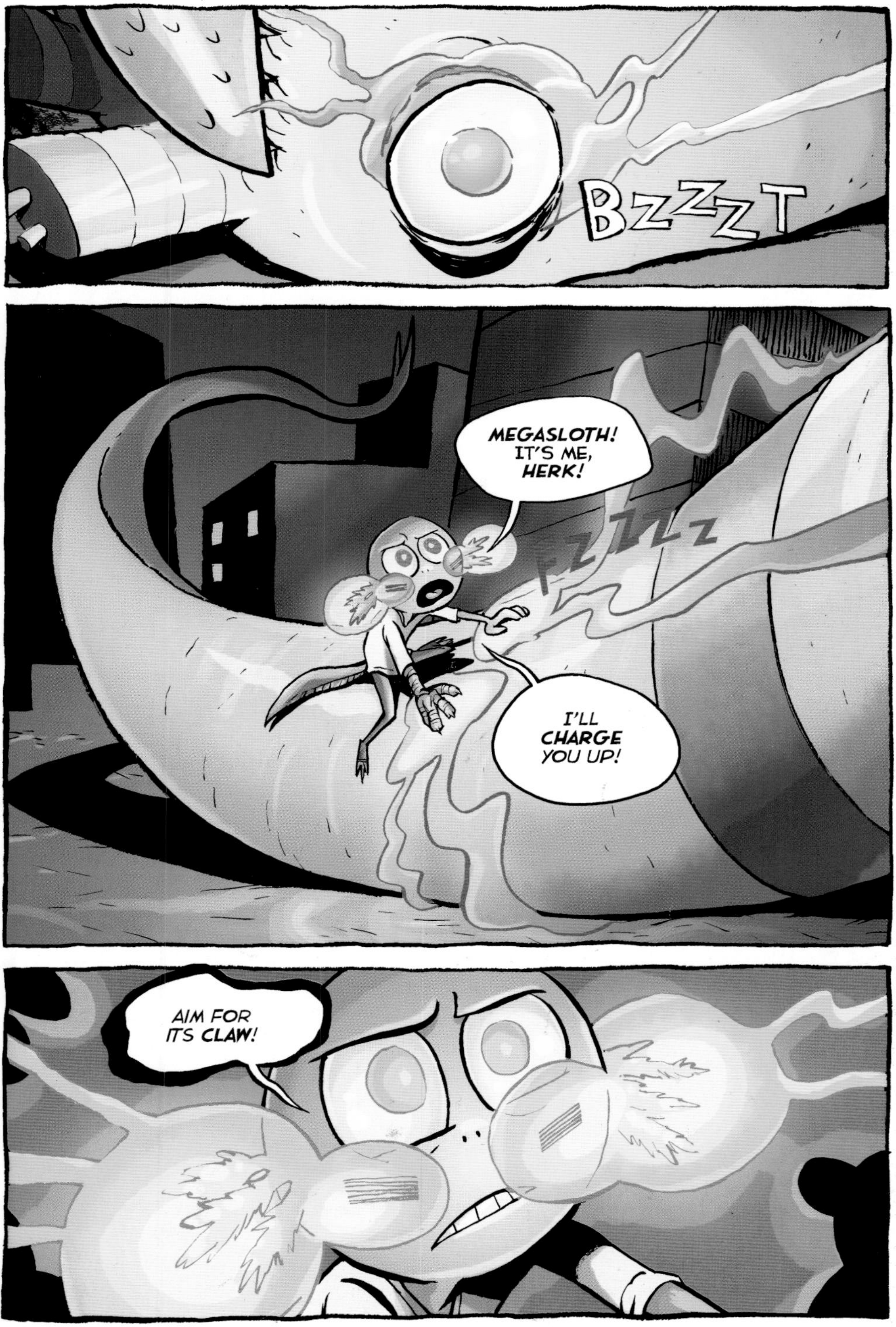
BZZZT
MEGASLOTH! IT'S ME, HERK!
FZZZZZ
I'LL CHARGE YOU UP!
AIM FOR ITS CLAW!

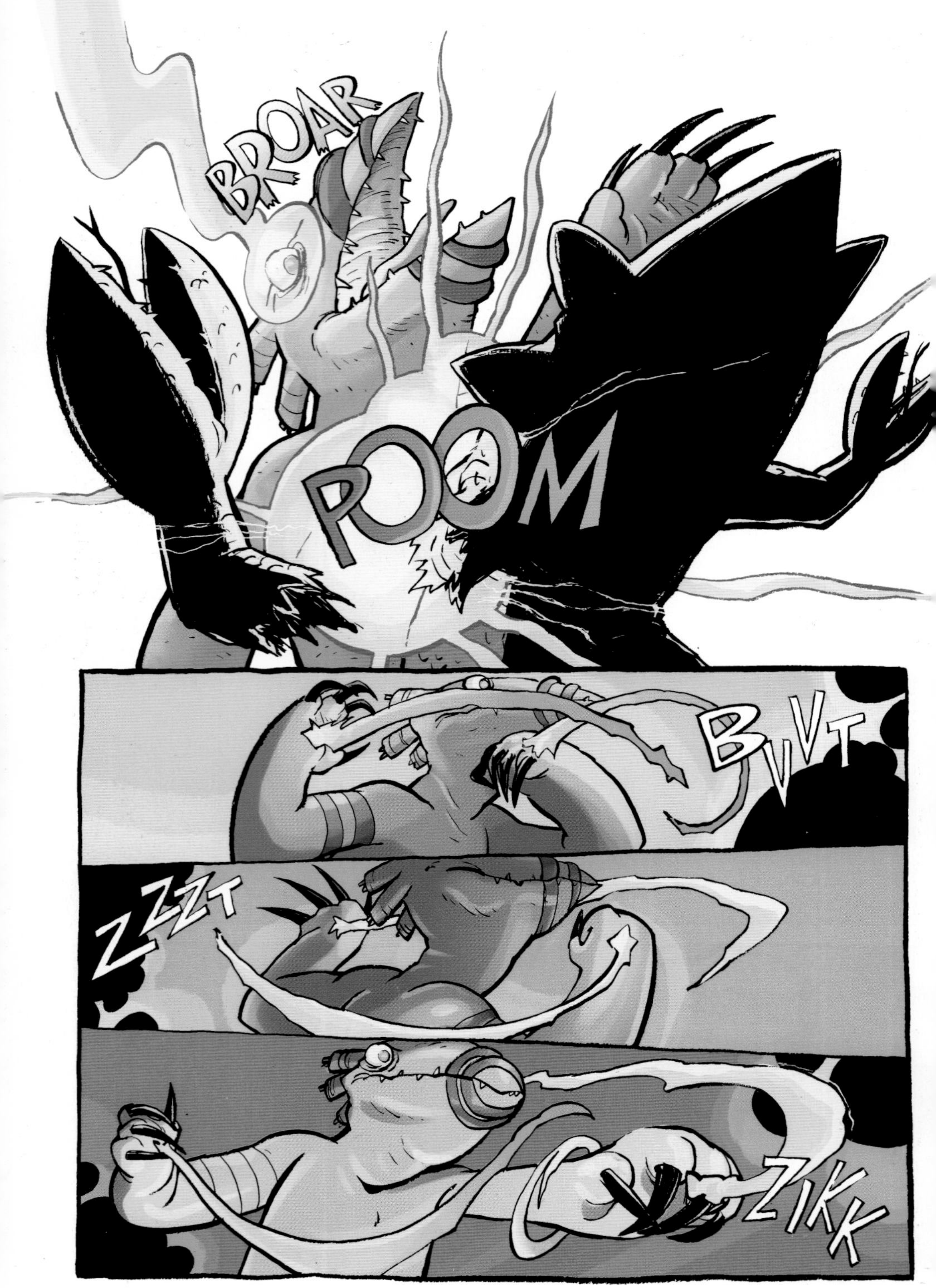
BROAR
POOM
BVVT
ZZZT
ZIKK

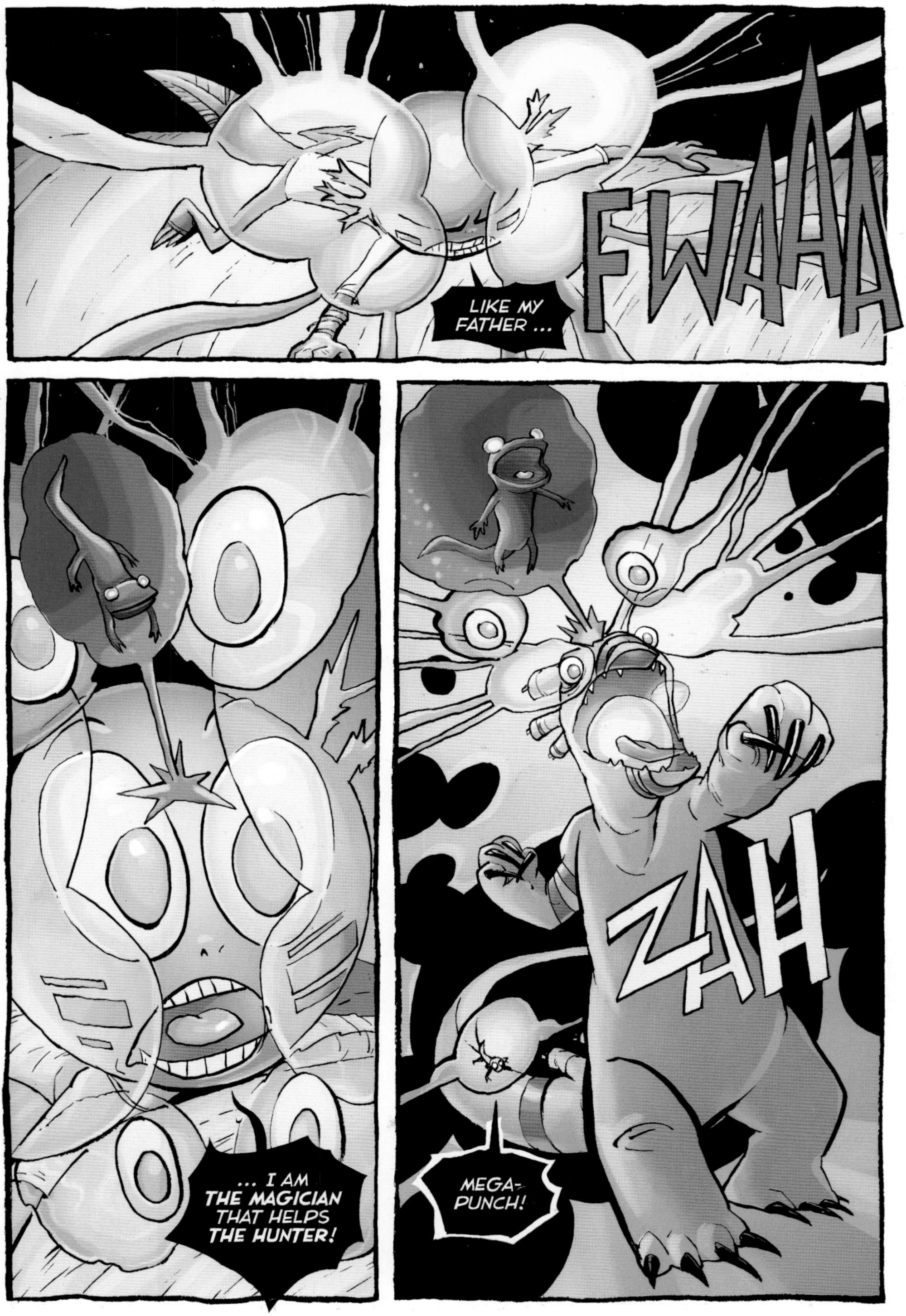
LIKE MY FATHER ...
FWAAA
... I AM THE MAGICIAN THAT HELPS THE HUNTER!
MEGA-PUNCH!
ZAH

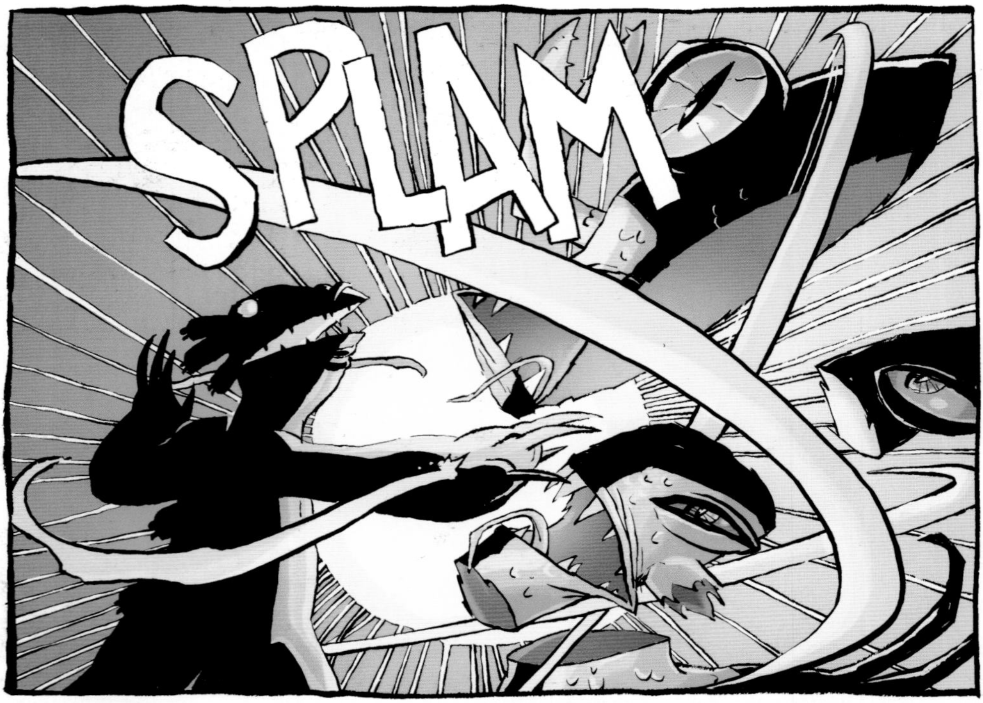
SPLAM

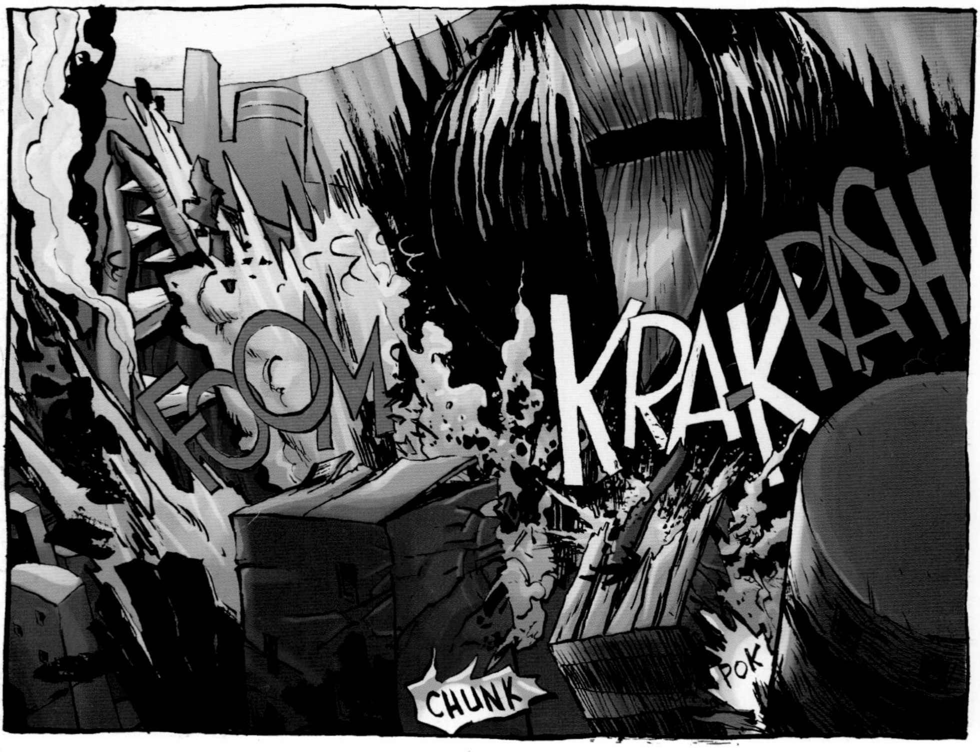
FOOM
KRAK
RASH
CHUNK
POK

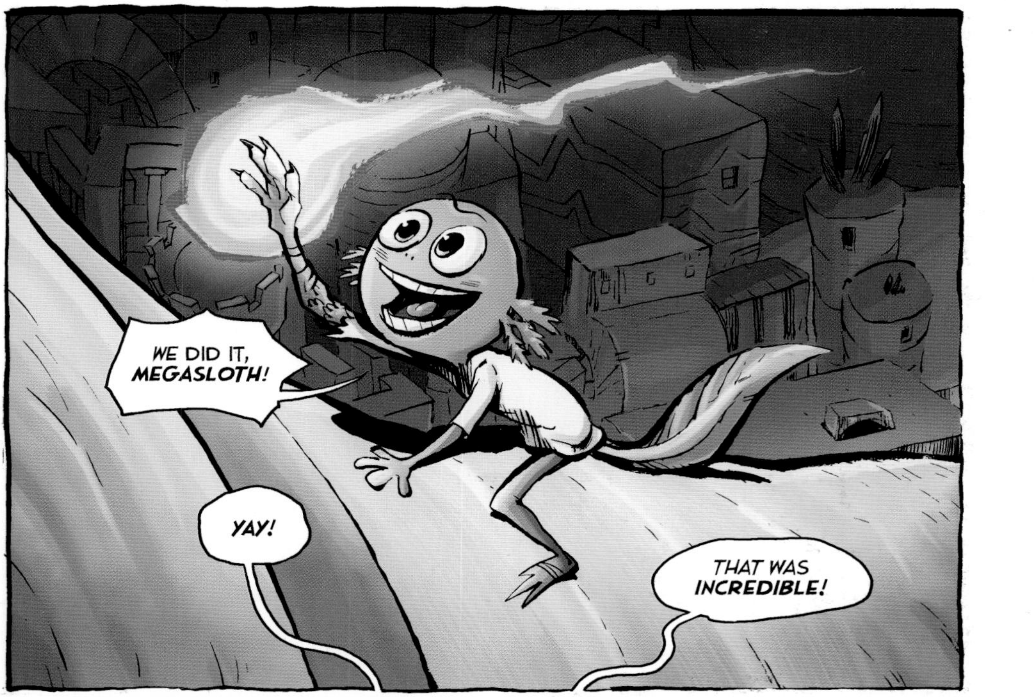
WE DID IT, MEGASLOTH!
YAY!
THAT WAS INCREDIBLE!

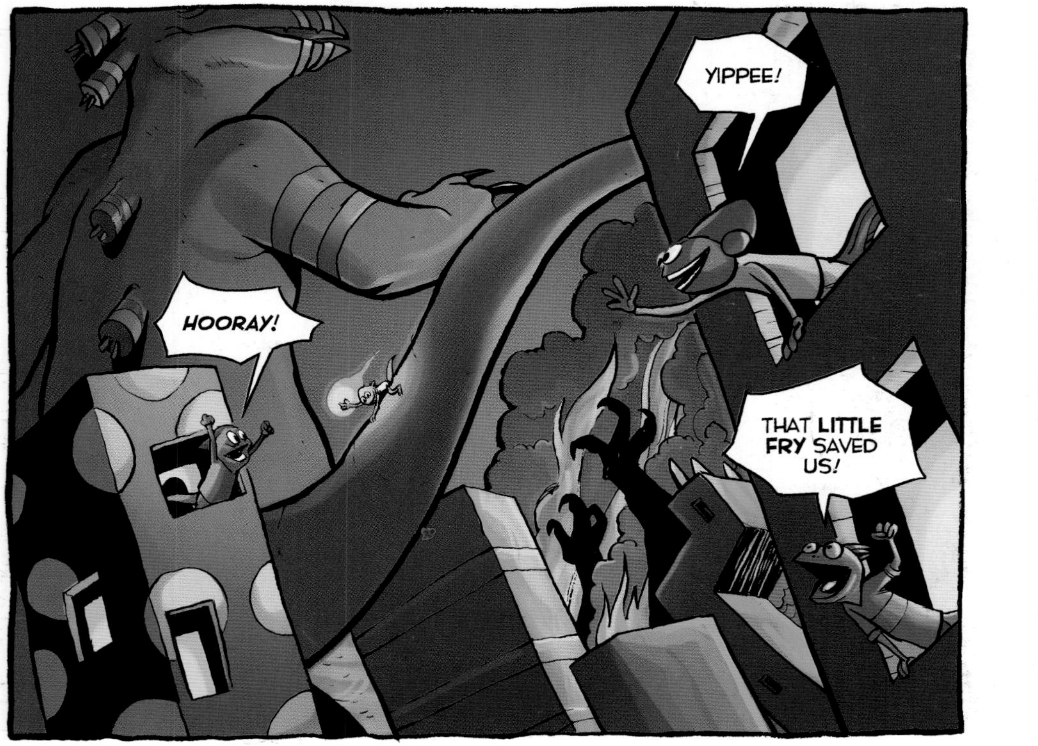
YIPPEE!
HOORAY!
THAT LITTLE FRY SAVED US!

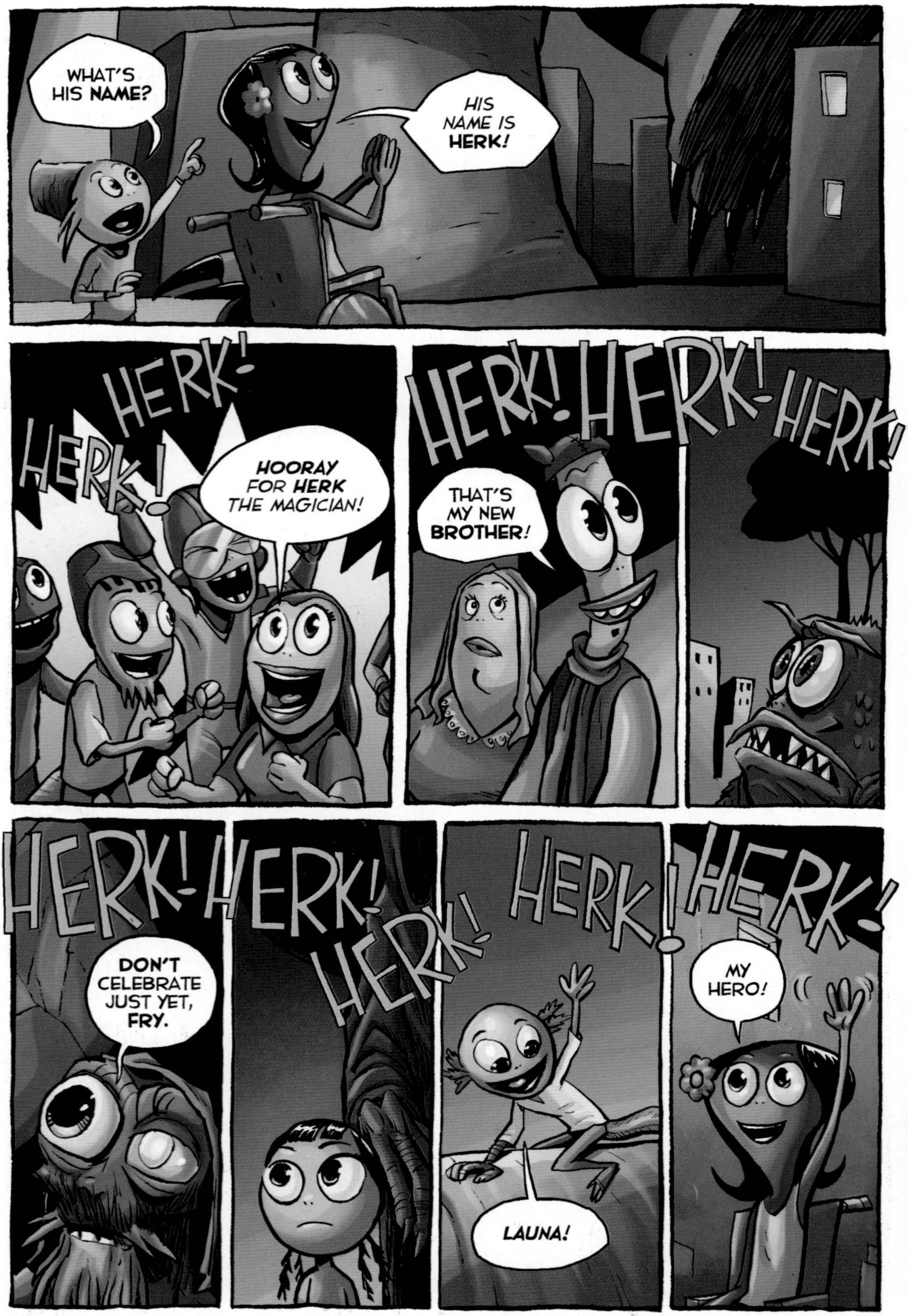
WHAT'S HIS NAME?
HIS NAME IS HERK!
HERK!
HERK!
HOORAY FOR HERK THE MAGICIAN!
HERK! HERK! HERK!
THAT'S MY NEW BROTHER!
HERK! HERK! HERK! HERK! HERK!
DON'T CELEBRATE JUST YET, FRY.
LAUNA!
MY HERO!

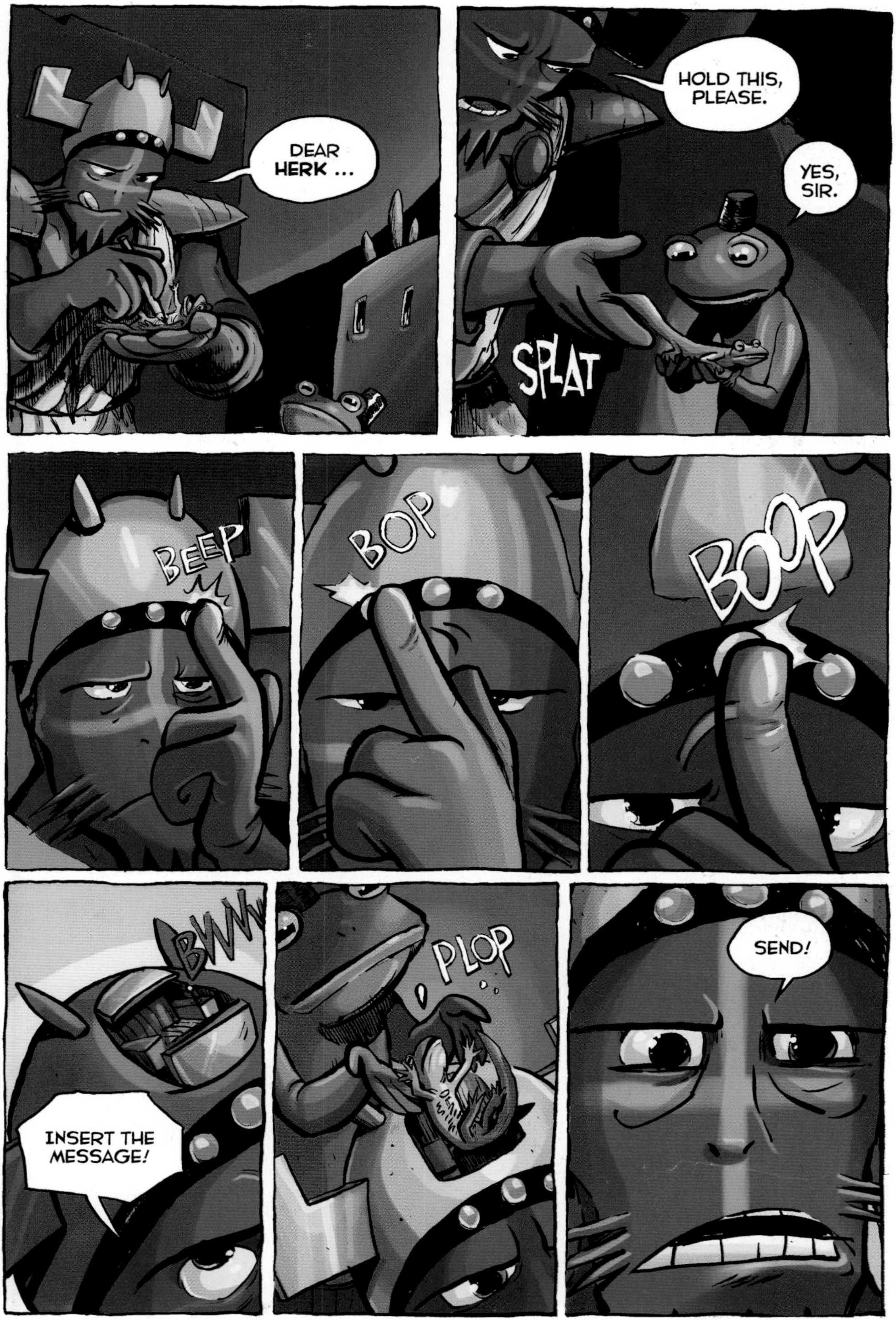
DEAR **HERK** ...
HOLD THIS, PLEASE.
YES, SIR.
SPLAT
BEEP
BOP
BOOP
BWW
INSERT THE MESSAGE!
PLOP
SEND!

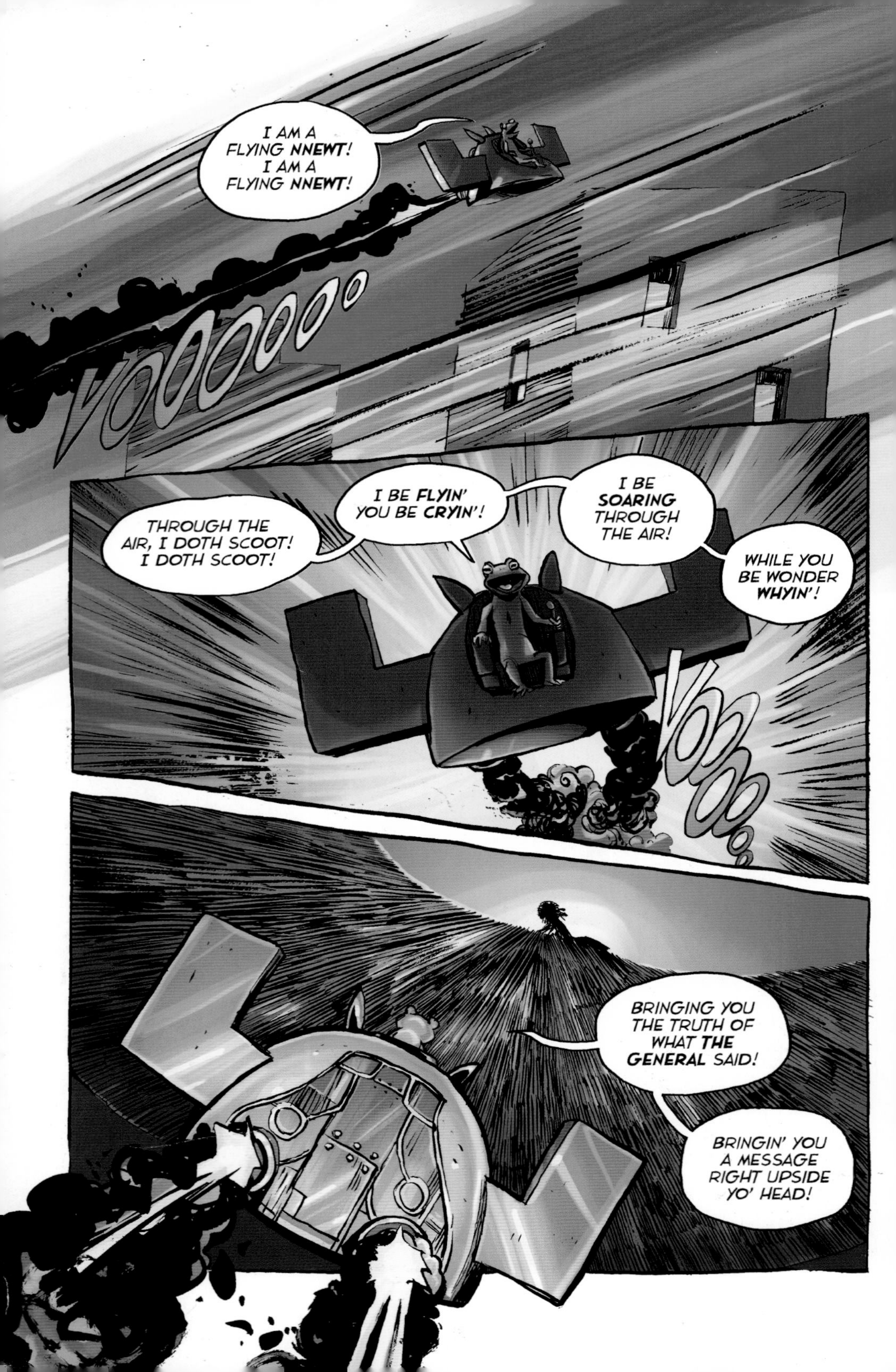
I AM A FLYING NNEWT! I AM A FLYING NNEWT!
YOOOOOOO
THROUGH THE AIR, I DOTH SCOOT! I DOTH SCOOT!
I BE FLYIN' YOU BE CRYIN'!
I BE SOARING THROUGH THE AIR!
WHILE YOU BE WONDER WHYIN'!
YOOOOOO
BRINGING YOU THE TRUTH OF WHAT THE GENERAL SAID!
BRINGIN' YOU A MESSAGE RIGHT UPSIDE YO' HEAD!

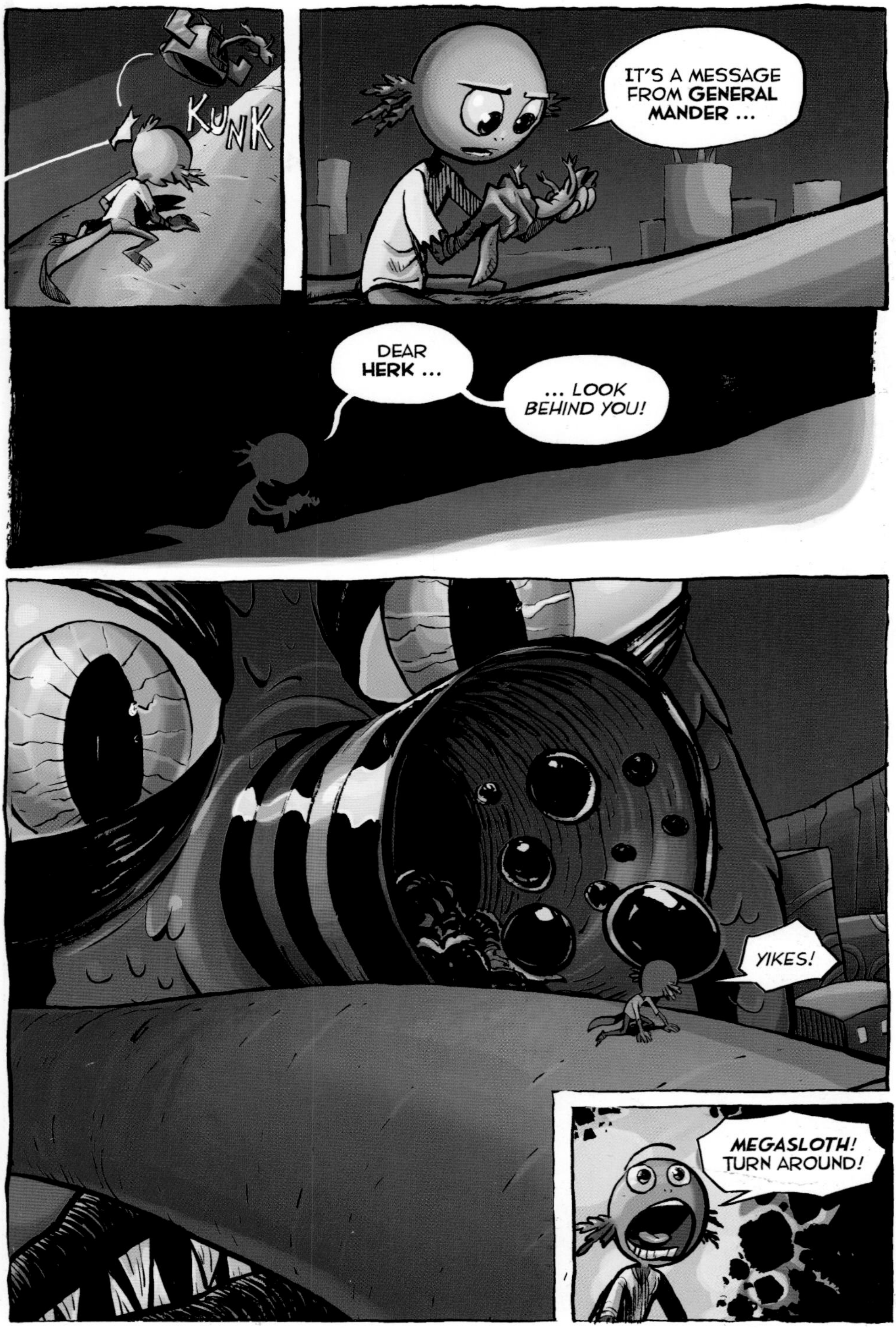
KUNK
IT'S A MESSAGE FROM GENERAL MANDER ...
DEAR HERK ...
... LOOK BEHIND YOU!
YIKES!
MEGASLOTH! TURN AROUND!

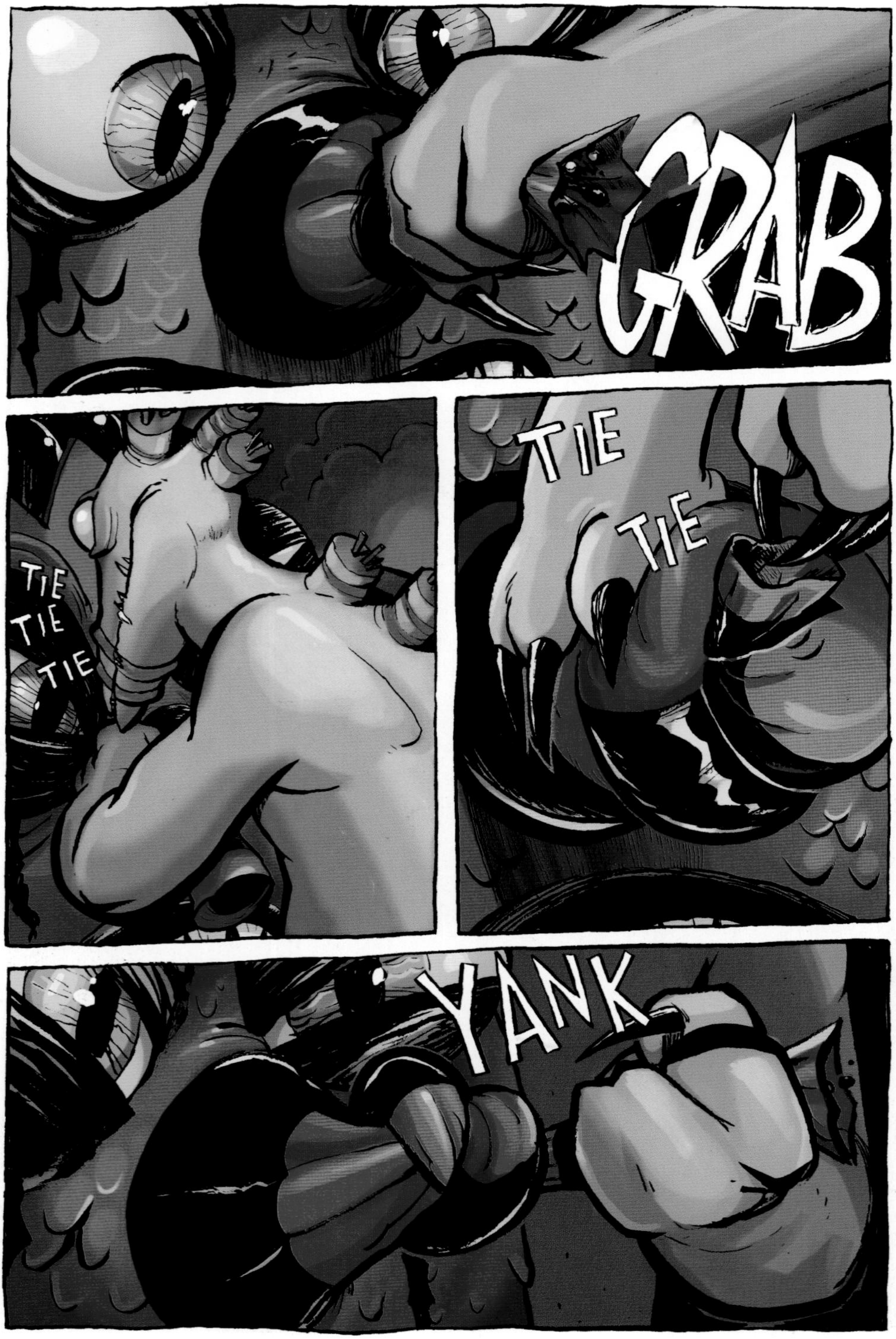
GRAB
TIE
TIE
TIE
TIE
TIE
YANK

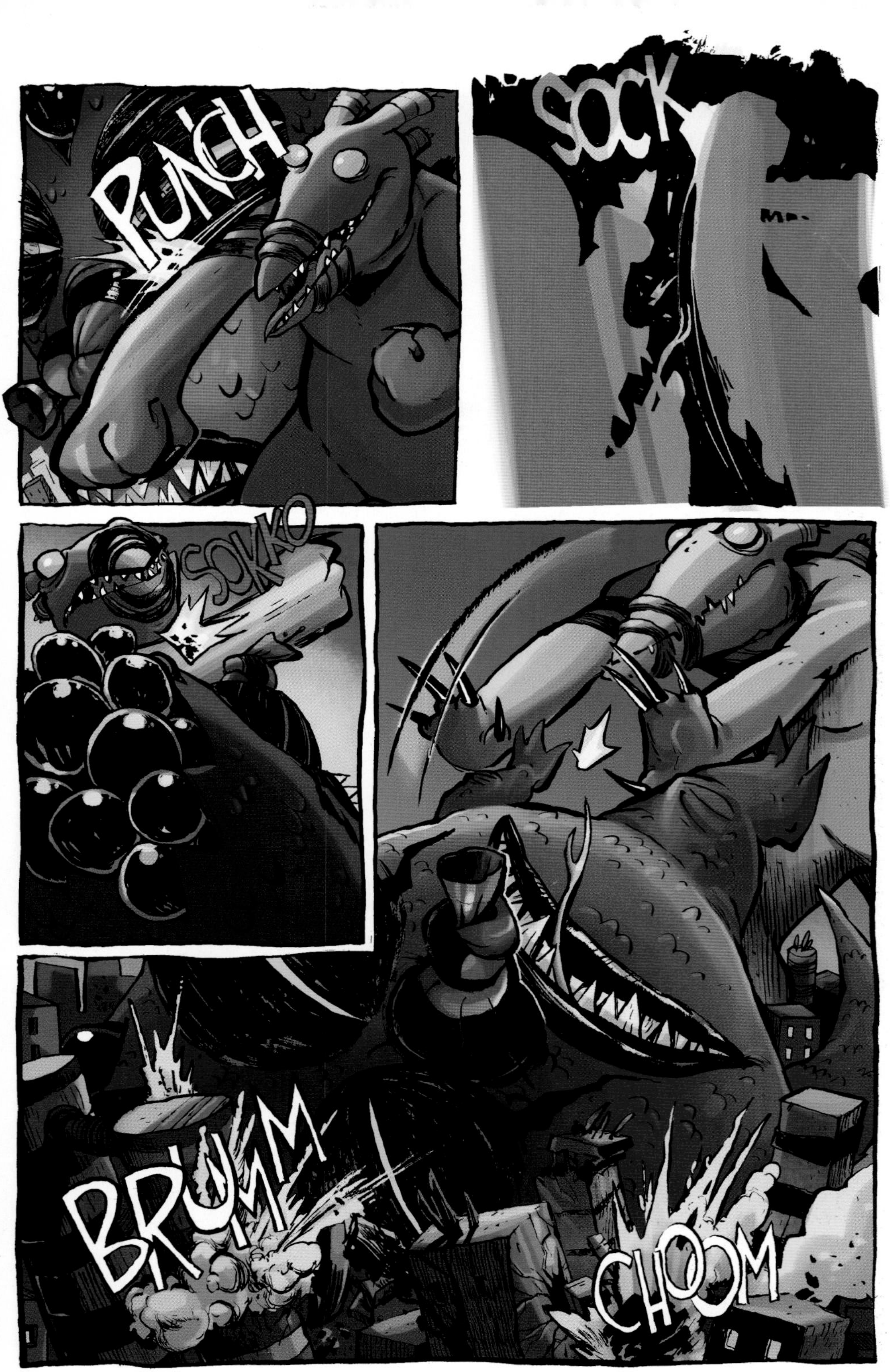
PUNCH
SOCK
SOKKO
BRUMM
CHOOM

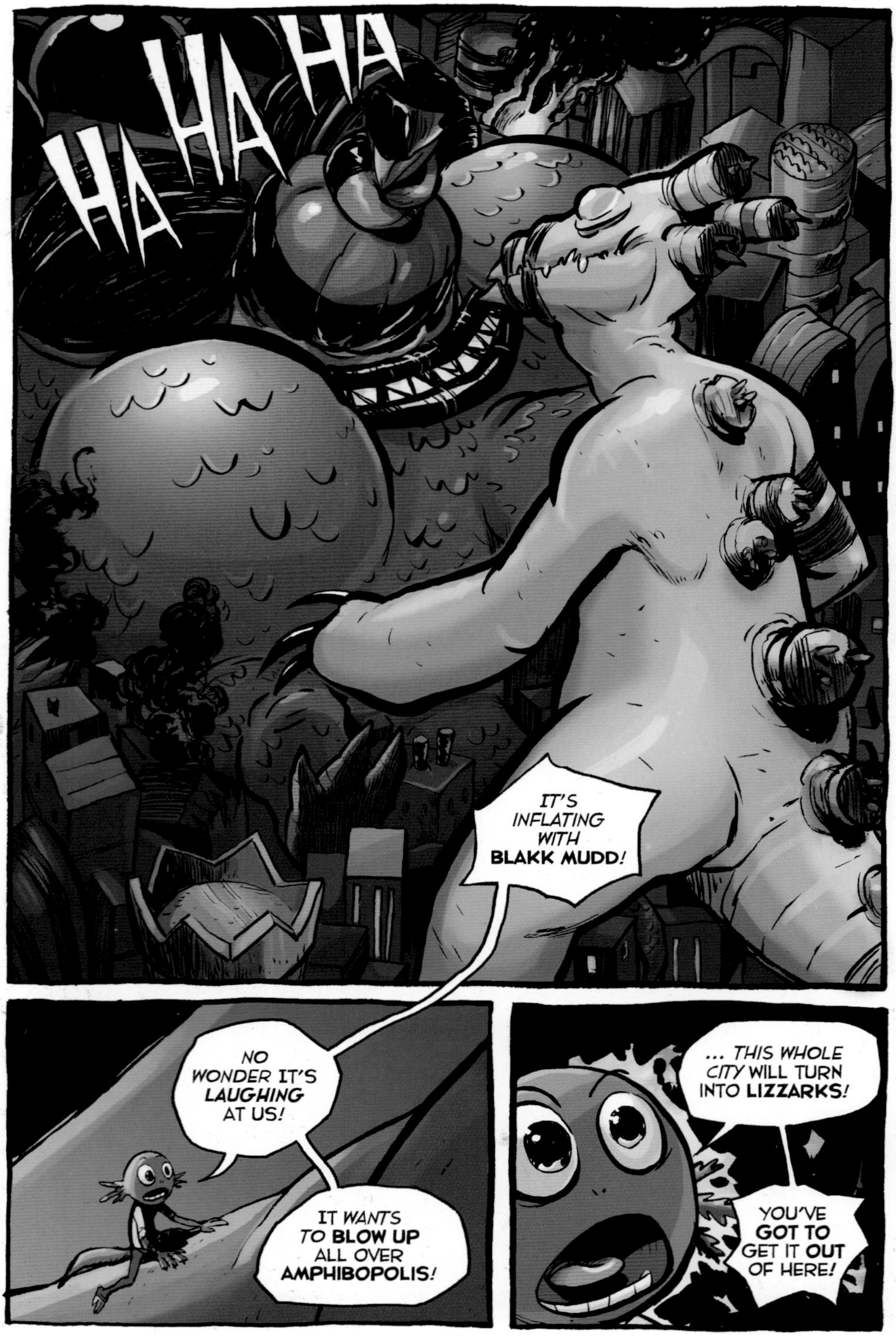
HA HA HA HA
IT'S INFLATING WITH BLAKK MUDD!
NO WONDER IT'S LAUGHING AT US!
IT WANTS TO BLOW UP ALL OVER AMPHIBOPOLIS!
... THIS WHOLE CITY WILL TURN INTO LIZZARKS!
YOU'VE GOT TO GET IT OUT OF HERE!

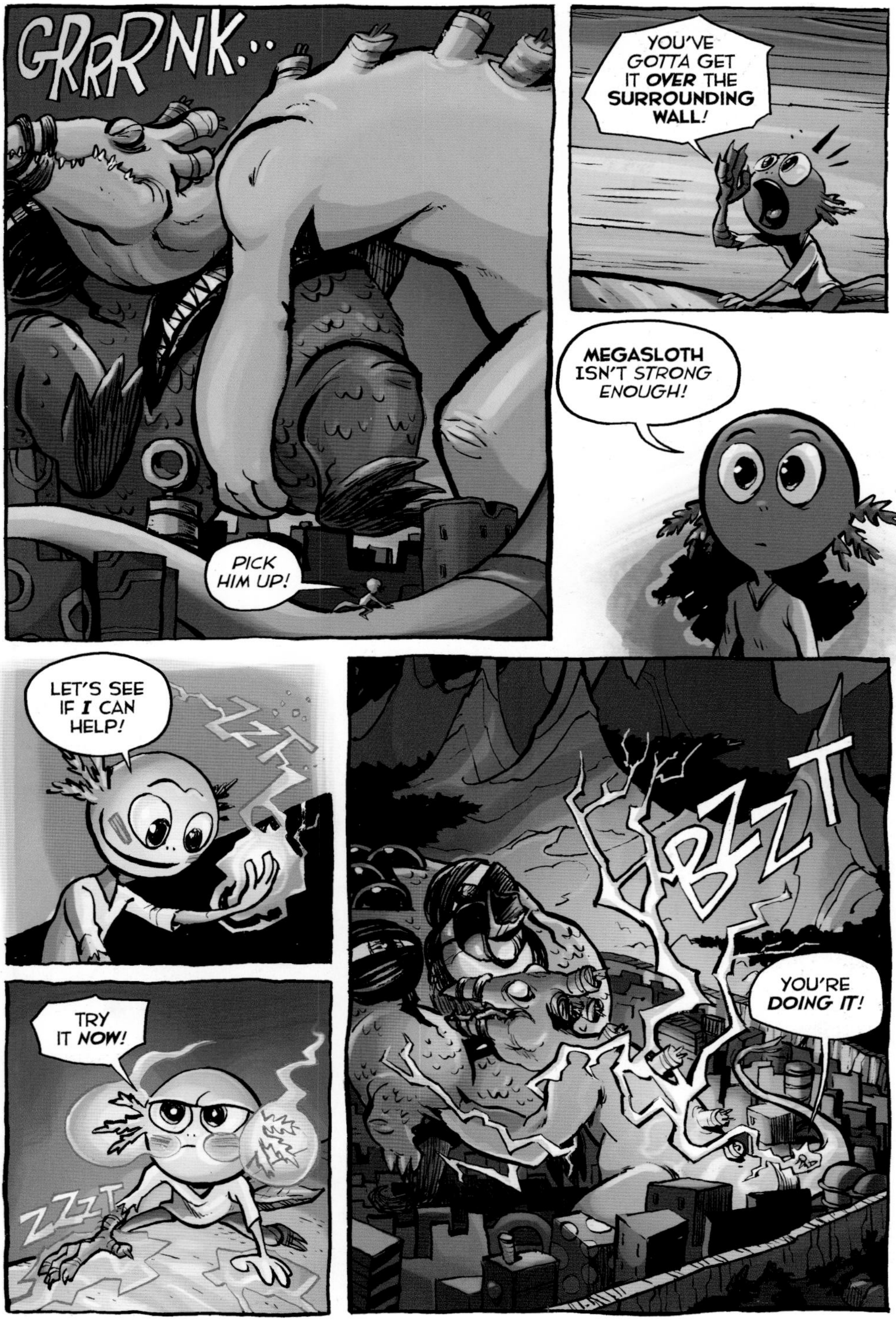
GRRRNK...
YOU'VE GOTTA GET IT OVER THE SURROUNDING WALL!
PICK HIM UP!
MEGASLOTH ISN'T STRONG ENOUGH!
LET'S SEE IF I CAN HELP!
ZZZT
TRY IT NOW!
ZZZT
BZZZT
YOU'RE DOING IT!

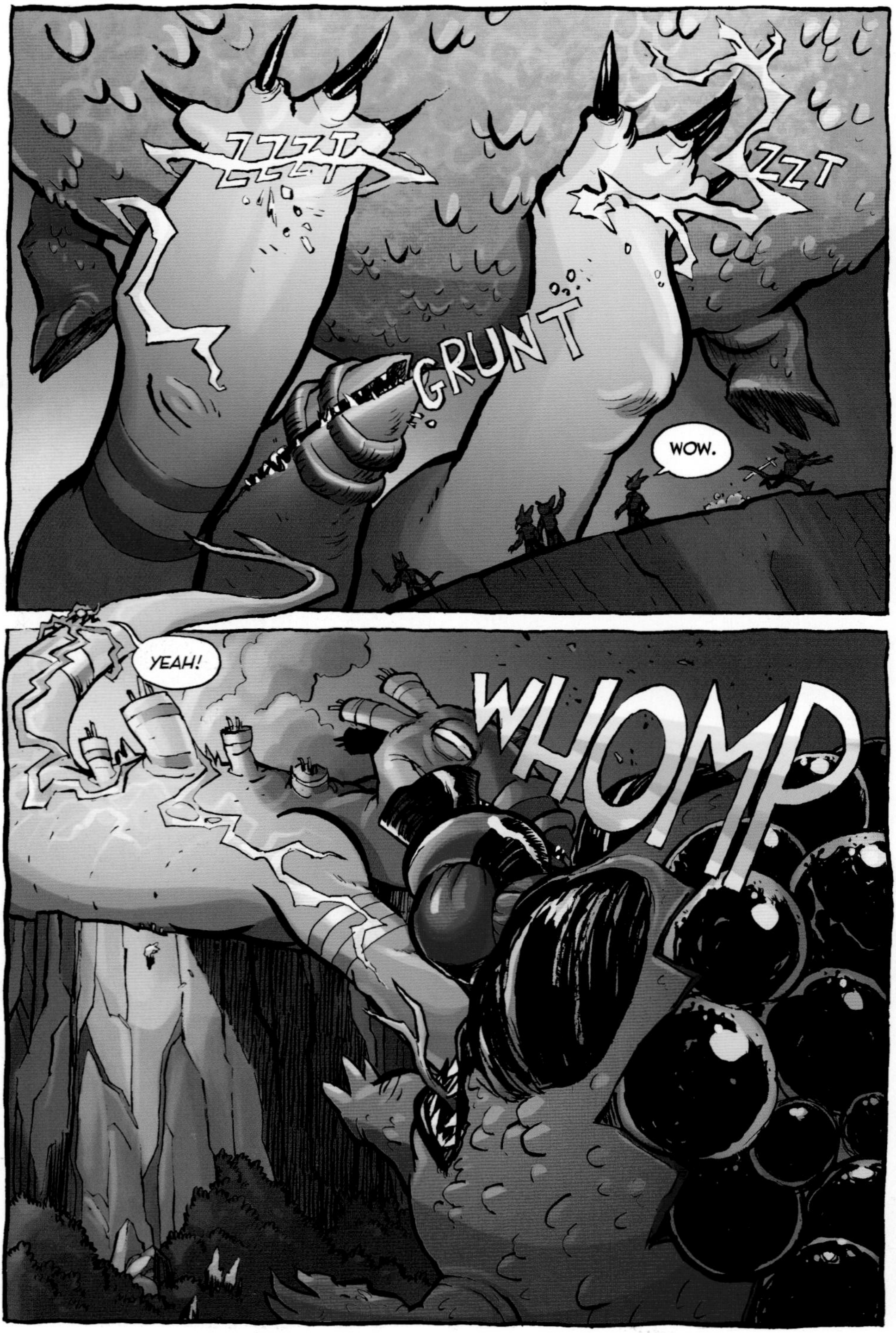
ZZZZT
ZZZT
GRUNT
WOW.
YEAH!
WHOMP

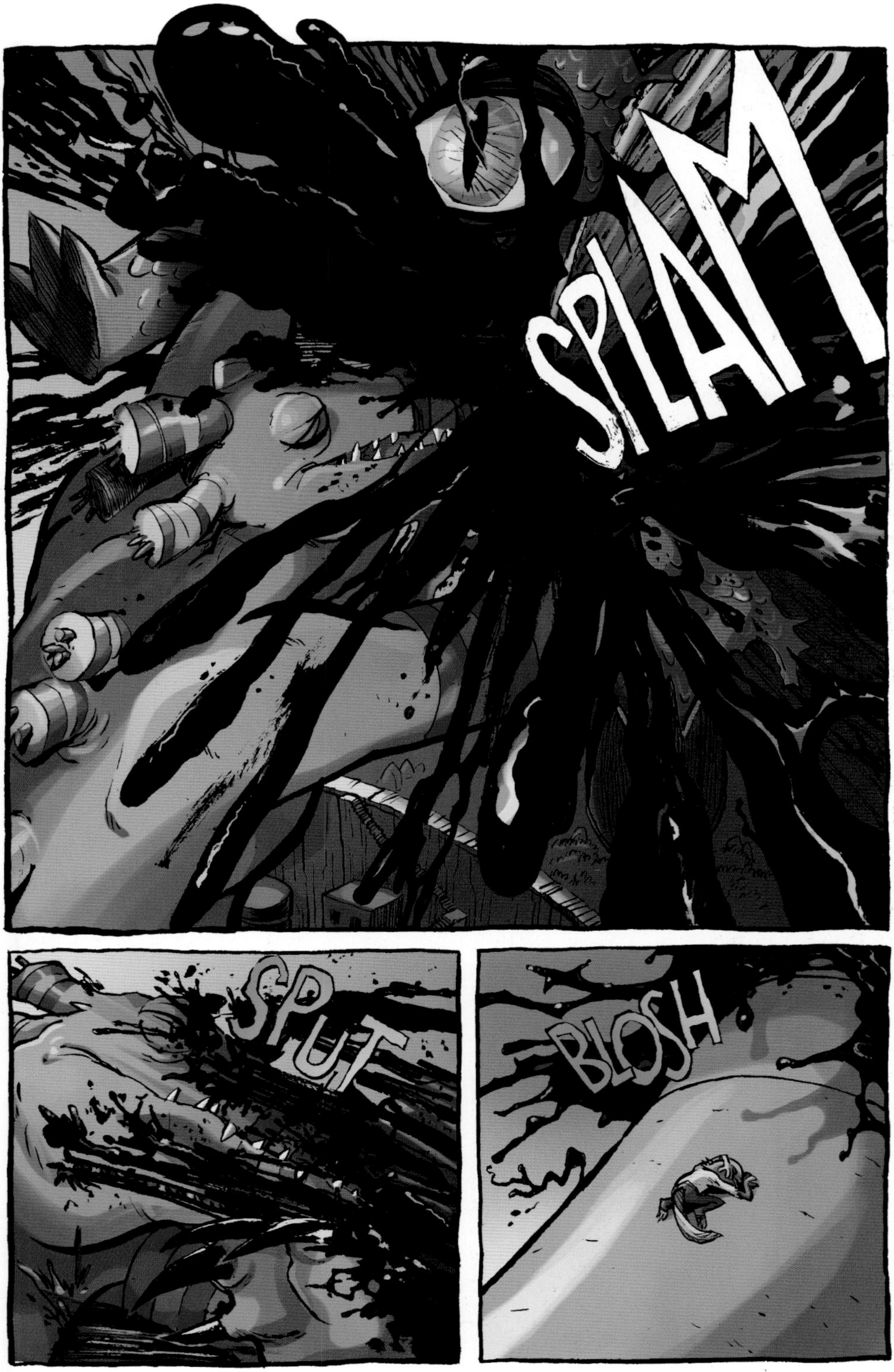
SPLAM
SPUT
BLOSH

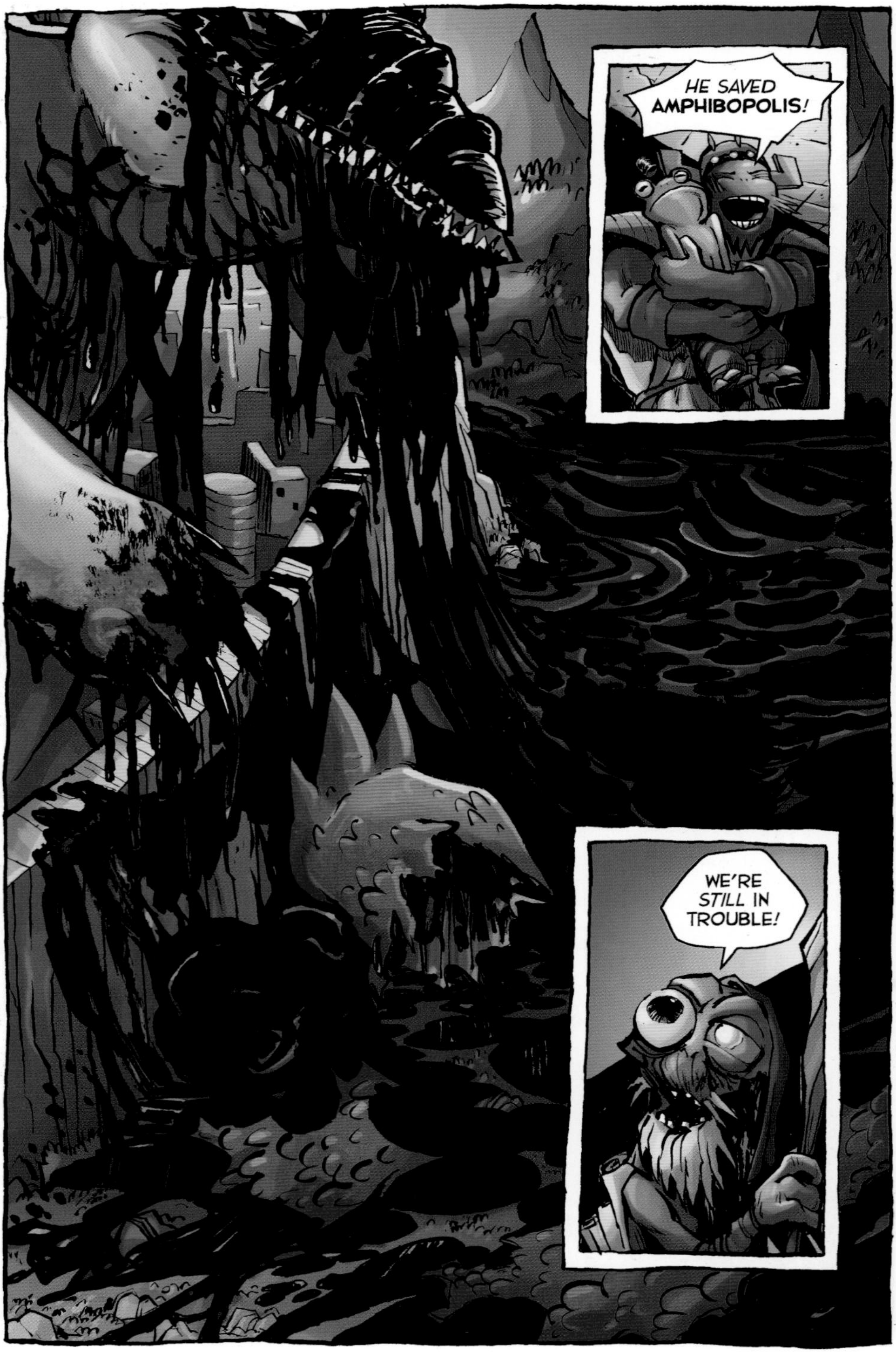
HE SAVED AMPHIBOPOLIS!
WE'RE STILL IN TROUBLE!

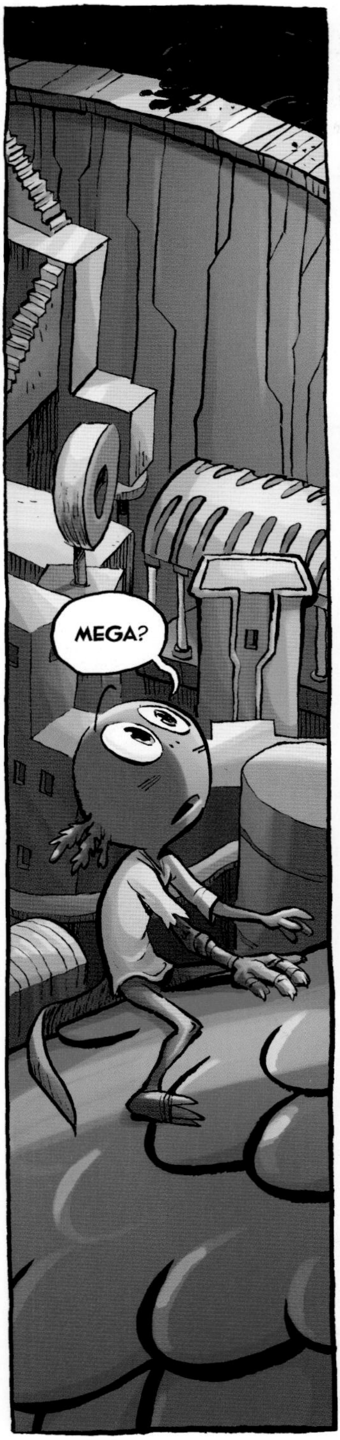
MEGA?

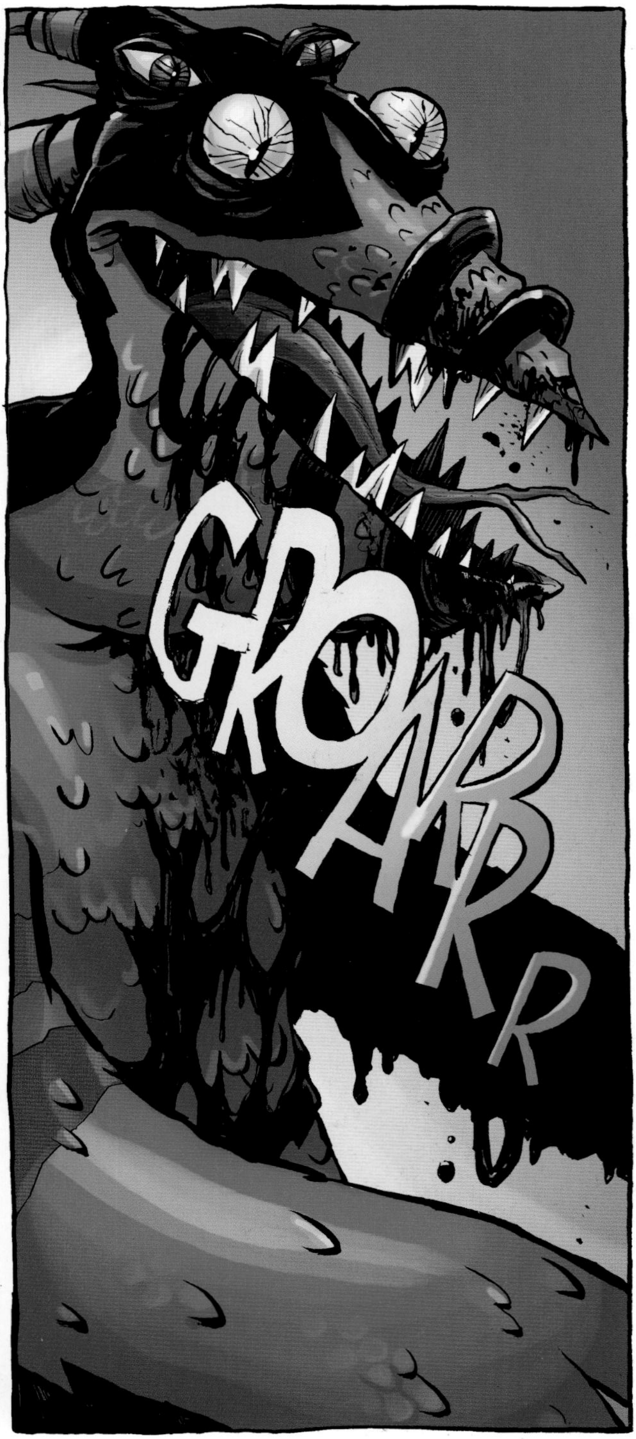
GROARRR

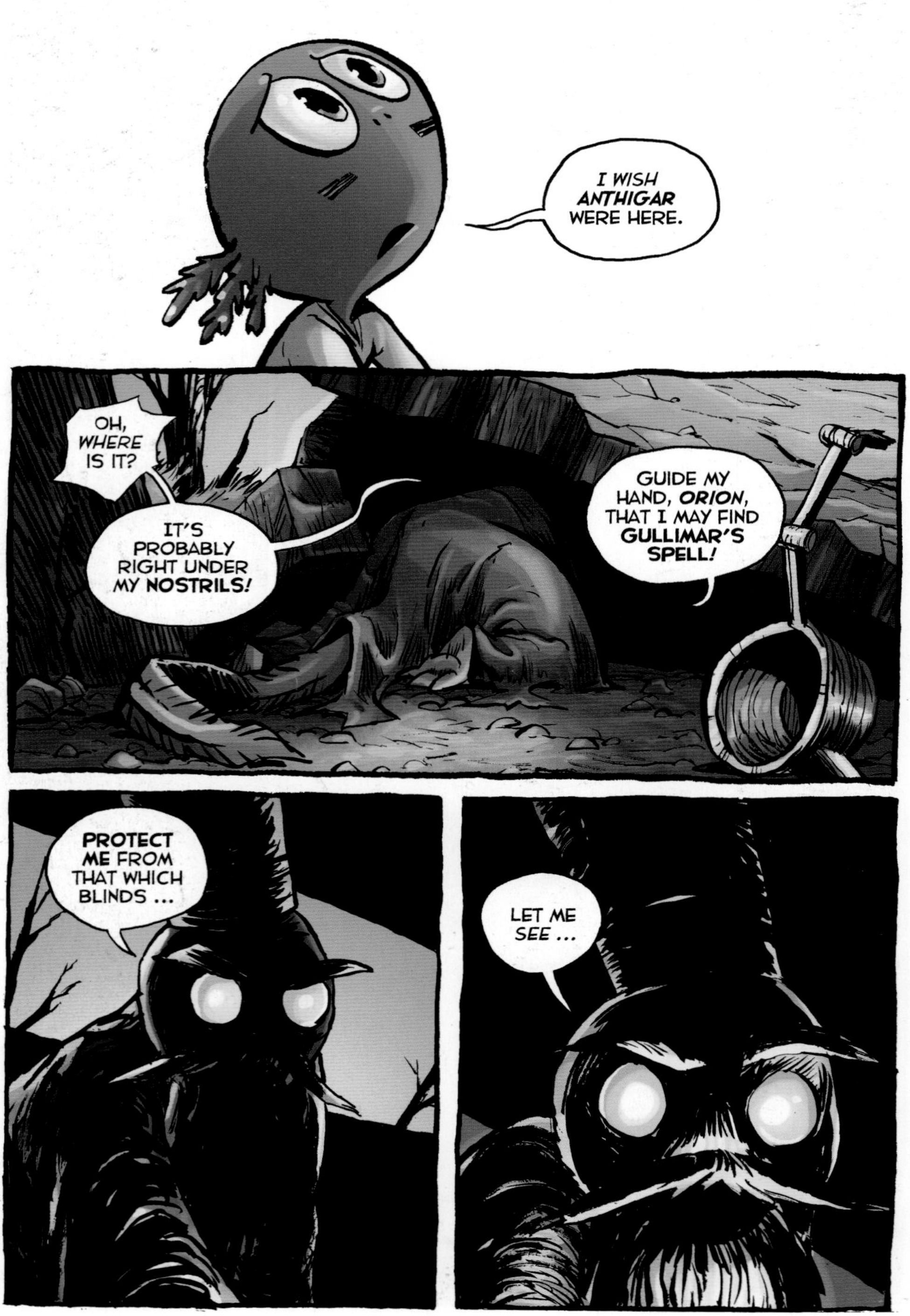

I WISH ANTHIGAR WERE HERE.
OH, WHERE IS IT?
IT'S PROBABLY RIGHT UNDER MY NOSTRILS!
GUIDE MY HAND, ORION, THAT I MAY FIND GULLIMAR'S SPELL!
PROTECT ME FROM THAT WHICH BLINDS ...
LET ME SEE ...

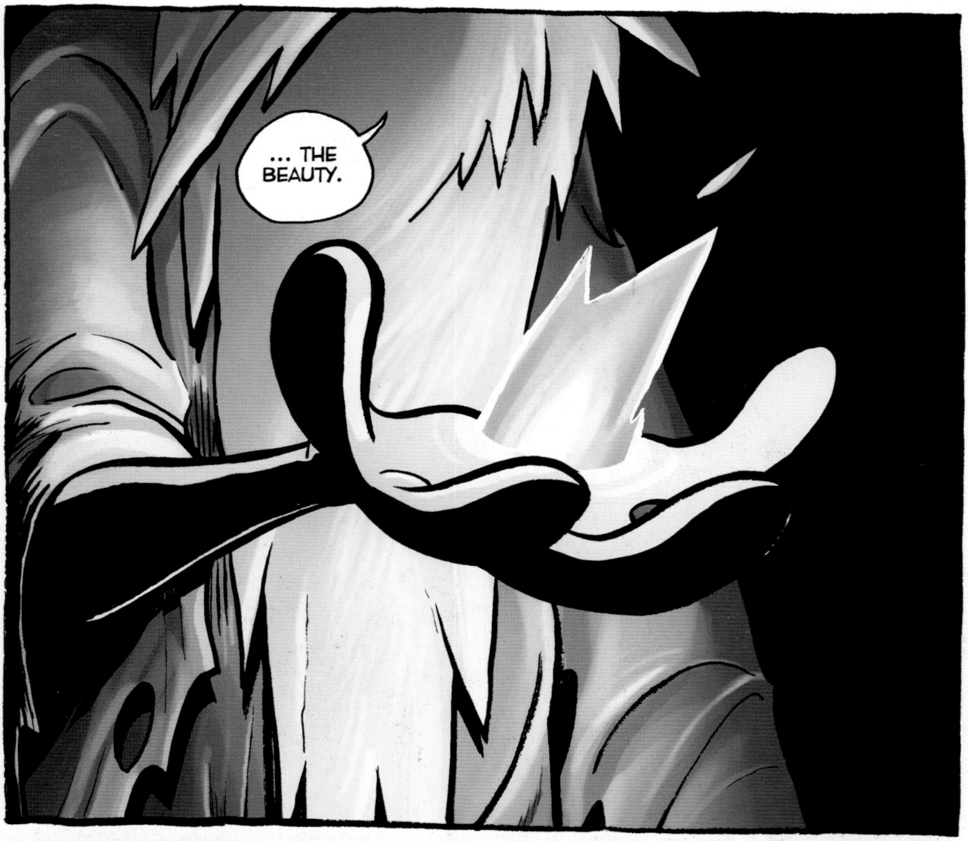
... THE BEAUTY.

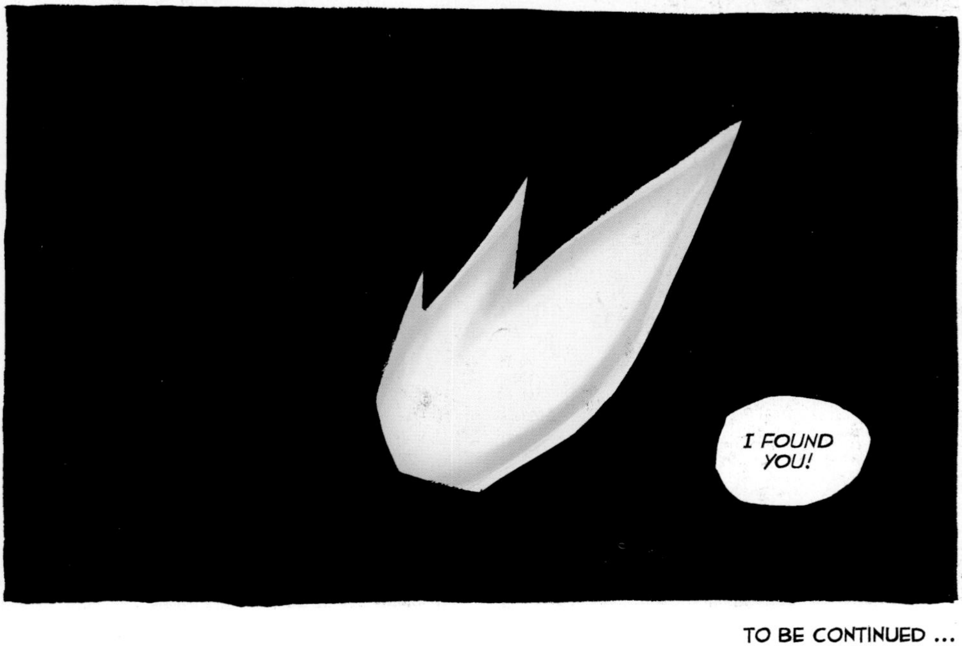
I FOUND YOU!

TO BE CONTINUED ...

DOUG TENNAPEL is the acclaimed author and illustrator of GHOSTOPOLIS, BAD ISLAND, CARDBOARD, and TOMMYSAURUS REX, all published by Graphix. Among other honors, GHOSTOPOLIS was an ALA 2011 Top Ten Great Graphic Novel for Teens, a 2010 *Kirkus* Best Book of the Year, and a *School Library Journal* Best Comic for Kids published in 2010. BAD ISLAND was a *School Library Journal* Top Ten Graphic Novel for 2011 and a 2012 ALA Great Graphic Novels for Teens selection. CARDBOARD was named to the list of *School Library Journal* Top Ten Graphic Novels of 2012.

Doug is also the creator of the hugely popular character Earthworm Jim. He lives in Franklin, Tennessee, with his wife and their four children.

KATHERINE GARNER, the colorist for NNEWTS, is an illustrator and colorist with a Master of Arts degree in Illustration. She loves to draw monsters and dragons. Katherine has worked on previous books with Doug TenNapel, including TOMMYSAURUS REX, BAD ISLAND, and GHOSTOPOLIS.

She lives in Shropshire, United Kingdom, with her family, dogs, and lovely hamster.